THE BEST
AUSTRALIAN
STORIES
2 0 0 1

THE BEST AUSTRALIAN STORIES 2001

Edited by
PETER CRAVEN

Published by Black Inc.,
An imprint of Schwartz Publishing Pty Ltd
Level 3, 167 Collins Street
Melbourne Victoria 3000
Telephone 61 3 9654 2000
Facsimile 61 3 9654 2290

National Library of Australia Cataloguing

The Best Australian Stories 2001
ISBN 1 86395 083 4
1. Short Stories, Australian – 20th century.
I. Craven, Peter.

A823.914

In memoriam
Amy Witting 1918–2001

CONTENTS

Introduction

Peter Craven

Realisms and counter-realisms dominate the landscape of Australian fiction as much as ever. We live in an age where the dominant established form of literary fiction (exemplified by Peter Carey as it is by Salman Rushdie and Gabriel Garcia Marquez) is called magical realism, an inscrutable oxymoron if ever there was one, and we are also open to the impact of fictional orientations enlivening and complicating the field of non-fiction as they do in Naipaul or Sebald and one or two factional pieces included here, where the curve and curl of the imagination enhances the writing and defies categories in something the way they are defied by a poem.

There is not that much in the way of magical realism in this volume and perhaps even less of the new postmodern fiction exemplified by David Foster Wallace in America though it's worth bearing in mind that short stories and extracts may not indicate the range of a writer's work or (in the case of extracts) the variegation of the whole work.

This collection includes short stories in the traditional (self-contained) sense as well as extracts from works in progress. Unlike its predecessor this annual does not include pieces of genre fiction though some of the pieces here are more potentially 'popular' than others. This represents happanstance rather than predilection though the decision, when it came, was deliberate.

My hope is that the work collected here will indicate the range and something of the power of the imaginative writing (most of it fictional) written by Australians in the last two years. Some of these stories have appeared in magazines, two in collections of stories and essays, but only one in a book of fiction and that book was an unusually short novelty hardback containing two short stories.

So what darkness and light can *Best Australian Stories 2001* shed, what pleasures might it yield, what sorrows might it enshroud in the form of art?

It begins with Thomas Keneally at his most sprightly, as a storyteller, narrating the business of how a young Australian priest meditates as he travels towards his parents' home in the early days of the Second World War and the diversions and difficulties he encounters as a young man and a spiritual counsellor. The writing is characteristically spry and lithe. Keneally makes us see his characters and he also makes us hear them evoking the blarney and the circumlocution of an Australia at once intimately sensed and historically distant.

That Australia, the Australia of more than half a century ago, seems always to have walked in the dreams of Amy Witting who died this year and who belonged to the generation that lived through the Second World War. The three chapters published here are what she completed of what would have been (had she lived) the last of the Isobel books and they show, with a kind of skeletal notation and economy, the hand of the bold humane realist who made the language and the moral climate of her own youth such an abiding richness for Australian literature even though her own fame was so belated.

If Witting captures the atmospheric and the verbal afterglow of an older Australia, Murray Bail is interested in the Second World War as the locus for a particular artistic individual, part stick figure and part representative hero, for one of his leisurely excavations of how the world of facts and the world of icons connect with each other, collapsingly and transfiguringly. This is a story full of wry humour which is at the same time as wrought and designed in its use of perspective (transposed to the domain of words) as any painting by Fred Williams. This is not realism though its detail – like the abstract scribbling of a Fairweather – is full of glimpses of lost worlds as well as animations of what is possible, with a nearly minimalist grid, in the art of fiction conceived of as a space to be improvised around and cajoled into being, a kind of parody (half joke, half act of faith) like an agnostic's apprehension of godhead.

If that sounds like a suggestion of spirituality inhering in the kind of bush modernism practised by Bail the theme is in some ways more overt in the case of Gerald Murnane, the writer he has most in common with and with whom the contrasts are instructive. Murnane is a minimalist but one who has less in common with the design of a painter than he does with the rhythmic patterning of the poet. The first of his stories is about a boy living in a rural Catholic enclave, a designed community in the 1950s, and it has all of the ceremonious drollery and sadness, as well as the teetering absurdity and the sense of ghostly paradigms performing their elephantine dances that we associate with this writer. In the second story a barer manner, rich with the evocation of every sort of emptiness, evokes the poignancy of an older man writing to a young woman, imagined but not glimpsed, with great spareness and depth and with a lame etiolated poetry which is nevertheless poetry of a high order. This is a story that remembers the Murnane of *Inland* and it shows him as a peerless master of whispered effects and engulfing shadows and sorrows.

For Robyn Davidson it is the sorrow and shadow of childhood and of her parents that whistles through the pages of this questing self-portraiture that follows the contour of the autobiographical but does so with a constant effort to pause, to analyse, to bring to life and to reconsider the art of commemoration and the mystery that goes along with it. This is part of a grand work of autobiography which one suspects can only be undertaken at some distance from the physical geography of Australia.

Patricia Cornelius is equally preoccupied with the face of parenthood but in this piece of fiction the face of the mother leers and rails at the daughter like a vengeance through all the pathos of a depleted condition. This is realism of absolute credibility, capturing the fragility and pain that goes along with the bond that links a daughter and a demented mother. This is writing of savage power and grace.

In the next story, almost a mood piece, at the edge of the essayistic mode, Nadia Wheatley, the great biographer of Charmian Clift who is also famed for her children's books, finds time to reverence a fellow female sower of seeds. This is an act of historical recapitulation that at first seems suave, even conventional, but which eventually turns into a kind of *tour de force* of homage, rather in the manner of Clift and perhaps consciously remembering her.

For Gillian Mears the remembering is done by a young black girl who ministers to the needs of an old stockman, who is dying, whom she loves and hates with some intensity. It is a story which completely inhabits the world it creates and which produces a kind of elegiac poetry, in the far interstices of articulation, finding words, with a sweeping plangency that is poetic and raw at the same time. This is the imagining of Aboriginal Australia from the woman's point of view with great individuality and pinpoint emotional authenticity that sweeps aside every generalised effect. It is a kind of pastoral epiphany that is also, with a keening undercurrent, a lament for things foregone.

Pastoral is central to the extracts from Kate Grenville's fiction which are in fact 'foregone' sections of a larger work. They stand on their own here as powerfully hopeful repre-sentations of a lame but decent people struggling towards a possible happiness (as well as a possible wisdom) in the weird environment – half-comic half-hostile – of bush Australia. This is realism with a romantic tinge but hinting not at the world of 'soaps' but at the underlying intimations of harmony that such things feed off.

Bush harmonies and disharmonies are central to the extract from Hannie Rayson's play which throws onto the stage a collection of characters linked by community and blood who are exposed to the apparition of a Hanson figure (one of their own) but who nonetheless make up their lives with a racketing mixture of improvisation and traditionalism. Rayson plays on the familiar idiom of the vernacular and on the quiet comedy of family life but manages to bring in allusions to globalisation, to suicide and hardship and the plight of young gays in the country thirty years ago. Her project seems comparable to Grenville's. The technique is all buoyancy but there are flickers of seriousness at every point in this foretaste of an epic bush drama that seems set to absorb and transcend the transfixing quality of the domestic serial.

The drama of families, of sisters in particular, is written all over the cross-textures and many colours of the fiction by Sue Hancock reproduced here. Hancock's novel is preoccupied with a group of sisters in New Zealand, one of whom has just returned from Australia. It begins with a lyrical passage of some splendour (reminiscent perhaps of Katharine Mansfield) and then details the by turns everyday and bizarre events of a daily round that is everywhere tinged with portent. This is intensely moody fiction swerving from one pole to the next, with crisp Garneresque social observation running up against intimations of daemonism and the Lord knows what.

Liam Davison, by contrast, sticks to a sober grid of realism but this story of a boy, a woman, a father and a motel is powerfully concentrated at every point so that its conclusion – which is epiphanic and satisfying at the same time – takes place within a generalised hush of disquiet. Davison is a contemporary Australian writer who shows what the short story, classically conceived, can do and this rite-of-passage story has an eerie brilliance which the sobriety of its telling does its best to disguise.

In the story by Sonya Hartnett a piece of uncomprehending childhood idiocy is suddenly fraught with moral consequence and the rite of passage becomes a loss of innocence. Hartnett is best known for her dark enigmatic books for young adults (which in fact are no such things or only among other things) but here she musters a nearly guileless style in order to notate something that is almost everyday but full of a trail of guilt and damage. The writing has the directness of skilled memoir but the symmetries are that of someone who makes fiction writing look easy.

That's true with bells on of Tim Winton's story which seems for its long first movement to be an almost triumphalist ode to childhood predictabilities but then grows dark, fated, the tail twisting everything towards calamity with a skill that never intrudes on the sense of reality generated. This is a master storyteller who seems to hum his way through the tale of being a boy but whose ultimate effect is one of appall and whose dark tug is one of guilt following on unwitting catastrophe.

In the case of Colin Oehring the gleam of adolescent experience and experimentation is presented close up so that we can see the fog of breath and feel the steam of desire in this 'Irish' story where the lilt of the language, expertly mimed and musically phrased, works to conjure up, as if in a cloud, a set of actions which are never quite clear, which by design suggest more than they disclose but in which a political game with explosives (terrorism and all its individuated insignia) somehow consorts with a girl on horseback who is suggestive of the desire for freedom, the licence to move, which the realistic faces and gestures of the actors in the story seem resolutely and stoically to contradict. This is a story which remembers Joyce in both its blarney and its refusal to allow rhetoric a more than strategic function, a story that allows itself to move through every wisp of confusion and suggestion while articulating each detail with great clarity.

Violence runs too like a pulse through the story by Anthony Lawrence that seems from its opening such a readerly (even a readable) depiction of a set of dramatic actions within a framework of narrative reassurance and 'comfort'. This is one of those stories a little in the manner of Tim Winton or Ian McEwan in which a cruel god seems to preside over a universe the stories of which can be told with maximum suaveness, with dramatic lighting and bite, but where everything goes awry, as if some original sin determined the flaws in the very clay of human likeableness and the fictional trick is one of creating characters who generate warmth only in order to chill to the bone, who compel identification only to confound it. Anthony Lawrence has a style as biddable as a television screen though you can also hear the crackles and eloquencies of a poet's way with language.

In David Brooks's story language is a mirror for atrocity imagined and made symbolic. This fissured fable of the Taliban's Afghanistan is a horror story that compels assent even as its nightmares act with a surgeon's knife.

Surgery (in its bloodcurdling early nineteenth-century mode) forms part of the charnel-house horror of James Bradley's two associated pieces of fiction – which both come out of work on the one novel. The first piece is a kind of inferno of dismembered ghastliness, transfigured and at the same time animated (to disturbing effect) by a tense, flexible invigorated prose that is at one with the wildness and the savagery of what sounds like a postmodern enterprise with fabulistic streaks. It is written so steadily and it is so barbarically focused that only its technical perseverance, its winging and swooping energy can save it and it does. In the second section the suaveness of the dialogue, the overheard quality of this nineteenth-century speech shows the fineness of Bradley's ear in this insinuation of how the spectres and scarecrows of Sweeny Toddism can cohabit with a sense of human slaughteryards that brings to mind the horrors of twentieth-century history. These are clearly the fragments – jewel-like or bleeding – of an extremely ambitious Australian novel, one that is wilder and blacker than our fiction is used to.

In the Wayne Macauley story something almost like allegory dances its way adeptly through what could have been the most deathly of clichés (the one about Death) and manages to do so with a delicacy and wryness, a sort of tough reversal of expectations, that relaxes the mind and sets it skidding on the thinnest ice of elegance.

If Macauley is black he's satiny whereas in Ellen Rodger's story the raw faces and rough play of professional sex are brought out for a compassionate airing in a way that compels belief while also remaining sharply observed and compassionate. This is writing of plain, cold-eyed authority.

In the Luke Davies story a particular woman is the locus of the narrator's appetite, his pity, his irony, his engorging gaze. This is a brilliant vignette, absolutely sharp and beautifully 'turned' which shows what a poetic novelist can do when he tapers his effects and creates a complex double-portrait of the perceiver and the perceived.

No masculine gaze could be more intense than Gerard Windsor's, whose essay is included here for the extreme artfulness and the dramatic energy – everywhere dark-cornered and intense – with which Windsor invokes a figure in a painting, and behind that the person painted, as a kind of emblem for the sensibility displayed here and the persona which is evoked with a sinister self-assurance reminiscent of a Browning monologue. Windsor is one of those writers who fictionalise compulsively but who do so with such mesmerising force that they seem too big for conventional fiction.

Graham Henderson follows Windsor not simply because painting is part of his subject but because he gets such powerful effect from the way he abstracts and subtracts from and plays upon what might almost be an allegorical chessboard of figures. Henderson is probably closer to Kafka than anyone else in our literature and this story has the quality of showing no excess of colour, of exactly disclosing an imaginary world.

The final story by Kim Mahood is a return to a more traditional – at any rate a different – frame of reference. This is a story of love and sex and violence and betrayal. It has the satisfactions of a traditional, nearly thrillerish novel, in conventional form and it is notable for the way in which Mahood has such a frontal approach to her characters, to great stretches of their being alive, as if D.H. Lawrence had mastered a method that could be handed on. This is an engrossing story that does have the breath of life.

This book would not have been possible without the co-operation of a number of people. Chris Feik and Sophy Williams were models of patience. My friend Colin Oehring helped, beyond the point of any duty. Andrew Rutherford made it all possible.

One Sunday in February, 1942

Thomas Keneally

This Sunday was in humid February. He had no car, but travelling by public transport gave him a sense of fraternity which he knew he would lose when and if he acquired the skills appropriate to a car, and a vehicle to go with it. Hard-bitten fathers of families raised their hats to him on Strathfield station, implying, 'We are one with you in the Faith.' He made in return a half-embarrassed gesture of raising his black felt hat to them. They were the ones who had fought the fight, had raised children in a harsh decade. But a fraternity of respect was established, even as people shuffled together towards the door of the red electric trains.

In the crowded Sunday morning carriage, young leading aircraftmen tilted their forage caps, and he nodded. The communion of Saints on the Western Line, thundered towards Central Station amidst showers of sparks from the electric lines above. Of course, from much of the population of the trains, those not party to the mysteries of faith, there were surreptitious stares and blankness. Mystification. A mute hostility to which he was utterly accustomed.

A beautiful young woman in a floral dress drew her six or seven-year-old son off the seat opposite her to allow Frank Darragh to sit. She held the child between her knees and told the boy in a lowered voice, 'Say hello to Father.' The boy had a small scatter of freckles on the same fine-grained skin his mother had.

Darragh said, 'Thank you for the seat.' The mother had that air of grace, and a particular light in the eye. She was not frightened of him. It was good not to be feared.

'My daddy's in the Middle North,' said the boy.

'The Middle East,' his mother corrected him, and kissed the rim of his ear. Darragh tried to remember if such easy exchanges had operated between himself and his mother. He decided briefly and with some unease that his mother might not have been so casual in the presence of a priest. 'Your father is a brave man,' Darragh told the boy.

Darragh saw that the woman nearly shrugged, as if Darragh's compliment did not serve her and her son much.

'We're going to Clovelly,' said the boy, resting easily against his mother's thigh. As the train rolled, this young woman, this pleasant boy leaned against his mother's body, evoked in Darragh the usual sharp and not too frequent pain of celibacy. His spiritual adviser, an elderly, gentle soul named Dr Cahill – for every seminarian had to choose a spiritual adviser from the staff of the seminary – had once said, 'The institution of celibacy is not a mere sacrifice of pleasure. It asks of a man that he will consent to be the end of the line. That he will not pass on his embodied nature …'

Darragh considered this apparently perfect, talismanic young woman who faced him. Besides what he read as an air of confident innocence, she had the character of having suffered without having chosen to. History had, without asking her, claimed her husband and put him at a fabulous distance from her.

On a rowdy stretch of line near Erskineville, she leaned forward by just a margin and told Darragh, under her breath, that she and her son lived closer to Flemington parish, but belonged to St Margaret's and preferred to go to Mass there. So she had recognised him as the curate of St Margaret's. Was she one of the young soldiers' wives who confessed to loneliness or temptation? Had he, unconscious of her loveliness, absolved her and imposed a penance – 'Say one decade of the Joyous Mysteries.' Darragh nodded, and the woman settled back and resumed a secret whispered conversation with her son.

Central Station that dangerous February was a melee of Sunday people, children in loose summer hats, beach-bound with their parents. Skylarking soldiers bearing kitbags made their way towards the steam trains which would take them – who knew? – to some banal camp in the bush, or to wounds in the Pacific. The warriors amongst whom he could not be counted. On the broad concourse at Eddy Avenue, a larger army of sailors, airmen and soldiers posed for the pavement photographer on the arms of their mothers, wives or girl-friends. The papers talked about Australia being stripped of troops, but there seemed enough to raise substantial regiments waiting with their womenfolk for the Bronte and Bondi trams. And amongst the crowd by the tramline stood the mother and son. She had the air of a woman who was used to waiting, of not resenting queues and crowds. Probably a country girl, he thought, building a history in his mind, whose husband had brought her out of the bush to the city. He saw her lift her son onto the running board of the Bronte tram. A militiaman who looked perhaps sixteen stood, doff-ing his slouch hat, and offered her a seat. She took it with a frank smile, and with a steely howl the tram bore her and her tribe of fellow travellers away to Elizabeth Street.

When his Rose Bay tram came along five minutes later, he too entered and a boy in a school blazer stood up to offer him his seat. Instinct that he should now separate himself from the memory of the lovely mother caused him to smile and say, 'No, I'm perfectly fine, thank you. You sit.' To the edification of any Catholics who might be on the tram, and the mystifica-tion of others, he pulled from the pocket of his black jacket his *Breviarium Romanum*. The volume he had was marked *Hiemalis* – Winter – since it was winter in Europe, winter in the Vatican surrounded by Italian Fascists, winter in Russia where Hitler's men correctly suffered at the hands of Soviet troops, winter over the bomb sites of England, and of course over the neutrally undisturbed and poverty-stricken farms of Ireland, from which his own ancestors came. This word *Hiemalis* in dull-gold lettering on the spine of the beautifully printed little book, when taken in conjunction with the humid summer day, told you that Australia was in a remote and inverted relation to the wellsprings of the European faith, to the locales of monasticism and mysteries of faith. That was the basic question which *Smith's Weekly* and the *Telegraph* kept asking: Could Mr Churchill be made to take an interest in the destiny of a place so distant? So far-off that a priest, reading the *Hiemalis* volume of his daily breviary, felt no shiver of northern wind but sweated instead into his black serge, in the close air of a tram beneath a ruthless February sun?

For each day, diocesan priests like Frank Darragh were required to recite their *Breviary* – the *office*, as it was called. In the tradition of those monks who sang the sundry hours of the office in plainchant, Matins, Laudes, Prime, Terce, Sext, Nones, Vespers, and Compline, busier souls like Frank and the monsignor were allowed merely to recite them. Times for the completion of the office were discussed on tennis Mondays the way athletic times might be discussed by runners. A jovial former seminary buffoon named Tim Murphy boasted that he could manage the whole thing in thirty-four minutes. If so, it showed a remarkable facility Frank Darragh couldn't match – the Latin seemed to him to demand a slower enunciation. Verses such as, '*Undique circumvenerunt me; in nomine Domine contrivi eos. Circumvenerunt me sicut apes; adusserunt sicut ignis spinas: in nomine Domine contrivi eos,*' did not rattle off the tongue. Neither did they off the mind, in their significance. *They surround me like bees; they engulf me like tongues of fire* ... He had got to say Matins, Lauds and Prime between his two Masses, and now on the tram he recited Terce from his Breviary, his lips moving, as required by Canon Law, to pronounce the Latin hymns and psalms and versicles.

Darragh was comforted to imagine that the purpose of having priests, the world over, from Nazi-occupied Belgium, where his Breviary had been published by the Benzige

Brothers, to the southernmost priest in New Zealand, was to remind the individual cleric that whatever business the rest of mankind might be engaged in – invention, invasion, impregnation – his job and caution, his only possible joy, was in pursuing the divine order. It was there in the Vulgate Latin version of the psalms at Terce, which he read with a slight, unobtrusive flutter of his lips, as he hung from a strap, expelling the words in minor whisper which the tram-clang drowned. *'And I shall walk on a spacious road because I follow at your precepts … I am reminded by light of your name, oh Lord, and I guard your law … I shall take delight in your mandates, which I guard.'*

He was towards the end of Terce, of the versicle and response, Darragh doing both, unlike the old monks with one side of the chapel uttering the versicle, and the other singing the plainchant reply. He had got as far as the words *'Averte oculos meos, ne videant vanitatum* – Avert my eyes that they should not see vanity,' when he felt in an instant cleft in two by the sharpest agony of loss. It arose from nothing, from a slight jolt of the tramlines, and carried not only the face of the young mother, but also the face of the boy generated from her, leaning confidently against her knees. He blinked and looked up. A proportion of the eyes of the tram-travellers, reverent and hostile, were on him. He felt certain they could see his extreme condition, the sudden axe which had divided him, crown to groin. How will I eat dinner with my mother? he wondered, though he hoped the extremity of feeling would depart by then. The rest of the office remained to be said, Sext, None, Vespers, Compline. How could it be completed before midnight if he felt as distracted as this? His legs ached too, for no good reason, and he wished he had taken the schoolboy's offered seat.

As the tram began the climb to Edgecliff, however, the pain retracted to become a dull, habitual depression, and he began reciting the hymn of Sext. *Extinguish the flames of passion, draw off the heat of poison, grant the salvation of bodies and the true peace of hearts.* He feared, however, that for him an age of automatic grace had passed.

The bungalow of Darragh's childhood, approached with this new feeling of having somehow aged and of being tested, stood on New South Head Road near Rose Bay. It was built of plum-coloured brick, and its street-facing windows had little segments of stained glass to relieve them of their banal transparency. His mother, a vigorous, lean woman, in, he surmised, her early fifties, tended the rose bushes that marked the way to the verandah and the front door. His parents had bought the house in 1923 from an old Scot who had placed by the front door a framed glass sign in which the word *Arbroath* was marked out in gold tinsel. They had left it there. The child Darragh had not realised it was the name of a true Scottish town, rather than a mystery formula for the hearth. In his present mood of at-best-wistfulness, though, on this still Sunday suffused with the smell of legs of lamb baking in a thousand kitchens, it failed to evoke much in him.

Baking legs of lamb were still offered up as a matter of course to Australian Sabbath appetites, despite meat rationing. One of them was inside *Arbroath*, and Darragh paused at the closed front door and let its savour lead him back to a more grateful sense of who and where he was, and what was his destiny.

When he rang, his aproned mother opened the door.

'Frank,' she said with a careful smile. She had always had this wariness in her affection. It did not mean she was not as generous as the young mother he'd met on the train. She was of a different temperament. 'Your mother is a brick, a true rock,' his father had told him once – approvingly. 'You know where you stand with her.' Darragh had learned from childhood to read her small signs, as now, when with her eyes modestly gleaming she led him through to the kitchen-dining room and his Aunt Madge. Madge, his maiden aunt, came through the curtain from the kitchen where she had obviously been assisting his mother with the bake. His late father's sister was a fuller and less-restrained woman with a plump, pleasant face. She believed in rouge, and her cheeks gleamed with that and with the sherry she always drank before Sunday dinner. While he admired his mother for taking quiet delight in things, Aunt Madge was rowdier. Her story, however, like her parents' story, had been shaped by the Great War. The family myth was that her boyfriend had been killed on some muddy patrol – he had been a mere eighteen years old. She had spent her adult life working in the millinery department of a store in the city – the highly trusted Miss Darragh who would have made a wonderful wife. When she loudly kissed him now, Darragh could smell the pleasant blush of sherry on her breath. Past her, he saw the table set with white linen on which cruets sparkled, and was fully absorbed and consoled now by the succulent smells of roast potato and moist lamb.

'We'll sit down in five minutes,' said his mother. 'I have beer if you would like it.'

After the long tram journey, he chose to have a glass. 'An aperitif,' said Aunt Madge, for the sake of elegance or of what his father called 'bush flashness'. While his mother went to get it, Darragh took off his jacket and went to the room he had occupied as a boy to hang it up. He also undid the press-stud at the back of his neck, and released the Roman collar and stock he had worn all the way from Strathfield. The underside of the stock was sodden with his sweat. So now he became an ordinary fellow in black pants and white shirt, about to eat spud and carrot, baked onion and lamb, with mint jelly taken from a cut glass bowl.

With the heaped plates before the three of them, Mrs Darragh asked her son to intone grace. He did so, and after a perfunctory sign of the cross as habitual as a kiss between spouses, Aunt Madge looked at her plate and said with an augustness of elocution which was her style, 'Who would believe there was rationing?'

'I would,' said Mrs Darragh, and half-smiled at her son.

Aunt Madge lived half a mile away but had a habit of inviting herself to meals at *Arbroath* so she would not have the fuss of shopping and dealing with books of ration coupons. In fact, Aunt Madge devoted a great deal of her time to film-going, and could always tell Darragh what film to see on

Monday nights after tennis. '*That Night in Rio* is a common-place little thing, but if you happen to like Carmen Miranda … *Dive Bomber's* not a bad war drama, a little unrealistic if that's what you're after. Errol Flynn, what a looker! They say he's an Australian. I met a fellow after Mass the other day who claimed to have shared a desk with him at Marist Brothers, Parramatta. I said to him, "Mr Henry," – that's his name – "Mr Henry, I wouldn't believe you, except I know a fellow like you wouldn't lie on the doorstep of the Church." But the beggar would, you know. *Blossoms in the Dust* … very touching. Greer Garson looks like a saint but from what I've read may not be one. *Love on the Dole* … now that's a real film about real people.'

'I'm surprised,' said Mrs Darragh, inviting Frank into the cautious joke. 'A woman of your age going to *Love on the Dole*.' It was said to be a notorious film. Priests and ministers who had not seen it had widely preached against it.

'Well, it's the way people live,' said Aunt Madge, her voice sweeping. 'If you treat people unjustly, they don't just offer it all up for the souls in Purgatory, you know. They try to find an outlet. Anyhow, where were all those priests who run it down when the working men and women were hard-up during the Depression? They weren't to be seen then. But they're quick to blame the poor for living close to the bone.'

Frank Darragh was used to Aunt Madge being an anti-clerical Catholic.

'The actors in *Love on the Dole*,' Mrs Darragh surprised Frank by saying, 'were never your poor working men and women, Madge. That Deborah Kerr. In real life she has a plum in her mouth like the Queen of England.'

'That's not what I read,' said Aunt Madge. 'In fact, I read that she had quite a hard upbringing as a shopkeeper's daughter. Anyhow, you'd approve of the newsreels.' Fork in one hand, Madge raised her other to trace phantom head-lines in the air. 'Rommel's army on the run in Libya, and our poor boys having Christmas in Egypt. Poor things. They look so young. Will they last the year?'

'Will any of us?' asked Mrs Darragh resolutely, chewing her lamb behind a delicate half-smile.

Darragh wondered whether she was really afraid, in the way the people in the confessional were afraid. She had never shown him any fear except when he was ill with whooping cough and pneumonia as a child. She looked levelly at her son.

'You should go and speak to Mr Regan.' Regan was the next-door neighbour, a thoughtful man, father of three daughters. Darragh had never seen him dressed, even at the most casual moment, in anything less than a shirt with detachable collar, a vest and watch-chain, and well-pressed, well-tailored pants. 'Mr Regan has room for me, and for Madge if she chooses, in his air-raid shelter.'

Aunt Madge declared, 'I might come over here, but it is half-a-mile. Whereas there's a shelter in the park right next door to me. I could be killed amongst strangers, I suppose, but ... well, God's will.'

Mrs Darragh murmured, 'Nice talk for a socialist. *And* for a friend of Deborah Kerr.'

'If you have read *Rerum Novarum*,' said Aunt Madge, referring to a famous social justice encyclical of Pope Leo XIII, 'you'll see that there is no conflict between social democracy and Faith.' Like many other Catholics, Aunt Madge had been a great supporter of the Labor premier of New South Wales, Jack Lang, and had given out 'How to Vote' cards in Rose Bay amongst what she called the *silvertail* voters. She was able to quote from the encyclical, as she did now, for it was the holy text of progressive, political Catholics. '*Hence by degrees it has come to pass the working men have been surrendered, isolated and helpless, to the hardheartedness of employers and the greed of unchecked competition* ... No one with eyes in his head would argue with that one.'

It was hard for Darragh to believe that all the particularity of Aunt Madge and his mother could be wiped out by a stray Japanese bomb. And Mrs Darragh had already told him, on previous visits, that in the event of the invasion itself, she and Madge had been invited to join the Sisters of the Sacred

Heart in their convent-fastness at Rose Bay. The nuns were confident that even the Japanese would not violate such an obviously august cloister. Indeed, Frank Darragh himself could not think of a better place for his mother to shelter should those terrible hosts that had sacked Nanking improbably arrive in the suburbs of Sydney. He feared he himself would be engaged with his congregation in Homebush and Strathfield. What place, apart perhaps from the abattoirs and the brickworks, Homebush and Strathfield could play in the grand plan of a Japanese South East Asian Co-Prosperity Sphere was difficult to imagine; but that might add to the peril of the event. Somehow he could imagine the soldiers of the Emperor becoming so enraged by the irrelevance of the suburb that they might be provoked to obliterate its people.

At his mother's urging, and before leaving, Frank Darragh went next door to see Mr Regan. Sweet-faced Mrs Regan sought to feed him another meal, and the Regan daughters who had known him in his adolescence quivered with excitement to have Frank Darragh, translated into priesthood, present in their home. The fact he was wearing shirtsleeves seemed to amuse them.

'I must talk to you, Father Frank,' said Mr Regan under his breath, and collected from his ice chest a bottle of Dinner Ale and led him out of the cooing and fluttering and teasing of the Regan girls into the back garden and down plank steps into the bomb shelter he had so industriously dug amongst rhododendron bushes. Frank felt already heavy with his meal, and hoped that Mr Regan, a man in his late fifties, was not about to embark on a moral and military weighing of this languid, humid hour in the world's plummet to a resolution. In the centre of the damp-smelling air-raid shelter, amidst harsh-timbered bunks, stood a coarse-grained wooden table, and Mr Regan sat at it, inviting Frank to take a chair on the far side. The air was dimmest umber. Mr Regan uncapped the Dinner Ale and poured two glasses. Apparently, in his experience, few priests had ever rejected the offer of a drink.

'Well, Frank,' Mr Regan reflectively stated, 'everyone knows that if they land it will be in the Eastern Suburbs here.' Darragh had not known that *that* had been established as military reality. 'I'm sending the women to my brother-in-law's place in Cootamundra. At least there's room to hide out there.' He sighed. The chance of bloody chaos threatened the fine-sown seams of his vest, the salt-and-pepper cloth of his pressed Sunday trousers. But he could never flee. He was a real estate agent and St Vincent de Paul man, who frequently slotted poorer families in Christ's name into houses and flats that awaited occupation. The Japanese might spare him for his expertise in finding them billets.

Mr Regan took out a packet of Capstans from his vest and lit sombrely and with a flourish, as if it would be the only one he would smoke that day. 'Did you happen to read the *Telegraph* today, Father Frank? The front page is all cricket and racing. People dancing on the edge of the abyss. The Australia Hotel and the Trocadero full of revelry. The divorce courts full, if not fuller. I read a piece this morning about an air force officer who went to his wife and said that he was not made for marriage. Just like that. Without any apology. And as if he hadn't already married her. The judge ordered him to return to her within twenty-six days.' Mr Regan shook his head. He considered the judge ultimately impotent in these matters. 'This is the problem as I see it. That we're a race that deserves punishment.' He lowered his voice to a confessional hush, and the words caused him pain. 'Myself as much as anyone. I do not exclude myself.'

Darragh said, 'I doubt anyone really deserves bombing, Mr Regan.' He was embarrassed to see this man who had been one of his elders when he was a boy now reduced by the times, and by Darragh's own dignity as a priest, to adopting a confessional tone. Mr Regan admitting guilt, regret and fear of unarguable doom. This man who had always been so certain and so venerable in the eyes of the fourteen-, fifteen- and sixteen-year-old Frank Darragh.

'Our god is a racehorse,' said Mr Regan, in explanation. 'Our god is a glass of beer. Our god is a dance or worse with a pretty girl. How can we complain if the true God shows us his harsher face? And if He chooses another power as his agent?'

Frank changed the subject. 'It's very kind of you to have Mum and Aunt Madge in here.'

Mr Regan gave a concessive brief smile. 'Oh yes. But they should go to Gilgandra or some such place themselves, you know. Somewhere that's negligible, you know. But your mother and Madge are very stubborn, you know.'

'They intend to shelter with you and the nuns,' said Frank.

'Well, the nuns feel bound to protect the mother of a priest. And Madge.' He laughed. Everyone seemed to have a wry affection for Madge. 'Madge comes along in her wake.'

Mr Regan took a sip of beer and peered into the mid-distance. 'I wanted to tell you … Pray for me, Frank.' Indeed the man had taken on what was to Darragh the now-familiar breathlessness of the penitent. 'I doubt my courage,' he said. Frank felt abashed – there was no wire screen between him and Mr Regan the patriarch, no curtain, no sliding wooden shutter.

'If the Philippines fall to the Japanese,' said Mr Regan, 'and there seems nothing to prevent it, Sydney will be even fuller of Americans than ever. And, you know, they *are* a corrupting influence. I had an American colonel come to my office the other day. He had with him a young woman, an American – she was in uniform. What they call their Army Air Force. The man had a smooth look. Very different from us – they're not as dowdy. The colonel wanted me to show him a flat. I could tell it was for the young woman, yet they seemed just about as normal and confident as a married couple. And I was embarrassed, but I did it. I knew, you see, he was setting up a love nest. I've always discouraged that sort of thing – I know how to put off a fellow Australian. But there was just something about the easy attitude of this chap I went along with. Just glided along. Like a weakling.'

He looked up with eyes in which shame and confusion were too naked. 'Sometimes,' Mr Regan continued, 'I think

Christ put the church into the hands of the wrong people.
The Europeans, the Americans. Us. It's possible to see everything that's happening as a judgement of our easy ways. The
races at Randwick while men die. Our general lack of fibre.
I felt that I must confess it to you, too, even though I knew
you as a little kid. Just to show you there are old fools as well
as young.'

He refilled his own glass, and Darragh's.

'I got a good rent, needless to say.'

Darragh felt bound to attempt to comfort him. 'You have
to do your job, Mr Regan,' he said. 'It's not your job to force
a confession from this colonel. The woman might have been
his daughter.'

Mr Regan shook his head.

'If anything,' Darragh persisted, 'it's the colonel who is the
sinner. You had no certain knowledge that he wanted the flat
for a bad purpose.' He was arguing like a Jesuit.

Mr Regan said, 'The worst sins are the most excusable.'

'I wouldn't say that, Mr Regan,' said Darragh, struggling.
'You're pretty hard on yourself.'

Mr Regan shook his head and seemed suddenly but too late
interested in his seniority. 'You may not understand what I'm
getting at, Father Frank. You're young. What concerns me is
this. Will I in a year's time happily be renting flats to the
Japanese? For the same reason I did to the American? For
that's what my office says it does, and it's what I do by habit.
Will their strangeness make me say, "All right, cripes, I might
as well."'

'I'm sure you'll behave like an Australian patriot, Mr
Regan.'

'I've been a real estate agent thirty-seven years.'

Eyes averted from this neighbour tormented by scruples,
Frank began to advise him that one of the great human errors
was to decide beforehand how we would behave in a given
situation. We could not predict beforehand what divine grace,
appropriate to the moment, would flow our way. This seemed
to give Mr Regan little comfort, and Frank Darragh was happy

in the end to be told by Mr Regan he ought to go and see his mother and aunt again. Mr Regan himself stayed on in his bomb shelter to finish his bottle of beer, and Frank passed through the household of lithe, Cootamundra-bound Regan women, so that he could go on his way to say goodbye to his mother and Aunt Madge.

Isobel, Anna and Stan

Amy Witting

I

In late afternoon, in the mezzanine gallery of a large city bookstore, Isobel sat at a desk, head down, pen poised, her mind only on the next person with an open book ready to be signed. These were the lovely people who had bought her latest novel and were going to put Anna through University. She loved them all dearly but could express her feelings only with a quick smile as she said, 'Do you want your name in it?' 'Happy reading, Winifred.' 'Best wishes, Olive.' A smile, a nod, and next please. 'Best wishes, Berenice. Lovely name. Don't see it often.' 'For Margaret, happy birthday.'

'Do you want your name in it?'

A man's voice said in confusion. 'Oh, I dunno. Just write in it.'

'Right.'

She signed the title page. The autograph was obscured at once by a newspaper clipping, the Speech Day photograph of Anna with her arms full of prize books, smiling with immodest delight at the camera.

'I want to talk to you.'

Oh, my god. After all this time she had almost forgotten to dread the moment. Now it had come.

She had known it was a mistake, that photograph. It had been tempting fate, but she hadn't been able to deny Anna her moment of glory, and after nearly seventeen years, her fear had seemed paranoid.

First, she thought of blackmail. She did not look up. Studying his Italian leather casual shoes and the fine lisle cable knit of what she could see of his socks below the tailored linen slacks, she dismissed that thought, which could not in any case have been serious. It had been a grotesque product of her own fear.

'I can't talk now. Can you wait?'

'Sure. I'll be at the door. See you.'

'What name, please? Happy reading, Jennifer.'

The voice hadn't matched the clothing.

Bea Fenwick's voice spoke from the past.

'An ocker. Isobel, darling, he's an ocker.'

What was his name?

She couldn't remember.

She could remember the place all right, the houseboat three moorings down from the Fenwicks' runabout. The place came back with the whisper and hiss of the Hawkesbury, the quality of the light, sun on still water, even the sensation of damp planking under her bare feet, but that didn't bring back his name.

It was like the old dirty joke. 'What did you say your name was?' But he wasn't part of her promiscuous phase. That had been long gone.

There was a gap in the procession of customers, giving her time to look for him in the doorway.

Ocker or not, what she had seen in him was still to be seen. The lean graceful body looked youthful still and the clearcut, harmonious features had lost none of their beauty. Only the raven's wing of hair that swept across his forehead looked tweedy as a tribute to middle age.

If only she could remember his name. Usually one took refuge in endearments, which wouldn't suit the occasion at all.

The last customers had lingered to chat, giving her a reprieve of ten minutes, but she had to stand up at last. She stretched, shook her fingers, put her pen in her handbag, gave a wave and a shake of the head to Lily from the publishers to indicate that the day's work was over. Then she made for the door.

No help for it. Oh, Lord, what was his name?

He said, 'You starvin'? You had about twenty to go, so I went round to Luigi's and got a table. Hope you like Italian. Thought you'd be needin' somethin' solid after signin' books for an hour.'

The voice was not so bad, indeed so pleasant in timbre that one might take the slipshod articulation for an affectation, a kind of defiance. *This is how I choose to speak, this is what I choose to be.*

His manner too was more composed than her own. At the head of the stairs that led down to Luigi's, he paused for her to go first, not claiming familiarity but walking close enough to take her arm if she should stumble.

She was finding it difficult to place him.

The waiter came to lead them to a corner table, where a carafe of red wine stood already along with place settings for two and two wine glasses.

'Hope you drink.'

'I drink.'

'Red all right?'

'Fine.'

They studied each other, seeking memories.

He prompted her, grinning.

'Stan. The name is Stan. Stan Paterson.'

There was a pause for something unsaid.

She spoke then, embarrassed.

'How did you know?'

'You'd a' used it, wouldn't you?'

She nodded.

'Well, hullo, Stan.'

The waiter had brought the menus. They ordered *fettucine boscoiola* and *risotto milanese*.

Isobel could not trust herself with long pasta in stressful situations.

He poured the wine, which was as hard to place as the voice. Certainly it was not the average house red, but a vintage decanted to await their arrival.

She sipped impassively. If he expected her to be astonished by the quality of the wine, he would be disappointed.

He took no interest in her reaction to the wine.

He had taken the newspaper clipping out of his wallet, smoothing it out on the table in front of her, then set another picture beside it.

It was a joke photograph, taken at some seaside fun parlour. Anna's head – low brow and laughing eyes, kitten nose and round chin, short upper lip now stretched in a beguiling smile and the cheeks which Anna compared dolefully to a baby's bottom, though Isobel declared firmly and with truth that they were the firm upward curve of the cup of a flower – Anna's face framed in the golden curls of her childhood, but projecting above a screen so that it appeared to belong to the grotesque body of an old-time beach belle, dressed in a striped neck-to-knee swimsuit.

What could Anna have been doing there?

But it wasn't Anna.

For a moment Isobel wished that Anna would do something so cheerful and so vulgar, instead of studying Japanese flower arrangements and copying the thoughts of great men into her day book.

Stan said, 'My ma on her honeymoon. You can't blame me for askin'.'

She saw now that the photo was a glossy enlargement of an old print, from which half, no doubt the image of a male companion, had been cut away.

'Those tablets you found in the first-aid box – they must have been out of date.'

How low key it had all been.

Dinner at the Fenwicks', with their weekend guests, the Tafts and the Lorimers.

Bea had begun it.

'I hate the thought of that poor young man all alone. I think we should have him up to dinner this evening.'

The other members of the party had been discreetly amused. Bea's curiosity about the visitors to the houseboat was well established.

Tom Fenwick had said, 'When she buys binoculars, we'll know that all is lost.'

Nevertheless, he had gone down to the houseboat, given the invitation and had it accepted. Then at dinner the beautiful young man had been so silent and so wary that Isobel had taken pity and devoted herself to him.

'Want to come fishin' tomorrow?'

She had looked to her hosts for permission.

Bea had been enthusiastic then. Isobel could bring back information about the floating palace of sin. What could you expect of a houseboat with the name *Time Out*?

Isobel had answered, 'Why not?'

'Want a swim? There'll be some togs around somewhere.'

So they swam.

They had sat sunning themselves on the steps that led to the private jetty.

'Want to play?'

He had run his thumbnail along her spine as he spoke. That touch had awakened a sharp sexual hunger.

'Have you got anything?'

'I'll have to look about. The old man don't spend all his time fishin'.'

Bea would be gratified by that piece of information.

So now she was saying, 'Must have been out of date,' and he was answering, 'Shoulda' checked. Sorry.'

Then they both looked down at the girl with her arms full of books and her eyes full of the future. They each felt a stirring, a soft wind as the wings of fate beat close to them. They looked at each other in a moment of awe.

'Did all right for myself that time, didn't I?' he mused.

'Top of the school and all, and Mum a famous writer.'

His complacency was infuriating. He was studying the photo again. The small pleat where the corner of his mouth met his cheek expressed intense private satisfaction.

She unclenched her teeth long enough to say, 'Not famous. Successful.'

She knew the length of the signing line indicated a degree of failure in the minds of her truest admirers.

He said, 'What's the difference?'

'Success brings in money. Fame lasts longer.'

He was interested in this new idea. He could have been looking about at the features of a house he had moved into.

Oh, no, she thought. No you don't.

'Pretty kid,' he said with satisfaction.

He folded the clipping and put it in his wallet as if he owned more than the piece of newsprint. The glossy photo went into an inner pocket.

The waiter brought the dinner.

They ate in silence. No doubt he was revisiting the past, as she was.

One thing she had remembered, vividly, at the moment when he had said, 'The name is Stan.' Why had it come back at that moment, her saying to Bea, 'If you were three floors up in a burning building and that man was down below shouting "Jump!", you would jump.'

Bea had answered, 'Well, darling, don't blame me if you spatter your brains on the pavement.'

Perhaps it had been to that feeling of security in his embrace that she owed her first experience of orgasm.

She had lain panting on the shore of that ocean of pleasure, gasping out at last, 'So that's what they mean by *coming*, and *being sent off*. I must say it's spectacular.'

That had brought a shout of joy. He had pulled her nose, nuzzled at her neck, ruffled her hair, all the time laughing. This she took to be a triumph ceremony, a ritual she had thought to be peculiar to geese.

'What's so funny?'

'You are.' He hugged and rocked her, laughing still but more gently. 'There you were with those longhairs and bigheads, all of them listening to you like you knew everything, and there you are like a kid that never done it before.'

She had noted at once the disagreeable fact that this extraordinary pleasure must be in the gift of someone else.

It was disconcerting to be so overwhelmed and so dependent.

It wouldn't do to give the experience too much importance.

Nevertheless, she had stayed behind on the houseboat when the Fenwicks went back to the city.

It was a relief to find that there was a Richter scale for orgasm. It wasn't always so violent, could be sometimes just a satisfactory conclusion to a pleasant exercise.

She looked across at him twirling spaghetti neatly on his fork and wondered if that was a smug look on his face. She hoped not.

Again, observing the practised table manners, she was puzzled, unable to fix his place in society.

'When can I see her?' he said.

She thought, 'Never. You know she's alive and that's enough for you. She's mine. There's no place for you in her life.'

She said, 'She's away just now. She likes to spend the holidays with her aunt and uncle in the country.'

'You don't go with her?'

'It's out West. Too hot for me. She likes the outdoor life with her boy cousins.'

He nodded.

'Did you tell her anything about me?'

They paused for the waiter, declined dessert and ordered coffee.

'I said that you were handsome and kind. I said that you were married and your wife was sick, so you couldn't leave her.'

'And that's not far wrong. When does she come back from the country? Anna, I mean.'

Of course her name had been in the newspaper, under her photograph: Anna Callaghan.

It still sounded offensively familiar on the lips of the stranger.

He paused, sensed her reluctance, was about to speak but did not.

They drank coffee in silence.

The waiter brought the bill.

He read the amount, added money, closed the leather folder and handed it to the waiter with the casual dismissive gesture which indicated that change was not required. Another oddity.

'She'll be back for the beginning of term. That's another three weeks.'

'Meet me again? We got more talkin' to do, I think. What about Thursday lunch? Meet here on Thursday, 12.30? I'll book the table now.'

'Thursday will be fine.'

'Good. Bring photographs, please.'

Oh, what a cad I am, she thought.

Well, at least he could have his photographs. She wouldn't grudge him so much.

II

Isobel turned the key in the lock of the front door which was not quite her own. She shared the house with her aunt Noelene. Though the upper floor had long ago been made into a self-contained apartment for herself and Anna, she was always aware that the house belonged to her aunt. Notices for rates, accounts for water, gas and electricity came addressed to Miss N.V. Callaghan, though it was Isobel who paid them. Only the cleaners Mr and Mrs Bailey saw Isobel as the proprietor of the house and her aunt as that funny old bird in the kitchen who resented their attentions.

As she went through the dark hall to the stairs, she saw a glimmer under the door that led to the kitchen where her aunt watched television, listened to the races, entertained and played cards with her friends. She made excursions to the bathroom, and on Saturdays to the telephone in the hall to ring her bookmaker, retiring late at night to her small bedroom. Isobel paused to listen at the door, assuring herself that her aunt was watching television, then she went on her way, feeling no urge to confide in the relative who had for most of her life been her support and her protector.

'Don't let me die alone, or in one of those places,' Aunt Noelene had said. She had not wanted any closer relationship, so far as Isobel could make out.

How empty that upper apartment seemed always, when Anna was away. Once again Isobel felt the ache of that emptiness, though it was she who encouraged the country holidays and the school excursions. She must not be possessive.

Possessiveness was the great danger to such a relationship; excess of love could soon become tyranny if one was not vigilant.

How unfair this was, to be asked to give up more of Anna. She was entitled to fight, to make him see that he must not disturb Anna's secure and peaceful life.

She looked at her watch: 9.30. Bea Fenwick would still be awake.

Phone calls after 8.00 were not encouraged. Bea's voice was sharp as she answered Isobel's call.

'Yes?' instead of 'Hullo' conveyed the message. This was one of Bea's minor talents. Come to think of it, all Bea's talents were minor, though they were always fully developed.

'Bea, sorry to ring so late.'

Bea's voice was milder.

'Oh, darling, that's all right. I'm dying to know how the signing session went. Plenty of customers?'

'One I wasn't expecting. Anna's father. That's what I'm ringing about. I don't know what to do. I'm afraid he's going to want to see her. I'm sure of it.'

Bea said, 'We can't handle this over the phone. Come to lunch tomorrow. We'll both have time to think beforehand and can decide what to do.' Bea drew a long breath. 'Stan Paterson! Oh, my God.'

'Bea! What is it you know that I don't know? What have you been keeping to yourself? I don't get this.'

'Darling! Keep it till tomorrow. We can talk then. And get some sleep. It's not the end of the world.'

She had put down the phone. Isobel rested the handset on its cradle, fumbling because she was shaking with shock. Bea seemed to know something Isobel didn't know. One would almost think that the name Stan Paterson was notorious. Was he a master crook?

This is what comes of sexual adventure. Ten days on a houseboat with an ocker – well, a handsome and charming ocker – who had come on in the world, by what means one must not speculate.

It had brought her Anna. Whatever had brought her Anna she could not regret.

She poured a whisky and drank it slowly, telling her teeth not to chatter.

Fortunately, the honest fatigue which remained from the signing session, along with the less honourable sedation from the enemy's vintage wine, combined to send her to sleep.

In the morning she was accustomed to pay her dues to Aunt Noelene, making tea and taking it downstairs to knock at her aunt's bedroom door.

Her knock at the door was firm and her voice as she called, 'Tea! Want a cup?' was not quite a shout.

She waited cup in hand for a sign of life from within.

'Hang on a sec, will you?'

Aunt Noelene did not wish to be seen before her hair was put up for the day. For all that, she wished to be reminded that she was not waking up to an empty house. According to ritual, Isobel set the tea on the small hall table beside the bedroom door, said, 'I'll leave it on the table. Don't let it get cold.'

She would be up and away, or at work at her typewriter, before her aunt emerged from her bedroom.

Today she was too restless to work on the new novel. She wrote two letters, one to her publisher to report on the signing session and her progress on the new book, another to a magazine editor accepting an assignment, beginning a third to Anna and abandoning it because of what she could not say.

City gear and make-up, stamped letters in handbag, at last she was off to the harbourside flat which sheltered Tom and Bea in their less active years. One couldn't apply to either the word 'declining'.

In welcoming Isobel with kisses to each cheek, Bea was not as composed as usual. Her greeting was too eager; she was dressed besides as for an ordeal, in a figured satin housecoat.

'You look like a lovebird,' said Isobel.

'Too small for a parrot,' Bea agreed. 'How kind of you, dear, to be so tactful.'

'Bea, come off it!'

Bea rescued their friendship with genuine laughter.

'Well, sit down and have a sherry. When you're settled, then we'll talk. You begin, and tell me about this meeting.'

Seated on the sofa, ordered to make herself comfortable, sherry in hand, Isobel began.

'He was in the line-up with a book to be signed. I didn't look up. He put the book in front of me. I asked him the usual, did he want his name in it? He seemed out of place then, didn't know what to say, just asked for my autograph. Then he put down that newspaper clipping, the Speech Day picture of Anna, and said he wanted to talk to me.' She shuddered. 'It was a dreadful moment. I think all my life – all Anna's life – I've been fearing it. I thought at first, blackmail.'

'I don't think you need worry about that.'

Her tone implied special knowledge which made that thought absurd.

'Oh, it was just for a moment. I was too frozen to look up, but the sight of his shoes and socks was enough … It was an ugly thought, born of anxiety, I think. Bea, you know something I don't know. You knew all the time, didn't you?'

Bea sighed.

'Of course we tracked him down. You said he wasn't to be told and we kept to that.'

'How kind!'

'That's all very well, Isobel. Suppose you had died in childbirth? You made a very good try at it, as I recall. And the TB coming back ... What about Anna? She would have had some rights, I suppose. Her father might not have rejected her. We had no reason to suppose that he would.'

Isobel had heard something like this before. It made her uncomfortable.

'We knew the houseboat belonged to Conrad Benning. We thought the young man must be a trusted employee, at best. We couldn't imagine that he was the great man's son-in-law. The family wouldn't have been likely to boast of that marriage.'

An old anger stirred in Isobel, lining her up beside Stan and against the Bennings and the Fenwicks.

'He told me that he was married. He didn't boast about it either.'

Bea said, 'Sorry, love. But he was a real ocker. "I been, I seen, I done." I was astonished at you, you know.'

'He come, he seen, he scored.'

'Oh, yes. I was a dreadful snob. And he must have been something more than an ocker. That's certain.'

After a pause, she added, 'Don't you ever read the papers?'

'Not often. Why?'

'Your Stan is involved in a very nasty court case about the Benning millions. The widow is trying to upset the will.'

'I did have a vague idea about it. The name Paterson meant nothing.'

She decided not to tell Bea that the name Stan hadn't come to mind either. To put such a morsel within peck of a gossip like Bea would be to provide an occasion of sin.

'I can't cope with this all at once. Give me time.'

'Well, you have to know the facts. It's the welfare of the wife that's the argument. The daughter ...' Bea shook her head. 'Julia Benning. The diagnosis is manic-depressive. They have always had trouble keeping her within socially acceptable bounds. For a while it worked, though some very nasty people made remarks about the husband's role. For years now, she's been in full-time care. Or so I gather. Then the old man had a stroke. He lasted five years. Then he died and left this will.'

'What was wrong with it?'

'A widow's portion to the lady, an income in trust for the daughter, to provide support and medical care. The rest to Stan. No strings. No arrangement for control of Julia's fortune. That means it goes automatically to the husband, without any real safeguards. I think that is what it's all about. This Stan makes an ass of himself on the stand, saying, "But he didn't have to spell it out. He knew I'd look after her."'

'What were the lawyers doing?'

'What the old man wanted. His own lawyer said the same. He didn't write down conditions for Stan because he didn't need them.'

'You have been following this very closely.'

'Well, knowing that he was Anna's father! I never mentioned it. If her lawyers find out that he fathered an illegitimate child while he was married to the daughter … he could be in a nasty position.'

'Thank you very much. You sound like the matron at that House of Correction for the unworthy poor.'

'Let us have lunch. And Isobel, dear, we were your friends then, as we are now, so if we make an error of taste, please forgive.'

Isobel nodded, too shamed for speech. At last she growled, 'I beg your pardon.'

'Granted.'

Smiling with true affection, Bea got up to take the casserole from the oven.

As she sipped claret, after the ritual reflection that she was drinking far too much, Isobel said, 'I had dinner with him last night. I suppose that was a mistake.'

'Perhaps it was unwise.'

'I wasn't to know that. I told him I couldn't talk then – he could have seen that for himself. I asked him to wait and he went and booked a table while I was finishing up. I wasn't thinking straight.'

While she ate the chicken Marengo, she reviewed the occasion.

'That's one thing explained. I couldn't place him. You know how it is – the kind of man who inspires respect in the waiter, the one a taxi will stop for while he hardly raises a finger … I was thinking he must be some kind of millionaire's bodyguard, or something – I don't know. Now I do understand.'

'Nothing like notoriety to help a man get a table at a restaurant. Nobody can place him. There's been some laughter in court, I can tell you. That wretched woman has dug up every bit of dirt she can find, even from his own mother. "Is it a fact that your mother has called you a faggot, a whore and a gigolo?" "But she's my ma. She's entitled." That brought the house down, and then he went on to say, "It was just the temper talkin'. Ma didn't want me to take up with the Bennings. Skin you alive, that lot, she said."'

'I like the sound of her, at least,' said Isobel.

'So did the courtroom. The judge threatened to clear the court. He is either making a fool of himself or of everyone else or simply stating the facts.'

'Wait now,' said Isobel. 'I remember something. That evening, Fay Taft was wearing an obscene brooch. A male figure in silver with a penis hanging down almost to his feet. You said, "That's a very interesting piece, Fay."'

'Between my teeth, no doubt. Fay was an irritating, pretentious woman.'

'She said, "I picked it up in Indonesia. An obvious phallic symbol, of course." Well, that passed. The conversation went on. Stan turned to me and whispered, "What's this about phallic symbols? Ain't that a prick?" I giggled and whispered back, "Couldn't be better put." I suppose that was the beginning of the closer acquaintance.'

'Oh, and I did encourage it. All because I wanted to know what was inside the houseboat.'

'I can't ever regret what brought me Anna.'

'And after all, the general feeling is that if Stan Paterson married for money, he surely earned it. The worst thing she's brought against him came from one of the maids. That is the worse story, I think. He is supposed to have watched his wife walk along the top of a balcony wall forty metres above the street without trying to talk her down. The maid said he stood and watched and never so much as moved an eyebrow. All he had to say about that was that he knew she had a good head for heights. Of course it didn't look good; he seemed to be waiting for her to fall. "Your wife was heard to say 'Shall I jump?' To which you are alleged to have answered, 'It's your decision.'"'

'Oh!' Isobel was shaken. This was Anna's father.

'But one still can't place him. His defence was that she chose to get down. That was pretty effective.'

The houseboat had been named *Time Out*. Isobel recognised the suitability of the name and felt a twinge of sympathy for the young man who had no doubt been seeking refuge there.

She wasn't going to let compassion take over. Anna was hers. She would fight for her.

'It's all been a shock, I know,' said Bea.

'Well, one thing. He can't afford to make waves. If I stand firm and tell him to leave us alone, he won't be able to use pressure. He's in no position to go to the Family Court.'

'You don't think, dear, that you might be being just a little bit ruthless?'

'I'm not going to have her messed about and upset.'

If Bea had any thoughts concerning fair dealing, she kept them to herself.

III

When Isobel entered Luigi's on Thursday, she was carrying a packet of photographs of Anna, intending to portray a life which required no intruders. That hadn't been an easy task, nor was she satisfied with the result.

There were happy photos enough: Anna (aged eight) at Truro, on pony Beanbag, Anna (aged ten) with Ken and Bobbie at Truro. There were others, but she didn't want to give the impression that Anna spent her life visiting. There were the large, full-colour photographs of Anna with Isobel, feeding the pigeons in Trafalgar Square, Anna with Isobel visiting the statue of Peter Pan in Kensington Gardens. Those were professional prints of magazine glossies, taken during that PR trip to London and therefore suspect. Famous author with enchanting little appendage (just a mother at heart, after all). She and Anna had had a wonderful time, six-year-old Anna in her white rabbit coat, blue eyes wide and for once almost dimmed with wonder. She had whispered to Isobel, 'Every moment of my life is different from every other moment' – an observation Isobel had thought decidedly advanced for a six year old. She had asked too many people to share her opinion, of course.

She had lingered over those prints, reliving moments of that wonderful fortnight and of Anna's happy memories. Anna hadn't thought herself exploited, had often asked if one day they could go to Europe together – yet the quality of the photographs suggested exploitation.

Finally, she had selected a handful of photographs depicting a happy, healthy girl, engaged in youthful pastimes, and hoped they would be adequate to her purpose.

The man was waiting, at a different table – wherever he had learnt manners, he had studied with an expert. Now that she saw him as a notorious person, she had to give him full marks for poise and presence – or for the lack of the latter. He was elegantly inconspicuous.

The waiter was leading her to the table. Stan Paterson stood up as she approached and remained standing until the waiter had seated her and she had performed the awkward little manoeuvre of placing her chair. He then sat down with ease, even with grace.

Damn and blast the man.

For want of conversation, she offered her packet of photographs.

His face brightened. This was not going to be easy.

The waiter arrived with the wine list.

Stan asked Isobel if she had any preference among the wines.

The waiter murmured that he could recommend the lamb liver with rosemary sauce – the chef's masterpiece.

Stan asked Isobel if she would care to try the dish.

She nodded, thinking that if there was any more of this syrup she might vomit.

The wine came, the little tasting ceremony took place. Stan sipped and nodded, the waiter poured.

Now they were alone with that packet of photographs.

He looked through them quickly, the little pleat at the corner of his mouth still the expression of joy.

'You don't have a partner? Nobody she calls Dad?'

So, it was the worst scenario.

She hadn't meant to make her stand so promptly.

'Isn't it better to leave it like that? You can see, she's happy, she's secure. Do you have to come into her life now? What good could it do? I can see that it's wonderful for you to know that she exists, but ...'

'Oh, no! Oh no!' He shook his head. His voice was calm. 'You robbed me once. You're not going to do it twice.'

Well! Isobel was silent but her inner voice was a screech of rage. Carrying bedpans and washing up greasy dishes in that beastly hospital, Lady Prudence Dogooder Home for Consumptive Sluts and their unfortunate offspring ...

'That', she said, 'is a funny way of putting it.'

'That is how I see it. And I'll fight if I have to. There are tests now; I can go to the Family Court, I can prove she's mine and I can claim access.'

'Of course she's yours. I'm not denying that.'

The waiter, showing a notable lack of interest in the conversation, served the lunch.

Both daunted by their moment of indiscretion, they ate in silence.

Isobel paused at length to play her last card.

'Considering your present circumstances, would it really be discreet to approach the Family Court? Is this quite the time for you to acknowledge an illegitimate daughter?'

'Are you trying a spot of blackmail? Forget it. I have met experts.'

His voice was calm. His articulation was perfect.

In a flurry of rage, she said, 'Do you speak two different languages?'

Three customers at a nearby table looked across at them with interest. They had not been trained as waiters.

'Luigi will be upset if you don't finish your lunch.'

She took a mouthful.

'It's very good.'

She kept her voice to a murmur.

'As for that,' he said, 'the two voices. It's not what you know, it's what club you're in. When I first took up with Julie, her mother kept at me. I was a real dose of salts to Sheila. "So you have seen something, Stanley. Tell us what you saw." I learnt verbs. Then Julie and I picked it up and made a game of it. Backwards and forwards. "Have you caught any fish today, Mr Fisherman? How many fish did you catch today?" "Have you broken any hearts today?" "How many hearts did you break today?" Then she'd say, "Oh, Stanley, you are very well spoken." And I would switch back to ocker and say, "You ain't seen nothin' yet." I swear we had the old girl gnashing her teeth.'

'Julie doesn't sound like a poor little waif, frightened of her own shadow,' said Isobel.

'Oh, that was when she was working up to a high. There was nothing like her.'

The hell with Julie! Who wanted to know?

Could she really be jealous of Julie? Did the human ego never give up?

However, she had regained some composure.

'If I didn't mean blackmail, what did I mean? How easy this is. When does the rot set in?'

He looked at her with sympathy, bearing no grudge. 'I don't want all that money. Money's a headache. What I think about it is, if you've got money and you didn't earn it, it gets back at you, keeps you awake at night and gives you ulcers, wondering if stocks and shares are going up or down, sweating in case somebody's cheating you. Never feeling safe. You could have twenty million and you'd think you need another million to be on the safe side. But there ain't any safe side. I've got enough. I've got my workshop. I owe that to you.'

'How come?'

He was indeed a kind man, helping to restore her self-respect.

'That night I met you. The other people there, they were old and up themselves, full of smart talk. And you half their age and … well …'

'Available?'

'Well, worth a try. You wouldn't have taken offence at a civil question. I'd never cheated on Julie, but you were different. You had something important for me. And you stayed, when they went away. That meant a lot to me. I thought I gave you a pretty good time.'

'You have a long memory.'

'How often do you think I would score, with someone like you? That lot, they all respected you. When you talked they listened. I was thinking it over, then, whether Julie and I should split. I didn't know if I could stand the life much longer. Conrad told me to go away and think it over. They all respected you because you did what you were good at. Your books. See, I used to be a top workman. Craftsman. I did hand finishing, wood carving on custom furniture. I was the best and I got top money, had all my own tools. I did outside jobs for decorators. I was paying off the house for my mum. I had cause to be proud of myself. Now I had everyone calling me the highest paid lady's maid in the country. I didn't want to leave her, poor kid, but I thought, if I could go back to doing what I was good at, I'd have something to be proud of. So I set up the studio, working for decorators and some shops. Working in wood. Lovely stuff, wood. Alive. I've worked up quite a business.'

'I know how much that means.'

She was vanquished. She was also chastened.

'That is how I came to meet Julie. Though I didn't even see her that first time. It was in Denver's workshop, I was working on a bedhead with a design of a bird on a branch. Denver was taking this man and his daughter through the workshop. They stopped to look. I straightened up. He said, "How do you like that one, Julie? Isn't it pretty?" I thought he was talking to a baby, for a minute. But she was a grown girl and she whispered, "I like it very much." Her head was down. I never saw her face. Denver said they should look at the catalogue and they moved away, but Conrad looked back, saying "That is splendid work. Thank you very much." I thought to myself, imagine being his son. My old man was King Arsehole himself, talked like an oily parson and spent half his life inside, conning old ladies out of their savings. Not much of a grandfather for her,' he added, seeing all things anew. 'But good and bad – they crop up anywhere.'

'Yes,' she agreed, concealing her dismay. 'There are no rules for that.'

The lamb had now been consumed, along with half of the bottle of wine.

She refused another glass and accepted the offer of lemon sherbet.

Stan ordered a cheese platter and continued with the wine.

'It was the next week, I think, when Denver's secretary rang down to the workshop and said I was wanted in the office. The last thing I could have thought of – there was Conrad Benning with the boss. The boss said, "Mr Benning wants to ask a favour of you." Benning said I would think it a strange favour, he wouldn't think of asking it in normal circumstances. His daughter had been very ill, was very depressed and they were having difficulty in getting her to mix with society again. There was a dance, a friend's twenty-first birthday – it was important that she should attend, to take up normal life again. What he said was a stunner. She wanted me to take her. Something about me had given her confidence. Of course it cost him a lot to ask. I couldn't have said no to him. Denver was giving me the nod, to say yes.'

They paused for the waiter bringing dessert, fruit and cheese.

'If you ask my mum where the rot sets in, she'd say, it's when you wear another man's clothes. But it all happened bit by bit. He said, it would be black tie. I thought a black tie was what you wore to a funeral, but I knew enough to keep my mouth shut, and it turned out that it meant a dinner jacket, with the whole suit and the shirt and the tie, which seemed to be the least part of it. Funny lot, aren't they? All that stuff named after a bit of ribbon. He said, you must let me take care of that.'

He took time for a full-blown laugh. 'Gawd, I was green. Turning up at a top gent's outfitters with a letter from Conrad Benning and now knowing why everybody was so interested. Maybe they thought the old man had given way to himself at last. But it was always girls with the old man. He used to say that a little discreet adultery was the oil that lubricated the heavy machinery of matrimony. He sounds like a bastard, but he wasn't. It seemed like he'd made up his mind long ago to make the best of things.'

'Time out,' she said.

'Yes. If you knew Sheila … He needed it. Well, they measured me up and pinned some alterations and a few days later the box came home and Mum went up in smoke.'

'First she wanted to know if I was going on the stage, so I said I was just doing a favour for the boss. Some favour! She'd heard that one before. "If you ain't good enough for them in your own good suit, worked for and paid for, you tell them to get lost." Maybe Mum was right. Everything started with that dinner jacket.'

"Fell in love with yourself, you faggot, when you saw yourself in that get-up." My mum has a fine flow of language. "Married a shit and reared a gigolo," she'd say. Didn't stick to words, either. Belted me out of the house with the broom handle, bless her old heart.'

He smiled fondly at this display of courage and energy.

'A formidable lady,' she said.

'She was robbed. She didn't get what she'd earned, for me to marry a nice working-class girl who'd give her grandchildren. That's one reason it's so important, I want to show her that she hasn't lost everything. I want her to know she has a granddaughter.'

'Go on with your story,' she said.

'I got to the big house in my new clothes and Julie was waiting in the hall with her mum and dad. She was frightened. So was I. I could see what he meant. She looked like, anxious, as if someone was watching. But right then, we had something for each other. She said – it was hard for her ever to speak, "You came. Thank you for coming." I croaked out, "That's all right." It seemed all right, you see. Because she was so sick, it was just helping a sick kid.'

He paused to spread brie on crispbread, to pour more wine for himself, respecting her shake of the head.

'Then we got to dancing. I suppose dancing is the other thing I'm pretty good at.'

Making three in all, she thought sourly, still irritated by her own walk-on part in the drama.

'The way we danced together, it seemed like our feet didn't touch the ground. Coming back to Mum and Dad at their table, smiling. You could see them looking at each other and nodding. Like they'd done the right thing.'

'They didn't foresee any danger in all this?'

'At that stage, they both believed in the quick fix. Sheila still does, that's the problem. Then, it was get her back among her own pals and she'll be right.'

'I think it was the most appalling piece of insolence towards you.'

'The rich, they can handle that so you don't know it's happening. Conrad said how grateful they were. And that should have ended it.'

'But it didn't, of course.'

'No. It didn't. Once more, twice more. Then at work the messages started. I used to find them pinned up in the wash-room, on my desk – once on the workroom door. Stan's Escort Service. So much an hour.'

'With quotations for optional extras?'

'There you are, you see. You can know things without being told. That was you, from the start. You want coffee?'

She shook her head, fearing that information might spill out of it. Any more would be excess.

'Right. I'll get the bill. You want to go to the Ladies? It's over there to the right.'

'What do we do?' she asked as she picked up her handbag. 'Here we are, two parents who don't know each other. You had better come home and meet Aunt Noelene.'

So he had won his way. His smile of joy celebrated the victory and expressed gratitude.

'You mean now?'

'No time like the present.'

Studying her face in the mirror above the washbasin in the Ladies, she asked, 'How come these things have to happen to you? Why can't you get away with things that everyone else gets away with all the time?'

The face made no answer.

He was waiting at the foot of the stairs.

As she had foreseen, he had no trouble in hailing a taxi. So much of the insolence of the rich had rubbed off on him – but not all. She had to admit that.

Camouflage

Murray Bail

All things considered, piano-tuning is a harmless profession. Working by themselves in rooms filled with other people's most intimate belongings, piano-tuners give the impression of wanting to be somewhere else. They're known to jump at unexpected sounds. At the sight of blood they'd run a mile. And yet early in 1943 Eric Banerjee, along with some other able-bodied men, was called up by the army to defend his country. 'Mr Banerjee wouldn't hurt a fly' – that came from a widow who lived alone in the Adelaide foothills, where her Beale piano kept going out of tune.

It followed that, if a man as harmless as Eric Banerjee had been called up, the situation to the north was far more serious than the authorities were letting on.

For the piano-tuner it could not have come at a worse time. He had a wife, whose name was Lina, and a daughter who was just beginning to talk. It had taken him years to build up a client base, which barely gave them enough to live on. Then almost overnight – when the war broke out – there was a simultaneous lifting of piano lids across the suburbs of Adelaide, and suddenly Banerjee found he couldn't keep up with demand. These were solid inquiries from piano owners he had never heard of before, in suburbs such as Norwood and St Peters, even as far away as Hackney. In times of uncertainty people turn for consolation to music. Apparently the same thing happened in London, Berlin, Leningrad.

'I'd say it was some sort of clerical mistake.' He patted his wife on the shoulder. 'I won't be gone for long.' She'd burst into hysterical sobbing. What would happen now to her and their baby daughter?

Already the city was half empty. Every day the newpapers carried grainy photographs of another explosion or oil refinery in flames, another ship going down and, if that wasn't alarming enough, maps of Burma and Singapore which had thick black arrows sprouting from the Japanese army, all curving south in an accelerating mass, not only towards Australia basking in the Pacific, but heading for Adelaide, its streets wide open, defenceless. And now it was as if he, and he alone, had been selected to single-handedly stand in front and stop the advancing horde.

This uncertainty and the vague fear that he might be killed gradually gave way to a curiosity at leaving home and his wife and child, although he was bound in strong intimacy to them, and entering – embarking upon – a series of situations on a large scale, in the company of other men.

Besides, there was little he could do. The immediate future was out of his hands; he could feel himself carried along by altogether larger forces, a small body in a larger mass, which was a pleasant feeling too.

Eric Banerjee gave his date of birth and next of kin, and was examined by a doctor. Later he was handed a small piece of paper to exchange for a uniform the colour of fresh cow manure, and a pair of stiff black boots with leather laces. At home he put the uniform on again and gave his wife in the kitchen a snappy salute.

It was so unusual she began shouting. 'And now look what you've done!' Their daughter was pointing at him, screwing up her face, and crying.

On the last morning Banerjee finished shaving and looked at himself in the mirror.

He tried to imagine what other people would make of his face, especially the many different strangers he was about to meet. In the mirror he couldn't get a clear impression of himself. He tried an earnest look, a canny one, then out-and-out gloom and pessimism, all with the help of the uniform. He didn't bother trying to look fierce. For a moment he wondered how he looked to others – older or younger? He then returned to normal, or what appeared to be normal – he still seemed to be pulling faces.

'I'll be off then,' he said to Lina. 'I can't exactly say, of course, when I'll be back.'

He heard his voice, solemn and stiff, as if these were to be the last words to his wife.

'You're not even sorry you're going,' she had cried the night before.

Now at the moment of departure something already felt missing. At the same time, everything around him – including himself – felt too ordinary. Surely at a moment like this everything should have been different. Turning, he kept giving little waves with his pianist's fingers. Already he was almost having a good time.

At the barracks he was told to stand to attention out in the sun with some other men. Later there was a second, more leisurely inspection where he had to stand in a line, naked. Then an exceptionally thin officer seated at a trestle table, whom Banerjee recognised as his local bank manager, asked some brief questions.

Banerjee's qualifications were not impressive. The officer sighed, as if the war was now well and truly lost, and taking a match winced as he dug around inside his ear. With some disappointment Banerjee thought he might be let off – sent home. But the officer reached for a rubber stamp. Because of his occupation, 'piano-tuner', Banerjee was placed with a small group in the shade, to one side. These were artists, as well as a lecturer in English who sat on the ground clasping his knees, a picture-framer, a librarian as deaf as a post, a signwriter who did shop windows, and others too over-weight or too something to hold a rifle.

Over the next few days they marched backwards and forwards, working on drill. They were shown how to look after equipment and when to salute. Nothing much more.

A week had barely gone by when the order came to report to the railway station, immediately. It was late afternoon. Lugging their gear they sauntered behind a silver-haired man who appeared to be a leader. As Banerjee hummed a tune he wondered if they should have been in step. From a passing truck soldiers whistled and laughed at them.

'I don't have a clue where we're heading.'

'Search me,' said the signwriter.

Banerjee took a cigarette offered, though he never really smoked.

Every seat was taken with soldiers. Most were young, barely twenty, but actually looked like soldiers. Tanned, tired-looking faces in worn uniforms. They played cards or sprawled about in greatcoats. A few gazed out the window, even after it was dark. A few tried writing letters. Some shouted out in their sleep. The motion of the long train and the absence of a known destination gave the impression they were travelling endlessly, while at the same time remaining in the one spot. To Banerjee, the feeling of leaving an old life and heading towards a new unknown life became blurry. A voice asked, 'What day are we?' Later another, 'Has anyone got the time?'

All that night, the following day and the next they travelled slowly, with frequent stops, up the centre of Australia. They were heading towards the fighting. The further north they went the more they stopped in daylight, waiting for hours on end. On the third day the train remained motionless all afternoon, creaking in the heat, and they saw nothing through the windows but low grey bush, a few worn hills in the distance.

A young soldier spoke for the first time. 'As far as I'm concerned the Japs can have it.'

The horizon remained. Nothing moved. And the low horizon may have spread the melancholy among them. Banerjee tried to picture his street, his front fence and house, the appearance of his wife. Their daughter was growing up while he waited in the train. The other men had fallen silent, some nodding off.

The train stopped. It creaked forward, stopped again. In the dark a sergeant came through, shouting his head off.

It was Banerjee's group which was told to fall in outside.

The cold and unevenness of the ground alongside the train had them stumbling and swearing. They herded together, hands in greatcoats, and waited.

'Put out that cigarette!' – meaning the light receding.

Banerjee didn't even smile. After it could no longer be seen the train could still be heard; but what remained was soon enough replaced by the immense silence. To clear a throat out there would be deafening, worse than a concert hall.

Banerjee was probably the first to pick up the sound, a smaller engine. Another ten minutes must have passed before the truck stopped before them, tall and vibrating. It took some trouble climbing into the back. They sat facing each other under a tarpaulin roof; and the truck turned, climbing over bushes, and made its way back along the same track, over low bush and rocks, and what appeared to be creek beds, pale stones there, while the dust funnelled out behind them, obliterating the stars.

After two hours of this – bumping about, grabbing at arms, crashing of gears – the truck slowed, the path became smoother.

Someone nudged, 'Stick your head out and see where we are.'

To no one in particular Banerjee said, 'I've never been in this part of the world before.'

Leaning forward he saw a large silver shed and other buildings in the moonlight.

They were shown into a long hut. Banerjee lay down in his uniform and slept.

At first light the desolate composition of the aerodrome was revealed. A runway had been cut into the mulga by a team of crack Americans. Here then were the nation's forward defences. And not a cloud in the sky. Already it was warm. Everything spanking new in the morning light. There were two large hangars, sheds and a long water tank. Down the far end were smaller buildings and men moving about.

A man wearing an officer's cap and khaki shorts stood before them. Eric could have sworn he used to see him at the recitals at the Town Hall, although there he wore a beard.

Clearing his throat he spoke casually, but firmly. He didn't expect much in the way of formality, he said. He did however expect their full attention. 'It would make our job a darned sight easier.' The enemy, he explained, was not far away and coming closer 'as we speak'. The aerodrome was one of a number along the top of the Northern Territory. Their task was to paint – every inch of the place. 'At the moment it is a sitting duck,' was how he put it. The slightest patch of bare metal, he explained, could flash a signal to the enemy in the sky. To demonstrate he fished around in a pocket and held up a threepence – 'like so'.

The camouflage officer then squinted at the new roofs shining in the sun. 'The art in all this is deception,' he said thoughtfully, as if the whole thing was a game. He spoke of the 'science of appearances', of fooling the oriental eye. It was a matter of applying the right colours in certain combinations and patterns.

Banerjee was handed a bucket of ochre paint, a wide brush, and assigned the roof of the main hangar. It took a while to get used to the height. And the roof itself was slippery. Close up it didn't seem possible that his hand, which produced a strip of rapidly drying colour, would make any difference to the larger situation, the advance of mechanised armies across islands and continents. Further along other men were slapping on industrial grey.

As the day progressed the huge expanse of corrugated iron warmed up, almost too hot to touch, and glittered more, straining the eyes.

The others had taken off their shirts and the signwriter nearby knotted his handkerchief at the corners and put it on his head. Now and then the officer in shorts appeared below and studied their progress through the reverse end of binoculars. Pointing with a long stick he shouted up to Banerjee to give more curve there to the red ochre. He made a parallel flowing movement with his hands. 'Like a woman's hips. Think of her hips!' Which allowed Banerjee in unpromising surroundings to wander over the softness of his wife's body – at that moment probably bent over their daughter. 'That's good, a little more to the left. Good man,' the voice continued.

At the morning tea-break Banerjee sat in the shade and closed his eyes.

The Americans were recognisable by their sunglasses. When he returned their greetings Banerjee thought everybody could do with sunglasses up on the roof.

And this thought made him realise he was doing his best, and he felt satisfied.

Piano-tuning hadn't been his first choice of profession. When Eric was about ten the *News* ran a photo of him seated at the Town Hall's Steinway, his feet barely touching the pedals, reeling off a mazurka by Chopin he had sighted only minutes before. That tabloid which always had a reputation in Adelaide for fearlessness came out and announced 'our latest prodigy'. A career in the concert hall beckoned. Accordingly his normal schooling was adjusted and his parents made the necessary sacrifices, going without small luxuries, such as extra clothes or holidays. The teacher appointed was considered one of the best available: Viennese, arthritic, cameo brooch.

Banerjee became accustomed to applause. His combed hair, jug ears. He hardly ever missed a note. As he went on playing here and there, as it all flowed more like water out of his hands, years passed, and he began to wonder, as did others, whether his playing was progressing. Flaws in his technique began to show. These were probably flaws in temperament; he didn't seem conscious of them. He was taller and heavier than most pianists.

By his mid-twenties Eric Banerjee had given very few recitals, at least not in the main venues. However hard he worked the world around him remained just out of reach. It was as if a steady invisible force held him in the one spot, and now began pushing him back slightly and to one side. Almost without noticing he was playing more and more at less demanding venues, weddings, church gatherings, schools and the like, and didn't seem to mind. He felt comfortable there. Both parents died. He hardly ever attended a concert. In the space of a few more years he retreated still further until, after taking in a few pupils, which is how he met his wife, he came to rest, it would appear, piano-tuning, which may be some distance from bowing in tails on the concert platform, but is in the general vicinity, and supplied a small, regular income.

For all this, Banerjee had escaped the bitterness endemic among piano-tuners. He was pale and had a small valley in his chin. One advantage of his profession was that it left his head permanently inclined to one side, which gave the impression he was a good listener.

Banerjee was close to forty. Looking back he wondered where it had all gone. What happened in all those years? Most people didn't know or care if a piano was out of tune; only a few could tell the difference. And yet there he would surely be, continuing into the sunset, crossing from one manganese brick house to the next, one suburb to another, adjusting the progressions of sound plucked out of the air, as it were. If anyone could understand it would be the officer who spoke of 'deception'. On the street between the dusty box hedges time itself seemed to have slowed to a crawl. Any sign of life was at mid-distance; and all so quiet it was as if he was going deaf.

Not that he wanted disturbance, disruption, surprise and so on. A certain order was necessary in his line of work. These thoughts he kept to himself. Yet increasingly he felt a dissatisfaction, as though he had all along been avoiding something which was actually closer to the true surface of life.

By early afternoon the officer had taken pity on them. The academic had lost his glasses. Further along another man was silently vomiting; Banerjee too felt dizzy – headache behind the eyes. There was paint on his fingers, elbows and wrists. Perspiration had also mixed with reddish dust and muck. The golden rule in his profession: clean fingernails. Now look at them. The one remaining sign of his previous life was the vibration in one leg, and he tried shifting his weight, for of course it reminded him of the final tremor of a tuning fork.

As they made their way down, Banerjee lost control of the bucket and paint ran all over his pattern.

'Leave it till morning,' the officer said. 'If the Japs come over we're done for anyway.'

'These blisters, I couldn't grip.'

'I take it you don't, as a rule, work with your hands.'

Banerjee was examining his palm. 'Piano.' He looked up. 'I mean piano-tuner, that's what I do.'

All he wanted just then was to drink a gallon of water, and shut his eyes to the light, which he did with the help of an elbow, only to see the roof in all its glittering endlessness. He didn't feel like eating.

But it only took a few days for his body to grow into the work. His hands soon enough hardened. With his shirt off and sun on his back he became absorbed in the task. The undulating pattern of red-grey was interesting in itself; the idea behind it made them merry.

A rivalry began with the men on the other roof to see who could finish first. These men Banerjee knew from the dormitory. In ordinary life some were successful painters of hills and trees – Horace, Arthur, Russell were names Banerjee heard. The picture-framer was apparently known to them. He suggested the artists sign each sheet of iron when they finished. The man with prematurely white eyebrows nodded. 'That's the only way you'll make a killing.'

Banerjee enjoyed this sort of banter, even if he was on the fringe. There was not much of it in the day of a piano-tuner; and it would never occur to him to banter with his wife Lina, who had anyway become curiously solemn after having their child.

Early one afternoon planes were spotted – three of them, high. Leaning back they shielded their eyes to watch. The officer on the ground had to clap and yell to get them down – 'For Christ sake!' – off the roof.

Later that same day they had a grandstand view of the first two planes to land.

And just when the dust had settled, and they were admiring the practised efficiency of the Americans parking the planes, they ran out of paint. There was nothing to do but come down on ladders and sit around in the shade, where it was still hot.

Without effort, Banerjee was a man who kept his thoughts to himself; preferred to stay back than join in. Yet there he was more or less part of the group mumbling and wise-cracking. Often they were joined by the camouflage officer. After all, he had nothing much to do either. Close up Banerjee noticed his face was infested with small lines.

The officer looked up from scratching the ground with his stick. 'I don't know what's happened to our paint.' To Banerjee he added, 'In war there's more waiting than shooting. Always was.' When the talk turned to music Banerjee could have said something, and with real authority; instead he listened while letting his thoughts wander among other things.

On the third or fourth day one of the pilots squatted beside him. After talking about his hometown (St Louis) and his parents, he held out a hand and introduced himself.

Banerjee married late. Lina was barely twenty-one. He had taken her away from everybody else; that was how it later felt.

All her privacies she transferred to him. The way their habits became one she accepted with busy contentment; while Banerjee composed his face, unable to find his natural state.

He was strong all right, in the sense that he practised a certain distance, the same way he had played the piano. But Lina, she knew more; she always had. It was part of her flow, along with blood.

Whenever he paused and considered his wife he first saw her name, then found he knew very little, virtually nothing, about her; what went on in her mind, the way she came to decisions – no idea. He could not get a firm outline; and he knew only a little more about himself. More than anything else he was aware of her needs, and how he reacted to them. She had a slightly clipped voice.

She had gone to him for piano lessons. When he appeared he said he was no longer taking pupils. But that didn't stop her. Marriage was a continuation. Later, she explained how she'd heard him playing in the next room, and then his voice, though unable to catch his words. Without seeing him she had turned to her mother, 'That man is for me. He will do.'

'Even though you didn't hear a word I said? I was probably talking nothing but rot.'

But then Lina's faith in situations invariably impressed him. She could be very solemn, sometimes. She was a woman who couldn't leave things alone; constantly rearranging things on tables, plates, sideboards. She also had a way of peeling an orange with one hand, which for some reason irritated him. Banerjee knew he should be thinking more about her, his wife; and their own daughter. She complained, as she once put it, he was 'somewhere else'. Very fond of her pale shape. Her spreading generosity.

One afternoon Banerjee and the picture-framer were invited by the pilot and another American for a drive to the nearest town, Katherine, about an hour away. The jeep had a white star on the bonnet; and, unusual for a pilot, he drove one-hand, crashing into bushes and rocks instead of driving around. 'Know any songs?' he called out over his shoulder. Both Americans began singing boogie-woogie, banging on the dashboard.

They reached the town – a few bits of glittering tin.

It was here the picture-framer spoke up. 'I've got a wife called Katherine,' he said. 'She's a wonderful woman.'

Leaning over the steering wheel the driver was looking for a place to drink. 'Well, we're about to enter Katherine right now. All of us. You mind?'

The other American was smiling.

Some time later Banerjee played the piano. Nobody appeared to be listening. The flow of notes he produced seemed independent of his hands and fingers, almost as if the music played itself.

The pilot and the picture-framer beckoned from a table. Between them were two women, one an ageing redhead. Her friend, Banerjee noticed, had dirty feet.

Both women were looking up at Banerjee.

'Sit down,' the pilot pointed. 'Take the weight off those old feet.' Leaning against the redhead he said with real seriousness, 'I've got my own aeroplane back at the base.'

'That beats playing a piano. Any day,' said the younger one.

The redhead was still looking at Banerjee. 'Don't smile, it might crack your face.'

'Hey, if a plane comes over and waggles its wings, you'll know it's me.' Taking her chin in his hand, the pilot winked at Banerjee. From the bar the tubby American constantly waved, touching base.

The drinking, the reaching out for women; the congestion of words. It was the opposite to his usual way of living. Banerjee went out and stood under the stars. He tried to think clearly. The immense calm enforced by the earth and sky, at least over this small part of it, at that moment. Also, he distinctly felt the coldness of planets.

When it was time to return he found the picture-framer squatting outside with his head in his hands. And in shadow behind the hotel he glimpsed against the wall the tall redhead holding the shoulders of one of the Americans, her pale dress above her hips.

On the way back the pilot kept driving off the track. 'I need a navigator. Where are the navigators around here?' He looked around at his friend asleep.

Seated in front Banerjee didn't know where they were. 'Keep going,' he pointed, straight ahead.

On the Thursday both hangars were finished. Everybody assembled on the ground and looked up, shielding their eyes, and were pleased with their work – about eight men, without shirts, splattered in paint. Still to be done were the long walls and ends of the buildings, the vertical surfaces. And there were sheds, the water tank, bits of equipment.

The camouflage officer unlocked one of the sheds. It was stacked with tins of beef and jam. 'Will you have a look at that? Not a bloody drop of petrol to send a plane up, but plenty of tinned peaches.'

He stood looking at it, shaking his head. He wondered if Banerjee and the picture-framer could fashion a patch of green water and a dead tree out of packing cases and sheets of tin, to be placed at one side of the runway. 'A nice touch.' Gradually the pattern was coming together.

For Banerjee these counted among his happiest days. The last time he had been as happy was when he had been ill. For days lying in bed at home, barely conscious of his surroundings; it was as if the walls and the door were a mirage. There were no interruptions. Now away from everybody, except a few other men, Banerjee with the sun on his back applied paths of colour with his brush, observed it glisten and begin to dry, while his mind wandered without obstacles. As the sun went down, the pebbles and sticks at his feet each threw a shadow a mile long, and his own shape stretched into a ludicrous stick-insect, striding the earth – enough to make him wonder about himself.

Since their trip into town Banerjee joined the Americans at tea-breaks or after meals. To squat down without a word emphasised any familiarity. The Americans were relaxed about everything, including a world war. Their talk and attitudes were so easy Banerjee found himself only half listening, in fact hardly at all. Without a word the pilot would get into the jeep, just for the hell of it, and chase kangaroos around the perimeter. A few times Banerjee and the pilot sat in the warm plane parked in the open hangar. When asked what exactly the plane was to be used for, the lanky American who was flicking switches and tapping instruments shrugged. 'Search me, my friend.'

In the few weeks that remained Banerjee formed a habit of strolling down the runway after dark, joined by the camouflage officer who came alongside in his carpet slippers. With hands clasped behind his back the officer recalled performances at the Town Hall, the merits of different conductors and pianists, but invariably turned to his wife and three teenage daughters in Adelaide. 'Imagine,' he said, in mournful affection, 'four women, under one roof.'

Banerjee had been receiving regular letters. Here were trust and concern he could hold in his hand – words of almost childlike roundness, beginning with the envelope. Willingly his wife expressed more than he could ever manage. For her it was like breathing. In reply he found there was little he could say. Months apparently had passed. It came as a surprise or at least was something to consider: what about him did she miss?

He mentioned to the officer, an older man, 'My wife, she has written a letter –'

'Not bad news, I trust?'

'She tells me the front gate has come off its hinges. A little thing. I mean, my wife would like me to be there now, this minute, to fix it.'

The officer put his hand on Banerjee's shoulder. 'A woman who misses you. The warmth in bed. There was symmetry, it has been broken.' He coughed. 'The symmetry we enjoy so much in music is illusion. That's my opinion.'

In the dark Banerjee found himself nodding. More and more he was conscious of a slowness within, a holding-back, as if he saw other people, even his own family, through pale blue eyes, whereas his were green-brown. Even if he wanted, Banerjee could not be close. Not only to his wife but to all other people, to things and events as well. It was as if the air was bent, holding him just away.

On the day in question the officer inspected the paint job from all angles, as the men waited. It took more than an hour. He came back, rubbing his hands. 'Well done. That should do the trick. Tomorrow we go onto the next.'

The Americans looking on had their arms folded.

'Only one way to test it.' The pilot put on his hat. 'You with me?'

Banerjee hadn't flown in a plane before. Soon the earth grew larger and the details smaller, reduced to casual marks, old worn patches, blobs of shadow. He twisted around to see the aerodrome. At this point the pilot tilted away and began diving; just for fun. He went low, then rose in a curve; Banerjee's stomach twisted and contracted. As always he composed his face.

Levelling out, the pilot now looked around for the aerodrome.

He gave a brief laugh. 'You sure as hell have done a job on the ground.'

Banerjee thought he saw wheel marks but it was nothing. The earth everywhere was the same – the same extensive dryness, one thing flowing into the next. When Banerjee turned and looked behind it was the same.

Climbing, the plane reached a point where it appeared to be staying in one spot, not making any progress. It was as if he was suspended above his own life. Looking down, as it were, he found he could not distinguish his life from the solid fact of the earth, which remained always below. He could not see what he had been doing there, moving about on it. Knees together, the dark hairs curving on the back of his hands.

Everything was clearer, yet not really. Plane's shadow: fleeting, religious. In the silence he was aware of his heartbeats, as if he hadn't noticed them before.

Now the earth in all its hardness and boulder unevenness came forward in a rush.

Briefly he wondered whether he – his life – could have turned out differently. Its many parts appeared to converge, in visibility later described as 'near perfect'.

Last Letter to a Niece

Gerald Murnane

My Dearest Niece

With this letter, our longstanding correspondence comes to an end. The reasons for this will become clear while you read the following pages. Yes, this letter must be my last, and yet I begin it with the same message that I sent in all my earlier letters. I remind you yet again, dear niece, that you are not obliged to reply to me; and I add yet again that I almost prefer not to hear from you, since this allows me to imagine many possible replies.

This letter has been the hardest to compose. In all my earlier letters I wrote the truth, but in these pages I have to write what might be called a higher truth. First, however, I must set the scene for you, as usual.

The time is evening, and the sky is almost dark. The day was fine and calm, and the stars will all be visible shortly, but the ocean is strangely loud. The weather must be bad far away in the west, because a heavy swell is running and I can hear, every half-minute, the loud crack as some huge wave breaks against the cliffs. After each crack, I imagine I feel under my feet the same tremor that I would feel if I were standing on one of the cliffs; but of course the cliffs are nearly a kilometre away, and the old farmhouse stands rock-solid as always.

As a child and a young man, I was known as the reader of the family. While my brothers and sisters were playing cards or listening to the gramophone, I would be sitting in a corner with a book open in front of me. I was always lost in a book, so my mother used to say. She, the wife of a dairy-farmer and the mother of seven children, had little opportunity to read, but that simple remark of hers stays in my thoughts as I write this last letter. What did my mother understand of body, mind, soul, that caused her to report of her eldest son, while his body and face and eyes were clearly in her sight, that he was somehow within the confines of the smallish object held in his hand and, moreover, unsure of his whereabouts?

Something else my mother said of me: I was a bookish person. After you have read this letter, niece, you may choose to understand my mother's remark in other than its obvious sense. My mother would have meant that I read a great many books, but she was, in fact, wrong. If my hard-worked mother had cared to look closely, she might sometimes have seen that the book I held up to the kerosene lamp at the kitchen table on some evening in winter was the same that I had shielded with my hand from the sunlight on the back verandah on some Sunday morning of the previous summer.

When I write 'book', I mean, as you surely know, the sort of book that has characters, a setting and a story. I have seldom troubled myself over any other sort of book.

In many a letter during past years, I named for you one or another book that had affected me. As well, I mentioned certain passages in each book and told you that I often took pains to recall my first reading of each passage. I wonder how much you divined of what I am about to tell you in full. The truth is, dear niece, that I have been, from an early age, powerfully drawn towards certain female characters in books. I am most reluctant, even in such a letter as this, to write in everyday language about my feelings towards these personages, but you might begin to understand my situation if you think of me as having fallen, and ever since remained, in love with the personages.

Picture me on the day when I first learned what it was that would inspire and sustain me from then onwards. I am hardly more than a child. I am sitting on the lowest of the tier of sandstone blocks that support the rainwater tank on the shady, southern side of the house. This is my favourite place for reading by day in mild weather. The bulk of the tankstand protects me from the sea-wind, and if I lean sideways I some-times feel against my face a trailing leaf or petal from the nasturtiums that grow out of the cracks between the topmost stones and down over the cream-coloured surface behind me. I am reading a book by an Englishman who died nearly fifty years before my birth. The book was presented to me as suitable for older children, but I was to learn much later that the author intended the book for adults. The action of the book purported to have taken place nearly a thousand years before the author's birth. Among the major characters of the book was a young woman who later became the wife of the chief character and, later again, was rejected by him. At one or another moment while I was reading from the later pages of the book a report of the circumstances of this female character, I had to stop reading. Rather than cause embarrassment to either of us, I will describe my situation at that moment by calling on one of those stock expressions that can yield surprising meaning if one ponders them word by word. I will tell you, dear niece, that my feelings got the better of me for a few minutes.

Do not suppose that a few moments of intense feeling of themselves revealed much to me. But after I had reflected for long on the events just described, I began to foresee the peculiar course that my life would take in the future: I would seek in books what most others sought among living persons.

I reflected as follows. My reading about the personage in the book had caused me to feel more intensely than I had previously felt for any living person … At this point, dear niece, you may be preparing to revise your previous good opinion of me. Please, at least, read on … If I had been utterly candid with you from the beginning of our correspondence, you might have broken with me long ago. To whom, then, could I have written my many hundreds of pages? To whom could I have addressed this most decisive of letters? My being able to write even these few pages today is justification a hundredfold for whatever reticence and evasion I may have practised before now.

You read and interpreted rightly just now. I declare to you freely that I felt as a child and have felt since more concern for certain characters in books than for my own sisters and brothers, more than for my own mother and father even, and certainly more than for any of the few friends I have had. And in answer to your urgent question: you, dear niece, stand somewhat apart from the persons just mentioned. You are, it is true, a blood relation, but our having never met and our agreement that we should never meet allows me often to suppose that we are connected through literature only and not through your father's being my younger brother. Then again, that you are a blood-relation of mine should lessen the strangeness of my revelations. You must have been from an early age not unfamiliar with aloofness and solitariness among the branches of our family. I am by no means your only unmarried uncle or aunt.

If you are still inclined to judge me harshly, dear niece, remember that I have done little harm to any living person during my bachelor's life. I was never a brute or unfaithful to any wife; I was never a tyrant to any child. Above all, consider my claim that I never chose to live as I have lived. My own conscience has reassured me often that I have dreamed and read only in an effort to draw nearer to the people who are my true kindred; the place that is my true home. My acts and omissions have had their origins in my nature and not in my will.

And now you wonder about my religious faith. I was not deceiving you whenever I mentioned in earlier letters my weekly churchgoing, but I have to confess to you that I long ago ceased to believe in the doctrines of our religion. I have read as much as I could bring myself to read of the book from which our religion has been derived. I was able to feel for no character in that book the half of what I have felt for many a character in books scarcely mentioning God.

Do not be dismayed, niece. I have sat in church every Sunday while our correspondence has gone forward, although stolidly rather than devoutly, and more as some English labourer of the previous century sat in his village church in one or another of my most admired books. I use my time in church for my own purposes but I cause no scandal. From under my eyebrows, I look at certain young women. My only purpose is to take home to my stone farmhouse and my bleak paddocks a small store of remembered sights.

You must remind yourself, niece, that I see very few young women. I spend a few hours each week in the town of Y... , where numerous young women are to be seen in shops and offices and on the footpaths. But I have observed during my lifetime a great change in the demeanour of young women. The weatherboard church in this isolated district is perhaps the last place where I could hope to see young women dressed modestly and with eyes downcast.

But I have not explained myself. I am interested in the appearance and deportment of young women in this, the everyday visible world, for the good reason that the female personages in books, like all other such personages together with the places they inhabit, are quite invisible.

You can hardly believe me. In your mind at this very moment are characters, costumes, interiors of houses, landscapes and skies, all of them faithful images of their counterparts in descriptive passages in books you have read and remembered. Allow me to set you right, dear niece, and to make a true reader of you.

I have had no education to speak of, but a man may learn surprising things if he spends all his life in the same house and most of that life alone. With no chatter or argument in his ears, he will hear the persuasive rhythms of sentences from the books that he keeps beside his bed. With his eyes undistracted by novelty, he will see what those sentences truly denote. For long after I had first fallen in love as a result of my reading, I still supposed that the objects of my love were visible to me. Did I not see in my mind, while I read, image after image? Could I not call to mind, long after I had closed this or that book, the face, the clothing, the gestures of the personage I loved – and of others also? Whenever I think of how readily I deceived myself in this simplest of matters, I wonder in how many other matters no less simple are persons deceived who will not inspect the contents of their own minds nor look for the source of what appears there. And I beg you, dear niece, not to be prevented by the welter of sights and sounds in the great city where you live; not to be deceived by the glibness of the educated; but to accept as truths only the findings of your own introspection.

But I am preaching at you, when my own example should serve. You will believe me, niece, when I tell you that I learned, in time, that all the contents of all the books that I had read or would read were invisible. Whatever personages I had loved, or would love in the future, were for ever hidden from me. Certainly, I saw as I read. But what I saw came only from my poor stock of remembered sights. And what I saw was only a scrap of what I believed I saw. An example will serve.

Last night, I was reading yet again from a book the author of which was born before the mid-point of the previous century but lived until the year before my own birth. I had read only a few words referring to the chief female personage of the book before the appearance in my mind of the first of the images that another sort of reader would have supposed to have originated by some means in the text of the book. Being by now well skilled in such tasks, I needed only a moment of mental exertion before I recognised the source of the image just mentioned. Note first that the image was of a detail only. The text referred to a young woman. Would you not expect that any image then arising in my mind would be an image of a young woman? But I assure you that I saw only an image of a corner of a somewhat pale forehead with a strand of dark hair trailing across it. And I assure you further that this detail had its source not in any sentence of the text but in the memory of the reader of the text, myself. Some weeks before, while I sat in my usual seat in a rear corner of the church, I observed from under my eyebrows a certain young woman as she returned to her seat from the communion rail. I observed many details of her appearance, and all were of equal interest to me. Neither in the church nor at any time afterwards did I think of any of those details as being connected with any personage in any book that I had read. And yet, dear niece, the image of a strand of dark hair and a corner of a forehead are all that I can see, for the time being, of a personage who has been dear to me longer than I have been writing my letters to you.

Much might be learned from all this, dear niece. I myself have certainly learned much from many similar discoveries. Item: if, for the sake of convenience, we call the subject-matter of books a world, then that world is wholly invisible to the residents of the world where I write these words and where you read them. For I have studied the images not only of personages but of those details we suppose to be the settings of books and suppose further to have arisen from words in the text. The same book whose chief female character is visible to me presently as only a strand of hair trailing across a forehead, that same book contains hundreds of sentences describing a variety of landscapes in the south of England. I have observed myself to read all of those so-called descriptive sentences while seeing in my mind only one or another of precisely four details from the scattered coloured illustrations in a magazine that had belonged to my dead sister and still lay about this house. All of the illustrations were of landscapes in the midlands of England.

But you have read enough of arguments and demonstrations, and I have almost lost my thread. Trust me to know that the personages I have been devoted to since boyhood have been invisible to me, as have their homes, their native districts, and even the skies above these districts. At once, several questions occur to you. You assume, correctly, that I have never felt drawn towards any young woman in this, the visible world, and you want me to explain this seeming failure in me.

I have often considered this question, niece, and I have come to understand that I might have brought myself to approach one or another young woman from this district, or even from the town of Y... if even one of the following two conditions could have been fulfilled: before I had first seen the young woman, I would have had to read about her, if not in a book then in passages of the sort of writing such as appears in the sort of book that I read; alternatively, before I had first seen the young woman I would have had to know that the young woman had read about me as described earlier in this sentence.

You may consider these conditions overly stringent, niece, and the chance of their being fulfilled absurdly remote. Do not suspect for a moment that I devised these conditions from a wish to remain solitary. Think of me, rather, as a man who can love only the subjects of sentences in texts purporting to be other than factual.

There has been only one occasion when I felt myself drawn to treat with a young woman of this, the visible world without any bookish preliminaries. When I was still quite young, and still not reconciled altogether to my fate, I thought I might strengthen my resolve by learning about other solitaries: monkish eremites, exiles, dwellers in remote places. I happened to find in a pile of old magazines that someone had lent to one of my sisters an illustrated article about the island of Tristan da Cunha in the South Atlantic. I learned from this article that the island is the loneliest inhabited place on earth, lying far from shipping routes. The cliffs around the island allow no ship to berth. Any visiting ship must anchor at sea while the men of Tristan row out to her. These things alone were enough to excite my interest. You know the situation of this farm: a strip of land at the very southern edge of the continent, with its boundary on one side the high cliffs where I often walk alone. You should know also that the nearest bay to this farm is named after a ship that was wrecked there during the previous century. But my interest in the lonely island increased after I had learned from the magazine article about a disaster that had happened some forty years before my birth. A boat carrying all the able-bodied men of the island was lost at sea, and Tristan became a settlement of mostly women and children. For many years afterwards, so I read, the young women prayed every night for a shipwreck to bring marriageable men.

There came to my mind an image of a certain young woman of Tristan da Cunha, and whenever I looked up from my paddocks to the cliffs I thought of her standing on the highest cliff of her island and staring out to sea. I was impelled to visit the library in the town of Y... and to consult a detailed atlas. I learned, with much excitement, that the island of Tristan da Cunha and the district where this farm is situated lie almost on the same latitude. I learned further than no land – not even the speck of an island – lies between Tristan and this coast. Now, dear niece, you must know as I know that the prevailing winds and currents in this hemisphere are from west to east, and so you can anticipate the conjectures that I made after I had studied the atlas. If the young woman on the cliff-tops of the island of Tristan had written a message and had enclosed the message in a bottle and had thrown the bottle into the Atlantic Ocean from a cliff on the western side of her island, then her message might well have been carried at last to the coast of this district.

You may be inclined to smile as you read this, niece, but after I had first conjectured thus, I began the habit of walking once each week along the few beaches near this farm. While I walked, I composed in my mind various versions of the message from the young woman of Tristan. I found no bottle, which could hardly surprise you, but I was often consoled to think that a message such as I had imagined might lie during all my lifetime in some pool or crevice beneath the cliffs of my native district.

You have another matter to raise. You want to argue that each of the personages I have devoted myself to had her origins somewhere in the mind of the author of the writing that first brought her to my notice. You suggest that I might have studied the life and the pronouncements of the author in order to discover the reality, as you might call it, beneath my illusions, as you might call them. Better still, I might read a suitable work by a living author and then submit to him or her a list of questions to be answered in writing and at length.

In fact, dear niece, I tried long ago but soon abandoned the line of investigation noted above. Most of the authors concerned wrote their books during the previous century and died before my birth. (You must have observed that I learned my own style of writing from those worthies.) I read just enough about the lives of the authors of my admired books to learn that they were vain and arrogant persons and much given to pettiness. But what of the present century? A great change has occurred in books during this century. The writers of those books have tried to describe what they had better have left unreported. The writers of the present century have lost respect for the invisible. I have never troubled myself to learn about the writers themselves. (I exclude from these remarks a certain writer from a small island-republic in the North Atlantic. I learned of the existence of his books by a remarkable chance and read several in translation, but I could not bring myself afterwards to compose any message for him in his cliff-bound homeland.)

I have come to hope, dear niece, that the act of writing may be a sort of miracle as a result of which invisible entities are made aware of each other through the medium of the visible. But how can I believe that the awareness is mutual? Although I have sometimes felt one or another of my beloved personages as a presence near by, I have had no grounds for supposing that she might even have imagined my possible existence.

On a day long ago, when I was somewhat cast down from thinking of these matters, I wrote my first letter to you, dear niece. I sought a way out of my isolation by means of the following, admittedly simplistic proposition: if the act of writing can bring into being personages previously unimagined by either writer or reader, then I might dare to hope for some wholly unexpected outcome from my own writing, although it could never be part of any book.

How many years have passed since then you and I alone know, and this, as I have told you, is my last letter. However little I may know of it, I remain hopeful that something will come of this writing.

Something will come of this writing. I was born in Transylvania in the seventeenth century of the modern era. I became in my youth a follower of Prince Ferenc Rakoczi. When the Prince went into exile after the War of Independence, I was one of the band of followers who went with him. In the second decade of the eighteenth century, we arrived at the port of Gallipoli as invited guests of the Sultan of Turkey. Shortly afterwards, I wrote the first of my letters to my aunt, the Countess P... , in Constantinople. We followers of Prince Rakoczi had hoped that our exile might not be for long, but almost all of us remained for the rest of our lives in Turkey, and even those few who left Turkey were never allowed to return to their native land, my native land. For forty-one years, until almost the last year of my life, I wrote regularly to my aunt. I wrote to her almost a full account of my life. One of the few matters that I chose not to write openly about was my solitary state. Only a few of the exiles were women, and all of those were married. Most of us men remained solitary throughout our lives.

Dear Reader
The following is adapted from one of the seven pages about the life and the writing of Kelemen Mikes in the *Oxford History of Hungarian Literature*, 1984:

The *Letters from Turkey* were regarded by critics for a long time only as a source for the history of the exiles. Much futile research was done in an attempt to find traces of the mysterious Countess P... who proved never to have existed. Mikes never sent his letters to any 'aunt' but copied them into a letter-book, which was found after his death.

As It Were a Letter

On the day before I began to write this piece of fiction, I received in the post two items from a man who was born when I was already eleven years of age. That man, whose name is not part of this piece of fiction, has the same urge that Vladimir Nabokov attributed to himself in the early pages of his book *Speak, Memory*: the urge to learn more and more about the years just before his conception and birth. The man often questions me about what I remember from the eleven years when I was alive and he was not. The man claims that what I tell him adds to the sum of what he knows about himself.

The first of the two items sent by the man was a clipping from a recent edition of a Melbourne newspaper that I do not read. The clipping consisted of a feature article and a reproduction of a photograph. The author of the feature article was, I supposed, a reader of the newspaper who had written the article and offered it for publication to make known the forthcoming celebration of the fiftieth anniversary of the founding, in the year when I became eleven years of age and the sender of the clipping was born, of a communal settlement in a remote district of south-eastern Victoria by a group of Catholic persons who wanted to live self-sufficiently and to bring up their children far from what they, the Catholic persons, considered a corrupt civilisation. The photograph reproduced as an illustration for the article showed about forty persons of all ages and both sexes. The persons seemed to be part of an audience in a hall and to be waiting eagerly to be addressed by someone who had inspired them in the past and was about to do so again.

The second of the two items sent by the man was a note from him to me. In the note, the man told me that he still recalled from time to time a certain few pages in an early book of fiction of mine. In those pages, the chief character of the fiction was reported as having visited, at some time in the early 1950s, a place called Mary's Mount in the Otway Ranges, in south-western Victoria. The place was a communal settlement founded by a group of Catholic persons, and the chief character found everything about the place inspiring. The man told me further that he had sometimes wondered whether or not this passage of fiction had been based on an actual experience of mine. Now, the man told me, he believed he had discovered the original, as he called it, of the place in the Otway Ranges of my fiction. He had been struck, wrote the man, by the similarity between the name of the place in my fiction and the name of the place in the feature article. He concluded, so the man wrote, that I had varied the name slightly and had moved the place, as he put it, to the opposite side of the state of Victoria.

Within an hour after I had read what the man had written, I had began to make notes and to write the first draft of this piece of fiction. Then, although I understood that the man who had sent me the newspaper clipping might be only a minor character in this piece of fiction, I found myself making notes about him for including in the fiction.

Since the previous sentence is part of a piece of fiction, the reader will hardly need to be reminded that the man mentioned in that sentence and in earlier sentences is a character in a work of fiction and that the newspaper clipping and the note mentioned in some of those sentences are likewise items in a piece of fiction.

While I made the notes mentioned above, I first noted that the man is himself the author of published pieces of fiction. I noted this in order to remind myself of the only conversation that the man and I had had about the writing of fiction. During that conversation, the man and I had agreed that the chief benefit to be got from the writing of a piece of fiction was that the writer of the fiction discovered at least once during the writing of the fiction a connection between two or more images that had been for long in his mind but had never seemed in any way connected.

I noted further, in my notes for my piece of fiction, that the man in question had at one time begun but had soon afterwards given up a course for the degree of bachelor of laws in a university and had often afterwards made remarks that caused me to suppose he held in contempt the persons who are sometimes called collectively the legal profession.

I noted further in the notes that later became part of this piece of fiction that the man who is now a character in this piece of fiction had become, when he was a young man, the owner of a guitar and that he had played his guitar often since then. The man owned many books of music for the guitar and many books about famous players of the guitar and many recordings of guitar music. The man had sometimes played his guitar in my hearing, although I had told him politely when I had first seen his guitar that I consider myself a musical person but that I have never been inspired by any sound of strings being plucked or otherwise handled.

I noted further in my notes that the man had at one time taken a course of lessons in the Spanish language and had told me at the time that he found the sound of the language inspiring. When I was making that note, I recalled for the first time in many years that I had spent more than a few hours at the age of eleven in looking through a newspaper printed in the Spanish language.

Towards the end of my notes, I noted that I had sometimes admired the subject of the notes as a result of my suspecting that he had been connected sexually with many more women than I had been, even though I had been alive for eleven more years than he had been.

I noted finally in my notes that the man had been for many years the owner of forty-five hectares of virgin bushland in the Otway Ranges and that he had sometimes told me that if only he could have found what he called the right sort of woman, he would have built on his bushland property a simple but comfortable house and would have moved there with the woman and afterwards lived what he called his ideal life.

I did not note as part of my final note, but I note here that I have never visited the Otway Ranges or wanted to visit them. I once wrote a passage of fiction the setting of which was a place in the Otway Ranges, but I have written many pieces of fiction the settings of which are places where I have never been.

After I had finished the notes mentioned above, I looked into the picture of the persons who seemed to be waiting in a hall for the person who inspired them from time to time. I was looking for what I looked for whenever I looked into one or another photograph or reproduction of a photograph of persons who had been alive during the first twenty-five years of my own life and who might have lived during those twenty-five years in places such that I might have met up with one or another of the persons while I was living at one or another of the twenty-five and more addresses that I lived at during those twenty-five years and before I decided to live for the remainder of my life at the one address. I was looking for the face of a female person who might have met up with me, or might merely have come to my notice, and whose words or deeds, or whose face observed merely from a distance, might have inspired me to become one of the many persons I might have become and to live for the remainder of my life in one of the many places where I might have lived.

In the illustration that I looked at, the female faces seemed to be those of married women or very young children. (I took no interest in the faces of the two nuns in the front row.) I supposed that the early settlers at the settlement had been families with small children. And then I read the text of the feature article beside the illustration. I found the text sentimental and dishonest, but in order to explain this finding of mine I would have to report certain facts that are not part of this piece of fiction.

After I had done all the things so far reported I made notes for, and later wrote, the following pages, which themselves make up a complete piece of fiction within the whole of this piece of fiction.

*

I was eleven years of age when I first heard of the settlement that I shall call hereafter Outlands. The settlement was in neither the south-east nor the south-west of Victoria but in the far north-east of the state, and it had already been established for several years before I first heard of it.

When I first heard of Outlands, one month short of fifty years ago, I was already living at a place that had been until recently a sort of settlement founded and managed by a small group of Catholic lay-persons who were, in their own way, inspired. This place, which I shall call hereafter the Farm, was in a northern suburb of Melbourne. From the front gate of the Farm I could see, only a short walking-distance away, a tram terminus; and yet the suburbs of Melbourne reached in those days so little distance from the city that I could look out from the rear gate of the Farm across a paddock where a few dairy cows had been kept until recently. On either side of this gate were sheds where tools and cattle-feed had been stored, and one shed that had been the dairy. Between the sheds and the house was a neglected orchard overgrown with long grass. Where the orchard adjoined the kitchen garden of the house was a small bluestone building that had been the chapel.

I was living at the Farm as a poor relation of the family whose home it then was. That family consisted of an elderly husband and wife, their only son, who was a widower in early middle age, and his only son, who was five years younger than myself. My own family – my parents and my sister – were scattered among relatives and friends because we had no house of our own. A few months before, my parents had had to sell the house they partly owned in a suburb not far from the Farm. They had needed the money to settle my father's debts. He had incurred these debts as a part-time trainer of race-horses and a punter. When my parents had put up the house for sale, they had believed they could move after the sale to a partly built house in an outer south-eastern suburb. Not all of my father's racing friends were luckless gamblers. One friend was what was called in those days a speculative builder. He was going to let my family live in one of his partly built houses while my father tried to arrange a loan from a build-ing society. But something had delayed this plan, and we found ourselves for the time being homeless. My mother and my sister went to stay with one of my mother's sisters. My father boarded with friends of his. I went to the Farm.

I remember no feelings of misery or even discontent. The Farm was a haven of order and neatness after the latest of the many crises that my father's gambling had caused. I was especially pleased not to have to attend school. I was tired of going to one after another school and being always someone newly arrived or soon to leave while everyone else seemed settled. I arrived at the Farm in the first week of November, and it was decided that I could do without school for the last months of the year. In the main room at the Farm was a tall cupboard full of books. I promised my father when he left me at the Farm that I would read every day, even though he seemed too concerned about his own problems to care how I might spend my time.

I was a relation of the people at the Farm because the widower's dead wife had been one of my father's sisters. I shall call the widower hereafter Nunkie. The name suits my memory of him as being always cheerful and helpful towards his nephew, myself. Nunkie might have been a scholar on the staff of a university if he had been born in a later decade, but he had been obliged during the Great Depression to train as a primary teacher for the Education Department of Victoria. He had met his future wife when he was teaching at the small school near the farm where my father and his sisters grew up. The school had a residence beside it for a married teacher, but Nunkie lived in the residence with his parents. Nunkie's parents had come with their son to the far south-west of Victoria for the time being because the father could no longer get work as a musician in picture theatres after the silent films had been replaced by talkies, and because he had been a reckless gambler on racehorses for as long as he had lived in Melbourne. I shall call this man hereafter the Reformed Gambler, because his years away from Melbourne had apparently reformed him. I never saw him looking at a form-guide or listening to a race-broadcast while I was at the Farm, and every Saturday he went off to umpire one or another local cricket match.

Nunkie and his mother always seemed united against the Reformed Gambler. The son and the mother mostly ignored him, or, if he tried to break into one of their many long discussions, put him off with short answers.

Every evening the people at the Farm, together with their many visitors, recited the rosary and a portion of the divine office for the day. The Reformed Gambler was obliged to take part in these prayers, although I could see that they bored him. He was a gentle, likeable man whose religious observance consisted of Sunday mass and an occasional confession and communion. One evening, after twenty or thirty minutes of prayer during which the word 'Israel' had occurred a number of times (*Remember, O Israel ... I have judged thee, O Israel ...* and the like), the Reformed Gambler looked in the direction of his wife and son and asked innocently who was this Israel, anyway: this chap who was always turning up in our prayers.

Much of what I know about the family at the Farm I learned at one or another later time from my father. According to him, the father at the Farm was the salt of the earth, the mother looked down her nose at the world, and the son meant well but had been turned by his mother into an old woman himself. On the evening when the Reformed Gambler had asked who Israel was, I actually saw his wife look down her nose. There is no better form of words to suggest the pose that she struck. Her son, Nunkie, tried to relieve the tension by saying, not directly to his father but into the air, that Israel was not a man but a people, and not even a people but a symbolic people ...

The Reformed Gambler has no further part in this piece of fiction, but I would like to report here that he lived a long life and that he spent much of his time in later life far from his wife and son and in the company of congenial relatives of his.

The person who looked down her nose sometimes I shall call hereafter the Holy Foundress. I call her this not only because she had founded the Farm, but because I believe she would have been, in many an earlier period of history, the foundress of a religious order dedicated to one or another special task within the Church; would have written without help from any adviser the compendious Rule and Constitution of the Order; would have travelled to Rome under trying conditions; would have gained at last official approval for her new order; and would have died long afterwards in what was called in earlier times the odour of sanctity.

My father had warned me before he left me there that I must not ask questions about what he called past goings-on at the Farm. I asked no questions, but I saw much evidence that the Farm had been, until recently, a small farm with a few dairy cows. I guessed that the cows had been milked and other farming tasks performed by the five or six male persons who had slept in the wing of the house which was obviously a later addition and which Nunkie sometimes called absently the boys' wing. I guessed that the boys, whoever they had been, had attended daily mass every morning in the bluestone chapel that was always locked whenever I tried the door but which Nunkie unlocked for me one afternoon, after I had questioned him about the chapel yet again, so that I was able to look at the empty seats and the bare altar and the cupboard where the priest's vestments had been stored and at the windows of orange-gold frosted glass that made a mystery of each view of trees or sky outside the place.

At the age of eleven, I never doubted that I would live for the rest of my life as a faithful Catholic, but I found it tedious to sit each Sunday in a parish church crowded with parents and their squirming clusters of children; to hear the priest preaching that the parish school needed money for an extra classroom; to read in the Catholic newspaper that the Archbishop had made a speech attacking communist-controlled unions after he had blessed and opened a new church-school building in a far-away outer suburb where the streets were dust in summer and mud in winter. From here and there in my reading, I had put together a collection of expressions that inspired in me what I supposed were pious feelings: *private oratory*; *private chaplain*; *gothic chasuble*; *jewelled chalice*; *secluded monastery*; *strict observance*. I seem to have been dreaming of a private place where I could enjoy my religion with a few like-minded persons. At the centre of the place was, of course, the oratory or chapel, but I was also concerned that the place should be surrounded by an appropriate landscape.

After I had been at the Farm for a few days, I heard for the first time about Outlands. The day was a Sunday, and a visitor from Outlands had arrived for the mid-day meal. The visitor was a young man perhaps not yet thirty years of age. He was pale and rather plump, and I was surprised when I learned that he came from a settlement of farmers but very interested when I saw that the newspaper he carried with his luggage was in a foreign language. Before I could learn much about the man or about Outlands, my father arrived to take me for a walk and to tell me news of our family.

While I walked with my father, I tried to learn what he might have known already about the Farm and about Outlands. My father would tell me only that Nunkie and his parents had been very kind to take me in but that I must not let them turn me into a religious maniac. My father, who could well be called for the purposes of this piece of fiction the Unreformed Gambler, was a Catholic in the same way that the Reformed Gambler was a Catholic. My father went to mass every Sunday and to confession and communion once each month and seemed to suspect the motives of any Catholic who did any more than this.

While we walked on the Sunday, my father told me that he knew about Outlands only that it was doomed to fail, just as the Farm had failed. Such places always failed, my father said, because their founders were too fond of giving orders and not prepared to listen to advice. He then told me that the Farm had been intended by its founder, the person called in this fiction the Holy Foundress, to be a place where a few men who had recently completed long terms of imprisonment could live and work and pray while they prepared themselves to find homes and jobs in the world at large. The Farm, my father reminded me, was only a few tram-stops away from the large prison where he himself had been a warder when I was born and where he had learned, as all the other warders, his mates, had learned, that almost every person who had been imprisoned for a long term was by nature the sort of person who would be later imprisoned again.

My father had ceased to be a prison warder in one of the first years after I was born, but he had remained friends with many warders. He told me on our Sunday walk, in the streets of the suburb where the Farm was at the end of the tramline that passed the front gate of the large prison, that all the warders who had heard of the founding of the Farm had · predicted that the Farm would fail and that the warders' predictions had been fulfilled. The Farm had failed, my father said, because most of the men who had gone from the prison to the Farm had not been reformed but had gone on planning – and even committing – further crimes while they lived at the Farm.

My father told me the story of the Farm with seeming relish, but I tried while he talked to compose in my mind arguments in defence of the Farm. I had lived at the Farm for only a few days, but each morning I had gone with Nunkie and his son, my cousin, and the Holy Foundress to early mass

in the semi-public chapel of a nearby convent; each evening
I had prayed with the others at dusk in the room where the
big bookcase stood; each day I had walked between the fruit-
trees for ten minutes, imitating the even paces of one or
another priest I had once seen walking on the paths around
his presbytery while he read the divine office for that day.
Perhaps I was discovering the power of ordered behaviour, of
ritual. Perhaps I was merely devising for myself one more of
the imagined worlds I had devised throughout my childhood.
Although I was hardly fond of the Holy Foundress, I admired
her for having tried to set up what I thought of as a world of
her own, a world apart from or concealed within the drab
world that most people inhabited, a small farm almost
surrounded by suburbs.

My own imagined worlds before then had been located
each on an island of the same shape and outline of Tasmania,
which was the only suitable island I knew of. The people of
those worlds had been devoted to cricket or to Australian
football or to horse-racing. I had drawn elaborate maps showing where the sportsgrounds or racecourses were situated.
I filled pages with coloured illustrations of the football
jumpers of the many teams or of the coloured caps of the
cricket teams or of the racing silks of the racing stables. I had
spent so much time in preparing these preliminary details for
each of my imagined worlds that I had seldom got as far as to
work out results of imagined football or cricket matches or of
imagined horse-races.

I had destroyed or lost all the pages showing the details
mentioned above, but sometimes during the year before
I arrived at the Farm I had felt a peculiar longing and had
wanted my adult life to be so uneventful and my future home
to be so quiet and so seldom visited that I could spend most of
my life recording the details of an imaginary world a hundred
times more complicated than any I had so far imagined.

The people at the Farm seemed not to read newspapers,
although I feel sure today that Nunkie and the Reformed
Gambler must have looked through the results and reports

of cricket matches during the summer. Perhaps they kept the newspaper out of sight of the children, or cut out the sporting pages and burned the rest. When I asked Nunkie, on my first day at the Farm, where the newspaper was, he told me that the people of the Farm were not especially curious about events in the secular world. Nunkie's expression, 'the secular world' gave me even then, on my first day, the pleasant sensation that I was inside a world inside what others considered to be the only world.

After Nunkie had answered my request for a newspaper, he had taken me to the bookshelves in the main room at the Farm. He told me I was welcome to read any book from what he called the library, provided that I first sought his approval of my chosen book. I saw names of authors such as Charles Dickens and William Thackeray on some of the nearest books, and I asked Nunkie whether the library contained any modern books. He pointed to a shelf containing many of the works of G.K. Chesterton and Hilaire Belloc.

On the day after Nunkie had shown me the library, I looked more closely at the books. When he arrived home that afternoon from the state school where he taught, I asked him whether I could read a book from an upper shelf: a book the spine of which I had looked at often during that day. The title of the book was *Fifty-two Meditations for the Liturgical Year.*

As soon as I had seen the title mentioned above, I had done, probably for the first time, two things that I have done many times since then: I first imagined the contents of a book of which the title was the only detail known to me; and I then derived from my imagining much more than I later derived from my looking into the text of the book.

I have to remind the reader that this piece of fiction is set in the year 1950. In that year, and for many years afterwards, the word *meditation* denoted only a little of what it has since come to denote. In the year in which I wanted to read the book mentioned above, there were no doubt a few scholars or eccentrics in the city of Melbourne who knew something about meditation as it was practised in so-called eastern religions, but neither Nunkie nor I knew of the existence of those scholars or eccentrics. The only sort of meditation that he or I was aware of was an exercise such as Ignatius Loyola, founder of the Society of Jesus, had devised: an attempt by the person meditating to bring to mind as clearly as possible one or another of the events reported in one or another of the four Gospels and then to ponder on the behaviour and the words of Jesus of Nazareth as reported in connection with that event and then to feel certain feelings as a result of the pondering and finally to make certain resolutions for the future as a result of the feelings.

Thirteen years after I had asked to be allowed to read the book mentioned above, I was anxious to have as my girl-friend a certain young woman who worked in a certain second-hand bookshop in the central business district of Melbourne. While I was thus anxious, I used to visit the bookshop every Saturday morning and to spend an hour and more looking around the shelves before buying one or another book and then trying to begin with the young woman while she sold me the book such a conversation as would persuade her that I was a young man who dressed and behaved unexceptionally but who saw inwardly private sights the descriptions of which would become in the near future the texts of one after another of the works of fiction that would make him famous. Whether or not I can claim that the young woman became my girl-friend, I can state that she and I went out together, as the saying used to go, for a few weeks during which time she sometimes described to me what she had seen inwardly as a result of her having read one or another book while I described often to her what I foresaw as the contents of one after another of the works of fiction of mine that would later be published, one of which works, so I promised the young woman, would include a character inspired by her. At the end of the few weeks mentioned in the previous sentence, the young woman went to live in another city, and she and I have never met up with one another or written to one another since then. However, I have learned from newspapers that the young woman later became a famous author, although not an author of fiction. The young woman later became a much more famous author than I became, and during the year before I began to write this piece of fiction, her autobiography was published. I have been told by a person who has read the autobiography that no passage in it refers to myself. Even so, the publication of the autobiography of the famous woman who had once been the young woman in the second-hand bookshop reminded me that I had still not kept the above-mentioned promise that I made. I am able to introduce the young woman into this paragraph, and so to keep my promise to her, for the reason that one of the books that I bought in the shop where she worked was a copy of the same book that I had wanted Nunkie's permission to read, as was reported above. I had bought the book, and had given the young woman in the shop to understand that I would look into the book, because she was still a faithful Catholic and I wanted her to suppose that I had not lost all interest in religion and even that she might win me back to a certain degree of belief in the Catholic faith if she became my girl-friend. The paragraph that ends with this sentence is, of course, part of a work of fiction.

After I had asked Nunkie whether I might read the book mentioned earlier, he had smiled and had told me that meditations were not for boys. He had then reminded me that it was time for our daily cricket match. This was played every evening between Nunkie and his son on the one side and the Reformed Gambler and myself on the other. We bowled underarm with a tennis ball on a paved area near the former dairy, and we observed complicated local rules as to how many runs were scored if the ball was hit into this or that area of the long grass in the orchard.

Even though I knew nothing about non-Christian sorts of meditation, I had already, at the age of eleven, heard or read enough about certain great saints of the Church to know that those persons saw more in their minds while they prayed or meditated than mere illustrations of the gospel story. I had heard or read that certain great saints had sometimes gone into trances or been transported. No priest or religious brother or nun had ever, in my experience, suggested that his or her congregation or pupils should do more while praying than talk to one or another of the Persons of the Holy Trinity or the Blessed Virgin Mary, or one or another of the saints. I sensed as a child that my priests and teachers were uncomfortable when questioned about anything to do with visions or with unusual religious experiences. Those same priests and teachers were never reluctant to talk about hell or purgatory and the punishments meted out to the residents of those places, but they were reluctant to speculate about the joys of heaven. A child who asked for details about the celebrated happiness of the residents of heaven might well be told that the souls in heaven were content for ever to contemplate the Beatific Vision. This was the term used by theologians, so I learned as a child, for the sight that one saw when one saw Almighty God.

For all that I was most curious to know what the souls in heaven enjoyed and what the great saints sometimes saw while they prayed or meditated, I was in no way curious to see God Himself. I write this in all seriousness. I had never wanted to meet God or to have with Him any more dealings than were absolutely necessary. I believed in Him; I was pleased to belong to the organisation that I believed to be His One, True Church; but I had no wish to meet Him and to have to make conversation with Him. I was much more interested in the place where God lived than in the Deity Himself.

For most of my childhood, I could only dare to hope that I might one day see the landscapes of heaven. I was rather more confident that I would one day glimpse some of those landscapes while I prayed with intensity or while I meditated. And, of course, I was able to imagine beforehand something of what I hoped to glimpse in the future. The landscapes of heaven were lit by a light that emanated from God Himself. Near its source, this divine light was of an almost unbearable fierceness, but in the distant zones of heaven where I was most

at home, it shone serenely, although by no means unwavering-
ly, so that the sky above the landscapes seemed sometimes like
a sky at early morning in summer in the world where these
details were being imagined, and sometimes like a sky at mid-
afternoon in late autumn in that same world. The details of
the landscapes themselves were by no means elaborate. I was
content to compose my heavenly vistas by extending further
and further into the background the simple green hills, some
of them with a few stylised, tufted trees on top, that I had
enjoyed staring at in pictures in the earliest of my picture-
books; by having a pale-blue stream wind between some of the
hills; by situating on this or that hillside a farmhouse or a few
cattle or horses, and behind just one of the furthest hills the
church-steeple or the clock-tower of a peaceful village.

The person who imagined the landscapes described above
could hardly have been satisfied to contemplate mere details
designed for infants, and nor was he. My looking at the landscapes of the outer zones of heaven was always accompanied
by the reassuring knowledge that heaven extended endlessly.
My looking over a vista of green hills was only an introduction
to the place that contained all places, even all unimaginable
places. Soon, the simple green countryside would give way to
unknown landscapes. And even more encouraging than the
knowledge just described was a certain feeling that I often felt
during my surveys of the little I had so far imagined.

The feeling mentioned above was a feeling of being accompanied by and watched over by not so much a person as a
presence. This presence was unquestionably a female presence. Sometimes I imagined that the presence and I were no
more than children who had agreed to be girl-friend and boyfriend. Sometimes I imagined, though I was still a child
myself, that the presence and I were adults and were wife and
husband. Sometimes I imagined the face of the presence,
sometimes even the clothes that the presence wore or the few
words that the presence spoke to me. Mostly, I was content to
feel the presence of the presence: to feel as though she and
I were sharers in a pact or understanding that bound us

together intimately but could not have been expressed in words. Although I would never during my childhood have asked such a question of myself, it occurs to me now to ask of the fictional child who is the chief character of this part of this piece of fiction the question what seemed to him the most desirable of the likely pleasures that he might enjoy in his imagined heaven. It is, of course, easy to ask a question of a fictional character but unheard of to receive an answer from such a character. Even so, I believe I should report here my belief that if the chief character mentioned above could be imagined as being able to answer the question mentioned above, then he could be imagined as answering that he most desired to discover, in a remote district of the landscapes mentioned previously, a place in which he and the presence that accompanied him always could settle.

If this piece of fiction were a more conventional narrative, the reader might be told at this point that the parenthetical passage that began in the fifteenth paragraph before this paragraph has now come to an end and that I, the narrator, am about to continue narrating the events of the Sunday when the chief character of this piece of fiction was walking with his father after having seen an hour beforehand at the Farm a pale and plumpish young man who was the first of the settlers at Outlands that the chief character had seen. Instead, the reader is hereby assured that nothing of significance took place during the rest of the Sunday just mentioned, and the same reader is further assured that the next paragraph and many subsequent paragraphs will contain not a narrative of certain events but a summary of the significance of those events and of much more.

I asked few questions about the settlement of Outlands while I was at the Farm, but I listened whenever a resident of the Farm or a visitor from Outlands said anything about the settlement in the far north-east of the state. Even years later, I was still able to learn details from one or another of my father's relatives.

The writer of the feature article mentioned much earlier

seemed to have believed that the settlement in south-eastern
Victoria was the oldest or even the only such settlement of its
kind. That settlement was founded in the year when I was
staying at the Farm, by which time Outlands had been in existence for at least one year. I have heard of another such
settlement that was founded in the late 1940s. These settlements were hardly rivals, but I suspect that the settlers in the
south-east, many of whose faces I had seen images of in the
illustration mentioned earlier, might have been called mostly
working-class persons, whereas the Outlanders might have
been called mostly middle-class persons. I suspect further
that the Outlanders would have wanted to be called a group
of Catholic intellectuals. My father called them long-hairs, in
accordance with his belief that men who had been to university wore their hair longer than did other men, had less
common sense, and were less able with their hands.

On the day after I had first met an Outlander and had
learned something about the settlement of Outlands, I walked
far out into the long grass between the neglected fruit-trees at
the Farm and founded a settlement of my own. I thought of
my settlement as having the same name as the settlement that
had inspired me, but for the sake of convenience I shall call
my own settlement hereafter Grasslands.

The founder of the settlement of Grasslands had never met
any other child or adult who was less skilled than he was at
representing things by drawing or painting or modelling.
Other children had often laughed, and even teachers had
smiled, at the distorted pictures and lumpish objects that the
future founder of Grasslands had produced in art and craft
classes. The same children and teachers praised the essays
and stories that the future founder wrote in English composition classes. On the day when he prepared to found his
settlement, the founder might have been expected to call on
his skills as a writer and so to write a detailed description of
the settlement and the settlers. But the founder knew he had
much more to fear if his writing were discovered by one of
the adults at the Farm than if one of those adults stumbled

on his model in the grass. The founder knew that his writing would report what the settlers saw inwardly as they lived their lives at the settlement and so, by implication, what he, the writer had seen inwardly while he wrote.

And so the settlement of Grasslands was founded not as the subject of a piece of writing but as a model or toy. And because the founder was so little skilled with his hands, he was unable to make from the excellent clay of the northern suburbs of Melbourne any sort of building other than a rough cuboid or trapezoid that later cracked apart in the sun. The animals in the paddocks at the settlement were pebbles. The settlers themselves were forked twigs found among the branches of the orchard trees.

I never learned how many persons had settled at Outlands. While I stayed at the Farm I saw two young men and three young women who might have been newly recruited to Outlands or, perhaps, returning briefly to Melbourne to settle some private business or who might even have been on their way back to the secular world after having decided to leave Outlands. The young men seemed thoughtful; the young women seemed more ready to smile or joke, but I noted that they were all what my father called plain Janes. All of these young persons were unattached. I never heard of any married couples at Outlands, although I cannot believe couples would have been prevented from joining the settlement.

I never met any of the leading settlers from Outlands. There seemed to have been two men prominent in the founding of the settlement: one a medical practitioner and one a barrister and solicitor. Of these two, the legal man was much more often talked about at the Farm, and always with reverence. His surname ended with the fifteenth letter of the English alphabet. So, too, did the surname of the Reformed Gambler. (And, so too, of course, did Nunkie's surname.) I understood that the Reformed Gambler had come to Australia from Italy as a young man. I concluded from all this – wrongly, as I shall explain later – that the surname of the admired legal man was an Italian surname.

The founder of Grasslands would have said at the time that he had founded his settlement as a place where he and his like-minded followers could live prayerful lives far from the dangers of the modern world. Or, he might have said that Grasslands was intended as a place from which heaven would be more readily visible.

If the founder of Grasslands had been asked at the time what were the chief dangers of the modern world, he would have described in detail two images that were often in his mind. The first image was of a map he had seen a year or so previously in a Melbourne newspaper as an illustration to a feature article about the damage that would be caused if an Unfriendly Power were to drop an atomic bomb on the central business district of Melbourne. Certain black-and-white markings in the diagram made it clear that all persons and buildings in the city and the nearer suburbs would be turned to ash or rubble. Certain other markings made it clear that most persons in the outer suburbs and the nearer country districts would later die or suffer serious illness. And other markings again made it clear that even persons in country districts rather distant from Melbourne might become ill or die if the wind happened to blow in their direction. Only the persons in remote country districts would be safe.

The second of the two images mentioned above was an image that often occurred in the mind of the founder of Grasslands although it was not a copy of any image he had seen in the place he called the real world. This image was of one or another suburb of Melbourne on a dark evening. At the centre of the dark suburb was a row of bright lights from the shop windows and illuminated signs of the main shopping street of the suburb. Among the brightest of these lights were those of the one or more picture theatres in the main street. Details of the image became magnified so that the viewer of the image saw first the brightly lit picture theatre with a crowd milling in the foyer before the beginning of one or another film and next the posters on the wall of the foyer advertising the film about to be shown and after that the woman who was the female star of the film and finally the neckline of the low-cut dress worn by that woman. This image was sometimes able to be multiplied many times in the mind of the viewer, who would then see images of darkened suburb after darkened suburb and in those suburbs picture theatre after picture theatre with poster after poster of woman after woman with dress after dress resting low down on breasts after breasts.

If the founder of Grasslands had been asked at the time why he had founded his settlement, and if he had been able to describe in detail to his questioner the images mentioned above, he would have assumed that the questioner would not need to question him further and would understand that he, the founder of Grasslands, wanted to live in a place where he need no longer fear the bombs of an Unfriendly Power and need no longer try to imagine the details concealed by low-cut necklines of dresses of female film-stars.

One of the young men who called at the Farm from Outlands wore a beard. Until I met him, I had never seen a beard on any but an aged man. I watched the bearded man while he worked with rolled-up sleeves to load some timber from a disused Farm building onto a truck that was going to Outlands. The bearded man joked and said such things as gave me to understand that he read often from the New Testament and the Fathers of the Church and Saint Thomas Aquinas. I thought of the bearded man as resembling a man from medieval times, and I supposed Outlands more resembled medieval Europe than modern Australia.

The newspaper carried by the pale and plumpish young man mentioned much earlier in this piece of fiction was in the Spanish language. Even before I stayed at the Farm, I had come to understand that Spain was the most admirable of all European countries, even though it was the most reviled by the secular press. It was the most admirable, so one of my father's sisters had once told me, because it was the only country in Europe where Communism had been fought to a standstill, and it was the most reviled because many journalists secretly sympathised with Communism.

Many years after both Outlands and Grasslands had ceased to exist, I read a statement by a man who had been a commentator on current affairs in various Catholic newspapers and on a Catholic radio program from the 1930s to the 1950s. The man had stated that he had taken many unpopular positions during his career as a commentator and had received many angry letters as a result but that the most numerous and the angriest letters by far had been those that reached him after he had written and had broadcast his opinion that the government of General Franco better suited the interests of Spain than any government that might have been installed if the civil war had ended differently.

The founder of Grasslands knew nothing of the causes or results of the Spanish Civil War, but he sensed that in this connection, as in so many others, the sort of Catholic who wore a beard and chose to live on a remote settlement possessed an inner, private knowledge of moral issues which was almost the opposite of what passed for knowledge with other persons. The founder hung about the pale and plumpish young man while he read parts of his newspaper. He, the founder, asked to have the dialogue in the Felix-the-Cat cartoon translated for him and laughed at the humour of it and learned from it the only five Spanish words he was ever to learn. The same founder was not at all troubled when the same pale and plumpish young man returned to the Farm two weeks later for another short visit and took out the same edition of the same newspaper (the founder identified it from the Felix cartoon) and began to read parts of it.

When the liturgical season of Advent was about to begin in the world where the settlement of Grasslands appeared as a few rows of cracked mud blocks and its settlers as a dozen and more forked twigs, the uncle of the founder of Grasslands, in whose eyes the settlement was a thriving village whose residents sometimes angered their neighbours by speaking the Spanish language instead of the English, took his nephew and the nephew's cousin into the garden of the Farm in order to choose leaves for the weaving of an Advent wreath, which was a custom, so the uncle said, that European Catholics had kept up since the middle ages and earlier. They chose fig-leaves for the wreath, wove the wreath, and hung it in the main room of the Farm. For a few days, the wreath looked well: a mass of green leaves hanging like a halo above the dining-table. On each of those days, the residents of the Farm had gathered at evening and had prayed beneath the wreath and had sung an Advent hymn some of the words of which can be found in a book of fiction that I wrote nearly twenty years ago.

Ten minutes ago, I took down from the bookshelves in this room a copy of the book of fiction mentioned in the previous sentence. I had not looked into that book for several years, although I see in my mind every day one or another of the images that caused me to begin to write the book, the title of which is *Inland*. I learned from my looking into the book *Inland* just now that the narrator of the book did not report that a certain wreath of fig-leaves mentioned in the book had become brown and withered soon after the wreath had been hung in the living-room of a certain house. I learned also just now that the narrator of *Inland*, which is a book of fiction in the same way that this piece is a piece of fiction, had reported in the book that a certain utopian settlement founded by certain characters in the fiction was situated between two rivers the names of which are identical to the names of two rivers on the maps of Victoria in the collection of maps in this room.

The wreath of fig-leaves that is part of this piece of fiction became brown and withered after a few days. Afterwards, the leaves seemed so brittle whenever I looked up at them that I was often afraid some of them might crumble and fall as a result of the vibrations from our hymn-singing of an evening. I was afraid that this would oblige Nunkie to have to explain to his son and to me that European people were able to make Advent wreaths that stayed green for much longer than ours had stayed, which was something that I might have found hard to believe, although I would never have said so.

All the settlers at Grasslands were unmarried. The founder of the settlement might have been only dimly aware of the power of sexual attraction between men and women, but he himself had for some years past felt a strong attraction towards one or another female person, which attraction he thought of as a falling in love, even though the female person was sometime of a different age than his. Accordingly, the founder had designed the settlement so that females and males lived at opposite ends of the place, with the chapel, the library, and all the farm buildings between. They mostly worked at separate tasks, but they met for meals and for prayers of the divine office, which they recited during their several visits to the chapel each day. This chapel was so arranged that the males and females faced each other, with each sex occupying a set of stalls to the side of the building. Males and females were permitted to look freely at each other. The founder expected that many a male would feel attracted to one or another female, but he supposed that such a male would be affected as he, the founder, would have been affected in such circumstances: the male would be continually inspired by the image in his mind of the face of the female as she appeared in the chapel or in the dining room; he would work more strenuously in the paddocks in order to impress her; he would study harder in the library so that he could discuss theology and philosophy with her. In the fullness of time, every male settler would be continually aware of the face and person of a young woman who was sometimes visible on the opposite side of the chapel or the dining room and was at other times an inspiring image in his mind.

One of the explanations that I heard long afterwards for the failure of the settlement of Outlands was that the bishop of the diocese where the settlement was situated would never allow any of his priests to be stationed as chaplain in a place where the presence together of unmarried males and females might have given rise to scandal among non-Catholic neighbours. The Outlanders had tried by every possible means, so I was told long afterwards, to obtain a chaplain. They had drawn up an eloquent petition at one time, and a number of them had travelled by horse and cart – their only available transport – from Outlands to the palace of the bishop, which palace was in a suburb of the city that was named Bassett in my first published work of fiction. The Outlanders had travelled for two weeks and had arrived tired and dishevelled at the bishop's palace, but he had rejected their petition.

This piece of fiction is as it were a letter to a man who was mentioned earlier in the fiction. As soon as I have finished the final draft of this fiction, I will send a copy to the man just mentioned. I mention this now rather than at the end of the fiction so as not to lessen whatever effect the last pages might have or to suggest that the whole piece is anything but a piece of fiction. While I was writing the previous paragraph, I intended to put marks beside that paragraph in the copy that I sent to the man mentioned above so that the man would not fail to note that a party of dishevelled Outlanders must have passed close by the house where he lived in the first year of his life. I understand now, however, that my having written the previous sentence relieves me of the need to put any marks in the margin of this text.

No one at the Farm knew about the settlement of Grass-lands. I was not anxious to keep the place secret, but I was mostly clearing the forest and building the buildings and keeping the twig-persons active during the daytime, while Nunkie and my cousin were away. Sometimes one of the young men or women from Outlands would be sitting with a book on the veranda or strolling up and down beside the house – praying, perhaps, or even meditating – and would ask me later what I had been doing out in the long grass. I would tell the questioner a half-truth: that I had a toy farm in the grass.

Grasslands had been already well established when a certain young woman arrived for the first time at the Farm. I shall call the certain young woman hereafter the Pretty-faced Woman. Perhaps I might not consider her so pretty if I saw her likeness today, but in the last month of 1950 she was the prettiest young woman I had seen. She was on her way to or from Outlands, busy on some secular or spiritual errand that I could never hope to know about. She bustled through the quiet rooms at the Farm, talking softly and earnestly to Nunkie or the Holy Foundress. Her noticeable breasts swung often behind her blouse. Her dark-blue eyes and dark-brown hair went strangely together. I stared often at the pale freckles above the high neckline of her dress.

The Pretty-faced woman was different from the other young women from Outlands not only because she was pretty and they were plain but because she seemed more curious about me. She asked me who I was, how I was connected with the persons at the Farm, where my home was, why I was living away from my family. She asked these things as though she was truly interested.

On the day after the Pretty-faced Woman had arrived at the Farm, I looked through the branches of the fruit-trees at the Farm in search of a twig to represent a new settler at Grasslands. The females at Grasslands were by no means all plain Janes; some of their faces had already begun to inspire some of the male settlers. But I had taken no special care in choosing any of the twigs that represented the females. Now, I found a twig with a certain shapeliness and symmetry and with a certain smoothness when the bark had been peeled away from the paler wood beneath. I placed this twig among the other representations of female settlers and looked forward to a series of events that would soon take place at Grasslands, the first of which events would be a long exchange of looks between the twig that represented myself and the twig that represented the new arrival when the settlers were next gathered in the chapel.

I did the things mentioned above on the morning of the day mentioned above. After lunch on that day, I was only just settling myself on my knees beside the settlement of Grasslands when I heard someone walking up behind me through the long grass.

I was a child, but I did not lack guile. I went on staring ahead. I pretended not to have heard her footsteps behind me. I sat back on my thighs and stared ahead of me as though I was contemplating fold after fold of an endless landscape.

She remained for a short while a female presence just out of sight behind me, and then she stepped forward and asked me what I would have expected any visitor to the Farm to ask about my dirt clearings, my lumps of cracked mud, and my forked twigs standing crookedly here and there.

I told her as much of the truth as she needed to be told: that I had founded a settlement in a remote place; that I had been inspired by the example of Outlands, even though I had only heard a little about it ... She reached down and drew her fingers through my hair and then told me she hoped to welcome me one day to Outlands, which was still hardly bigger than my own settlement in the grass but which would grow and thrive. And then she went back to the house.

After she had gone, I began to modify somewhat my original ground-plan for Grasslands. Somewhere at the edge of the settlement there would have to be space for a house, and perhaps a small garden, for the first two of the settlers who were a married couple. Later, other such houses would be needed for other couples and their children. But these plans of mine were never carried out. On the next day, my father arrived without notice at the Farm. The electricity had been switched on in the partly-built house on the far side of Melbourne where my parents and my sister and I were going to live happily together during the foreseeable future. (In fact, we lived there for four years, until my father, who had become for several years a reformed gambler, became again a gambler and had to sell the house in order to pay his latest debts.)

I suppose the last traces of Grasslands would have melted away several years after I had left the Farm. And yet, the settlement of Outlands did not outlast Grasslands by many years. At some time in the 1960s, I heard that the settlement no longer existed, although several of the married couples who had been among the last settlers still remained on the site. They had bought a share each of the land and had survived as farmers.

At some time in the early 1970s, after I had been married for several years and was the father of two children, I decided I had better make my Last Will and Testament with the help of a legal practitioner. While I was looking into the telephone directory at the pages where legal practitioners advertise their services, I saw a very rare surname that I had only once previously come across. I understood from what I saw that the bearer of the surname was the principal of a firm of legal practitioners in an inner eastern suburb of Melbourne, where the value of the most modest house was three times the value of my own house. After I had looked at the initial of the first given name of the principal just mentioned, I became convinced that the man I had heard of twenty and more years before as one of the founders of Outlands was now a prosperous legal practitioner in one of the best suburbs of Melbourne, so to speak.

Only a year or so after the events reported in the previous paragraph, I heard of the death of Nunkie. I had seen him only occasionally during the years since I lived briefly at the Farm, but I took steps to attend his funeral service.

I sat near the rear of Nunkie's parish church and saw hardly anything of the chief mourners until they came down the aisle with the coffin. Among the leading mourners was a man of middle age whose appearance could only be called commanding. He was very tall, strongly built, and olive skinned. He had a mane of silvery hair and a nose like an eagle's bill. He looked continually about him, nodding to this person and that. He did not nod at me, but I was sure he took note of me. And while his black eyes measured me, I was aware of what a weak, ineffectual person I have always been and of how much I have needed to be guided and inspired.

At the side of the commanding man was a woman with a pretty face. She was perhaps ten years younger than the man and was herself approaching middle age, but I could readily recall how she had looked twenty and more years before. She kept her eyes down as she passed.

Behind the couple mentioned above were four young persons who were obviously their children. I estimated from the seeming age of the oldest that the parents had been married in the very early 1950s.

In one of the last years of the twentieth century, I pressed by mistake a certain button in the radio of my motor car and heard, instead of the music that I usually hear from that radio, the voices of persons taking part in what was probably called by its makers a radio documentary. I was about to correct the mistake mentioned above when I understood that the actors taking part in the program were reading the words previously spoken or written by several persons who had been among the settlers at Outlands almost fifty years before. After I had understood this, I steered into a side-street and stopped my motor-car and listened until the program about Outlands had come to an end. (The program was one of a short series. The following week I listened for an hour to a similar program about the place mentioned in the second paragraph of this piece of fiction.)

I learned less than I had expected to learn, except for what will be reported in the last paragraph of this piece of fiction. The details of the daily lives of the Outlanders seemed to have been hardly different from what I had imagined while I lived at the Farm. Even when the actors spoke the words of the early settlers (who would have been aged seventy and more when they were interviewed) explaining why they had left the secular world for a communal settlement, I was not surprised. The Outlanders too had felt that the world was becoming more sinful and that the cities of the world were in danger of being bombed flat. I was beginning to be disappointed while I listened. But then a number of younger female voices began to report the recollections of the earliest female settlers at Outlands while they asked themselves what had finally persuaded them to leave the world and to join the settlement in the mountains. The reports were at first rather predictable. But then a name was mentioned: the name of a man. The surname had a musical sound and ended in the fifteenth letter of the English alphabet. The reports from the young female settlers became more specific, more in agreement, more heartfelt. I shall end this piece of fiction with a paragraph reporting my own summary of what I understood the female actors to be reporting from the females who claimed still to remember their feelings of nearly fifty years before.

He was the sort of person who would be called today charismatic, truly charismatic. He had graduated in law but had declined to practise. He was a cultured European in the dull Australia of the 1940s and 1950s. He had a Spanish father, and he spoke Spanish beautifully. We had never heard such a musical language. And he played the guitar. He would sing Spanish folk-songs for hours while he played the guitar. He was inspiring.

The First Sense

Robyn Davidson

Hearing, they say, is the first of the senses we develop in the womb. For a certain time, inside our mothers' bodies, the entire universe is a soundscape, nothing else exists.

As soon as we are born, our mothers speak to us in a special lilting way, and we respond to those sounds – to their rhythm, pitch, intensity and timbre – the musical or prosodic features of speech. Our brains are already organised to decipher them. They convey emotional rather than grammatical meaning. Perhaps, back in the shadows of geological time, such exchanges between mother and infant arose in order to bond them still closer, and from this evolved into a form of communication between adults. Perhaps this is the ancient root of music, and of speech, the first language lying coiled beneath the later, gatekeeper to more primal realms.

My career as a concert pianist ended with the two final chords of Brahms's rhapsody in G minor. The chords, delivered fortissimo, sound something like *Take That*. I was nineteen.

Three years previously I had won a scholarship to the Queensland Conservatorium of Music, but it was not quite enough to live on, even with part-time work. My father, suddenly aware that he was the sole parent of, and therefore somehow responsible for the future of, a girl, declined to contribute financially, suggesting that I get a job as a secretary, or something, anyway, respectable, until marriage. I hitched a ride on a truck going to Sydney and lived, initially, on the streets and in the parks of that sparkling city. Eventually I found work as an artist's model, then as a croupier and poker player, then as the de facto manageress of an illegal gambling club. This gave me enough money to enroll at the Sydney Conservatorium of Music, in order to rejoin the path my mother had set me upon long ago, in an infancy beyond conscious recall.

I trudged along it for about a year. I was obliged to transform my technique, single finger exercises requiring transcendent patience and concentration. The playing of actual music was forbidden. Surreptitiously, I had learnt the Brahms Rhapsody – a troubled, passionate piece that suited my temperament and style. Bunuel's heroine plays it stark naked in *That Obscure Object of Desire*. Fortunately I had not seen the film at the time of my own performance.

I am sitting at a concert grand halfway through the rhapsody. There is an audience of sorts, I don't remember who, or where. The epiphany arrives during a difficult passage that I am not confident I have fully mastered – 'You do not have the makings of a great pianist, and you are revealing that fact in front of a lot of strangers.'

My body carries through to the end, but my head has completely vanished. *Take that!* I bow, walk away from the piano and do not touch another for over two decades.

In all that time I did not experience one moment of regret. I was not, in any case, given to dwelling in the past. I seemed always to be in a present that sheered off from the past like an iceberg, and floated into the future carrying a new version of myself.

But one evening, I was listening to Glenn Gould playing Bach. I closed my eyes and gave myself over to music I had heard before, but this time it was almost unbearably moving.

I suppose I was already primed. My mother died when she was forty-six. As I approached that age, an indeterminate sadness had begun to settle over my life. I began to wish that she, a stranger to whose scanty memory I had previously felt indifferent, could be retraced, reconstituted, as the person I must once have loved.

I was sitting in my father's old chair which had travelled in his family's wake all the way from Scotland to Australia, accompanied him through all our various Queensland houses, and had now ended up with me, a dreg of the Davidson line, back in Britain. Through large industrial windows, the view was of an East London skyline. There was a familiar bittersweet sensation in my body, characteristic of musical attention – states of anticipation, deferral and reward which seem to occur all at the same time.

As I penetrated deeper into the sound, or it into me, I began to 'see' the music – a 'hearing' of architecture or landscape, as if sensory channels had misfired and were hitting each other's targets. I had always experienced mild forms of this phenomenon – assumed that everyone did – but nothing as intense, or as unnerving, as this. Then, the main event – a bolt of awareness which tore open memory all the way to the root.

*

It is shimmering over the downs country. A white sand riverbed ascends from the house towards the brigalow ridge. The banks are lined with eucalyptus trees, their grey leaves hanging vertical to the sun. A man on a horse moves along the riverbed towards the brigalow forest. Every day he sets out early from the house, with his axe and saddlebags. A cattle dog follows behind. Every evening they return, along the same track, always stopping at the same bores, the same gates, trailing the same spume of dust, and again, the next morning, as before.

Brigalow wood is springy and hard. The percussion of iron on brigalow produces a unique timbre. You can hear the wood's elasticity and resistance, blunting the axe with each strike.

The man whistles without awareness, always the same tune, ground into his memory when he was a boy, and unleashed into immediacy by certain kinds of concentration. His attention is cut by a bird's call. He looks up to follow the sound which breaks into smaller and smaller fragments until it disappears into the midday silence of insects and a friction of leaves.

On his way back from ringbarking the brigalow, he catches sight of a building undulating on the horizon, but this is an illusion created by heat pouring into the sky. When the real house comes into view, it is no more than a rent in a curtain of eucalyptus trees on the far side of the river of sand.

A woman is singing, accompanying herself on a piano. She sings beautifully and without inhibition – an 'aria'. As he approaches the lonely house, other sounds stir in the air – the luffing of sheets on a line, a windmill creaking. The sounds of her world have their silences too, just as, at midday in the forest, there is a silence of the axe, of insects and leaves.

I sit beside her on the piano stool, in front of the German upright. I press the keys with her hand over mine. Now she is at the window staring out at the drought which penetrates the house as a fine powder, as if the house itself were a wreck beached far from shore, into which sand seeps threatening to bury the survivors …

*

No, these are not the memories that erupted out of me that night in London. I don't recall now what, specifically, I remembered then, if indeed it was as straightforward as that. Certainly the sites of my childhood and the people who lived there returned to me, and the sensation was something akin to a mental avalanche. But a lot of time has passed since that night, and much work has been done breaking the crust of the past and fathoming its depths, the consequence of which is that I now have a facility for calling up its contents. I could have gone on and on with the 'ringbarking' sequence, pulling scenes from my mind with the ease of a magician pulling scarves from a pocket. It is perhaps the same mechanism by which dreams become easier to recall if you make a habit of noting them down.

The scenes seem to exist as if a flash of light had fallen on the original episode, illuminating and congealing it. Each scene sprouts, as it were, tendrils of story which link it to the next, giving the illusion of a seamlessly flowing sequence. Sound pervades the memories like a mirage.

That child who, glimpsing her father setting out on his horse, or who, hearing her mother's voice, was perhaps already transforming 'father' and 'mother' into actors, on some imagined stage adrift in time, was perhaps already making stories to contain the emotions stirred by certain sounds – an axe's thud, a piano, sheets on a line; was perhaps already creating images out of such fertile new words as 'ring-barking', 'brigalow', 'aria'.

Inside the pocket of bone, beneath blonde curls caught up in a bow, an electrochemical gale was sweeping signals along loops and switchbacks of unfathomable complexity, embedding mind and world together in a configuration that, in spite of ceaseless changes wrought by new information, by experience, nevertheless would maintain a continuity that felt like me-ness, and in some way that seems even more uncanny, was laying down the basis for a past which could later be exhumed by music, and remodelled as a synthesis of fact and fantasy.

It is not important to me any more that my 'scenes' aren't true, though it was at first, when I thought the past could be reconstructed. Paradoxically, it was when I gave in to the inevitability of fiction that I gained insights which had a deeper and more subtle authenticity, were more valuable to me, than facts.

For example, if I look again at the sequence of story that emerged from the seed image of the man on the horse, sure enough, I notice something to which I had not previously given sufficient attention – the extent to which my parents' spheres were discreet, the rigidity and formality of the separation. The either/or-ness of it.

My father lived in the paddocks; my mother lived in the house. I see now that this segregation of the manly (free, outdoors, undomesticated) from the feminine (restricted, interior, tamed) has influenced me deeply, prefiguring the opposing inclinations in my own nature.

*

My father was born in 1900. The moral structures under-pinning his personality and beliefs were formed before the First World War, that is to say, by the nineteenth century. The whole of his life's journey was an extension, a playing out of that epoch. One of his beliefs was that certain beliefs amount to natural laws because they are upheld by science, notably Darwinism. Men are superordinate to women because natu-ral selection made it thus, and whites are superordinate to blacks for the same biologically determined reason. These laws have predictable, though often regrettable, even tragic, consequences. For example, Aborigines were destined to die out in the face of invasion by a fitter race. My father was neither aggressive nor cruel – he admired and respected Aboriginal culture and knew as much about it as most anthro-pologists of the time. But admiration and respect, even friendship and love, were no match for Natural Law. Similarly, the self-evident truths of Darwinism informed his relations with women. Ambition and aspiration in females, beyond their biologically determined roles as homemakers, was folly and bound to lead to unhappiness and disorder.

His family were squattocrats who had opened up grazing land in Queensland during the previous century. The women tended to be eccentric, imperious, and jealous; the men, evasive and good-natured. They were all tall and strong and led marvellously free lives. Indoors was where you resentfully went when you couldn't be outdoors, galloping bareback down a beach, going for picnics in the first T-model Ford in Australia, mustering cattle on some vast holding. They looked down comfortably from an elevation that was moral and social as well as physical. They despised weakness of any kind, hoarded and squabbled over money, and were constitution-ally incapable of humility, introspection or self-pity.

My father's choices however, made him something of a misfit in this milieu. He inherited the amiable indifference of the male line, but cleansed of snobbery. Just after the First

World War, he slipped out from under female dominance and went jackarooing and dead-wool picking in the outback. Then, abandoning all responsibilities and betraying his family's expectations, he set sail for East Africa with his savings. There he lived a youth of high Romance – prospecting for gold and diamonds, going on safari with his 'boys', harpooning crocodiles, wrestling with death in the form of blackwater fever and charging elephants, and looking breathtakingly handsome in pith helmet and khakis. He sailed a ketch home for the next war, met and, contrary to the wishes of both families, married a woman seventeen years his junior – and I was born in his fiftieth year, on a droughty cattle station called Stanley Park, in western Queensland. Being conventionally Victorian in his views, he left all things domestic, including the raising of children, to my mother without, however, allowing her ready access to his purse. In short, he was an inadequate husband and father in many ways, but an adorable hero.

On those rare occasions when I was allowed to accompany him through the paddocks, reaching up to hold onto his thumb, (half of it was missing), I would pester him to tell me, yet again, about igneous and sedimentary rocks, about stars and planets and Magellanic patches, about the conceptual difficulties of space and time, about the formation of crystals, about the cretaceous and malachite and radiolaria and basalt, and I would strive to impress him with my latest dilemma about my choice of futures – should I be a zoologist, astronomer, geologist, astrophysicist, botanist? He chuckled and seemed to approve, although his attention, as always, was partially elsewhere. If we passed a snake, poisonous or not, he would quietly pick it up behind its head, so that it wrapped around his arm, and invite me to stroke it. 'No need to kill the poor old Joe Blakes,' he would say, and throw it far away from us. Thus by example rather than instruction, he taught me to be unafraid: of snakes, spiders, cyclones, ocean waves, solitude and the dark. He taught me how to listen to the silence of nature so that its silences opened all the way out to the rim of our exploding universe.

Of course I do remember him being in my mother's territory. But he had the status of a special visitor. He might sometimes, of an evening, allow me onto his lap as he sat in his armchair, or come to read to me at night – Edward Lear verses, most of which we knew off by heart, or essays from Marvels of the Universe, popular science volumes published in the '20s. Yet there was always the sense that he was doing what was expected of him. She sat him at the head of our table (serviette rings, table manners), and tried to establish him as the disciplinarian. But he was hopeless. His authority inhered in him more subtly – by having the right to disappear to some inner place unavailable to us. That is what set him above us, like air above land.

Only once did I witness his anger. He was in the horse paddock. He thought he was alone. I peeked at him from around the corner of the sheep shed. He had the reins of the horse in one hand, and with the other he was laying his stock whip, again and again, across the terrified creature's back as if he would flay it alive.

The atmosphere inside my mother's time is modern; her journey begins just after the First World War and her gaze is fixed firmly towards the fresh new century. I have a photograph of her when she was a girl, dancing in the style of Isadora Duncan. The possessions which defined my father – prehistoric stone axes, fossils, rare geological specimens, African spears and an elephant gun – were perfectly antithetical to hers – a silver fox fur, a crystal bottle of eau de cologne, a trunk full of sensational ball gowns that her children would use for dressing-up, a piano. She was exquisite, comic and full of nervy vitality.

She was raised as a Protestant though her father, at least, was a Jew. Whether anyone thought this important I shall never know, as it was never mentioned. But I sometimes wonder if it contributed to the disdain with which she was treated by my father's family, or whether they simply believed her the wrong class and temperament. It was not, after all, the barbarism of Aborigines of which they were scornful. They related to their black stockmen as to aristocrats of a separate and doomed order. No, it was the 'civilising' values of the middle class they disliked. My mother's aspirations – her concern with clothes and accomplishments, her care to define herself against all things 'common' – would only have compounded their disdain.

I know that by the time I came along she was ground down by country life and yearned to return to the city and all that it represented – lively conversation, light opera and friends; doctors who weren't a couple of day's journey away; opportunities for her daughters. I suffered croup as an infant and I know that she spent countless nights walking me up and down the corridor, willing me to breathe. Snakes terrified her and they were everywhere – on the path to our outdoor dunny, in the rafters of our bedrooms, coiled in the corners of her kitchen, basking on the verandahs. Loneliness engulfed her and there was no relief from it. Except music and I suppose, to some extent, me.

Whenever she wasn't working – and both my parents were industrious to the point of illness – my mother was making music. She played the violin, the piano and had a lovely soprano voice. The German upright that had followed her from her previous life was the hearth of all our houses.

For something that played such an important role in the family, music received very little of my curiosity. It was just there. A background accompaniment weaving in and out of our lives, as unremarkable as breathing. Yet one of my first uncontestable memories is being on the swing in the back yard of Stanley Park composing a 'symphony'. I must have been less than four. The event exists as a series of seed memories – the swing, a hot sunny day, eucalyptus trees, the awe and exhilaration of creation, the enormous scale of the back verandah steps as I struggle up them to inform my mother. I hear her words, 'Hum it for me.' But when I listened for the melody again in my mind, it had vanished. She laughed and hugged me to her legs, but some losses are inconsolable.

I think as a child I provided some solace for my mother. I remember, quite vividly now that I attend to it, an afternoon that I presented her with a routine I had been working on. We had moved to the coast by then, so I was probably six or seven. I dressed myself up in her old ball gowns, led her in from the kitchen and made her sit in my father's armchair. I put Gracie Fields on the wind-up gramophone, and mimed ... 'I'm a char and I'm proud of it too and that's that, though charin's a thing that I 'ate' ... There she is, a little, elegant, worn-out woman collapsed backwards in an armchair, a tea towel across her knees, laughing, as she would have said, 'to beat the band'. And I can feel the echo of what I felt then – the open, willing sympathy that is a child's love. I notice, too, with a little shock that she is much younger than I am now.

It is some time after this that I begin to be consciously aware of the rift between the two worlds, and of its implications. In my mother's world my vocation was obvious – I was a musician, singer, dancer, actress. In my father's world it was equally obvious that I would solve the riddles of nature through scientific enquiry. By then I was beginning to show real musical aptitude, but I was also finding my mother's realm stuffy and restrictive, and longing for the freedom of the paddocks.

And there was something more ominous in the air. A pressure, as if the two continents were grating against each other, and something was going to crack. There were little releases from time to time. As when my parents flicked each other with wet tea towels in the kitchen, and my sister and I joined in until we were all chasing each other around the house laughing so deliriously we ended up gasping for breath on chairs and floor.

Or when neighbours visited and we gathered around the German upright for a 'sing-song'. Then it was as if we all breathed an eternal air of friendship and goodwill. When we sang together, each of us, immersed in inner worlds as real to us as the objective world we shared, felt the boundaries of our individual solipsisms dissolve and we were one with each other and all things.

I watch us gathered there, through the transfiguring light of years. It is the late '50s. The colours are a little muddy. There is a new 22-inch screen television in the corner which will gradually parasitise our sing-songs. But for now, it's *Roll Out the Barrel* and *How much is that doggie* and *Bimbo Bimbo where you going to go-e-o,* and everyone has forgotten their wounds and worries and is warmed through. Music is a kind of compassion I think. It lives in the depths of us as a subtle solidarity, consolation for the separation from each other and from the Supreme.

In the afterglow we offer our solos. My sister is doing her *Vilia oh Vilia,* and then my red-letter moment arrives with *I heard a robin singing.* It is touch-and-go whether I will hit that top A or land a good half-tone below it.

And then it is my father's turn. He is self-conscious standing there beside his wife, with his pipe clutched in his right hand, singing *Sare Mare* in what is probably bad Afrikaans. Surely anyone can see what we in the family already know, have always known. That our beloved hero is ashamed of his own gentleness, which he thinks of as effeminate, a weakness. The man's man, unwilling to burden you with his emotions, is an idealised version of himself; and his need to prove (to himself) that he is not afraid, is what makes him obdurate. The general remoteness of his breeding is in fact the expression of an impregnable obstinacy, and it is wearing her spirit out.

By the time we moved to the suburbs of Brisbane, she was very ill. Her eyes held a perpetually bewildered and haunted look and she did not make music any more. We lived in a new sound collage – the silence of ticking clocks, of stifled weeping, of a car passing slowly down a tarmac road, of things going wrong quietly, and very fast.

I remember one day she came home from an appointment with a psychiatrist. She said, 'He told me I should be happy. I have everything a woman needs – a husband, two lovely children …' She trailed off as if I would not bother to listen. I was ten years old, and even if I had not been distancing myself from my drowning mother, trying to save myself, I was still too young to have been able to find the words to comfort her, to assure her that I perfectly understood the sadism of the doctor's words. A sadism induced by anxiety – a woman who was not satisfied with a husband and two children was, by definition, unnatural, diseased. And coded into his words was the message that she could never be happy unless she agreed to be docile, to be asleep to her own predicament. I don't imagine my mother was much of a thinker; her rebellion was instinctive and therefore profoundly honest. I wish to hell she had chosen to live, yet if, for her, it was a choice between the death of her body or the death of her meaning, then I admire her for choosing the former. It is not necessarily true that where there is life there is hope.

I have never assumed that my mother's suicide made my existence worse than it might otherwise have been, only different. In fact, it would be just as legitimate to describe the act as her last gift to me – the gift of becoming a puzzle to myself.

I was sent to live with my father's twin sister – my mother's bitter enemy. I barely saw my father again until I was in my twenties.

Under those circumstances it was inevitable that I would lose trust in the world of appearances – the so-called 'real' world – and withdraw further into my private world, the key to which was the secret of how things really are. Early on I understood that most people are happy because they do not know how things really are. They are happy in the way that dogs are happy. By the time I got to boarding school I was in the grip of a paralysing inertia and I don't think anyone had an inkling of the magnitude of my retreat from life.

Those years are obscured by a kind of mental fog. Through the fog the only glimpses I catch are of a faintly autistic girl hiding out in the music rooms, missing classes and playing Chopin badly but with feeling. I did not shed a tear for my mother, I don't recall ever thinking of her. Yet somehow the music mothered me, by playing an essential part in my emotional development. It was like a hand to hold until I had passed safely through a perilous place, and reached the shore of adulthood.

There are assets to every liability, and one of the assets of my fractured childhood was that I had no regard either for the securities of the status quo, or for conventional ambitions. And such things as identities, which people with normal histories took for granted as a natural unfolding of first causes, as something contiguous with the past, I could invent from scratch. It took time to grasp that I could make myself over, but when, at the age of seventeen, I hitched a ride on that truck that would take me away from my past, I was laying the first stone in the creation of an individual.

*

In his final years, my father's emotional life rose closer to the surface. He strove to conceal it, yet it was that never fully disguised vulnerability that had always made him so loveable to me. We had grown very intimate by then, yet he never made reference to my mother except in the most oblique terms. Once, on a trip back from London, I gave him a tape of Willie Nelson songs – *Stardust Memories*. We sat together in the lounge, he in his old chair, me at his feet. The music, sentimental and nostalgic, which I had hoped would give him pleasure, instead opened a vent. He began to weep, that old man's weeping that comes from some unreachable cavern deep within. The music had brought her back to life in him, and at the same moment, made him aware, again, of her loss.

I suppose you could say that something similar happened to me. Music gave a mother back to me but also made me aware of an irreparable loneliness, the asset of which was a greater range of thought and feeling. What Bach's music made possible that evening in London was an imaginative or literary engagement with a past that had been so undisturbed by contemplation that it was stagnant.

For a long time afterwards, that engagement took up most of my mental life. I had been exiled too early from childhood, and like all exiles found myself obsessed with a place that could never be reached. It was as if those who could not be reconstituted as they truly were, were now represented by actors whom I brought on stage to help investigate the meaning of a text – a scrappy, incomplete document of traces and clues.

How many combinations and variations we experimented with in that theatre, how many arguments and contradictions, tantrums and reconciliations we endured. Any final under-standing was an illusion, of course. One has simply to live with the fundamental ambiguity that is the nature of all things.

I have less and less to do with my actors these days, but I came to like them very much.

Sweet Parting

Patricia Cornelius

When the baby comes, and it lets you know it's coming, loud
and clear, and it's covered in this white shit and bits of blood
and it's sucking its fist and its eyes are slits and it's got this
repulsive blue white and thick cord attached to its belly and
then someone's sticking its mouth on your tit and your cunt
is screaming because it's cut, there is one thing that is very
clear. You think, I'll never forget this.

Which one's your bed, she says. Which bed are you sleeping
in, she says. Or are you going to sleep with me?

I look hopefully over my shoulder for someone to bail me
out. They've snuck off and left me to get through to her: how it
is, how it is going to be from now on, how there is no way back.

Listen, I start. Listen, I repeat. Listen. I'm looking for the
right tone. This is where you live now, got it. Not me. Just you.
Got it?

Got nothing. I recognise the pucker in her brow. Rubbish,
she says. What absolute rubbish. I'm going with you.

I say, have some chocolate. She sticks a block of eight pieces
in her mouth and I've got a few moments until it melts down
to a reasonable suckable size.

We rang you, the nurse says. We left a message on your phone.

I didn't go home last night I tell them.

The hands that undress my mother stop short. They think I've been out fucking all night.

I didn't get the message I tell them. They continue to peel off her clothes.

My mother groans. Oh don't, don't, she cries. A blue bruise bracelets her upper arm.

Deep ravines and dark pockets and bald hills of clavicles and hip bones and elbows and wrist bones is the barren and dry land of my mother's body. Flesh has deserted her. A damp cloth rushes in under the deep pits of her arms and under the flat flaps that were once her breasts, and down between her legs where strands of grey hair unexpectedly shine, long and silky.

Wash under your arms. And between your legs, she says.

I hold the yellow soap in my hand. Its edges are rough, freshly torn from the long rectangular block kept under the trough in the laundry. I am cold. Only sometimes and only bits of my body are blessed with the warm trickles of water which fall from her elbows or between her breasts, onto my face when I lift it to breathe. It is not possible for her to make room for me. She fills the space and, in fact, has billowed out the shower curtain so it won't cling to her skin. Occasionally she cups the warm water and empties it over my shoulder or down my back. In front of me is her belly. It is folded and stacked. And down I can see only her feet with their bunions and her toes with nails that are thick and badly clipped. She lifts both her arms to shampoo her hair, and when she rinses one breast sits for a moment on the top of my head, a snug and weighty cap.

You'll hear stories they told me, wonderful stories, stories of childhood, detailed with moments of joy, with moments of grief.

A young girl, about three years old, stands precariously in her pram, her small hand clutches the hood and she calls, at the top of her voice, at anyone who might pass. It is impossible to keep her quiet, with that voice, like a foghorn, and an unstoppable will to be heard.

A young woman of fourteen sits at her mother's bedside and gags at the fetid smell on her mother's breath. She weeps while her mother tells her things, hurriedly, in a long list, and insists that her daughter remember because she will not be there to remind her.

A woman in slacks, freshly painted luscious lips, hair pinned back off her face, is telling a very earnest young man to go jump. She tells him she doesn't belong to him, that she has her own life to live and doesn't need him to live it for her. Go jump she says, and then she laughs and bounds inside, absolutely carefree.

But these are the stories that I make up to make more of her. There were never any I-remember-whens. I prised information from her. There were no stories. Not before … And certainly not now. We sit in silence and it is not strained. It is familiar, comfortable even; we've been trained by years and years of sitting on floral lounge chairs, our eyes fixed on a television screen.

You're my mother she says.
What! I say.
You're my mother.
No. You're my mother.
Don't be silly, you're my mother, she goes again.
I want to shout at her, no, you are my fucking mother, but I might cause some hearts to stop in the bodies which surround us.

Who's that? she says. I'm holding a photograph of her husband in my hand.
He's the man you married and lived with for forty years.

Did I? she says. Where is he? she says.
I say, He's dead.
Oh, she says.

Who am I? I ask her.
Don't you know, she says.

She is rubbing her fingertips when I approach. It's something she does a lot. I don't know why but it drives me crazy.
Hi mum, I say.
Oh, she says in surprise. Hello love. Back to the fingers.
How are you going, I ask her.
Oh, she says in surprise. Hello love. Back to the fingers.
How's things, I say.
Oh, she says in surprise. Hello love. Back to the fingers.

I read her newspaper. I don't actually read it because there is no need to go beyond the first couple of lines. There's a woman who is pregnant with five babies, there's another one who lost one but had another one, there's a man crying because they killed his dog because it killed someone, there's a new drug to stop something, an old cure for head lice, Jack Nicholson's mother was actually his sister and there's a brilliant play about low life. I read mum her horoscope: 'From one viewpoint it would be easier to gloss over certain differences and let some issues work themselves out. Consider this strategy carefully, however, since with things moving quickly, what are now minor misunderstandings could soon become important.'

There's a bowl of tomato soup, a plate with some sort of stew which swamps an ice-cream scoop of mashed potato and a dish with a sweet of custard and cake and jam and jelly. She picks up a spoon and scoops a little meat on it and takes it to the bowl to add the sweet to it. She continues this process of sweet and sour but most of it never reaches her lips.

Eat your lunch, I tell her. You've got to eat.

Her eyes become bird-like and her mouth purses and her brow of course puckers. I take the spoon from her and attempt to shovel some stew into her mouth. She slaps my face. Not hard. It doesn't hurt. It's just a sharp short slap on my cheek which instantly brings tears to my eyes. My mother looks very pleased. I swallow a sob, I swallow another, and another. The old duck in the next chair warbles, Good night Irene, Good night Irene, Goodnight, and a sob escapes my throat and others follow, ridiculously and theatrically heaving accompaniment.

I see her in the mornings sometimes when she's still in bed. She moves over and pulls back the covers. I get in. There are some raised eyebrows from the man with the vacuum cleaner. We lay there napping and I wonder whom she thinks she's invited into her bed. My body is enormous around hers.

I fear I might smother her or push her out of bed onto the hard linoleum floor. I cup her body and we lie quietly. I pick up a lock of her white hair and place it behind her ear. Mum, I whisper. Mum.

Seeds

Nadia Wheatley

Lately I have often found myself dreaming her story. I remember waking a couple of nights ago with the whole thing clearly formed inside my brain. By the time daylight came, it was lost. I have never been one for jumping out of bed to write stuff down (especially not in a place such as this, where the draughts and damp rise up through the cracks between the bare floorboards) or even for keeping a pencil and notepad handy on the bedside table. (I like to believe that, if an idea is any good, I'll think it again.) And yet, although I keep losing what her story is about, I go on waking with her in my mind, morning after morning …

I do not know her name, but I do know that she is the first woman who lived in this house. I watch her in the garden – her serviceable brown dress protected with an apron she has fashioned from a clean hessian sack, neatly edged with a faded strip of floral cotton – as she squats down to plant the seeds which she shakes out from a number of little paper spills that she has brought in her portmanteau all the way from the country which lies across the ocean. When she stands upright again and reaches for the rake, she can see through the cleft in the hills that same ocean (or the edge of it) – cobalt blue today in this springtime weather, with a small white sail patched against the horizon.

(I can see it too. Through the window of my workroom.)

She would have sailed along that line of water towards the end of her journey, as she and her fellow passengers quaked in the storms off the notorious Shipwreck Coast. Only twelve months previously, the Yankee ship *Eric the Red* had foundered on the edge of the Cape, sending to the rocky bottom all the sewing machines and other American newfanglery which it was transporting to the Great Exhibition. She feels a kind of personal connection with the event because her husband took her to the building where it had been held, the very same day she arrived (or husband-to-be he was still, that morning), for he was keen to prove that this was a proper city that he had summoned her to. *See the dome*, he advised her, *just like St Pauls*, but she had not been to London, apart from the docks, and found her mind swelling with the shape of a gigantic breast; then blushed at the thought, for she was still a virgin, of course, before that night. But since those first few days in the city, life had been here, in the one-room slab hut where the dirt floor had turned to mud through the winter and where it's so lonely, you can sometimes hear your own thoughts. Sometimes, too, she finds herself wondering about the other women who must have lived here once (she saw some of them in Melbourne, with grey blankets clutched around them like cloaks; they looked as if they felt even more lost than she was) but according to the husband's father, there weren't any. This was no one's land.

I would love some company, nevertheless.

And if wishes were horses she would love a sewing machine as well, yes she would, and often thinks of them whirring away uselessly beneath the waves. (Sometimes, in an easterly, you can still hear them.) It would be such a help, with all the shirts and trousers that she will make over the years. What with nine sons, not to mention a husband, and the husband's father and the two brothers who will never marry, not they – well, why should they, with a sister-in-law to tend to their every need? Besides, women are scarce as hen's teeth here; and heaven knows, even hens are hardly plentiful, what with the foxes prowling through the night. (She sees their eyes glittering, like bright coals.)

When the storms are huge off the Cape (as they are now with the equinox due any day) the sand of the beach at the river mouth washes back and you can still see some of the spars of the upside-down hull of the American ship, like the rib cage of a beached whale.

(I have seen it, myself.)

And in months to come she will name her first son for it, Eric, who grows silently inside her like a seed inside the earth or her story inside my dreams. When summer comes she will feel him kick on the same day that she sees her first snake. *Oh what a start I got, I felt the blood go chill in my veins and the hairs rise up straight on my arms and I could not run to save my life and we were both staring at each other, the snake and me, for god only knows how long,* she would tell the tale for years to come, *and then I felt the baby kick, it was the very first time that ever happened, and it was as if the snake felt him too, for the next second – off it slipped into the bush.* (She always felt that there was something more in the tale, than what she could tell.)

But now in this first springtime she sows seeds in the garden, in lieu of shirts, for the children are not born yet and just a husband and father-in-law and the husband's two younger brothers are not too much trouble, not when they are away down the bottom of the block for weeks at a time, burning off. That's how they turn the forest into farms here. With a box of matches and a broadsaw. They've been working all through the winter and are flat out now, of course, in their last chance before summer sets in. By day the hills stream with smoke, and at night the fires glow like eyes along the ridges. The blackened stumps of the big trees stand reproachfully around the house site.

Manna gums, that is what they call them, she explains in a letter to her sister which she will never write down, let alone send. (Women like this one leave no traces on paper.) *Manna, like the food in the bible, but here the men burn it as if it were a plague.*

In place of the native grasses that last year grew on the open ridge that her husband has chosen for their home, she plants the seeds that she has been collecting since the marriage was arranged and the commitment made to come to this outlandish place where *not a skerrick of anything grows that anyone would want to eat or look at* (her husband-to-be had warned in his letter of invitation). And so, with the help of her sister who worked at the Big House, she raided the kitchen garden up there as well as the garden that grew around her home cottage, and the hedgerows nearby. She always fancied herself as having a green thumb, maybe it was hereditary, certainly her father spent enough time on his favourite pew at the Green Man.

I pick some of her legacy now, apple mint from the patch near the tank-leak, a bay leaf from the mighty tree near the shearing shed, lamb's lettuce and rocket for a salad, rhubarb from the ancient crowns that are flourishing near the septic (they're greedy feeders, rhubarb, that's for sure). Any day now the hills will blaze gold with one of the plants that escaped outside her picket fence, to establish itself in competition with the thistle and the blackberry. I had the man from the Department here only the other day, reading the Noxious Plants (Control Thereof) Act at me. Since then I have spent hours pulling the pests out by hand. You can be fined thousands of dollars, it seems, for owning a paddock full of feral flowers.

Into the beds that she has dug and raked and dug again, she scatters foxgloves and granny's bonnets, nasturtiums and shasta daisies, love-in-the-mist and sweet William and poppies and cornflowers and forget-me-nots and honesty and babies' tears and columbines and snapdragon and sweet Alice and agrimony and hollyhocks and wormwood and birthwort and ragwort and stocks and busy Lizzy and bouncing Bet and lavender and candy tuft and lady's bedstraw, Canterbury bells, golden rod, hellebore, sunflowers, catmint and catnip, rosemary and rue, speedwell and sweet pea, teasel and yarrow and heartsease and anything else she can find to fill the emptiness where the big trees once grew.

It gets so lonely that sometimes I find myself thinking out loud.

There! I have said it. And if that is a sign of madness, it cannot matter, for there is no one who can hear.

Her husband spits as he returns from this last month in the forest where they've been cutting logs for the house posts, timber for the floor (these same boards that let the night air rise through the cracks) and finds the beginnings of little green shoots poking through the earth around the house site. *What're you trying to do – make work for a man?* Already he can see that there will be demands for water tanks and a picket fence and all those other things that wives seem to want. Besides, where's he going to fit the house? She's gone and put the cart before the horse, or the garden before the cottage, trust a woman. She's even made a blooming path all the way to the front door that doesn't exist yet.

Going out the door now to do some weeding before sunset, I unearth the white seashells which she used to border the edges of the pathway that leads up to the road. Beside this she planted clumps of belladonna lilies, or naked ladies as I have heard them called around here, which nod their pink fleshy heads as I go up to check the mailbox. (No one has written to me, once again.) At the corner near the gate she has placed a large, flat ornamental stone, which over the years has gathered earth into a sort of concave pocket at its centre. And in this miniature garden bed there has sprouted yet another of the cheeky yellow flowers that have spread like wildfire across my paddocks. After yanking it out (getting that sour ragworty smell on my hands from the sap in the stem), I scoop the soil from the rock to make sure that the intruder cannot seed itself there again. I even fetch the hose and, as I give the stone a thorough wash, I realise what purpose it once served.

This night the woman is not wearing her brown dress and her hessian apron but a patchwork cape of skins as she kneels on the earth, turning seeds into flour with a smooth oval rock that fits comfortably into the concave depression in the grinding stone.

Waking, I realise that I have lost the story once again.

La Moustiquaire

Gillian Mears

The girl crouches in front of a fire about the size and circular width of the leaf she intends to wrap around some of the beans that she has stolen from the man. She has his little silver flask too. The veins of the leaf seem to glow with a green fire that's nothing to do with the burning twigs. If I could become very thin, she thinks, thinner even than the man, then I'd slip through this leaf to become its sap. The beans are on a metal spoon, smoothed by the innumerable tongues and fingers of girls who've accompanied the stockman.

This girl has been with the stockman for nearly five years but sometimes they are still such strangers the girl thinks it's as if they've been sealed off from each other in candlewax. On other occasions, there's no separation between them. Being with the man then is like cantering on the smoothest horse imaginable. The man puts his nose against the girl's and holding only one nostril shut breathes out and in so that their breath becomes the breath of one creature – neither girl nor man but the animal whose shape she has seen only in dreams, or in the moving leaves of a tree against the stars. It has a horse's head but its ears are soft and round in a way that reminds the girl of the love poem the stockman once wrote. 'La moustiquaire', the man said it was called. 'For you,' he said, reciting, but the girl could understand nothing of it, as it was in the language he'd learned when he went away to the long ago war. Mosquito net girl, he says it means. Mozzie, he calls her or Ginny, the name he called the other girls.

Yet not even the night with the rodeo boy on the last full moon in town can equal what the girl feels for the old stockman. The man can't live much longer and although she hates the man more than she has ever hated anything, she also loves the man more than she has ever loved. With the boy she'd pretended to laugh at his jokes about old men but even as is hands were finding her again, she'd felt the pang of her betrayal. Wondering if the stockman was over his sudden sickness, she'd suddenly lost all interest in doing anything more with that rodeo boy. Even as he was throwing his leg over like she was another of his rides for the day, she was wishing she was inside a mosquito net with the stockman, listening to him reading.

The girl sighs. Already it's light enough to see a line of trees about fifty horse lengths to the right. Hovering in this way between day and night, the land looks downy, as if old stockmen have multiplied out there and lain down with their finely haired shoulders turned towards the sky. The three horses are tethered near another tree and look over. She waves a hand at them, trying to convey that she won't get to them for ages.

At least there are no mosquitoes here. The girl bows her head. It isn't often when they travel away from the town that she doesn't have to stay up all night with the switch made of wild grass, waving mosquitoes off the man.

The old travelling net rotted about a year ago and although it could've easily been replaced, now the man prefers to call the girl, La Moustiquaire. Or 'Ginny,' he calls, stretching her out over him as if her skinny limbs are cotton net. He jokes that girls like her are more beautiful when tired, with the purple skin under the eyes deepening in the way of the coast at dusk. 'Your father must've been one of those really black black-fellas,' he speculates, but she won't ever say who that father might have been or where he got to or if she even remembers him.

She mashes the beans into a paste and pinches some salt out. Her hands come together. 'Thankyou beans. Thankyou leaf who is a little like me. Thankyou God.' She wraps the leaf into a parcel and eats.

For a moment the girl's jaw stops chewing and with alarm she listens. The air has filled with the moaning noise of insects. Then she looks up and grins. For it isn't mosquitoes after all. She's sitting under a tree full of flowers and it's just bees, floating around the yellow blossoms.

Everything seems to be playing with me! she laughs. In a spiderweb there seems to be a heart shape on a string. And look at the sun! The more she stares, the more the sun pokes out its tongue. Even the sun desires me, she thinks, and then worried by the brazenness of this thought, she picks up the hip flask.

The rum almost instantly dries out all extraneous thoughts. So that's why the man has never allowed her any. She tips it into her mouth again and rocks back on her heels. Selfish, selfish, she thinks. Crazy old slutfish. She utters a few more obscene words and suddenly hopes that when she returns to the tent, the man will not want to get up immediately but will order her to take off her clothes and lie down on the square of blue cloth. I will pretend I'm with the boy. I will suck his old so-and-so until it goes foamy like the sea. Although she hasn't seen the boy for a while, she feels he isn't far away and that his face, smiling this way, contains all the haziness of a summer.

As the vision of the boy fades, she drinks all the rum and lies down. Suddenly she feels the mixed animal whose name she doesn't know is very close. It half hops, half runs but no, it is clearly a young bridal veil wallaby, she sees that now. White people are killing wallabies with knives and clubs. It's the time of blood and in the distance she can hear human babies crying. She knows they are babies with skin as black as her own and that like the wallabies, they're going to be harmed.

Oh, but it's too much. White women laugh and show their teeth. Even though they are only watching their men, the girl sees the power that the killing bestows. Under their dresses, she senses their breasts becoming even whiter, like huge dampers rising, threatening to smother the land altogether. She sees that the killing makes them powerful in the same way she feels power over all the mosquitoes she's destined to kill, or the mice in the horse's oats whose tails she sometimes seizes, swinging their heads against a stone with a sharp crack.

When she kills mice the stockman smiles and loves her and says she's like a bloody good dog. Good at anything. His best Ginny ever. And he tousles her hair like it is indeed the ruff of a dog.

The girl sits up and spits. The twig fire's gone out. It's time to creep back to the old man's tent. First she goes across to the horses who prick their ears hopeful of an early feed. She scratches their tails instead and the favourite spot behind the wither and tells them that probably by this time tomorrow, they'll be back in town. 'There,' she says, pulling off two bottle ticks, 'that must feel better.' She licks her horse's neck where the salt from yesterday's sweat has gathered, in the hope that it'll hide the taste of her mouth.

When the girl ducks down into the tent, she sees with horror that the stockman is as if carpeted in mosquitoes. He has come out from his cover, the better it seems to feed the numerous mosquitoes that have been feasting in the tent. Panic-struck, she picks up her switch but it's of utterly no use. It's simply a miracle that the man sleeps on through such moaning. Surely there can only be one explanation. The man has fallen into that which he has always most dreaded. He's in the mosquito fever from which there is no return.

The mosquitoes, at the presence of the girl, rise for a moment like little blood suns, like a multitude of demon spirits with fiery gold wings and red bellies. 'But I am to die first,' she says. The stockman has always said this. That it's the fate of her race. That if she leaves him she'll end up buried young in a shallow reserve grave the dogs'll dig up. She utters the man's name which even though it is ridiculous and ill-suited is the only one she has to use.

The girl puts her mouth onto the man's but there is no resp-onse. The girl slaps the man and shouts that at the very least he could've fallen into a normal fever first. 'They'll think I killed you and stole your booze and bible.' The girl lets forth a volley of violent words. The man seems deep in his own breath and has tucked his hands into his armpits in the way of a sick bird.

Now she holds the man in her arms, the way the man has never allowed. He is just a tiny little fella really. Without his boots on, not much more than her size. She cradles the face. She forces open the stockman's mouth, trying to induce him to take a nipple. At the touch of the old man's lips, one nipple forms a drop of whitish dew. She looks deeply and sees the face his mother must once have seen, when he was just a baby. For a moment it seems that the man's going to suck but his lips loosen and, skinny though he is, he's too heavy to hold up anymore. Then she wipes the brylcreem from his hair off her breasts with sudden disdain. 'Funny, seeing you without your hat on,' she comments but he doesn't reply.

The day inches along. Now the girl grows impatient, wishing that the man would hurry up in the taking of his last breath. And what a rotten breath it has become. If God is breath as the man has said, then God is surely rotten. The girl feels the familiar revulsion. A wasp flies down towards them and then out of the flap to the outside. Then another.

'The bible's hatching!' The girl in one leap is at the book, sealed up last visit to town by a pottery wasp building her nest along the pages. The man had taken it as a sign. That not until the wasplings had hatched and flown safely away would it be time to resume his readings.

Two perfect holes now pierce the mud and from within comes the humming noise. The girl goes back and leans down to the man's ear to convey her excitement. The hair of the man's ear shimmers as if traced in late evening water seen from a track, but he doesn't appear able to hear. The girl feels bitter. Her shoulders slump down in the most downcast of ways. After all their waiting, for the book to be released but for the reader to be dying.

Throughout the day, more wasps hatch and many memories come and go. Then the man grows suddenly much older when the sun's right overhead and just like that, like that little bay filly that got lockjaw, is dead before dusk. The girl spits at the man's feet because not once during the entire length of the day has the man so much as acknowledged her presence or joined in the excitement over the wasps.

'What do you do anyway, with such an old man?' the rodeo boy had wanted to know.

'We're waiting for a book to hatch,' she'd replied, completely sick of the boy and his fingers.

When she cries it's because she always knew much more than the man. She, not the man, has lain on the earth and felt the strong lines moving through her like God and the waterbird with wings as outspread as the big altar, flying through darkness to enter through her hands.

Now it's too late. She can never tell the man about this or look directly into the man's eyes. Cautiously, the girl pushes her thumbs over the lids and pulls them down. As soon as she lifts her fingers, though, the eyes come open again.

Remembering how the man once seeled the eyes of a brown hawk, she thinks that this is what'll have to be done. He'd found the book on French hunting birds in that green bedroom above the pub and for weeks had been determined to get a brown hawk to catch rabbits for them. The baby hawk he got out of a nest never did any hunting. 'It died didn't hit,' utters the girl sadly, not bothering to correct her pronunciation the way he'd liked. She searches around in the saddlebag for the mosquito-net mending needle and thread, hoping that the man has thrown it away, but it is more or less in the place where it always was. Grave now, she threads the needle. There's not much light left. Old man skin must be tougher than hawk lids. She cries. For the man. For that poor hawk and how its eyes got full of pus.

Another wasp finds its freedom and hangs low beside them. The girl wishes that she could read something from the book for the man. 'Well, you were quite a nice man,' she says instead but the words come out sounding like an accusation.

The bird the stockman used to call The Cup Overfloweth Bird begins to call and there comes the feeling of bright uncontained liquid running in every direction. It calls and calls like liquid and seems to belong to no specific time at all. It could be two thousand years ago or two thousand years ahead. The bird leaps out of the purple tree and its wings look to her like the rodeo boy's dark red shirt when he's in the shute for the last ride of the day.

She drinks all the rum in the big bottle and feels so sick she thinks she too will lie down and die for a while.

Later, gulping down water at the tent's opening, trying to dissolve her uncertainty, she claps her hands and clicks her tongue.

'By and by,' she tells the man, 'we'll come back for you,' knowing that no such thing will happen and that after this night she'll never see the stockman again. 'I know,' she says, and finds his stash of black jellybeans. 'We'll leave you these.' But then one by one she eats them.

'I'll ride your horse,' she says, 'and you'll see how smoothly she travels for me.' She makes a dismissive gesture with her hand. 'I was always a better rider than you.' In the town she can sense it's that time when the dust is hanging in the air and the mandarins the man likes to eat from the tree by the travelling stock route would probably still be too green.

In the last light left she takes the bible into her hands and examines how perfect and round are the leave-taking holes of the insects. Nothing has ever looked so simultaneously complete but empty, so full of potential but so spent. One chamber was never filled and sealed and she pokes her finger into it before tapping the whole nest off the book. On the underneath of the nest she can see where the mud the wasp collected was dark and where it gleams with silvery river sand. She has covered the man in the blue blanket. When she looks underneath she jumps backwards, for the man's feet have taken a different position. Even when dead the man tries to keep his feet in the stirrups, thinks the girl and feels a grudging kind of admiration. The man's face looks like a rock now blank but vast and excessively salty. She drops the bible that as much as it brought them violently together, helped shamefully to hold them apart.

In the light of the fire she builds, the horses look like they're preparing for an end of show parade, dancing at the end of their ropes. Below his forelock, Boney the white gelding's face looks rosy, as if his cheekbones have been rouged. Big horse yawns seize the girl. She hopes the fire will last until morning.

The mosquito when it comes towards the skin of the girl's arm comes tentatively at first, then more surely. I can feel the wings, she marvels. Like a small mouth blowing. Like a little breeze.

She watches the mosquito's beak tapping, then experiences a small sting. Gradually the abdomen of the insect fills with blood. When the girl sneezes in response, she feels every particle of moisture as it lands on her body and the mosquito flies off, only half full. If the stockman was alive the girl would have to hide that she's no longer the extraordinary black girl from the coast that mosquitoes won't touch. Now, like any other girl, the mosquitoes form in a spiral above her head. Now she just watches.

The unknown animal hops across the night without moving, formed of stars. The girl waits for morning which seems longer away than ever before. On the caps of her elbows, on the edges of her ears and toes, the welts of the mosquitoes are already rising and beginning to itch. More mosquitoes arrive. When she chucks the bible into the fire she is sad all over again. One day, she'd thought, like a perfect leap on old Boney over a fallen tree, their separation would be severed. Now all the possible moments have passed. Now the bible burns like a grey fan; the colour plate of Jesus in the Lily of the Fields going into ashes; red coals taking away all those little words in the way of ants taking eggs.

Bushfire

Kate Grenville

The radio said that Minnamurra was in *no immediate danger,* but the television had a different message. There were pictures of walls of flame flickering and leaping up into trees. *Ringed by fire* was a phrase the journalists seemed to like. Against the ragged angry blaze, ant-like silhouetted figures scurried ineffectually, flapping wet bags and squirting water from backpacks.

No immediate danger. Louise repeated the words to herself. But Minnamurra was such a little place, with hillsides of bush all around. It was easy to imagine a fire swallowing it down without missing a beat.

As she walked down Homer Street towards the shops, brown smoke hid the contours of the hills over in the distance and smudged the sky. After a term at Minnumurra Public School she had got used to seeing the hills, always there at the end of Homer Street. It was unsettling to have lost them now.

They were hoping for a change in the wind. A man from the Weather Bureau had come on and pointed at isobars with a ruler, but he had not committed himself on the matter of a change in the wind.

With the town in crisis, it had seemed the right thing for

the new teacher to offer to help. But Valda in the school office had looked doubtful.

Got any First Aid, love? She had asked. Class B licence? Anything like that?

Valda did not want to be rude, but it seemed that the only place for a person without such skills was down in the Country Women's Association Hall, helping with the sandwiches.

Grand Street, Minnamurra, did not normally generate a lot of traffic, but today as Louise turned the corner, there was quite a bottleneck: three cars and a lorry, and then one of the old red fire trucks from the Volunteer Bush Fire Brigade. A man on the back, half-hidden among hoses and tanks, lifted a hand to her, but he took her by surprise and by the time she waved back, the truck had gone.

She thought it could be that Lloyd. The one who'd bought her a cup of tea at the Picnic Races.

Valda had more or less made him do it: she loved to matchmake. Valda had already tried to set her up with her cousin from Gulargambone, and then with the man from the Pastures Protection Agency. Neither event had been a success.

Lloyd had agreed willingly enough, but she felt herself going stony. She had sat at the wobbly table in the Refreshments Tent, staring into her cup of powerful Ladies' Auxiliary tea, watching Lloyd stirring the sugar into his. Behind her, she could feel everyone skirting around them – Valda, and Mrs Mitchell the principal, and John the man from the garage. They were ostentatiously not watching. It was like grown-ups leaving children alone to *make friends*.

It never worked. She could have told them that. It didn't work with kids and it wasn't going to work any better with two wary frumps past their prime. *Frump*: that was how she thought of herself. She knew how she looked: too big, too plain, and with that uncompromising set to her mouth. This Lloyd was a frump, too, with his ears that stuck out, his big freckled face, his awkward smile, the way he kept fiddling with his spoon. They were two of a kind, but the wrong kind.

She'd always hated being paired off, hated the way people thought you'd be grateful. No one seemed to realise that a failed marriage wasn't like a broken plate. You didn't just go out and get another one.

Lloyd seemed no more comfortable than she was, but with the whole of Minnamurra watching them sideways, they felt obliged to exchange some information about themselves. It turned out that Lloyd was something with the Water Board. He was here to check the reservoir.

As conversational material, Louise felt this was less than promising.

Oh, the Water Board, she said, and heard it as the other kind of *bored*, the one that they both seemed to be experiencing there and then. She hurried on before she could laugh.

Been with them for long?

It was only to be polite.

Few years, he mumbled, and it seemed as if that was going to be that, but he suddenly blurted out:

Take Mozart!

Pardon? She'd had to say.

Dead of typhoid at thirty. Just think – if they'd had decent water! Another six symphonies!

He was radiant at the thought of it.

Yes, she'd managed to say, feeling the startled look on her face, hearing it in her voice.

I wanted to write music, he said. But Dad thought I ought to go into something solid.

He cleared his throat unnecessarily, glanced at her. She was too much taken by surprise, could not rearrange the muscles of her face into a more welcoming expression in time.

So here I am.

He picked up the spoon and made a big show of putting sugar in his tea and stirring it, even though he'd already put two spoonfuls in before. Her mouth refused to make any of the encouraging sounds she wished to make.

And now he was blushing through his pale freckled skin. Even his neck was blushing. And his ears. She had never seen such a blush. It was like ink spreading through water. She looked at where his shirt opened at the neck, where she could glimpse soft fair skin that the sun had never roughened. She caught herself wondering how far down the blush went.

Then he met her eye, and a funny thing happened: she felt herself blushing as well. It was ridiculous. There was nothing to blush about. She was angry with herself for blushing, and with this man, for watching her. He was not bold, but he was paying attention. She tried to take a sip of tea, to stop him looking, but the tea was scalding, and only added heat to her blush.

She had no reason to blush: it was just her skin doing it. It was as if her skin and his were having a conversation with each other, all by themselves.

*

Down in the Hall it was all sandwiches and hearsay. It was so hot up at the fire, they said, that you could fry an egg on the front of the truck. A fireball had jumped right across the highway, from the top of one tree to another. The paint had been burned off the number-one fire truck as neatly as with a blowtorch.

Mrs Cartwright, mother of Lee-Anne in second class, was mass-producing the sandwiches. It was easy to see she had done it before, for other fires, for floods, for any kind of disaster requiring sandwiches. Her hands moved quickly and deftly among the bread, the wrapping-paper, the beetroot and shredded lettuce. Her finished parcels were as smooth as little pillows.

Being the novice, Louise was given plain cheese to do. You would think you could not go wrong with plain cheese. But she forgot to put the wrapping paper under first, so the wrapping took twice as long. Or, when she cut them in half at the end, she cut through the paper as well. Her finished packages were lumpy, and unravelled as soon as you let go of them.

She imagined the fire-fighters, sitting on the running board of the fire truck eating the sandwiches. Lloyd would be there, perhaps picking shreds of sliced wrapping paper out of his. She did not think he was the sort to laugh at a failed sandwich, but someone else might.

A man with a soot-dark face, his eyes bloodshot, rushed in to pick up a load of food. He took a sandwich in each hand and spoke with a wild look in his eyes.

Not bloody burning, he was insisting. Bloody exploding!

His hands flew out, demonstrating, and a baked bean landed in Louise's bowl of cheese.

We lost two last time, Mrs Cartwright said, her face gone grim. The wind changed on them.

She laid out another couple of flaps of bread.

They said it looked like they'd tried to run. Dropped the backpacks and that. But you can't outrun a fire.

Louise had seen the fire trucks standing in their garage. They were very shiny, with the words *Minnamurra Volunteer Bush-Fire Brigade* in fancy letters on the doors, and some kind of coat-of-arms thing. They were picturesque, but now that she thought about it, she saw that they were picturesque because – to put it bluntly – they were old. They'd be a disaster. Stalling, boiling over, every trick in the book.

So what should you do? Louise asked. She'd learnt that city people were expected to ask the stupid question.

You find a little dip in the ground, Mrs Cartwright said, and get something over your head, a bag or whatever. It does go over real quick.

She glanced at Louise.

You'd be inclined to give running a go, but, wouldn't you?

It was easy to imagine how it would happen. There would be a few of you working in a line. You'd be flapping away with your wet bags and your little squirters, but the fire would suddenly come up at you from behind. Its size and power would make the idea of wet bags and squirters absurd. You would shout to each other and climb aboard the truck, but it would not start.

You would have just a few moments, after you saw it was hopeless and before the fire got you. There would be no time to think any great thoughts or to review the shortcomings of your behaviour. There would be no point in scribbling a note to anyone. In the moment before the breath was sucked out of your lungs, you might turn and hide your face in the person beside you. In that moment of extremity, it would not matter who it was.

The idea that a man who checked reservoirs for the Water Board might have once wanted to write music had seemed nothing more than ridiculous, that day in the Refreshments Tent. Now, watching her hands automatically buttering bread, she saw how interesting it was that his way of *going into something solid* had been to *go into water*.

At the time it had seemed merely silly. It occurred to her now that it could be a kind of heroism.

*

One of her ex-husbands had made a hobby of apocalypse. He'd done a chart in coloured pens, extrapolating forward from the fifteenth century, and had announced that another big war was due any time. He was ready. He kept a knapsack packed ready in the garage, with a compass and a knife and something he called *iron rations*. At the weekends he ran up and down hills, and practised lighting a fire with a magnifying glass and two dry leaves.

If the bomb drops, he had told her, and we get separated, I'll meet you at Gunnedah Post Office. It's far enough out to be safe.

Gunnedah Post Office, she had repeated, but doubtfully.

Don't forget.

She had not forgotten. But if a bomb dropped, she did not think she would go to Gunnedah Post Office. He would have made other plans now, with some other woman.

And he was not the man she would want to find, in the event of apocalypse.

She did not really know anything about the man who'd gone into water because it was solid. Lloyd. From the Water

Board. That was all she knew about him: that, and the way he had of looking at you with a kind of intensity, as if wondering.

She hardly knew him, had only met him the once. She did not have any arrangement with him about the steps of Gunnedah Post Office. Or anywhere else. Why was there, all at once, an emptiness, thinking that it might be too late now to have any arrangement with him, of any kind, about anything at all?

She had got the hang of the sandwiches now. She was churning them out, fast, faster, as if racing the fires eating up the bush. He would not be burned alive. He would come back down as he had gone up, perched in among the hoses, and she would be ready for him this time. He would wave, and she would be there, waving back. Then, perhaps, they could continue the conversation that their skins, so much wiser than they were themselves, had already begun.

Mate

He'd bought the Akubra and the elastic-sided boots but anyone could see he was a city bugger. Boolowa knew all about Will Bashford, the city bloke who'd bought the Phipps place for a hobby farm.

Hobby farm. He'd heard the way they said it.

The neighbour, Norm, would have told them all about him. *Nice enough bugger,* he'd have said. *Bit of a no-hoper, but.* Norm had seemed to know all about him as soon as they shook hands. You could tell Norm had never been a *no-hoper.* His grip was so strong that Will winced. *Sharpe's the name, sharp's the game,* he'd said, and laughed, so Will had felt obliged to laugh too.

Will had stopped wondering how people knew straight away. It was like a smell he gave out, the smell of diffidence and uncertainty. He knew he smiled more than a man should, and knew it was the wrong kind of smile: too eager to please.

He was not stupid, he knew that. But his face often was.

Boolowa was a little town like dozens of others out in the bush. Ridiculous wide main street, empty except for a dog crossing slowly from left to right. Shops all crammed up together outdoing each other with pretentious plaster facades. And over everything, the huge sky, pale with heat, and the crows taunting you.

There was a drought on – well, there was always a drought on. But over against the blue hills in the east, big heavy clouds built up every afternoon: heavier and bigger each day, dense-looking sharp-edged clouds with flat bases as if sanded smooth.

Looks like rain, he had suggested to Norm, that first day, meeting him at the gate down on the road. It was just for something to say, but Norm turned straight away to the men in the back of his broad dusty car.

Will here reckons we're in for rain, he said, and a man sunk deep in the back moved his mouth around his cigarette in something that could have been a smile.

Rain, eh? he said, and turned to tell the man next to him. Reckons we'll have rain.

Then they all looked at him.

It was rather more response than Will Bashford would generally have wished for.

It was hard to get it right, with these country folk. You had to be *matey*, of course. If they thought you were *stand-offish*, you might as well pack up and go home. But getting the exact degree of *matiness* right was something Will never seemed to manage.

The country was another planet, though he had got to know the theory of it at Kogarah Public School and they had learned the poem. *I love a sunburnt country, a land of sweeping plains, of something something something, of drought and flooding rains.* They had made the cartridge-paper bullock-dray, the balsa Pioneer Hut, the cardboard shearing shed. They had learned that *Australia Rides on the Sheep's Back.* It had been explained that this was in the nature of a meta-phor. Miss McDonald had made damper at home in her oven and brought it in. She had forgotten the salt and it had not been eaten, but they all knew after that what a damper looked like – scorched, unappetising – and admired the pioneers all the more.

So the streets where they lived, the little houses cheek-by-jowl, the lawn-mowing, the rush-hour crowd in the bus, their fathers hot and cross from hanging onto the strap all the way from Central, the man in the back lane with his bag of lollies – all that was not really there. That was just an accidental, temporary thing. Australia was *that land of sweeping plains*. It was *Click Go the Shears* and *Once a Jolly Swagman*.

It brought on a certain guilt. Will Bashford's natural – almost pathological – diffidence was amplified here in the country, where the very air felt foreign in his nostrils. He was not a proper Australian, in spite of having once memorised what a *blue-bellied joe* and a *coolabah* were, and he knew it showed.

*

He'd got it hopelessly wrong yesterday. He'd gone for a walk, along one of the back roads that led out of town. It was early enough to be cool and pleasant, the sun only just up, the flies half-hearted, the birds carolling away in the trees. The paddocks were soft and silvery in the early slanting sunlight, like something off a calendar. *Communing with Nature*, he told himself. This is *communing with Nature*.

He was all alone. It was hard to be all alone in the city. Someone was always watching you from between the venetians. Whatever you did, you had to assume it was being done in public. This – being all alone on a little back road, not having to keep the right sort of expression on your face, or look as if you knew what you were doing – made a nice change.

Click go the shears, boys, click, click, click, he sang. It was exhilarating, belting it out into the stillness of the morning. *Wide is his blow and his hands mo-ove quick*. He heard his voice wavering, drifting up and down. *Tone-deaf*, Miss McDonald had announced to 3B. *William Bashford, you're tone-deaf*, and he had felt a clutch of fright, wondering if being tone-deaf was something you got sent to the principal for. *Stand at the back, William, and just move your lips*.

He'd been an obedient boy. Being obedient was half of being a no-hoper. He had stood up the back and just moved his lips for years.

But he loved to sing. *The ringer looks around and dah-di-dah-di-dah, and curses the old something with the blue-bellied joe!* A cow lifted its head from the grass and stared.

Things had gone wrong when he saw a house he thought was derelict. He'd stopped, his hand on the cool metal of the gate, tempted to explore. This old place had its roofing iron curling at the seams, the grass was long around the rotting veranda, the house and the faded old red truck beside it all up to their ankles in dry grass. He liked poking around old places, but he'd been caught out before. You'd think a place was abandoned, but suddenly there'd be someone coming down off the verandah, and you'd have to wave in a casual way, and call out *morning, how's it going mate*, and they'd come down to the gate and you'd have to have a conversation about who you were and what you were doing there. By the time you'd got through all that, any idea of *communing with Nature* was well and truly finished.

There were cows in the front yard of this place, tearing at the grass around the water-tank, tilting dangerously on its stand. As he watched, an old woman in a long pink nightie ran around the corner of the house waving a stick at a few flustered cows that were lumbering along in front of her. In a surprisingly big voice for such a frail old thing she was shouting *Garn! Gaaaaaarn! Git!*

He watched, frozen to the gate, as she herded the cows around to the side and into a paddock. Her nightie, drenched and dark with dew along the hem, swung heavily around her bare feet as she strained to close the ramshackle gate. Her wispy white hair stood up in a ruff around her head, with pink scalp showing through.

She did not see Will, but disappeared around the back of the house. The cows gawped at the place where she had been. Will felt he was gawping too, and reminded himself to blink.

Coming back along the road later, the sun was in his eyes and he kept his head down. The dew had dried on the grass and the birds had been replaced by the cicadas that were starting up one by one, each one drilling away a different note. The flies were taking it in turns to get up his nose.

As he came near the house again he made his stride more purposeful and did not look around. The old woman was in her yard again, still in the pink nightie although there was a pink cardigan over it now. She was standing near the powdery old truck, looking up at the face of a young police-man writing in a notebook. Near them, another policeman bent over with a spring-loaded tape measure, measuring something along the ground. As Will watched, the tape snapped back and the policeman grabbed his hand. His mouth made the word FUCK.

Will walked faster and did not glance over towards the house again, his neck stiff with the ungainly look of a tall person trying to be inconspicuous. He stared into the dusty bushes, at the dusty roadside grass, at the dust itself on the roadway. He was tremendously interested in the dust. But even a man as interested in the dust as he was could not fail to hear the old woman, speaking with one of those well-bred penetrating kinds of voices.

'If I was going to pinch his bloody cattle, d'you think I'd do it in my bloody nightie?'

He had not pinched any bloody cattle, had not been caught trespassing, had got no further than putting his hand on the gate. Had done nothing wrong, in fact. Why did he feel so guilty, scurrying along with bowed head?

The thing he had done wrong was going for a walk in the first place. Going for a walk was not something you did, out in the country. That alone was asking for trouble.

At least there had been no one listening to him sing.

*

He had the Akubra and the elastic-sided boots, but he had not thought to bring a raincoat with him from Sydney. But the clouds were there again, at the end of Hill Street, as they had been on the first day, big dramatic clouds with serious dark-grey folds that looked full of rain.

He imagined himself out on the paddocks – his own paddocks! – in the rain. He would have to huddle under a garbage bag. Word of that would soon get around. *That Bashford bloke, saw him out on his place in a bloody garbage bag!* It was easy to get off on the wrong foot in a new place.

Looking down Hill Street, he could see the Criterion Hotel and the Milk Bar. No raincoats there. There was the butcher, and a Draper and Mercer that looked as if it had been closed for years. Further along were the Stock & Station Est 1919 and the General Store. The General Store had a window full of faded and flyspecked cornflakes boxes. It did not look a promising prospect for a raincoat. That left the Stock & Station, whatever that was.

A tall skinny bloke like a long drink of water, all chin and nose, was leaning on the War Memorial cairn watching him as he walked slowly along to the shop, carefully, as if he expected to have to give evidence. *Brown hair, brown eyes, big ears.*

Quickly, as if he knew exactly where he was going, Will crossed the road towards the Stock & Station. His walk felt jerky as he crossed the vast expanse of Hill Street under the gaze of the chin-and-nose man. *Funny kind of walk.* He forced himself not to *look to the right and look to the left and look to the right again.* Only a no-hoper would think a car could take you by surprise on Hill Street, Boolowa.

Inside the shop he paused, hearing the door bell jangle above his head. He was going to be Norm Sharpe. Front up to the counter and say *mate* a lot. Easy.

The first problem was finding the counter. After the glare outside, the shop was dark. It would be easy to think those grey overalls were a person. That would get back to Norm. *Feller comes in here, says g'day to the bloody overalls.*

There had been a teacher at school called Mr Overall. Naturally, the kids had called him Mr Underpants.

It was the kind of thing you tended to remember at the

wrong moment. He instructed himself not to laugh. *Feller comes in here, laughs at the bloody overalls.*

Beyond the overalls there were shoulder-shapes. It was hard to be sure of anything in the dimness, his eyes straining to adjust after the scalding light outside, but he thought the shoulder-shapes were not a *mate* either, just a row of checked shirts, with caps on a stand beside them.

He was working out that there must be a counter over on the far wall – there was a gleam of something horizontal cutting across the verticals of the shelving behind – when a voice came from the direction of the gleam.

Help at all, mate?

He thought of laughing and calling out *bit dark in here, mate, nearly talked to the bloody overalls!* His mouth open for the laugh, he thought better of it. Over the years, he had learned that not everyone thought the same things were funny that he did. New place, new people, no offence intended. Better to play safe.

Ah, yes. Mate.

He dodged around a tower of brown blocks of cow-lick. He could see the man behind the counter now, two blanks of reflected light from glasses turned at him, another long nose, long chin, like the Johnny over the road. Inbreeding. Small gene pool. Probably a lot of long noses and long chins in Boolowa.

After a moment he realised there was a customer at the counter too, a big solid man in a red-checked shirt, standing as still as a pair of overalls.

Sorry, mate, Will said. Didn't see you there.

He made an ushering gesture with his hand, palm up.

Go ahead.

But the man shook his head.

You're right, mate, he said.

Will turned to the shopkeeper. The glasses sat cock-eyed on his face so you wanted to reach over and straighten them up. Tufts of grey hair erupted out of his nostrils. *Eye contact,* Will told himself. *Make eye contact.* But he could not look.

I'm after a raincoat, mate, he said. It sounded a bit on the loud side. Got a raincoat at all? Mate?

Somehow it was not quite the way Norm Sharpe would have said it. The shopkeeper did a peculiar thing with his face that made the glasses twitch back up his nose. After a long blank-glassed stare, in which his hand smoothed over the empty counter, he said:

Nope. No raincoats.

It seemed that this was going to be all. Will nearly turned to go, but the image of himself under the garbage bag was vivid in his mind.

Oh well, he began.

But the shopkeeper cut across him quickly.

Not at the moment.

There was another pause. Will started again.

Oh well.

But the shopkeeper might have been waiting for him to speak.

 Sold the last, some time ago now.

His words were like a force of nature. Will was silent. He did not think he would say *Oh well* again.

The glasses were slipping down the shopkeeper's nose again.

The man in the red shirt moved now. He turned slowly and methodically and had a good long look at Will Bashford, all the way from the elastic-sided boots to the Akubra. Then he crossed his arms over his big checked chest and gave a short deliberate laugh like a cough.

Not had a drop of rain here for three years.

He turned to the shopkeeper.

That right, Lance?

Lance nodded and stared at Will.

Before he could explain about the big flat-bottomed heavy-looking clouds, and the way they were heaped up against the hills, the shopkeeper cackled and pushed his glasses back up with his thumb. You could see he was enjoying the anticipation. He was going to make a joke.

Not a real lot of demand, for a raincoat, just at the minute.

He and Lance both laughed thoroughly. Will tried to smile but it felt like a snarl. He wished he could think of something else to ask for, so he could leave with dignity, but he did not want a cube of cowlick.

He tried a joke of his own.

Be prepared, that's what I always say!

It was not what he always said, and it did not sound as if it was. His witticism was received in silence.

Will felt his mouth shaping a stupid meaningless smile.

Oh well, he found it saying again. Okay mate. See you later.

He was turning away from the counter when Lance gave him a fright by saying suddenly,

Pump's pressing charges, you know.

Will was confused, his mind full of anxiety to get outside and check the clouds. Surely he had not imagined them. He felt as if his mouth was hanging open. *Pump? Pressing?*

The shopkeeper said loudly, as if he thought he was deaf, or slow:

Charges. About the cattle.

He and Lance exchanged a tiny smirk.

When you was out for your walk. This morning.

Lance gave Will a fright, slapping his hand on the counter suddenly.

Been bad blood there for years.

Will turned from one face to the other as if he was lip-reading.

Business about an easement. Reckons he'll sue this time, but.

They both watched Will. Even if he could still remember what came after *sweeping plains*, he had a feeling it would not help him now.

Um, he said, and wished he had not. They were both watching him as if he had something more to say.

After a long silence, the shopkeeper said kindly,

So, if you saw, mate, you should say.

Will was feeling congested, as if his pipes would burst from sheer incomprehension.

Yes? He tried.

Don't want to see her go to jail, do you, an old thing like that?

He twitched the glasses up his nose again.

Mrs Quincy, mate. You give a statement, she'll be right. Small, in at Willoughby.

He was speaking very slowly. Each word was beautifully clear. No problem at all with the words.

The man in the check shirt broke in impatiently.

The cops, mate. Go to the cops, give a statement.

A statement, Will repeated. The cops.

They were waiting for him now.

He imagined himself going into Willoughby and finding Constable Small. Norm Sharpe had introduced him to Constable Small, outside the Criterion. Gregory Small did not seem like a young man to hurry or cut corners. He had shaken Will's hand at length, as if testing it, and inspected his face closely.

Bashford? he had asked. Or Brashford?

He would be slow on the big black Remington that the Willoughby Police Station would be managing with. *I was proceeding along Seven Mile Road in an easterly direction at about 7am on Tuesday the 14th of February.* Read out in Gregory Small's loud flat voice, it would make Will sound more of a no-hoper than ever. *At Lot 84 known as Braeside I saw eight cows proceeding through a broken fence.*

The exact number of cows would cause a bit of a bottleneck. *About eight* or *approximately eight*, Will would want to say. But he did not think Gregory Small would be the sort of man likely to be comfortable with approximations. Cows were either *eight cows*, or *nine cows*, or *seven cows.* You could not have *approximately eight cows.*

They would sit there at the desk with the Remington between them and Will would feel himself going red in the face and his ears swelling, the way they did when he was embarrassed.

Course, your mate Norm's on Pump's side, the man in the check shirt suddenly said. They're cousins through old Grant Pump.

Plus Norm married the sister-in-law's girl, the shopkeeper said. They own that, where you was going this morning. For your walk.

There could have been another little smirk exchanged. *Click go the shears, boys, click click click.*

Will stared at the dusty boards between his boots. He could feel the blood pouring up into his cheeks, his neck, his ears. He seemed to be radiating heat, as if these two could warm their hands at him. *And curses the old something with the blue-bellied joe.*

There was a little jump on *blue-bellied* where his voice always cracked. It would have been funny if you had been a person behind a tree, listening.

Well, he said. Okay.

They did not ask him exactly what it was that was *okay*, but watched with interest as he backed away from the counter, got himself turned around, and headed for the doorway. It seemed to have got lost among the shelves of dim things. Dodging a pyramid of something in big tins, he lost his balance and had to put a hand out to save himself, knocking a big box of Ratsak on to the floor. His bottom felt a huge ridiculous target for the two faces watching as he bent over to pick it up. Then he could not find the right shelf for it and had to stuff it in next to a bundle of axe-handles and some funny-looking leather appendages.

He felt he would never reach the hard white glare of the doorway. It seemed centuries ago that he had set off in the cool of the dawn, when he had not known that there was no such thing as a private walk in the country.

Hooroo, mate, the shopkeeper called, but he could not bear to turn.

Inheritance

A Rural Family Saga

Hannie Rayson

Family Tree in the Year 2000

Nollie (1890–1960) *m.* Norm MYRTLE (1880–1934)

The HAMILTONS

Farley HAMILTON **80** (b.1920)
m.1942
Dibs MYRTLE **80** (b.1920)

The DELANEYS

Lucky Joe DELANEY **80** (1925–1995)
m.1943
Girlie MYRTLE **80** (b.1920)

Hamish
divorced
Julia **44** (b.1956)

William **50**
(b.1950)

Nugget RILEY **45**
(b.1955 adopted
Aboriginal)

Felix **19** (b.1981)

Bridget **56**
(b.1944. Nun living
in Bangladesh)

Rory
(1946–64)

Maureen **55**
(b.1945)

Lyle **48**
m.
Libby Ferguson **42**
(b.1952)

Ashley **16**   Brianna **15**

Main Characters

The HAMILTONS:

DIBS HAMILTON, 80 years
FARLEY HAMILTON, 80 years, husband of DIBS
WILLIAM HAMILTON, 50 years, oldest son
JULIA HAMILTON, 44 years, daughter
NUGGET RILEY, 45 years, adopted son (Aboriginal)
FELIX, 19 years, JULIA's son

The DELANEYS:

GIRLIE DELANEY, 80 years, twin sister of DIBS
'LUCKY' JOE DELANEY, (Deceased), husband of GIRLIE
MAUREEN DELANEY, 55 years, daughter, MHR, Member for Murray (Independent)
LYLE DELANEY, 48 years, son, farmer
LIBBY DELANEY, 42 years, wife of LYLE, hospital matron
ASHLEY, 16 years, daughter of LYLE and LIBBY
BRIANNA, 15 years, daughter of LYLE and LIBBY

Secondary Characters

NORM MYRTLE, father of DIBS and GIRLIE (1890–1934)
NOLLIE MYRTLE, mother (1902–2000)
GIG RYLIE, stockman
DULCIE, Nollie's sister
WORMIE McCALLUM, Dulcie's husband
BRIDGET DELANEY, oldest daughter of GIRLIE and JOE, nun, living in Bangladesh
RORY DELANEY, son of GIRLIE and JOE, killed in a farm accident

ACT I

PART ONE

Sunset in the Mallee. A country road. There is an almighty explosion. A Toyota Corona has shuddered to a halt. Smoke pours from the engine.

The driver is a woman in her forties, JULIA; the passenger, her son, FELIX. They are clearly inner-city folk.

JULIA: Fuck. *Pause.* Fuck fuck fuck fuck fuck.

They get out. As Julia slams the door, the car explodes again. This time the bonnet springs open and water gushes out.

A black crow comments: Faarrk. Faarrk.

Silence. They stare at the car. FELIX surveys the landscape. They are miles from anywhere. He goes to release the radiator cap and burns his hand.

FELIX: Fuck!

He kicks the tyre.

JULIA: Felix!

The car radio springs to life and in the vast Mallee silence we hear a tinny version of Noel Coward singing 'Don't Put Your Daughter on the Stage, Mrs Worthington'.

FELIX: Where are we?

JULIA: About 20 k. north of Birchup. On the Berriwollock Road.

FELIX: And how far is Rushton? Approximately.

JULIA: About 40 ks.

FELIX: Too far to walk. Obviously.

JULIA examines things under the bonnet. FELIX leans on the roof of the car and squints into the distance.

JULIA: Black smoke means a fuel system defect.

FELIX: *(To audience)* I hate cars.

JULIA: Blue or blue-white smoke means internal engine problems.

FELIX: *(To audience)* I don't even have a licence.

JULIA: And white smoke is the result of coolant getting into the cylinders.

FELIX: My mother did a course in Car Maintenance For Women, so we should be back on the road in no time.
I'm Felix. I live above a Turkish takeaway in Sydney Road – The Cosmic Kebab. I live with my girlfriend Hiroko and this other guy, who's just moved in – DJ Dumpster. He's a turntabler.

JULIA: I think it's the head gasket.

FELIX: That did occur to me, but I didn't want to be alarmist. *(To audience)* This is my mother Julia.

JULIA: Felix, can you pass me a spanner? In the glove box.

FELIX hands her a screwdriver.

JULIA: That's a screwdriver.

FELIX: Right.

He dives back into the car and hands her a spanner. She holds the two tools up.

JULIA: Spanner. Screwdriver.

She returns to the business under the bonnet.

FELIX: *(To audience)* Living above the Cosmic Kebab is pretty interesting. There's this giant plastic kebab rotating outside our bedroom window. It's got this 1,000 watt light inside. It's a kind of landmark in a way. Just up from Ali Baba's Variety Store. Opposite the Parthenon Bridal Emporium. Anyway one night it was squeaking in this really irritating way – the kebab – and DJ Dumpster thumps it with a broom to make it stop but he just smashes a hole in it. So now there's this pink light that flashes into our bedroom, all night, every 3.7 seconds. It's sort of like a search light in a POW camp.

JULIA: Oh God. Look at the size of that hole.

FELIX: *(To audience)* Hiroko said if I didn't negotiate with Mostafa to fix the kebab, she'd move out. Which is why she is currently living with her friend Megumi. And which is why, when my mother rang – Hey Mum.

JULIA: Hi darling.

FELIX: I agreed. To her irritatingly passive-aggressive request:

JULIA: I don't suppose you'd want to come with me up to Allandale this weekend?

FELIX: Even though I hate Allandale, which is my grandparents' farm. Sure. Why not?

JULIA: It's just that it's your grandmother's eightieth birthday and everyone would be so sad if you weren't there. *Pause.* But if you really feel you've got more important things to do then –

FELIX: – Then what?

JULIA: Well. We'd all be very disappointed, that's all.

*

DIBS walks across the stage with a wheelbarrow of dirt.

DIBS: *(To audience)* We were all very disappointed when Julia and Hamish separated. Julia's my daughter. She's coming up this weekend, for our birthday. Girlie's and mine. We're eighty tomorrow. Old as God's dog.

She tips the dirt out.

But it's a terrible thing when a marriage ends. Mind you, I don't think Julia tried hard enough. I think she just got bored. That's the thing with young women. Too selfish by half.

I thought he was lovely, Hamish. I miss him. He came up one Easter and helped me plant the lavender hedge, over there. Sometimes in the spring when I come out for herbs and I see the lavender in full bloom, I say 'Hello, Hamish.'

*

GIRLIE'S house. LYLE knocks on the door, looking for his mother. On the front path is a large object with a blanket over it.

LYLE: You there, Girlie? Mum? You there?

GIRLIE: (Off) Only just.

An old lady shuffles out onto the porch using a walking frame.

GIRLIE: What's this?

LYLE: Happy birthday.

GIRLIE: What is it?

LYLE: Nah nah!

LYLE unveils the object. It is a motorised lawn mower that he has converted into a little drive-bike for his mother.

Long pause. GIRLIE stares at it.

GIRLIE: Do I have to do m' own lawns now?

LYLE: It's for getting around town. Hop on.

GIRLIE: Don't be ridiculous.

LYLE: Come on. This is going to make all the difference to your life, Mum.

GIRLIE: Too right it is. I'm gonna be the town idiot.

LYLE: Look. Hop on. Pull the cord. And away you go.

LYLE demonstrates.

GIRLIE: Where d'it come from?

LYLE: Never you mind.

GIRLIE: Fell off the back of a truck, did it?.

LYLE: I bought it at a garage sale.

GIRLIE: Kirby's?

LYLE: Yes, if you must know.

GIRLIE: You expect me to ride down the main street on a dead man's clapped-out motor mower.

LYLE: It's not clapped out. It's beautiful. I reconditioned the motor. Nice soft seat. Good brakes. Know how much those motorised bikes cost? On the TV ads?

GIRLIE: How much?

LYLE: Two hundred a month. Whereas this cost me sixteen bucks – tops. Oh, bit more for the seat. What d'you reckon?

GIRLIE: I reckon you're a whacker.

LYLE: Just try it.

GIRLIE: Lyle.

LYLE: Don't be a piker.

GIRLIE: Jesus Christ.

LYLE: That's the spirit.

She makes her way down the path with LYLE's help.

GIRLIE: D'you see where Kingston Boy came home in the third at Cranbourne.

LYLE: D'you have any money on it?

GIRLIE: I gave that silly sister o' mine ten quid. D'you think she remembered to go to the TAB?

LYLE: She's got a lot on her plate, poor ol' Dibs. Hop on.

GIRLIE: Poor ol' Dibs, my arse. Came in at seven to one.

LYLE: Jesus and Mary.

GIRLIE: Always had the luck of a speckle-arsed rooster.

She clambers on, refusing his assistance. Lyle pulls the starter cord and the machine roars to life.

GIRLIE: Jesus H. Christ!

LYLE: Put your foot on the pedal!

The bike leaps into action, carrying GIRLIE offstage.

*

In the garden outside the HAMILTON's farmhouse kitchen.

DIBS comes out in her gardening clothes and big hat. We hear the slap of the flywire door. She is humming 'Two Little Girls in Blue'.

WILLIAM comes up the path carrying bags, surprising his mother.

DIBS: Will! I didn't hear the car.

WILLIAM: Deaf as well as everything else.

DIBS: I was on the phone. Hello darling.

They embrace.

WILLIAM: Happy birthday.

DIB: Thank you. Julia not with you?

WILLIAM: No.

DIBS: She's broken down on the Berriwollock Road.

WILLIAM: Not again.

DIBS: I thought you might have passed her.

WILLIAM: No. I never come that way.

DIBS: You turn off at Wycheproof, do you?

WILLIAM: Yeah. And up through Quambatook. I suppose I'd better go and get her.

DIBS: Come in and we'll ring Nugget.

WILLIAM: Why does she persist with that ridiculous bomb?

DIBS: She likes old things.

WILLIAM: Handy for you.

DIBS: Things, darling. Not people.

*

GIRLIE hoons across the stage sitting atop her new motor.

GIRLIE: Crikey O'Reilly, where's the brakes?

LYLE: On the side. On the side!

She lurches to a halt.

LYLE: What d'you reckon?

Pause.

GIRLIE: I'll think about it. Maybe if it didn't have that thing on it *(the grass clippings catcher).*

LYLE: I had a call from Val Barker, by the way. They're all coming.

GIRLIE: From Chinkapook. Oh Gawd. How many's that, now?

LYLE: 'Bout sixty.

GIRLIE: Have you told Dibs? We're gonna need more grog, Lyle.

LYLE: Everything's under control. All right?

GIRLIE: You don't know those Barkers. They drink like fish. Here give us a hand. I remember one night after shearing, Toddy couldn't get his ute going. The gear box was buggered. So he reversed it into Sea Lake to get to the pub before six. He reversed that car fourteen miles.

LYLE: That'd be right. That was Toddy backed his truck into the Methodist Church, wasn't it?

GIRLIE: No. That was his brother. In more trouble than Ned, that lad.

LYLE: Emu.

GIRLIE: Emu Barker. What's he want, coming to our birthday?

LYLE: Someone must have asked him.

*

DIBS: I asked the Barkers, by the way.

WILLIAM: Jesus, Mum, that's a bit desperate, isn't it?

DIBS: You don't mind, do you?

WILLIAM: Why? Because Brian Barker stoushed me in primary school.

DIBS: He broke your nose. The little thug.

WILLIAM: That was thirty-eight years ago, Mum.

DIBS: You don't think he'll try it again, do you?

Pause.

WILLIAM: Why did you invite them?

DIBS: Well, I saw Mrs Barker at the CWA –

WILLIAM snorts.

DIBS: It's not just a group of narrow-minded old biddies, you know.

WILLIAM: It's a hotbed of lesbian radicalism.

DIBS: You'd be surprised what we get up to.

WILLIAM: Do I want to hear this?

DIBS: Honestly.

WILLIAM: These roses are looking good, Mum. I like that bright red one.

DIBS: That's my favourite. The Tammy Fraser.

WILLIAM: What about the Margaret Whitlam? Have you got her?

DIBS: Don't be ridiculous. We've got Maureen Delaney.

WILLIAM: Not yet you haven't.

Suddenly, the back doors roll open. Accompanied by triumphal nationalistic music, Maureen Delaney rides in on a tractor which rolls down the stage toward the audience. She is waving to a crowd of enthusiastic supporters who clap and whistle and stamp their feet. A large banner reads:

VOTE ONE MAUREEN DELANEY
Putting *Australia First*

MAUREEN addresses the assembled crowd.

MAUREEN: Thank you. Thank you. Thank you. Bless you.
It's great to be home.
You know you're with city people when you say, I worked every summer back home, stripping. And they look at you funny. *(Laughter.)* You realise there are certain things that city people just don't understand. And after you've spent a fair while with them, you learn that there is *a lot* that city people don't know and *that* ignorance is destroying this country.
Now as most of you know, I used to run a caravan park and the press has had a field day with my caravan park. But I learned a great deal about people in those seven years. And I learned that what people want from the manager of a park is the same thing they want with their government: they want fair treatment, they want to feel safe and they want rules.
Let me tell you a true story. One night, a gang of bikies rode into my park. Stirring up trouble, making one helluva racket.

Taking over the Amenities block and helping themselves to the communal fridges where the other campers keep their food.

Anyway I had this young fella working with me and he says, 'We're just gonna have to sit tight. There's nothing we can do.'

And I thought, 'Bugger that. I'm the manager here and I am not going to be intimidated by a band of thugs.'

So I marched down there and I said 'Out!' And this big hairy bloke in a leather vest with tatts all over him, he's goin' f—ing this and f—ing that.

I said, 'You heard me. I'm in charge here. This is my park. On yer bike. Now.'

I said, 'I'm not gonna ring the police. I'm just telling you, myself. Out.'

And he stares at me long and hard this bloke and then he says, 'Yes Mam. Whatever you say.' And he gives me a little bow and he gets on his bike and they all ride off down the road and we never saw 'em again. True story.

LYLE and his daughters, ASHLEY and BRIANNA, inadvertently cycle downstage on their bikes with pigeons in a basket.

Ladies and Gentlemen, the people of Australia are being held to ransom by foreign interests – who are no different from those bikies. I'm talking about the bullies of international capital who come riding into *our* country and help themselves to *our* resources. These multinational corporations have no loyalty to our country. Why should they? Why should they care about the wellbeing of ordinary Australians? In fact it is in their interest to lobby for the kind of trade regulations and international treaties which are designed to ensure that decent hard-working people are deprived of the rewards of their hard work. Ordinary Australians don't stand a chance.

And the tragedy for our community is that the people we've got running this country are a mob of city pansies who will *not* take the responsibility to tell these global thugs to get on their bike and bugger off.

LYLE and the girls cycle across the stage and find a grassy spot to dismount. LYLE squints into the sky.

BRIANNA: D'you think she saw us?

LYLE: Who?

BRIANNA: Auntie Maureen.

LYLE shrugs.

ASHLEY: Why didn't you want to go?

Pause.

LYLE: I don't like crowds.

BRIANNA: She's your sister.

LYLE spots a pigeon flying high in the sky.

LYLE: Well, well, well. Look up there. I reckon that just might be our girl. Your great grandpa was a marvellous pigeon man. D'you know that?

BRIANNA: Nup.

LYLE: One time he sold a pair of pigeons to this bloke in the city, and the bloke got TB and had to go into a sanatorium. His mum just opened the cage and let all his birds go. Anyway, Grandpa Norman's out in the yard and he can tell a pigeon flyin' in the air. What number it is. And he says to Nanna – I think that's 357. And Nanna says 'But you sold that bird in Melbourne.'
'That's right, 357.'
But when he sold the bird he was using a different loft. About twenty-two mile away. In Sea Lake.

Anyway, the bird lands down on the ground and Norm throws a bit o' seed around and he's calling it and then he says to Nanna, 'There y'are. Have a look at that.' 'Cos she'd boxed it and sent it down for him. 357 all right! Found its way all the way back from Melbourne and to a different loft.

That went on to be a very good pigeon, that one.

BRIANNA: Can I do the first toss?

LYLE: Can't see why not.

ASHLEY: What happens if it doesn't come back?

LYLE: Well. You've put in all the work. Training him up. So provided there are not too many hawks up there, he'll fly straight back. Yeah. You put in the work and you get your rewards. But you gotta have a bit of faith too.

BRIANNA: Dad?

LYLE: Yeah?

BRIANNA: Why did Grandpa Norm hang himself?

LYLE: You're full of questions, today.

BRIANNA: Mum says it's good. To ask questions.

Pause.

ASHLEY: Was it because of his pigeons?

LYLE: No.

BRIANNA: Maybe he put in the work and didn't get the rewards.

*

We hear the sound of a motorbike roaring along the road. JULIA and FELIX get out of the car preparing to hail down the motorcyclist and her passenger. When she takes off her helmet, JULIA recognises her.

JULIA: Libby!

LIBBY: Thought I reckonised you. How you going? Having a bit o' car trouble.

JULIA: *(To FELIX)* You remember Libby? Lyle's wife.

FELIX: The pigeon bloke.

LIBBY: That's right. I've just been in Swan Hill hearing Maureen address the locals.

FELIX: Maureen Delaney?

JULIA: She's in town?

LIBBY: There were about 300 people at the Town Hall. She can pull a crowd all right.

FELIX: What was she like?

LIBBY: Got a standing ovation.

JULIA: Jesus.

LIBBY: They can't get enough of her, up this way.

FELIX: What do you think of her?

LIBBY: I think she's an extremely dangerous woman. But I keep that opinion pretty close to m' chest.

JULIA: So I suppose she's coming to Mum and Girlie's party now?

LIBBY: 'Fraid so.

JULIA: Fuck! Excuse me. Mum didn't mention it.

LIBBY: She prob'ly guessed that if you knew, you wouldn't show up.

Pause.

JULIA: You still matron, at the hospital?

LIBBY: Yeah. Working away so we can pretend we make money off the farm.

JULIA: How is Lyle?

LIBBY: Same as ever. Working himself into the ground. Going backwards fast. What's the story with your car?

JULIA: It won't go.

FELIX: I think it's the head gasket.

LIBBY: I'll give Nugget a ring. He'll sort you out.

She reaches for her mobile.

LIBBY: You all geared up for 'the big talk'?

JULIA: What 'big talk'?

LIBBY: I really don't get your family, sometimes. *Pause.* Your mother wants to put the farm on the market.

JULIA: What!? Allandale?

*

DIBS: She's polling well, Will. People round here are fed up. They're not getting any joy from the Nationals.

WILLIAM: As if Maureen Delaney's going to deliver anything. Except ignorance and prejudice.

DIBS: At the party tomorrow – ?

WILLIAM: – I thought I'd say, 'Cousin Maureen, have I ever told you what a repellent, narrow-minded, ugly bigot you are?' What d'you reckon?

DIBS: You might find there are certain issues where you line up on the same side …

WILLIAM: She's become a gay activist?

Pause.

DIBS: She's anti-globalisation.

WILLIAM: I'm not against globalisation.

DIBS: Well you should be. We've lost our bank. Our post office, our library, the Water Board, the school bus.

WILLIAM: That's just the way things are, Dibs.

DIBS: It's the way things are, if you believe greed should be allowed to run riot. And rule everything. The town's dying Will – don't you feel anything? Anything at all?

WILLIAM: I feel anxious, that my car might break down. And I'd be stuck here.

Here's the olive oil you wanted.

DIBS: *(Looking at the bottle)* Calabrian? Goodness.

WILLIAM: Good peppery flavour, apparently.

DIBS: I was talking with Gerald Cogsley the other night – he's our new financial counsellor. He's in Rotary with Dad. A very decent fellow actually. *Pause.* Bit boring.

WILLIAM: Boring? Gosh. I'm surprised they let him into Rotary.

DIBS: Gerald says that nearly half the middle-aged men in the bush are earning less than $300 a week. Don't you find that staggering? Men with families.

WILLIAM: Well you know what I think. You're making the right decision –

DIBS: This isn't about us, Will. This is about a whole series of little communities that are just being wiped out. At least Maureen is going in to bat –

WILLIAM: Look, what Maureen Delaney and her stupid nuff-nuff supporters have to understand is that globalisation has affected every country on earth since the end of the Cold War. Protectionism won't work any more. We're too small an economy.

DIBS: Hang on a minute. If you think about my rose garden – this is what I said to my ladies at the CWA – it's beautiful because it doesn't have to compete in the free market with all sorts of other plants. It's been protected so the roses can bloom and prosper in conditions created just for roses.

Pause.

WILLIAM: You should be locked up.

DIBS: Why?

WILLIAM: You are a social menace. Telling those old boilers that their gardens should be kept only for English roses.

DIBS: I am not.

WILLIAM: You are. You are urging them to weed out their indigenous plants.

DIBS: That's not true.

WILLIAM: It is. Admit it. You are –

DIBS: I am simply saying –

WILLIAM: And as for *foreign* plants …

DIBS: I am simply saying that careful borders are important.

WILLIAM: Careful borders that keep out foreigners – like those little yellow ones from Asia.

DIBS: Oh, honestly.

WILLIAM: This is the White Australia policy at work. You are gardening for racism.
   Here's your balsamic vinegar.

DIBS: They're a damn side more progressive than the men. I'll tell you that for nothing.

WILLIAM: Who? The CWA.

DIBS: It's the men who won't budge.

WILLIAM: Cajun spices. Wild rice. The Tamari. What else …?

DIBS: You can buy Italian olive oil in Swan Hill, you know.

WILLIAM: Not this one, you can't. But when you come to town, you'll be able to buy all these things yourself. At the corner shop. On the way home from the theatre.

DIBS: Incredible.

WILLIAM: You're not getting cold feet are you?

DIBS: No.

*

GIRLIE and LIBBY walk down the main street of Rushton. GIRLIE on her frame, LIBBY assisting in her matron's uniform.

GIRLIE: Here. Cross the road. I don't like walking past the pub.

LIBBY: They know it was you who dobbed them in, you know.

GIRLIE: Serves them right. Pack o' cheats.

LIBBY: The Health Inspector told George Pappas that the complainant sounded like a little old lady who knew the pub very well. I wonder who that was?

GIRLIE: You can't tip out half your vodka, fill it up with water and expect to get away with it.

LIBBY: You made that up, Girl.

GIRLIE: I did not. *Pause.* Fifteen dollars for a plate of steak and chips. That's robbery. There are people in this town who can't afford to buy a raffle ticket.

LIBBY: Everything's gone up.

GIRLIE: We never charged anything over ten bucks.

LIBBY: What with the GST and everything.

GIRLIE: Food's food, Lib. People gotta eat. Thirty years I ran that pub. They're thieves those Greeks. They're just blow-ins and what's worse – they got no morals. It's their culture. I'm sorry to have to say it –

LIBBY: All right. Settle down.

GIRLIE: No, bugger it. Where they come from, you don't help a bloke who's fallen over in the street. You pinch his wallet.

LIBBY: Now you know that's not true.

GIRLIE: I saw it on the T.V. They're shifty.

LIBBY: By the way –

GIRLIE: Not as bad as your person of Asiatic extraction.

LIBBY: I've ordered some extra quiches for the party.

GIRLIE: They're the worst. Those Asiatics.

LIBBY: I just got the small ones.

GIRLIE: But I wouldn't trust a Greek. No way. They'll pull the rug out from under you –

LIBBY: Girlie, listen. I ordered two dozen spinach and two dozen asparagus.

GIRLIE: You should have got the quiche lorraines. I like them the best.

LIBBY: They've got bacon in them.

GIRLIE: So?

LIBBY: We needed something for the vegetarians.

GIRLIE: Oh bugger the vegetarians.

*

DIBS hands WILLIAM some bedding.

DIBS: Don't forget to tuck your eiderdown in tight. We're having a bit of trouble with mice.

WILLIAM: Not again.

DIBS: Dad found one in the toaster this morning.

WILLIAM: Ugh Gawd. How is *der Führer* today?

DIBS: He's out in the paddock, helping them shift.

WILLIAM: Nugget told me the old boy misplaced the ute yesterday. He said he found Dad wandering around The Gums looking for a mob of ewes.

DIBS: I know. Yesterday he didn't recognise Lyle Delaney at the back door.

WILLIAMS: He's bunging it on.

DIBS: Oh for goodness sake, William. He is not. This is what happens. Some days he's lucid and some days he's not.

WILLIAM: He just hears what he wants to hear.

A feisty weather-beaten old man enters, FARLEY.

FARLEY: Here's trouble.

WILLIAM: Dad.

FARLEY: When d'you get here?

WILLIAM: I've just arrived.

FARLEY: Want to give us a hand down at Burns?

DIBS: He's just got in, love.

FARLEY: That inch last week'll bring on a green pick soon.

WILLIAM: That's good.

FARLEY: Depending on how hot it gets. *Pause.* You don't know where the air compressor is, do you? That side tyre's a bit flat. *(To William)* You'll need to pump it up.

DIBS: We'll give him a cup o' tea first I think, love.

FARLEY: D'you get that thunderstorm down your way, few weeks back?

WILLIAM: No.

FARLEY: Green barley shoots all through the stubble. Coming up bloody beautiful down there. Where's Darcy? *(Farley's dog).* Darcy!

He looks out the window

Ah! Come 'ere you ol' bugger. Don't think you can get out of it that easy. Go on. Ay! Outta there.

FARLEY walks off. The flywire screen slaps shut.

WILLIAM: Hello William. How are you? Are you well? How nice of you to come all this way to see us.

DIBS: At least he remembered you.

WILLIAM: Instead of 'Hey you, Slave Boy!'

DIBS: Let's not go down that track. Please.

WILLIAM: No. Let's pretend that he has the capacity to treat his son slightly better than his dog.

DIBS: You can say 'No,' William. You're an adult, remember.

DIBS follows FARLEY. The door slaps closed again.

*

WILLIAM enters his memory. It is 1959.

MAUREEN comes into the woolshed. She is wearing her school uniform flanked by a group of kids. She is fifteen years old. WILLIAM is twelve.
    WILLIAM is cornered. MAUREEN starts to undo the buttons on her uniform.

MAUREEN: You can say 'No,' Willy. *(Long pause)* If you're a faggot. Are you?

WILLIAM: What?

MAUREEN: Are you a faggot?

RORY: A homo?

WILLIAM: Nuck.

MAUREEN: Prove it.

WILLIAM: What?

MAUREEN: I said prove it.

Long pause.

WILLIAM: What?

MAUREEN: If you were normal you'd know.

She stands there posing menacingly in the guise of sexual provocation.

MAUREEN does her buttons up determinedly.

MAUREEN: I'm very sorry to say, ladies and gentleman. William Hamilton is a homosexual.

RORY: You sicko poof.

WILLIAM: I am not.

BRIDGET: Rory. Sssh. Will, listen to me. Neither fornicators, nor thieves, nor homosexuals will inherit the kingdom of God. You have to ask Jesus for forgiveness.

RORY: I should bash yer fuckin' head in.

WILLIAM: I'll bash *your* fucking head in.

BRIDGET: William! Stop it. We've come to you as Christians because we *care*. You're our cousin and we don't want to see you burn in Hell.

RORY: I do. Fuckin' pansy.

MAUREEN: Rory. Shut up will ya.

BRIDGET: It really hurts God, what you're doing.

WILLIAM: Shut up, you frigid nun.

MAUREEN: Shut up yourself, you pervert.

*

JULIA and FELIX wait by the side of the road with their car.

FELIX: How long does it take before you die of thirst, do you reckon?

JULIA: See that line of trees over there. That's Pearson's Creek. You won't die of thirst.

FELIX: This really sums it up. Everything I've ever experienced about country life. You sort of wait, don't you. Wait for something to happen.

JULIA: When you were a little boy I used to get you to walk to the shops, by saying, 'Let's pretend we're Burke and Wills.'

FELIX: Conveniently omitting to mention that Burke and Wills get lost and die of thirst. You are a *very* strange woman.

JULIA: If you follow the line of the creek, that's the southern fence of the Maloney's. I went to school with Pete Maloney.

FELIX: Mm? Pete Maloney?

JULIA: Yep. Donger Maloney.

FELIX: Oh purlease.

JULIA: We had a level of sophistication of which you could only dream.

JULIA takes a deep appreciative breath.

FELIX: This whole open-space/peaceful thing you've got happening – it's really overrated. In the city you do not have to be constantly vigilant in case some reptile darts out and sinks its venomous fang into your leg. I'm starving.

JULIA: *(Rifling in her bag)* Here. Sink your fangs into that.

He holds up a takeaway sandwich which is wrapped in plastic and looks decidedly unappetising.

FELIX: The idea that country food is healthy. Hello? I see a sign, 'Wholesome country food', and I think, *that* is an oxymoron.

JULIA: Your generation is just soft.

FELIX: Excuse me?

JULIA: You want your experiences to happen in the safety of your own room.

FELIX: Yeah right.

JULIA: You want *ersatz* adventure. Experience you can get from playing games on the computer or from drugs. But you don't actually want to leave home to get it.

FELIX: Where do you get this stuff from?

We hear a tooting of a ute in the distance, whirling up dust as it barrels along a dirt road.

JULIA: That looks like Nugget.

FELIX: I still can't believe you guys call him *Nugget.*

JULIA: That's his name.

FELIX: His name's Neville.

JULIA: Yeah, well he's never been called Neville in his life.

FELIX: It's like calling him *Coon.*

JULIA: It is not.

FELIX: It is. It's off.

Silence. NUGGET pulls up and ambles over.

JULIA: Nugget. G'day.

They hug.

NUGGET: How are ya, Sis? Jeez I would'na reconnised you.

JULIA: Why not?

NUGGET: You're lookin' good.

JULIA: Get off.

Pause.

NUGGET: *(To Felix)* How are you mate?

FELIX: Not bad.

They shake hands. NUGGET laughs.

NUGGET: That's the way. Still a real asphalt fella. Eh? Still eatin' your greens? *(FELIX frowns.)* I remember when you were a real little tacker and Nanna Dibs goes 'Eat your greens.' *(To Julia)* Remember? And you go, 'I have. I've eaten …' – what was that thing called?

JULIA: A caper.

NUGGET: That's it. 'I have. I've eaten a caper.' Aw, laugh. I tell you what.

Pause.

NUGGET: Yeah. You're lookin' good, mate. Divorce agrees with ya.

JULIA: Sorry about Annie.

NUGGET: You heard, did you?

JULIA: Mum told me.

NUGGET: She cleared out about a month ago. I lost me missus, you lost your bloke. What's the matter with us, Jules?

JULIA: William's still with Kevin.

NUGGET: I'll just get the rope. Mum's been lookin' forward to you coming.

JULIA: Forgetting to mention that Maureen Delaney is coming tomorrow night.

NUGGET laughs.

NUGGET: She is Girlie's daughter.

JULIA: She's a fascist. And a racist.

NUGGET: Every family has them.

He ambles back toward the car. JULIA and FELIX watch.

*

GIRLIE: *(To audience)* We had some people up here from the University. They were staying in the pub. This is a few years back and they were doing some study or other into the Aboriginal history of the area. I said, 'You should talk to my nephew, Nugget. He's an Aborigine.'

Oh, quick as you like, this young fella, his eyes lit up. 'He must be one of the stolen generation,' he says. Rubbing his hands together.

Stolen my arse. His mother was killed in a road accident. It was a tragedy. And my sister, Dibs, who's the most Christian woman you'd ever meet – took on this young boy. In fact she adopted him and looked after him like he was one of her own. And he's a good boy, Nugget. He's done them proud. Mind you, it hasn't been all beer and skittles. They've had their rough patches.

But they come round here, these university people, askin' farmers if they've ever found any evidence of an Aboriginal presence on their land– you know, stone axeheads, flints, bones. That sort of thing.

Nothing. They're wasting their time. Nobody in this district has ever found anything at all.

And even if they had, they wouldn't bloody tell 'em, would they?

*

WILLIAM *is playing the piano in DIB's lounge room, 'And The Angels Sing'.*

DIBS: Aren't you glad now, I forced you to learn?

WILLIAM *and DIBS sing the chorus together.*
  DIBS remembers 1934:

Two little girls climb up the fence on the home paddock and watch their father with a water divining rod.

YOUNG DIBS: Find one for me, Daddy.

YOUNG GIRLIE: Me too.

After a while, Grandpa Norm's divining rod begins to shudder and bend. He leans down and picks up something. He strolls over and cleans the dirt off a coin. He hands it to YOUNG DIBS.

NORM: Here you are, Princess.

DIBS: A halfpenny.

The girls look at the halfpenny with awe.

NORM: What year is it?

DIBS: 1928.

NORM: Ooh. Crikey O'Reilly. You're in luck. That is a *very* lucky sign.

GIRLIE: Why?

YOUNG DIBS: What is it?

NORM: That was the year Bert Hinkler flew solo from the United Kingdom. In his Avro Avian. February, 1928.

YOUNG GIRLIE: So?

NORM: So.

YOUNG GIRLIE: What does it mean?

NORM: It means that your sister (if she plays her cards right) is going to marry a very handsome airman.

YOUNG DIBS: Really?

*

WILLIAM: It never occurred to you that he had the coin in his pocket?

DIBS: No.

WILLIAM: No, what?

DIBS: He didn't. He had a gift, Will. Everybody said so. You ask Girlie. He was the dowser who found water at Wormie McCallum's place. Good stock water. Saved the McCallum's farm. We've got letters from people all over the place thanking him.

WILLIAM: All that proves is that there is a great deal of water under the earth.

DIBS: Well how come the McCallums drilled all these dry holes, before they called Dad in? Hmm?

WILLIAM: The better question would be to find out whether he could actually find a dry spot within a hundred metres of a well that he'd dowsed.

DIBS: You've got a very closed mind, you know, when it comes to anything that falls outside of logic or science or rational explanation.

WILLIAM: Ya.

*

GIRLIE sits with an old case on her lap. She is sorting through papers.

GIRLIE: 'Dear Mr Myrtle, your divining has been entirely satisfactory. Our bore on the site you have chosen is providing us with gallons of beautiful water. Our windmill will be one more memorial to your learning and deep penetration of the mysteries of underground water.'

LYLE: Here you are, Mum. Get that into you.

GIRLIE: What is it?

LYLE: Barley soup. Yeah, he had a gift all right, Grandpa Norm.

GIRLIE: Do you think anyone's gonna want all this stuff?

LYLE: What is it?

GIRLIE: Just a few odds and sods I kept when Mum died. Look. Little shoes and a curl, from our baby brother. He died of scarlet fever when he was three. Dibs knitted him this little red cap (*she holds it up*) so we could always see where he was in the wheat.

There's all the letters that Dad wrote to Mum during the War. He was on the *Southland*, you know, when it was torpedoed off the coast of Egypt.

Rabbit tickets. A hundred pairs – two and six. You could only sell them in pairs. All these tags. He loved his pigeons, didn't he?

LYLE: Yeah. He was a great pigeon man.

GIRLIE: There's a crib board. They used to love playing crib, Mum and Dad.

GIRLIE remembers her Dad:

Grandpa Norm and Nollie and her sister Dulcie and Wormie McCallum sit around a table playing crib. The two little girls in blue, YOUNG DIBS and YOUNG GIRLIE are doing the dishes. It is 1934.

GRANDPA NORM: How 'bout a cup o' tea, you girls? An some o' those cream horns your Mum fixed.

NOLLIE: In the pantry, Girl.

GRANDPA NORM: I was closin' up the butcher shop this morning.

DULCIE: You're lookin after it, aren't you, for Mr Peel.

NOLLIE: How is he by the way?

WORMIE: Pretty bloody crook, by the sound of it.

GRANDPA NORM: Yeah. Any rate, I only had a coupla minutes before the footy bus, when Mrs Barker comes in and she says, 'I want a chook, Norm. I've got some unexpected visitors.'

Well I've only got one chicken left. 'Two and six,' I said.

'Ooh it looks a bit small. See if you've got something bigger.'

So I ran out the back, put the chicken on the block and I smacked him a couple times with the flat of the meat cleaver. I stretched his neck, pulled his wings out and put me fist inside the carcass and punched him out a bit, and then I ran out and said, 'How's that for size, Mrs Barker?' and she says 'How much is that one, Norm?'

And I said, 'Four and six'.

She said, 'Good, I'll take it. And you may as well wrap up the other one too.'

*

LYLE: Eat up, Mum.

GIRLIE: Something must have just snapped, you know, Lyle.

LYLE: Yeah.

GIRLIE: It was all too hard, tryin' to make a go of it. He was gettin' one and six a bushel. And then on top of that – running the farm – he was doing every dead-end job he could get. Tryin' to scratch a living. Water divining. Trapping rabbits. Chopping wood. Hard yakka. But he'd be laughing away, life of the party and then he'd get a visit from the black dog.

LYLE: Yeah.

GIRLIE: I remember there was this dust storm on the morning he died.

LYLE: Come on, Mum. Get stuck into it, before it gets cold.

GIRLIE: You're not having any?

LYLE: No. I gotta shift some ewes with Nugget. They've been up at Cleary's being crutched.

GIRLIE: You've got to eat, love.

LYLE: I'm right.

GIRLIE: You remind me of him, you know.

LYLE: So you said.

GIRLIE: Do you want this stuff? *(the case)*.

LYLE: Nah.

GIRLIE: Turf it?

LYLE: Yeah.

GIRLIE: We're all just memories, you know, and then one day, there's no one left to remember.

LYLE: Yeah. Well. This won't buy the baby a dress. I'm off.

GIRLIE: OK.

LYLE: Oh Mum. I might be a bit late with tea. The girls have got choir.

*

Lights come up on the choir which is practicing in a Church Hall. Brianna and Ashley are ushered in by LYLE. They are late. The cast sing (as choir).

Meanwhile at the Hamiltons, FARLEY is standing on a chair as DIBS pins up his trousers.

FARLEY is restless. DIBS has pins in her mouth.

FARLEY: This won't buy the baby a dress.

DIBS: Just a minute.

FARLEY: Some of us have got work to do.

DIBS: Hold your horses. *(To William)* I got these *(trousers)* at Kirby's garage sale. Fifteen dollars.

WILLIAM: Dead men's trousers?

DIBS: I don't think they've ever been worn.

FARLEY: She wanted me to get new ones. New trousers for *one* night. Bloody ridiculous.

WILLIAM: That's what people do, you know. When there's a special occasion. They buy themselves some new clothes.

FARLEY: Is that so? Aren't I a fool.

DIBS: OK. Hop down.

WILLIAM: It's not as if you can't afford it.

FARLEY: No, I'm just a miserable old skinflint.

DIBS: OK. All done.

WILLIAM: It's not like you've spent your whole life throwing parties.

DIBS: Hop down, Farl.

FARLEY: Oh what a fool am I. Good lord. I can see that now. To think that all these years I've been scrimping so I could send my children to Geelong Grammar. When I could have been poncing about –

DIBS: Pop into the bedroom, love.

FARLEY: How the scales have fallen. What a buffoon. What an imbecile.

DIBS: Put your old trousers back on.

FARLEY: Frittering away all that money. On education. Good God. The waste. As if we ever saw any results. Ha! As if you ever showed yourself to be anything –

DIBS: Into the bedroom.

FARLEY: Anything. Anything at all but a –

WILLIAM: But a – what?

Silence.

FARLEY: Obviously there are people in this world who can't overcome their own narcissism. Their own weakness.

WILLIAM: Their own moral turpitude?

DIBS: Off you go now.

FARLEY exits, ushered out by DIBS.
She returns.

WILLIAM: How can you stand it?

*

GIRLIE: *(To audience)* Every Christmas we'd do a nativity play at Sunday school. Dibs always got to play Mary. I was usually the back end of the donkey.

Anyway, there'd be a party in the Mechanic's Institute and everyone in the district'd come. Santa would show up on the fire truck. And all the trestle tables'd be groaning with food. Our Mother would bring everything in two lined suitcases. Cream horns – they were her thing – ginger fluffs, asparagus rolls, lamingtons, cheese boats. But every year our Dad was unable to make it. He'd always be working. We'd beg him to take a day off but he never could. We sort of felt sorry for 'im, Dibs and me. Missing out on all the fun.

It wasn't till I was about ten that I caught a glimpse of him and the penny dropped.

GIRLIE enters her memory. It is 1934.

Father Christmas enters ringing a bell and throwing sweets into the audience.

Little GIRLIE stands shyly watching.

FATHER CHRISTMAS: Happy Christmas, Little Girlie.

LITTLE GIRLIE: Happy Christmas … Santa.

A spotlight roves around a velvet curtain.

Voice-over and organ music: Ladies and gentlemen, please put your hands together for the winners of the 1934 Archie Kirkwood Award for the Best Sibling Duo – Dibs and Girlie Myrtle.

The two little girls in blue open the curtain, holding aloft a trophy. The crowd goes berserk.

The music plays 'Keep Your Sunny Side up' as the two little girls run through the auditorium holding the trophy.

DIBS: Dad? Dad?

GIRLIE: Daddy?

Lights change.

The girls run and run to the woolshed. They push open the big door at the back of the stage.

Their father, still partly dressed in his Santa Claus suit, is swinging from the rafters.

Dominion

Susan Hancock

You see they were always there, the Red Queen and the Peastick girl, the Red Queen howling in the wind that came banging up the valley. But the Peastick Girl never made a sound, falling down in the long rows. Here where she was the earth was dark and clogged, the mud soaked her face. Her legs were bent behind her. Over she fell, her little triangular dress with the spot at each corner, like a butterfly's wing.

Something had happened to the Red Queen that made her howl like that in the air above the sandpit where the tunnel of wood came down. Her eyes bulged, the wind blew her face away. But here where the Peastick girl lay soon would be green leaves, and the lip-smooth pods. In black empty triangles the peasticks stretched away.

How they first got there no one knew, but no one could remember a time when they weren't there, the wind blowing, and the Peastick girl falling down.

Book One: The Dialogue of the Insects
Cass's Prologue
There were two dolls. Sometimes they stood side by side on the mantle piece, their cheeks just touching; and sometimes they were on the tallboy, on either side of the green speckled vase. They were made from wood, like little tree trunks; only

their heads were enamelled; the boy's head had a topknot and the girl's had a small round bump. Her head was heavier, and when they stood together it lolled against the boy's, because his neck was thicker and fitted firmly like a plug into the top of the little trunk. And when she was on her own the girl doll's head could be kept straight with a piece of paper stuffed into the hole. And later, when it was invented, Blue Tack. Like Builder's Bog, said Cass, rubbing the sleek silky ears of her dog, called DogWog, all those words, Tack and Clag and Bog, all the things you keep your life stuck together with.

On calm days they stood there on the tallboy, in the bland weather. But whenever the wind was blowing and the light swarming all over the walls, she put them on the mantle piece as if it was a raft in a sea moving, and the light moving all around them, rushing over the green walls, in spots and circles and long running waves, and the wind inside and outside, the wind rushing the house like water, splitting along its prow, and Cass dreaming of the tiger, how it sailed in through the window in a graceful loop. And in the early morning from the same window you could see where the dawn was coming, and at night the moon floating up through the crystal bowl of the air like a rising pearl.

Blackbird

Though the sunlight is already brilliant over the front of the house it is the back that interests us more for it is here that the cold is coming from, making its way down the long hall, stealing forwards along the shadowed walls. The small back window over the sink is open; the water lies quiet under a coat of grease, like a wintry pond. Although yesterday it was summer, overnight the autumn has come. And with it comes the past, moving in shadows over the bags and the boxes that are scattered everywhere, rising in cool breezes and eddies of air.

Because of the hill's steep pitch the house is like a wedge, one-storeyed at the back, two at the front. A verandah at second-floor level crosses the front of the house. Shards of white paint are flaking from its wooden posts, splintering the way frost splinters. From a distance, walking towards the front room all you can see between these posts is the sky. But as you get closer to the window, when you step out onto the worn wooden boards, there is the Harbour, rising almost to eye level, like a curtain of wet light. Below it lies the city, cast in a deep pit of shadow. Lines of sun are snaking in from the eastern ranges and rising up out of the shadow the spires of St Mary of the Angels are rusty in the sunlight, smoking with frost and damp.

You may turn round and face the room through which you have just come. Behind you as you prop yourself on the rail are the dizzying movements of the sky, reflected in the mirror in which you now see yourself. A cloud sails by in the glass. If your dressing gown slips open, for it's old and the cloth is thin, you may even see a portrait of your own body, a full frontal nude. Your hair, if it is short and fair like that of the girl who now faces herself in this way, stands out in a halo of gold-lit spikes. The thin light fabric of the dressing gown, blue patterned with gold leaves, lifts and stiffens in the wind. As you stand there, looking at the shape of yourself outlined in the mirror, you realise you cannot see the reflection of your face, because of the light. You are seeing yourself as others might see you, a visible mystery.

The girl who stands looking at herself this way is Teresa, younger sister to Mollie, older to Cass. She has come back to New Zealand after five years away. In Australia she has written a book, had a love affair with someone else's husband and met a demon. It is partly to escape him that she has come back. Does she hope that he will find her? Secretly track her down? Secretly maybe she does – there is nothing like the attentiveness of a demon after all, his eye worming into you. Her flight through twelve hundred miles of air has left a vapour trail twisting like a worm, or the shape of a tornado. In her mind's eye she sees it shining red-gold, a whole trail leading from her to him.

She tips her head back into the full sun. The sky is a diamond, full of facets, her eyes fill with sharp diamond tears.

Air puffs into her face, cold slides and insinuates itself under her dressing-gown, feels her breast, drapes its arm round her neck, fingers her hair. On the lip of the gutter above her a bird stands still as a cut-out, its chest feathers rosy. It flips away, wafting across the valley, then arrives on the roof of another house, whose perfect diagonals are shining in the sun. Behind the house a magpie slowly climbs the cold hill of air.

Oh, the air, the air, pure and clear the air is like music, the starlings rattle on the thin tin roof, the white shards of paint rustle, the verandah, a pathway of boards hangs onto the air itself, its blue support, a hill. Wintry pangs of light wink from the water and answering them from every corner and angle of the hillside, windows of light wink back. Another bird flies from the lip of the gutter and swings away.

Although it is still early there are people about, making their way along the damp black paths that line the hill. Those who know who she is glance up, then look away, keeping their conversations discreet, wondering what it must be like to be someone so different from themselves. Seen from a distance, in the circles of light and birds, she seems to be walking the sky. But they soon forget, making their own way along and down the hill, for the roads are shining like rivers and the wind comes in. And now as she leans both arms on the cold rail, as she almost sees the wind moving towards her from the mountains, as she watches it tossing the gardens of the houses spread out below, she almost forgets, herself.

Below her the front of the house drops thirty feet into the steep garden. The poor leafless tree that leans in from the bank nods at her its poor old head, old woman tree, sad thing, its branches a few sparse strands. Old women in homes nod their trembling heads, waiting for the tea-trolley. The wind, wandering along the front of the house comes in fits and starts. In the stronger gusts the whole tree sighs.

And now the wind is picking up. It shakes the tree woven with a mat of creeper that grows in under the shelter of the house. It tosses the clump of dahlias standing in a little patch of sun. The air is so clear that you can see the worm casts in the grass. And there, spread-eagled on the convolvulus that waves its tendrils all over the top of the tree is Jake's jersey, forgotten from yesterday, spangled with damp. Above it and across it the bees travel in and out of the purple trumpets, great black-and-yellow-striped bodies with their blundering hum, their dark legs working, their spiny hair covered with pollen, for they are always busy in the sunlight, the bees.

*

So that's where Jake's jersey had got to, lying there now with its arms spread wide on the dense thick mat of the convolvulus. He drove them nearly mad with it yesterday, tying the sleeves together in a knot and whirling it into the air so that Florian had been uncontrollable, shrieking and laughing in fits. Then it disappeared. 'I think the sky took it,' Jake said. This made Florian even wilder, running round and round, laughing artificially.

'For God's *sake!*' Mollie said.

In the end, of course, Florian, running in smaller and smaller circles slipped and hit his head.

'It's not Jake's fault,' Teresa said. Though it was.

'It's not my fault he gets excited,' Jake said.

Florian stopped crying and started to laugh again, 'Jakey-wakey, you could go up like a rocket, you could flip through the air. I could've gone up the other way, like a rocket.'

'Will you just stop working him up,' Mollie said, trying to cuff Jake's ear as he ran past.

'Ooh, duh, SCARE me,' he said.

'Leave them.' Teresa took Mollie's arm and dragged her out onto the verandah. 'Have a vodka with me. It all looks Russian enough.'

'The sun's over the yard-arm,' Mollie said, draining her glass.

'What yard-arm?' Teresa said.

It was nearly dark; the air was a deep olive, the Harbour a black hole ready to swallow things up. They leaned on the verandah rail; a wind shivered through the line of brassy poplars below their mother's old house.

'What does it feel like to be so near Mum's?' Mollie asked.

'I don't know yet,' Teresa said, 'it's too soon. Who bought it, by the way, do you know?'

Mollie shook her head. 'I don't know.' There was a finality in her tone.

'Am I boring?' Florian said, putting his head out through the gap. 'Jake says I'm boring, but I don't know what that is.'

'Florian!' said Mollie, 'Don't EVER stand under the sash, it could come *crashing* down!'

He looked at them uncertainly, wondering whether to cry, then withdrew. Crashes resounded from the further room.

'I don't think he knows what you mean,' Teresa said, refilling Mollie's glass. 'What are you doing Jake?' she said, raising her voice. A particularly loud glassy crash was followed by dead silence. After an interval Florian put his head out again. 'He's looking for his jersey,' he said.

'I'm looking for my jersey,' Jake confirmed from within the room. He sounded muffled.

'I'll find it tomorrow,' Teresa said.

'I don't care,' Mollie said, the pale indistinct outline of her face an oval. She straightened up and stared directly ahead. 'I don't want to care,' she said, in a voice as faint and brassy as the poplars.

In the hall she picked up her string bags, the onion skins leafing through the gaps. In the last of the light that still lingered along the side of the house, you could make out dim purple flowers against an amber ground; the air in the hall was dusky, amber, thick.

Florian sidled up to her, to hold her hand. 'It's scary-time,' he said.

'He was in our bed all last night,' Mollie said. 'He said he'd dreamed the ghost of a prawn.'

'That wasn't my fault,' Jake said.

'You take the onions, Jake,' she said. 'Nothing is ever your fault.'

'Onions bunions,' Florian said, swinging on Mollie's hand.

'Stand up straight both of you,' Mollie said, for Jake had thrown himself on the floor, rolling over and over down the length of the hall. Marching them down the path she looked back up to Teresa who stood on the balcony the way their mother always did, her weight leaning on her hands. 'See you tomorrow, maybe,' she said.

'Maybe,' Teresa said.

Now she puffed out a breath, looking down at the jersey. Bracing herself against the rail she leaned over as far as she could and dangled her hands but it was far too far down. Even if she got over the rails and tried she wouldn't reach it. Besides which it could be insanely dangerous. Quite childishly she hung there, looking straight down into the red flowers of the dahlias that loomed up towards her, like open red mouths. The world tilted, turning itself over. The sky rushed past her, whirling luminous blue.

She straightened up. Black specks swarmed in the blue space. On the Harbour a small boat began to crawl over the glassy water like a fly. She watched it as it moved this way and that, moth-like in the water, before it disappeared into the haze off the further shore. Then, almost without thinking, she climbed over the rail and felt with her feet for the top of the fire escape down.

*

'If the soul is a fountain,' he had said, 'or a clear spring, then of course a demon in the form perhaps of a dragon will coil itself there.' He paused to pick a shred of tobacco from his tongue. Bud lights wound through the trees. Under the green flare of the streetlight even his pallor was tinged; his eyes flickered, assessing the traffic; he held her arm in under the elbow.

This was one of those almost warm nights in the Melbourne autumn. Every now and then, at the mouth of this alley, for instance, they walked into a colder patch that had to be negotiated like a river. At the end of the alley a mass of building, whose bulk blocked their view, held high above their heads its radio masts, its silent listening posts and towers, lit in a phosphorescent chemical light.

'You're in a prison,' he said. 'With your demon. I know him. His name is Arkeum. He makes you feel you are fascinating, but you are not fascinating.'

A wind bounced out at them. Her arm was held tight against him; she could feel his breath, a dark rag moving through his ribcage, in and out. 'You silly baby Westerners,' he said. He took the cigarette from his pale mouth. His secret was never to look at her while he was talking, never to meet her eyes. 'You think you know all about freedom, but your minds are changed.'

'Don't you mean chained?' she said.

'No, no,' he said, smoothly; lightly, delicately he took her hand. 'They are *changed* – they are changed for you – by T.V., by political party, by prime minister's secret gang.'

'*Secret gang*!' she said. 'We don't have secret gangs.'

'Oh-ho,' he said. He permitted himself a thin smile, 'so you are not like America, you are not democracy.'

He sent her a postcard that he'd made himself, something he'd cut from a magazine. In it a golden dragon with a jewelled eye strangled a little palm tree in its spatulate paws. 'When he has finished with you,' he wrote, 'your Arkeum, you will only be selfish and full of greed.'

She went to see him. 'I know only three words in Russian,' she said, '– left, right and hell.'

'You are intelligent,' he said, 'but your mind is silly, it cannot concentrate. You must give him up for me.'

'Is this literal?' she said. 'Or is it a metaphor?'

'Oh yes,' he said, nodding, 'of course you would like it to be metaphor, you would like me to be metaphor too. I'm just crazy Russian, aren't I. I'm just crazy stranger.'

'*A* crazy stranger,' she said.

Now, as she flipped almost unthinkingly down the first few rungs, everything to do with him seemed to vanish. From round the corner of the hill she could hear a steady roaring like the sea, the shining lines of it, the coursing of the currents through the open Strait. She felt free, backing down the outside of the house like a thief, out in the wind and air, holding on to the smooth sides of the ladder. Starlings whistled like conspirators from the nearby houses, like a robber band. She swung herself around, one arm flung out as she let go, as if for applause, and braced her back against the ladder, her feet slipping on the worn rung.

From this position she could see along the hill as a bird might see it, the tops of trees opening up a path, the lines of wires. A flag billowed monstrously on a turret, then collapsed its great tent of air. In her mother's house, high on its headland, a curtain like a sail flapped hard in a window. Below her the garden swung giddily; the breeze that was moving along the front of the house now played with her, wrapping her in rags and scarves of icy cold. The ladder shifted slightly under her weight.

The top of the tree was now only a few feet down. Stretching she gave the edge of the creeper a shake with her foot. The ladder seemed to be holding. The jersey didn't move. The world was stable after all. Hooking her hand under the strut she gave an even more vigorous kick. The whole mat of the creeper moved. Bees rose, blundering, and the jersey flopped over the edge and into the garden underneath.

She turned round to go back. But when she looked up, holding on to the slippery sides of the old ladder, the house loomed out suddenly like a cliff. She seemed to be hanging backwards at a dangerous angle; above her the peak of the verandah jutting out, the sky behind and above on every side speeding and everything coloured around its outlines with an unpleasant yellow edge.

She pulled her head in and leaned her forehead against the boards. There was no room for her knees. She couldn't turn round again and go back up that way, shuffling upwards like Charlie Chaplin in his ridiculous spats. She couldn't let go and drop down, because the crooked narrow bank at the end of the ladder was still ten feet above level ground. She would land hard and unevenly and break something even before the further fall. Yet for a moment the garden was calm – a little line of creeper warmed itself in the sun; the dahlias stood patiently in their pale brown patch.

Then everything tossed and jumped. From along the side of the hill the wind was swimming towards her, almost visible, like a current of clear water. It hit the side of the house, fell back again, then returned, picking her up, a huge clear swelling against the wall. All around her on the hillside trees humped and bowed, and the wind rushed the house again, delivering itself in a series of stunning, vibrant blows, whistling along the weatherboards.

The building was groaning now, shaking in all its planks. She heard the boards knocking and somewhere close to her ear something gave out an ominous grinding sound. The ladder shifted sharply to the left, and she lurched with it. Something dark sucked at her heart. The ladder shifted again, this time slightly to the right and she looked up to see two of the metal brackets above her head pulling themselves out slowly, impersonally, from the wood.

She made herself stand upright on the ladder and closed and opened her eyes. A slight movement off to the left made her turn her head. In the high window of the house on the corner, now miles above her, its massive bulk sprawled all across the hill's profile, the curtain was withdrawn and the house itself, as if at a signal, began to move out slowly under the canvas of blue, making headway with its great orange roof like a prow.

She stood there upright, barely breathing, her feet squashed in against the side of the house. She wondered what she must look like from the distance, a small upright shape against the white gleam of wood, on the high white cliff of the house. She seemed to see herself crouching there like a spider, something tiny that could be blown away by a puff of air. A bird cried faintly from the hill behind the house and above it, far away the sky moved in a slow, sickening vortex, its clouds drawn in round the sun.

She began inching upwards, closing her eyes. There was a heart-shaking jerk and she opened them just in time to see two more brackets pull out. She couldn't be far now from a catastrophe, the ladder wouldn't hold much longer; she tried to angle her neck so that she could see if the top hold was still there but the sun defeated her, shining in a brilliant blinding stripe along the guttering. Soon she would be falling backwards, fastened to the ladder as it turned end to end in the air on its final fall down. A sudden rush of liquid filled her mouth.

And then it was next to her, a deep calm presence. It came close to her, like a living figure, next to where she stood – in the air, with the world fallen away, fastened by a few metal staples to a board. All around her everything grew peaceful. She felt her face melting from its bones. She looked up into the burning sun, the sky with a few sun-ringed clouds floating in it quite near. Behind her a body of water, deep and steady, waited to carry her away.

Another of the brackets came away; the ladder sagged to one side; she watched this dreamily. She thought of her mother out there on the shining lines of water, all alone. The sea sounded in the hollow shell; large time went by; the sound of the sea roaring, the wind, diminished to a whisper, rattling dryly against the boards. Half-closing her eyes she felt herself drifting away, arching herself backwards from the ladder, its slippery sides loosening her hands. A spider looked out at her from a crack between the boards. She saw its eyes, its greedy pursed mouth, the brown stripe that ran down its back. Tentatively it put its legs out onto the back of her hand and a violent revulsion ran over her; the world came rushing back; the air slapped her face. She shuddered and flipped the spider off, almost taking both her hands away.

She was eight feet down. Only three brackets still holding, two on the right. Any minute now and she might swing across the face of the building like a comedian on a clock. She gave a sudden crazy laugh.

To her surprise it was echoed from above. There were foot-steps on the verandah, then Cass and a dark-haired girl looking down. Their faces, cool and foreshortened, didn't seem surprised.

'This is Dorothy Ollie, I brought her to meet you,' said Cass. 'This is my sister,' she added, 'she's just come back from Australia. They don't use doors over there, they just climb in and out like this all the time, like kangaroos, getting into their pouches – well, not their own pouches of course, the babies I mean. It's the marsupial factor.'

'Please Cass,' she said faintly. ' Do you have to be quite so … hilarious?'

'Don't tease her, Cass,' the other girl said. 'Look at the state of the ladder, she's in trouble. Be serious.'

'But what's she doing down there?' said Cass, studying Teresa who was stuck there in a posture with her head tipped back not unlike that of religious adoration.

'Can you move at all?' the other girl said.

'No, I can't,' she said. 'Something really terrible is happen-ing to me.'

'We need the other ladder,' said Dorothy. 'We saw it when we came in through the back – remember, it was leaning against the shed.'

'There isn't time,' she whispered. 'You'll have to get me now.' Had they heard her? How strange her own voice sounded, rustling in her skull. Her eyes filled with small dry diamonds, she could barely see. Again she felt herself drop-ping upright through the world's long fall, like a figure falling against a cataract, down and down in the rainbows of haze, the watery golden light.

'But we can't,' Cass called back, her voice thin and reedy. 'You need to be higher. We can't reach you from here.' Her face darkened with anxiety. It was like a crucifix, that ladder, she thought, hanging over the Abyss, 'like that Dali painting.' She screamed.

'Listen, Teresa,' said Dorothy very quietly, 'You are going to have to get up those two rungs, and you're going to have to do it now because the whole thing is about to give way. Rush – think about running uphill, and we'll have one chance to get you, GO FOR IT – NOW.'

It was touch and go, Teresa swinging horribly from their stretching arms and her feet slipping on the boards. And the trouble was both Cass and Teresa wanted to laugh. 'It's like the three stooges,' Teresa panted. The top of the falling ladder had grazed her shin. It would have knocked her backwards if she'd been a second slower.

'Grip the wood,' Dorothy said. 'Use your bare feet.'

But they were all helpless and for a terrible moment it seemed that the only way this would end would be with a plunging forward together over the rail and down the front of the house.

'Like a symbol', Cass said later, 'of the failure of feminism.'

'Like the Immortals,' said Dorothy, 'falling through space and time.'

'Like three dickheads,' said Rangi, 'behaving like dickheads. If it hadn't been for me ...'

For coming in the gate at the crucial moment she had picked up the broken side of the ladder – 'I would've torn it off if I had to,' she said and running up the side path had shoved it up underneath Teresa's backside just as she was about to drop back again bringing the others with her. So that making a desperate upward lunge at the wall she got high enough for them to drag her arms across the rail and half-pulled, half-prodded from below, she rolled herself up over the railing and fell heavily on her shoulder on the other side, onto the soft wood of the worn boards against whose yielding, nearly sentient surface her flushed cheek, rolling with tears, smacked hard down.

She lay there, inside the rail, on the soft silvery boards that seemed as she watched them to rise and swim, floating in the air beside her like a satin sheet. She was almost naked, what was left of the front of her dressing gown shredded away, and a long red scratch starting to show along her stomach. Her eye seemed to fall wider open, staring at Cass's yellow espadrilles and Dorothy Ollie's scarred and scuffed climbing boots. A pair of red peeptoes with long protruding toenails arrived, joining the espadrilles.

'This is Dorothy Ollie,' said Cass, intoning clearly. The red peeptoes said Hello and smiled. The mountain boots said nothing, they stood still.

'Is this your sister?' said the red peeptoes; they shifted interrogatively. 'Yes,' said the espadrilles.

'Funny habits,' the peeptoes said.

'Jetlag,' said the espadrilles.

'But she's only come from Australia – you can't get jet lag from that.'

'Yes you can,' said the boots. 'You can get it from anything. I've had bus lag living up here. You have to wait for hours.'

'What about waiting-for-your-benefit-to-come-through lag,' Rangi said. 'It's a new phenomena – I've had that.'

'It's part of the patriarchy, keeping women waiting for their money,' said the boots.

'… or the bus,' the peeptoes said.

' Anyway, get up and talk to us,' said Cass, prodding Teresa with her toe. 'We've come over to see you. We can help you unpack. I've got thinner, I can probably fit into most of your clothes.'

'I can't,' she said. 'I'm too tired.'

'Don't go to sleep,' said Cass.

'I can't help it, I'm knackered,' she said. Her body felt so light, *Floating in, under the deep shadow.* 'Sport in the wind!' she said in a sudden loud voice.

They put a blanket on her but not before noticing the line of little bruises like fingerprints along her thighs. Cass saw the other mark too, hastily twitching what was left of the dressing gown across.

'What was she saying?' Cass said.

'She's your sister,' said Rangi, who gave Dorothy a significant look over Cass's bent head. 'You tell me. Is she eccentric, or what!'

Out in the small cold kitchen they stood around making tea.

'You don't think she's passed out, do you?' said Cass.

'No,' said Rangi, looking at Dorothy again, 'It's all right, she's just crashed.'

They opened the fridge. 'Oh,' said Cass happily, 'there's quite a lot of food.'

'Could be love-affair-lag,' said Dorothy. 'I get that.'

'Or one-night-stand lag,' said Rangi. But they could see she was losing interest. Her expression had become rather fixed and she was flicking the fingers of her right hand, and glancing about.

Dorothy left soon after, her boots straggling on the path.

'She's a bit too pleased with herself, that one,' Rangi said. 'She's got tickets on herself.'

'She's just ambitious,' Cass said. 'I can sympathise with that.'

They glanced out the window to where Teresa could be seen sleeping, still on the boards of the verandah, her hair sticking out of the end of the check rug like toi-toi in the wind, a shining plume. Above their heads in the hall, little prisms of light floated off from the glass lampshade, covering the walls, the ceiling, the floor and their own faces with rainbow circles and dapples, making everything seem less solid than usual, more airy, more pervious.

'It's crazy to be ambitious,' Rangi said.

And everywhere the shining points of light and floating, gauzy colours seemed to confirm this, and agree.

> Whether you go up the ladder or down it
> Your position is shaky.

said Lao-tzu.

*

They wandered back into the kitchen and made some more food.

'Nice clothes,' Rangi said, looking at the suitcases in the back room, then at a photograph, which she picked up. 'She doesn't look like you. She looks more like Mollie. Maybe you're adopted.'

'No such luck, I've got the blood,' said Cass. 'Watch out, you're dropping your bread and cheese.'

'So are you,' Rangi pointed out. 'There's a big glob of it in the suitcase.' She laughed, showering out some crumbs.

'God, she'll be furious,' Cass said. 'She always knew when I borrowed her things. Once she came home early I had to hide behind the shed.'

'Were you younger than her?' Rangi said.

'Yes I was,' said Cass.

'Is your name short for Cassandra?' said Rangi, fishing out a striped hat and trying it on. She pulled a face at herself in the mirror then bulged her eyes. 'I look like you when I do that,' Cass said. 'No, it's Cass – it's near where Dad grew up. But I am a bit psychic, you know.'

'Uh-huh,' said Rangi, abstractedly, pulling out a piece of long shining dark blue fabric which turned out to be an evening dress, very narrow. 'Very narrow,' she said. 'She's skin and bone.' She put her bread down to hold the dress against her with both hands. 'Look at this,' she said, jiggling her hips, 'it doesn't even cover the middle of me. Here, you try it on.'

'Oh God, you've got butter on it,' said Cass. 'Look, they're your finger marks. She'll be pissed off. She'll wish she hadn't come back. I think she went away so no one could get at her clothes.'

'That's all right,' said Rangi. 'We can clean it and put it back. A few little butter marks aren't going to make her change her mind.'

They thought about tidying up. 'I wish she'd wake up,' Cass said.

'What are you going to do now?' said Rangi. They went into the study. The screensaver was on. Twenty, it said, turning over and over in small blue print on the screen. Cass pushed Enter.

'I'm not quite sure,' she said. She reached down to the keyboard and changed the screen. 'I'll probably stay.'

They went down the hall. In the fresh air from the window the glass ornaments that hung from the lightshade were still tinkling; the small prisms of colour circling over the walls and radiating from the mirror with its bevelled edge.

'Bye,' they said to each other, one from the verandah, the other from the side path. Rangi, who moved lightly for such a big woman, simply disappeared. Cass looked for her further down the hill but even after five minutes she hadn't shown up again.

After Rangi had gone she wandered through the house, at the edge of discontent, stirring through the currents of air, then back out onto the verandah again. The day was still early, not even eleven o'clock. The mist had gone from the seaward valleys and the wind, crossing from hilltop to hilltop, made everything clear. There was traffic, now, moving along the Hutt road. Tiny flashes came from the cars as they moved in and out of the sun. On the highest ridge of the hill a white curtain floated at an open window. A fern stood still as a sentinel in the sheltered place inside the gate. In and out the curtain blew in the sun and wind, but where the fern was, in the greenish light of the hollow, nothing moved.

She'd written to them, *In Australia the wind is always burning.* She'll come back, their mother said. Their mother went from room to room, waking them up, *'morning has broken ...'* In the garden across the hill the breeze caught at the tree fern, blowing its arms about. Fronds blew against fronds, saluting. Even here, the fern said airily, things will change. She woke Teresa up and made her get into bed, then hung around on the verandah for another five minutes waiting for things to change. She could see her sister's peaceful face in the mirror, and behind it, on the lip of the gutter above the verandah, the small dark head of a bird. How deeply she was sleeping in the mirror, and how silently.

And silently Cass stole past the foot of the bed and let herself out, padding down the path in her soft-footed espadrilles. On the road she stopped and changed into the boots from her backpack and began to run, her feet thudding. At the corner where they used to turn off for school the wind came roaring up through the pine plantation. Leaves and birds blew from the trees like sailors. The plantation formed a deep vee and the wind tore through it so hard that it pushed her off her balance. Fighting it as Wellingtonians do she hurled herself along, through blinding pulses of light bounding on the road and the deep roaring. Clouds bowled by overhead and swarmed over the city. And on all the further hills, each crowned with its dark shag of furious trees so that the whole city seemed to be beating, more and more quickly, to the heartbeat of the world. And then she was through the last of the corners and down out of the wind's way; and here she could slow down, for the last stretch of the hill plunged straight down like a ruler and everything levelled out and the trolley bus lines began.

*

All New Zealand cities have a deep colonial heart, visible in the architecture, the great bronze of Victoria, the terraced streets. In Central Park the walks are lined with red-flowering trees; ornamental iron gates guard the entrances to the Botanical Gardens; there are ornate fountains and deep stone basins holding cool green ponds. Ducks float in flotilla formations, like photographs of the Allied fleet in Scapa Flow.

Down here on the flat land, though the wind is coursing the hilltops, all is still. The sun penetrates here and there through the chinks between narrow buildings. There are very few people about, walking through stripes of yellow light, rectangles of shade. Cass walks more sedately now, though people look at the wild state of her hair, her bare legs and boots. At the Quay, where the Harbour ripples against wooden boathouses and piers, she is taken by the idea of catching the train to the coast, but a cold wind ripping off the water makes her decide against that, and turning right she starts in on the final stage of the long walk home, a fair stretch along the Esplanade to the further side of the Harbour where up under the shadows of a thick stand of old trees the windows of her house can just be seen, the glass of them faint and dim, like old eyes weary with looking out too much on the world.

*

She settles into a walking gait, a bit dogged for such a slim girl, her boots hitting the footpath firmly, her shorts making a rubbing sound. There are people already drinking wine outside the shipping warehouses, in the sun that shines like so many silver dollars off the round metal tables. At the concrete amphitheatre set low on the waterfront where often the wind singing sweetly remembers Oceania, *suonare, says Hugo, the swooning of guitars,* a group of art students is hanging out a banner for this week's Palm Tree Festival. *Hopefully involving coconuts, Hugo says to Florian, who cries, not knowing what that means. 'It's a kind of modern pagan version of Palm Sunday,' Hugo says.*

The amphitheatre is newish but it looks old, standing there in worn grey concrete next to the sea, the saxe-blue, sage blue sea; the Art Deco sea. You can imagine anything while you're standing there. Teresa sees a bare place with two men standing. Cass sees a grove of loquat trees splayed in golden light.

She walks on. Ahead of her more and more of the hill revolves into view, the houses above Oriental Bay presenting themselves like rows of ceramic houses arranged on shelves, each one a different colour and shape, like a catalogue of all the possible houses in the world. She much prefers her own; the old brittle glass of the windows is water cast, full of bubbles and flaws, like memories. The outside world appears through them as if through rain, even in the hot weather, which Cass doesn't much like, a cool rainy subtle sort of look.

She stands on her verandah in the sea damp weather wearing her mother's dress. 'Saved from the fire,' she always thinks, whenever she puts it on. Her feet are bare on the cool bare boards. In the salt air, in the overcast weather, her hair is frizzing with damp. She loves this weather. Everything feels possible on these rainy days. Inside at the mirror she puts her favourite colours, lilac and green, around her eyes, then tipping her head to one side she looks at herself in the glass. It is old and worn thin, like the windows, whose rectangles appear in the side wings. She moves them this way and that to change the view, all made up of momentary angles and surprising shifts. And from the centre of the mirror, with its softly spotted surfaces, her own face is composed for her, a portrait of herself caught in mournful Time, which has little to do with the actual light outside.

Amphitheatre

Something woke her – what was it? The closing of a door? An adroit definite sound. She sat upright, listening. In the mirror she saw her headless body, like a classical torso, swathed in drapes. The wardrobe door swung further open revealing a segment of the hall. The air was dusky, swarming with half-shapes. She slid her feet to the floor. Her body was sore, as if strips had been torn off it, but her head was light and clear – too light, she realised, as her feet slipped unevenly and the floor, skittering like an ice rink, came rising then slipping away.

A faint roar came up – the city at evening? the sea? Not evening, she saw, grabbing a quick glance at the clock as it came sliding by, only two o'clock, yes, the room was reeling, the shelves above the fireplace circling, the door leaning in the shape of a tall astigmatic tower, now this way, now that, red spots were dancing where only seconds before the mirror had been, the tinny sound of the phone.

She fell back on the bed and closed her eyes, her head whirling the way it used to when they rode the witch's hat, gift of the Bishop to his Virgins, the cage crashing again and again against the central metal pole while they hung, so many Sibyls hauled aloft, screaming like parrots, blue-eyed crows in the barebones crowsnest, the furious cries of the nuns oddly distant, faraway. Common of a Holy Woman Neither a Virgin Nor a Martyr, what sort of woman is that, Sister? Cheeky cow-eyes in the class as Sister Aloysius, young, luscious, blushed and adjusted her veil.

Coming in through the window cold air calmed her down, and sounds too, winter sounds, the double knock of hammers rocking from side to side of the cradled afternoon. There were dogs barking in German, *Zwolf ... Zwolf, Zwolf ... Zwolf.* A motorbike buzzed off, fuzzily burring, winding round and round. Asleep she dreamed herself asleep, her body wrapped round and round.

Seconds later she startled awake again. Straining for it in the silence she heard the sound quite definitely this time. Was it someone coming in or going out? *Comeone someone Florian said.* Silently she swung her feet to the ground. The floor was steadier this time, only beneath it the hill, the deep rock itself, felt uneasy. Trembling with hangover she put her hand to the phone which rang of its own accord. 'Hang on a sec,' she said, 'I've got someone here.'

But a quick scan of the back rooms revealed no one. Under the painted-out window her papers had stirred, slipping out of their acid-yellow folders over the floor. Through a worn patch a small illuminated version of the back garden shone pale and milky. She picked up the phone. There was breath-ing on the line. She waited, and the other waited too. She held the receiver away from her; a small faint voice piping; she put it to her ear.

'Are you there after all?' Mollie said. 'What are you doing? I've been waiting here for hours. Are you screening your calls?'

'Oh,' she said, 'it's you.' The garden hovering foreshort-ened, white and gold.

'There's been someone ringing,' she said. 'But no one knows I'm around.'

Mollie laughed. 'Everyone knows. Everyone knows every-thing here, have you forgotten that?'

'I suppose I have,' she said. 'Can you wait while I go to the other phone?'

Back in her room, though, she couldn't find anything to put on, all her clothes seemed to have disappeared. She stood there, fiddling with the phone cord. In the mirror she arched her back, looking at her body, its hipbones standing out, her stomach hard and thin, the pale rat-like shadow of her pubic hair.

'Are you listening or not?' Mollie said.

She'd wanted to come back, but not to *be* back. Was it so impossible, she wondered, pivoting in the mirror.

'Clearly it is,' she said.

'I can tell that you're not listening,' Mollie said.

The sea took everything. It rose up swift and silent and opened its glassy maw.

'I don't think I am,' she said. 'Sorry, I meant to – I'm feeling really spaced.'

'Anyway, I found Jake's jersey,' she said

'Oh, good,' she said. 'I'm very cross with him.'

'Well, you don't have to be cross now. It's found.'

'Yes I do,' said Mollie. 'I'm a mother, I have to be cross all the time.'

'Well, I'd better go,' she said, Teresa having said nothing. 'This place is a mess. This house is behaving like a hovel.'

'So's mine,' Teresa said. Through the open door she saw her clothes falling out of the suitcases in every direction, like bad girls at a dance.

'Bloody Cass,' she said, 'she's been going through my things.'

Mollie laughed. 'Better face it,' she said, 'some things never change.'

Everything changes, he said, And nothing stays the same. He helped her set fire to the shed. Oddly, there'd been no flames. After a long interval it had simply emitted great sheets of smoke. Only towards the end when the back wall collapsed inwards did some orange appear, flames pale in the sunlight, pale ashes, faint roses of the past, crumbling, broken to embers.

'Well, I'd better go,' Mollie said. 'Before we know it'll be night again.'

Where Mollie stood now in her own house a pane of amber sunlight came in from under the trees. Soon it would be evening coming towards them under the calm brown light of the pines. There was a loud thump from the boys' room, followed by an immaculate silence.

Unseen below them the sea rose silently then fell again.

Teresa had started on another subject.

'Really I have to go, I've got to get ready,' Mollie said.

*

Once she was dressed she went outside to the shed and hauled at the door, dragging it outwards over the thick grass, its bolt scraping a pure arc exactly like a geometry lesson.

Something needs to be said about the genus, Shed. New Zealand is covered with them, small almost windowless places, dark the way earth is dark, made of wood or red tin. There are things in there that no one has looked at for years, men's things; things that have come in; things that have never got out.

'The shed,' says the man of the household, the man of the forties, the fifties, 'I'll just go out to the shed.' He disappears. Do women have sheds? They never used to, she thought. A male precinct for decades, this shaggy darkness. No light ever seems able to penetrate and square the corners; there are things in here that have never seen the light of day – that nameless lump shrouded in spider webs that seems to have been extruded from the walls, a Minotaur in miniature, beating its head. Sheds are truer than houses and in some cases they are where their owners keep their minds, the private thoughts of a man whom not even his best friends know; the paedophile grandfather; the demon who stands beyond the reach of words.

She tugged the door wider, keeping her hand on the hasp. What was she looking to find – a prowler? an object? a sign?

Somebody or something, she was sure of it, was starting to hang about. She examined the lock. On Monday she'd get a new one and seal it all up. If there was an alternative mind for this house it could live out here. And one of these days, when she had a mind to it, she might just burn the whole thing down. She put her shoulder to the door and began to push it hard, lopping off more heads from the daisies and the clover that grew so thickly in the grass. It was no use; the door, dropping off its hinges, would not shut. Now it was open forever, a gate in the universe.

Inside the house that afternoon stood empty. From time to time she came and sat at the top of the stairs. She felt nervous and far too much on edge. A steady draught of air blew in from the back. The afternoon pushed by, the glass pendants letting out brief, bellbird-like sounds, that stinting sound that is like a perfect clear diagonal, a slant of rain on a window, that sort of sound.

She stood up impatiently. She'd already checked the basement out – there was no internal access, only an outside door half-wedged in against the bank. The very first day she'd come here she'd slid around it and looked in. There in the dead grey dust that dirt turns into under houses she saw part of the hill's profile, like a buried head.

Now she took herself through the rooms – no hidden doors, no cupboards sunk in panelling where something might hide. The house felt inhabited, but a lot of old wooden houses felt like that, having spent more time as forests than they have as planks, bowing in both incarnations, however, to the winds. It was nothing more than that, she thought, standing in the kitchen vaguely contemplating the sink, only a neurotic in a T-shirt staring at the sink. *Your demon Arkeum.*

The yellow clock fastened to the wall gave out its peculiar tock. It was just on four – time to call it quits. She ambled down the hall, over the patterns of the sea-grass, the coir, copra and coir, through the leaf-patterned light, Fiji. At the top of the stairs she sat down and fished out her papers again.

I'm over-sensitised, she thought. *Angels and devils, good and evil. Signs.*

Too many horror films

But it wasn't just that. The others all watched films.

Silly baby Westerners, he said.

'Is it superstitious,' she asked them, 'to look for signs?' Munch, munch, munch, they went on their lettuce, like a bunch of poor old cows, *one day we'll be thin.* 'Probably not,' they said.

'You worry too much,' they said.

'It's because I grew up in a country that committed a great crime,' she said.

'So did we,' they said. 'Is it true that henna is actually bad for your hair?'

'It famishes it,' said Gloria, 'inside a coating of fat!'

'That's just like us,' they said.

Out of a clear sky one night came a single thunderclap.

You will run away. You are cowardly, and a liar, these are your faults, being cowardly, lying and running away. He took her by the elbow and steered her across the street. It was lined with trees; the bud lights woven through them were already on. It must be a kind of torture, she said, for the trees. You are foolish, he said, your mind does not concentrate; you are like all the other babies, you don't know what things mean.

He lifted a shred of tobacco from his tongue. His face in the pale malevolent light that came off the buildings, green and mauve, was slick with its own pallor; he ate terrible food, tinned pork from China that went grey when they opened the tin.

'Pigs from China are fed on human offal,' she said, 'it's as close to cannibalism as you can get.' He could have been even closer, for all she knew, in Vorkutsk.

'He's too young for Vorkutsk,' her contact said. 'You don't have to have an affair with him.'

'I'm having an affair with Russia,' she said.

She felt listless, the tobacco packet drooping in her grasp. Her elbow was aching where she'd jarred it and she seemed to have pulled a muscle in her thigh. She sat there rubbing at it vaguely; her mind active but blank. And as she watched, it seemed as if a cloud or a mist passed across the leadlight above the door, leaving it faded. Sunlight faded too from the smaller window, round as a porthole, set into the wall on the higher side of the door. An aqueous green entered, making the hall watery.

Silently a head almost in full face appeared in the little window as in a portrait frame.

She sat quite still. He peered in through the glass, unable to see anything in the gloom inside. Like a peephole it allowed her to see out even as he couldn't see in – Jake had established this difference the other day, mouthing at them from the outside while they all, even Florian, sat quiet inside. The path sloped steeply where he stood; the green leaves of the bush on the bank behind him stood out like something startled. He turned in profile and lifted his head, as if to listen. Then he swung his face back again and stared in so hard she was sure he was looking directly into her eyes. Under its red hair the pale face with its absurd full lips contorted in the frame and the eyes under their shaggy brows swivelled. Then just as suddenly, he was gone.

She struck another match. The little flame flared up then dwindled straight away. When she looked up from it she saw a dark shape move across the glass and then, framed in the round window, the face appeared again.

The match went out. She felt her heartbeat thudding through her blood, but nothing from outside, no sound, not a footfall on the grassy path. Above her head a faint tinkle came off the glass shards hanging from the light. The wind blew again. The deepset eyeballs resolved themselves into leaves, the hair was foliage, the face had gone.

A fitful gleam of sun sent the shadow of the japonica bush on the bank outside playing further into the room. Suddenly the whole hall lightened; the leadlight shone with flowers and twining leaves; the porthole window turned blue and green. She rushed down the steps and flung the door open. Outside a bird was crying, the year was turning on its spindle,

the phone behind her began to thrill and ring. With a thrill
of her own – excitement, panic, relief – she sprang up the
side path and out into what was left of the broad wide world
of the afternoon. It was only as she began the steep trot up
behind the house that she realised that the phone was still
ringing and that she had no idea who it was who was being so
persistent, or even if what she thought might be happening
was happening at all.

*

She jogged, she positively jumped, over the contour lines of
the sheep tracks that were like hard thin ribs barely skinned
over by grass on the cold shiver of the hill. Above her a corridor of gorse opened up, then another and then, by now
slightly out of breath, she was out onto the open flanks, a
great broad spreading paddock of rank grass on the eastern
side of the hill, the kingdom of their childhood, accessible,
sunlit, unchanged. For a long moment she took it all in – the
grass, the sunlight, the wide line of the hill Even the air was
the same. She pulled her T-shirt straight and stepped out
across the margins into the thick grass.

Around her everything was shining, water sparkling everywhere – on the rough ends of the grass, on the clusters and
spikes of gorse, on the silken tents of spiders stretched like
minarets. Opening them as children, they had seen a world
where hundreds of baby spiders the size of pinheads lived in
a luminous mall. Looking up, worrying about what they'd
done (*will they get cold? Mollie said, will they die?*), they saw
where the rocky top of the hill poked into the sky. It always
looked as if you could get up there in two or three jumps,
three turns of the skipping rope, but dourly it eluded them,
trailing upwards in a diminishing of great grey rocks.

She remembered skimming up on her own, climbing at a
cracking pace, longing for company. But no one had really
wanted to go up with her, though they'd started out. They
hung about in the long grass, making up their minds. You
don't want to go up there, man, it's not too cruisy up there.

Winding up through the rocks and the rough parts, stepping over the sunken wire fences, turning about and about to take in the expanding circle of the view.

Standing here now she felt the same odd temptation, to get up there, on her own. At first she took only a few steps, slowly, as if not really going anywhere at all, strolling, gliding movements, without energy. Then she was on the track, the climb getting steeper, harder, hanging on to the cutty grass over the slippery bits. Looking down she half-expected to see some of the smaller kids, crying uncertainly, their gumboots stuck in rabbit holes, or sitting stubbornly at the base of the flax, looking away, out over the Harbour, their mothers already calling them from houses down the hill

She went on up, higher and higher, into the revolving view. From time to time she stopped to take it in. Things shrank and diminished below; the hill fell away into patterns of gardens and roofs and houses; the sea opened up. And now the wind that was blowing over the top was close. She shouted into it and it blew her voice away, off over the valleys of the city to the ranges and beyond, these sounding ovals, words.

A cat popped its head up out of the undergrowth curiously and looked at her She called to it, crouching down, but it slunk away, looking back at her once or twice, its tail stiff with a white spot. And then suddenly, after all this steadiness and looking, she put on a burst of speed, as you always do, as the hill takes you, propelling you up over its final incline, hurling you across the last of the rusting wire fences designed to keep you from flinging yourself off on the other side, the far side, the wild side, where plummeting in ledges it turns itself perpendicular and plunges down. And where at last except in the thickest weather you come face to face at eye level with the standing heights of the sea.

Out here on these final slabs of rock it was cold and very clear.

She stepped out carefully. The rocks were slippery in the shadow. Grey lichen scrabbled across the edge. Ahead of her stood the sea, rigid, pintucked. Behind her the city was cast in a fabulous light. She seemed to stand at a fantastic altitude on an exact dividing line between two worlds. She edged further out. On the ledges the stiff light-filled feathers of the toi-toi were hardly moving. Further down the roofs of houses tucked in an almost permanent shadow beneath the hill. As she hung over them a glassy level of air, like water, seemed to rise rapidly towards her, like a bottle filling; she straightened up and stood back.

And the devil took him up into a great mountain and showed him all the kingdoms of the world. The First Sunday in Lent – which could easily be today, she thought, vaguely ransacking her memory. Natalie Nansett fainting in the church, with a dead spider in her dress. But what could have been his sin, weren't they already His? Had he been giddy with it, forgetting who he was, whirling down the vertigo of thought, was that the sin?

Crabbed writing limned in gold straggled down the hill.

Something cracked behind her, or a stone fell on another.

Someone? She turned. But there was nothing.

Methought

She turned again. The air weightless, an outline, a sense, something moving over rocks.

Methought his eyes ...

She shivered. Something unnatural. Her flesh felt light and thin.

This had always been forbidden ground, treacherous at evening, sinister in the sun. Their parents must have been half-mad with fright at the thought of them going up there, but they didn't stop them, how could they, short of tying them down? In the end, of course, they got bored with it; sliding down on pieces of cardboard on the inland side, over the corrugations, the hard bumps, throwing stones down, putting a cat inside a suitcase and throwing that down too. Little habits of cruelty, and something else beside, something that lived up here, the Maori kids wouldn't go up, Not up there, man, they said. Something lurking, a particular configuration: rock and water, a secret.

What lived up here?

The devil, waiting in the rocks.

Below her the landscape was luminous; the pine trees on the ridges stood up like hair. Laid out before her, divided one from the other by ridges and valleys, were all the kingdoms of the world. Her head which had been aching steadily for the last few minutes suddenly seemed to swell, her feet miles away, so pale and weak on the edge. Her head falling from her body, bounding down from ledge to ledge. From the city below, the city standing in the tarnished dish of the sea, the sound of the carillon came pulsing up; hundreds of tiny spiders moved in unison through their minarets; a flare of heavy sunlight consumed the inner side of the hill in a liturgical gold.

She shouldn't stay up here.

'Mooning around up there,' her mother said, furious; 'throwing stones down.'

'Only the moon moons around, when you think about it,' she said, dodging the slap.

On the ledges below, the toi-toi began to dodge and shiver. A squall almost at eye level was blowing in across the Strait, moving directly towards her in a palpable mass, blotting everything out. Silent and swift it came, releasing damp tendrils of mist; she listened for the break in the weather but there was no sound, only the mass growing larger and the field of the sea smaller as it came.

On the Way Down

On the inland side, however, nothing had changed. The light was warm, the air blue and calm, the music from the carillon, playing strongly, washed across the city in concentric rings of sound. But she felt weird and displaced, in the warm sun, prickled by the gorse, crossing over the worn edges of the tracks. She watched her feet making their own movements, picking their way down; there was something pernickety about them, something a bit too dainty about the ankles, like a cow's.

She stopped and took stock. She was more than halfway down. Below her was the yellow roof of her house. In a gap that showed clear all the way down to the sea she saw the Monastery, inches high on its harbour point. Thin sails hung in the water like nail cuttings. Other people's lives.

How was it possible to feel you knew so little about yourself, even though you thought about yourself all the time?

'I do,' she said, 'you're right, I do think about myself all the time.'

'Your Arkeum,' he said, 'too much language and not knowing what you mean.'

So what if he was right, she thought, turning sideways to get down through a narrow gap in the gorse. What if you were quite wrong about yourself, how would you really know? What if you weren't your true self at all, whatever that is. Maybe you were only ever the most recent of all your possible selves. A line of false selves all made up and noisily crossing the stage like girls at the Moulin Rouge.

Well, if that's the case, she thought, inserting herself carefully into an even narrower place between two tough old clumps, I'd be the last one to know.

She stopped again and tried to figure it out. She seemed to have veered off onto the steep side, she didn't remember this. It was too high, and thick enough to get you stuck. She turned round and looked doubtfully back but the gorse closed over behind her; all she could see was the top. Whipsnakes of cloud were already whizzing up from behind, and soon with a *whoompf* the wind would come up too, like God's forehead rising. She was way off course.

I'm getting nowhere, she thought; two steps sideways and I'll completely disappear. She couldn't see a thing she recognised from here, her view completely fringed by gorse. It gave her a rectangular view, neat but empty. It was as if the hill had turned her footsteps, winding her round in its course, like a screw with a crooked thread. She knew that somewhere below, or maybe further round to the left, the hill dropped away in a series of rough cliffs and bare faces far more frightening than anything on the seaward side. She would have to renegotiate the whole climb. Just then her right foot slid sideways on a worn edge and she pulled herself up, grabbing at a gorse branch a few feet down. I'll be covered in wounds, she thought. She picked some spikes out of the top joint of her thumb; a shoal of little splinters lay just below the clear surface of her skin.

She was now completely hemmed in, with only a little window of view. It was oddly comforting, standing pinned in by tough old plants, with no option except to stay and turn into a tree. If this was a myth, she thought, I'd be ravished now by a god, a bull, maybe, or a golden snake. But maybe not a bull. Something lighter, more airborne; a winged being of some sort – something that didn't actually get in.

Warm and sunny she stood in a little niche of the universe. All she needed now was the right kind of lover, and a breath (*sweet scented zephyr of the gorse*) of the divine. She pushed off to the right in what she hoped was the safe direction, although the growth was so thick and immediate that she couldn't see the configuration of the land. Just in case she had it wrong with the cliffs before her and not behind, she forced a fairly steep path upwards, inching through the scrub. And it worked. Within minutes she found herself back in the clear.

Things were beginning to alter. A spatter of rain flung like stones hit the bushes. The grass in the deep corridor below her to the right turned a brilliant green and the roof of her house, which was at the end of it, shone a deep orange, so that the direction she was meant to go in was banded in vivid stripes of colour. Directly beneath her were the beginnings of a little wood, its silvered trunks and branches jutting out over the plunge into the valley. Sick of hiking upwards then inching downwards again, taking care to direct herself so that a headlong rush would not send her over the edge to the left, she let the hill take her, and running, dodging the last runnels, she began to speed down towards the line of trees, her breath bouncing in her chest. And just as the light began to deepen she hurtled into the wood, catching at a branch where a bronze light shone, and landed on her knees in the soft, wet, layers of the soft, wet, deep and leafy earth.

Wild rays of sun were poking in through the wood's western end. Straight ahead glimmered the milky garden of the Unicorn. On her knees she moved forward, like a hunter in a tale. Brambles rose before her, and rose haws. A flash of white caught her eye and reaching sideways into a scratch of blackberries she pulled out a crumpled piece of cloth, soft, freshly washed, a large white handkerchief. Underneath it, half-lost in the mulch, was a silver key.

It looked familiar, the key; its weight and shape felt known to her hand, but she couldn't place it. It was quite long, quite old, made for a mortice lock, but smaller than she might have thought. Or did she remember it in a smaller hand? Well, she probably didn't 'remember' it at all. She spread out the handkerchief and looked for some clue – but there was no reason to think the two were connected; washing blew away on the winds up here, winding up in trees and under bushes just like this; other people's stockings like knots of snakes, once even a whole tablecloth; and once, Cass maintained, a cow, truly, a black and white one, blown up the hill by the wind, which their father had – that, was it their father, that shadowy male outline – a jacket, maybe a pipe, a figure leaning on a spade. 'What was Dad like?' they asked their mother, 'Elusive,' she always said.

A thrush hopped away; something bigger rose, cawing disconsolately. She moved forwards, still clutching the handkerchief but leaving the key.

Just inside the last thin line of the trees she stopped, still on her hands and knees. She giggled, wondering what anyone else would make of her, mad in the woods. It was in this position that Hugo spotted her, emerging out of the brush on all fours. 'Covered in mud!' he said.

Standing at the back door he had turned and peered. 'Am I in the right place?' he said. 'Are you who I think you are?'

'None other,' she said, standing up and brushing at her jeans, 'or if you like it better, the very same.'

She stood on the lawn four feet above him, looking down. The grass was covered with daisies and at her feet small sprays of flowers growing out of the retaining wall were perfectly balanced.

'I'm Hugo,' he said.

'Help me down,' she said, reaching out her hand.

Behind her the bad weather came howling down the hillside, the trees thrashing in the crazy yellow light.

'Better get in,' he said. 'Here comes the storm.'

But she didn't move. He noticed how vivid the rim of blue was in her eyes, pirate eyes, like a pun for Paradise. There was a faint growth of fair hair along the line of her top lip.

'Go for it,' she said.

They got in the back door just instants ahead of the rain. They jostled, vaguely, breathily, in the narrow space.

'I need a drink. Or something faster,' she said.

In the weird dim light of the kitchen the green of the water-tossed garden seemed to penetrate. It was hard to see anything under the thrumming of the roof and the great watery gusts of air that kept bursting in.

'It won't last long,' he shouted.

'What?'

'It'll be over soon.' He yelled right in her ear.

'Don't do that,' she said, recoiling. But he pretended not to hear. Nodding and smiling like a figure from something Japanese he led her by the hand out through the hall and into the front room.

More rain hit the roof, the light turned olive green. From the front windows they watched as the squall moved rapidly across the city and the Harbour, then off, like a swarm of demons, over the northern hills. Miraculously everything emerged looking rinsed and clean; windows shone like shy rubies in the last of the light, sails came rushing home as if drawn together on a thread, like Gulliver towing the ships. Golden clouds floated in the last of the blue and along the edges of the balcony single drops elongated, fell into ovals and came lapsing down.

They propped their vodkas on the rail.

'So, what's it like to be back?' he said. 'Hard work?'

'A shade over-symbolic,' she said.

He looked at her.

'Don't even ask,' she said. 'If I wrote it in a book nobody would believe me anyway.'

'It's a hard country to come back to,' he said.

*

If ever there was a night for the carillon this is it, people said, coming to their windows to look at the moon, the reflections on the harbour, the trace of the ferry. If you took a fish-eye view of the city from a certain angle, sweeping all the new buildings off to the periphery, you would see the carillon standing on its own, a tower in moonlight, every projection on it standing out sharp. On a night like this you can almost see the notes issuing, round and black into the moonlight, like cartoon notes. The music inside the tower is a living thing, trapped in there, humming. And the city is its amphitheatre, the land of bees. Bees in the wind; bees humming and singing through the moonlit dark, and the land swooping up steeply on every side.

The music of the carillon is like the past, echoing and hollowing, threading through people's lives.

Sometimes when she has time and the children aren't with her, Mollie goes to visit someone who loves her, someone who remembers her from the time before. They climb the tall stairs, then they take the lift even higher, through the dusty shaft. Now they are in the chamber where the keyboard is; above them and below them are the bells.

'It's not carillion,' he says. 'It's pronounced differently, you know.'

She nods, leaning in her long coat against the high bench. Outside, below them, the little city is circling by.

'It's pronounced the French way,' he says.

'Yes,' she says, 'I know.'

'*Tu sais?*' he says.

'*Oui, je sais.*'

He plays for her, a long piece, beating the wooden keys.

In this weather (it is cold, it is blue) the held bells sing like captives from the high tower. Across the listening city the high hills resonate. Afternoon light inserts itself like orange glass in the open belfry slats. In this narrow slit in time Mollie stands listening.

Weaker than all the others the last note fades away.

He looks at her, his hands still close to the keys.

'*A quoi penses-tu?*' he asks her.

'*Je ne sais,*' she says.

Motel Morning-Star

Liam Davison

Angelo remembers this place. Even as his father turns the car into the forecourt of the Morning-Star Motel, he knows he's been here before. He can't say when: before his mother left, before the motel was built? He can't be sure. But he's been here before.

He remembers the curve of the bay beside the road, the water shimmering in the distance. It touches something in him, some half-forgotten link with family and home and travelling together, the three of them in his father's car, only it's not the one he sits in now. It's an older car. His mother sits in the front, her dark hair falling over the back of the upholstered seat, and he's a smaller version of himself, cushioned in the back with the smell of his father's cigarettes wafting over him.

He remembers the statue of the Virgin lit up against the night sky by the side of the highway. It stood, perched on its column, sixty foot or more above the turn-off to the beach – the turn-off he looks at now from the car-park of the Morning Star Motel. He remembers seeing the statue from a long way off, hovering above the road like an apparition. It drew the car towards it. And when they passed below it he remembers looking up through the back window to see it floating above the car, shining like nothing he'd seen before. The whole car was bathed in light.

'The Big Virgin!' his father said. 'Like up in Queensland. The Big Banana they have, now this. The Big Madonna.'

And his mother hushed him. 'Don't,' she said. 'What will Angelo think?'

Further down the peninsula, they had passed caravan parks shut down for the winter months and beach-side kiosks with flaking stucco walls. At the top of a hill, his father had stopped the car. Angelo remembers now, as his father shuts the car door behind him and walks slowly across the stones towards reception, how he'd looked back across the bay to where the shining Virgin seemed to float above the water.

It's not there now. Outside the car, the air is filled with light and movement. Insects with shining wings float past the window and he can feel the heat of the afternoon through the glass. The highway runs behind the straggling line of oleanders at the edge of the car-park and he can see the empty column at the turn-off to the beach. It's not as tall as he remembered it to be. Lines of rust stain the white paint and he can see the empty platform at the top, the open expanse of sky where the Virgin used to stand. The monument rises like something out of memory, drawing him back to a half-remembered past which stops short against the sky. He thinks of his mother's dark hair falling across the back seat of his father's car, the light from the statue washing across her face. And he knows that, somehow, his memories end with her; that if he traces them far enough back he will come to the empty space she occupied before she left.

Angelo sees his father walk from reception towards the car, a short, overweight man in a dark suit, shielding his eyes from the insects. As he draws near, Angelo can see his face and the beginnings of a relieved, self-satisfied smile, as though a weight has been lifted from his mind. He sees him peering in at him, the cigarette stuck to his bottom lip, and for a moment it's the face of a younger man, the man who sat beside his mother all those years ago. She might be there even now in the room his father's come from, pulling her hair back into a plait, putting her make-up on, getting ready to walk out into the bright light of the day as though she's never been away.

His father bangs the side of the car with the flat of his hand and moves round to the back. He throws the boot open and Angelo can hear his bags being lifted onto the stones – the same bags Nurse Bird had carried into the ward when his father arrived. Most of the others had already gone, their few belongings packed into similar bags by bewildered-looking parents. 'Wicked shame,' they said as they carried the bags out to their waiting cars. Angelo watched them go, wondering whether his mother would come. And when his father walked into the ward without her, with Nurse Bird carrying the bags, he thought, 'She'll be at home. She'll be getting things ready.'

Nurse Bird had told him as much. 'You'll all be going home,' she'd said, with her small, sharp face daring them to defy her. 'They're closing us down. Back to your mothers and fathers. Back to the family unit. God only knows what they'll do with you now.'

But they hadn't gone home. Instead, his father had driven around the bay, through the low-lying land where unfamiliar houses clung to the railway line, and out into open country. He kept the radio on and his eyes on the road. And now, it seems they have arrived. His father opens the door and Angelo steps out, onto the stone carpark of the Morning-Star Motel. He can smell the bay on the hot wind as he carries the smaller bag towards reception. His father walks two steps ahead with the other bag.

Inside, the room is cool. The glare is cut by heavy drapes and an air-conditioner rattles against the panelled walls. Behind the counter, a woman with long, dark hair is leaning over papers with a yellow light beside her on the desk. Angelo starts when he sees her. She appears to glow with the reflected light and, when she looks up, he's surprised to see how young she is, no more than a girl, with a vaguely familiar face. His father stubs out his cigarette in the Morning-Star ashtray on the counter as she moves towards them. The

smoke curls around her face. She might be his mother looking across the back seat of the car at him all those years ago.

'There's just the two,' his father says. 'There's not much
else he needs.'

She leans across the counter to look at the bags, and
Angelo sees her smiling down at him with the light from the
window across her face.

'This is Lena,' his father says. 'She'll look after you.' Lena
turns the smile towards his father as if some tacit understanding has been reached between them and his father
smiles back. They're comfortable with each other, as though
they've met before. 'She'll show you where your room is.'

Lena moves out from behind the counter and takes
Angelo's bag from him. He sees his father's eyes drift to her
legs and feels the softness of her hand against his.

'Hello, Angelo,' she says. 'You'll like it here.' And the sweet
scent of her perfume stays with him as she straightens up and
moves towards the door.

Outside, it seems hotter and brighter than it had been
before. The light bounces off the white stones of the carpark
as they follow Lena along a concrete path to a row of doors.
Each door has a blue star with a number stencilled onto it.
Angelo counts them as he goes. Seventeen is open and he can
see a man lying on the bed in underpants. A television blinks
in the corner with the music turned down low.

'Victor,' Lena says. 'You won't need anything to do with him.'

At twenty, she stops and reaches for the key. She twists her
body to get to the tight pocket of her skirt.

'I've made it ready,' she says as she pushes the door open,
and Angelo can see a towel folded on the double bed with a
miniature soap on top of it. Inside, there's a vinyl couch, a
chair and a television set which Lena switches on.

'Do you like the telly, Angelo?'

The walls are the same wood panelling as reception. An air-
conditioner makes the same rattling noise against it.

'It gets hot in the afternoon,' Lena says and stretches across
the couch to draw the blinds. 'Keep these shut and you'll be

alright.' Angelo catches a glimpse of the bay before they close. 'There's cold water in the fridge.' The room has a closed-up smell of Pine-O-Cleen and other people's cigarettes.

Angelo watches his father put the two bags into the wardrobe and close the door. The bed's bigger than any he's ever slept in, a bed like the one his parents used to share, and he moves away from it, intimidated by its size, unsure of what's expected of him. He moves towards the vinyl couch. Lena laughs and runs her fingers through his hair as though she's always known him, as though she can put him at ease by touching him.

'He's like you, Joe,' she says, and it takes Angelo a moment to realise she's talking to his father. 'He's a lot like you.'

She walks to the bathroom at the back of the room and his father follows her in. Angelo can hear her giggling behind the door and the low sounds of his father's voice.

'Don't,' she says.

He looks at the T.V. with the sound turned down until the toilet flushes and she comes out, smoothing down her clothes, smiling at him.

'I'll see you this afternoon,' she says to Angelo. 'Just to see you're settled in. You'll like it here.'

His father follows her to the door. As she opens it, Angelo sees him rub his hand along the inside of her leg. She pushes him away and shuts the door. Angelo hears her footsteps on the path outside and his father turns to face him. The two of them are alone, with the television blinking in the corner.

'Your own bed,' his father says, pushing the mattress down with his hand. 'Your own T.V. A clean towel every day.' He picks up the miniature soap and smells it. 'Those buttons there,' he points to a console beside the bed. 'That's a radio. A radio and T.V.' And he turns it on to prove the point. The music sounds like the piped music from the hospital, and already Angelo can imagine the slow hours he'll spend listening to it or watching daytime television.

His father is like a salesman. He moves from feature to feature in the small room, opening the wardrobe to reveal the bags again, pointing to the half-sized fridge beneath the bench, the jug of water.

'It's comfortable,' he says. 'Your own bathroom.'

He looks everywhere but at Angelo, who stays seated on the vinyl couch and looks, not at the things his father shows, but at the man in the dark suit who's brought him here.

'You'll like it here,' he says, taking Angelo's shirts from the bags and hanging them in the wardrobe. 'Lena will look after you.' The hangers are fixed to the metal rod and he struggles to keep the shirts straight. 'I'll be back in a few days. I can't stay long today.' There are only four hangers and, when they're full, he folds the clothes back into the bags. 'I'll bring some hangers when I come.'

When he leaves, Angelo turns the television off and pushes the buttons on the console. Each channel is the same – the same music, the same pre-set volume. He switches it off as well and settles back into the vinyl couch. Outside he can hear the wind off the bay and the occasional crunch of car wheels over the stones – the same noises he will hear for most of the night, along with the opening and closing of doors, the footsteps on the concrete path, the muffled voices from the room next door. He will lie awake in the dark room watching the glowing numbers of the digital clock in the console by his bed.

When the cars swing in off the highway their headlights flare into his room, shining through the curtains and lighting up the back wall like a screen. He sees, for an instant, the tray that Lena brought him, still sitting on the couch with the sausages half-eaten on the plate, the box of Panadol she calls his medication, the glass of water she's placed beside his bed.

'There, there, my angel,' she'd said to him as she ran her fingers through his hair again. 'My sweet little angel,' and she'd tucked him into bed as if he was a child. 'Lena will look after you.' He'd felt her soft lips against his cheek and resisted the urge to nestle into her.

Then it is dark again and the numbers float before his eyes. He drifts into uneasy sleep and wakes with the headlights to see the shapes of people moving outside his room. Their shadows are thrown up on his wall. Lena's shape is there. He wakes in the middle of the night to see her, surrounded by light, floating in front of him, shedding a yellow glow across everything in the room. He watches as she hovers above him then drifts away. And when he slides into unconsciousness again he takes her image with him – a shining figure watching over him as he sleeps.

Angelo comes to recognise the cars that pull in each day to the Morning-Star Motel. He recognises the particular sounds their tyres make on the stones and the slamming of their doors. He knows which ones will leave their engines running outside room seventeen while their drivers disappear inside; which ones will park around the back and leave an hour later, nosing innocently out into the traffic. He knows the men and women who arrive in separate family cars for the afternoon; the women who arrive in taxis, dressed as though they're going out at night. He knows the sales reps' cars with placards in the back which park outside reception, waiting for Lena to unlock a room and slip inside, leaving the phone unanswered for half an hour or more. And he knows the sound of his father's car. Once a week he hears it pull into the carpark to check that things are working out.

He smooths the bed and waits for his father to come into his room. Sometimes his father comes before he visits Lena. Other times he goes to reception first and Angelo hears the rattle of the key in one of the empty rooms. He turns the television on and waits for the two of them to walk into his room together. His father puts whatever he has brought onto the bed – a magazine, a tube of shaving cream, a box of handkerchiefs – and sits down on the couch.

'You're happy,' he says, and Angelo is never sure if it's a question or an order. 'You have everything you need.'

'Of course he's happy,' Lena says. 'You're happy, Angel, aren't you?' and she holds his hand or strokes his arm. 'He likes it here.'

His father looks uneasily about the room. There are no pictures on the walls, no photographs, nothing to suggest it's his son's room. He knows that if he opened the wardrobe door, the shirts would be hanging in a neat row, the bags would be where he'd left them. He thinks about bringing something from home, something of Angelo's but he can't think what. His son's not the boy he used to be.

'What would you like me to bring?' he asks, but Angelo doesn't answer. He acts as though his father isn't there. 'Talk to me, Angelo. Don't do this to your father.'

They sit, the three of them on the couch or Lena will lie across the bed, and struggle for conversation. Eventually, his father stands and walks towards the door.

'I'll come next week,' he says. 'I'll bring some socks for you.'

Lena brushes Angelo's hair when he's gone and wipes a mark from his cheek with a tissue. When it doesn't move, she rubs it with her tongue. Angelo feels the moist strokes against his skin and a tightening in his groin.

'Your father loves you, Angelo,' she says. 'He comes all this way to see you. You should talk to him.' He feels her hair fall across his shoulder and reaches out to touch it. 'You should make more of an effort, you know.' And she steps away from him. 'You really should, my angel boy.'

In the mornings, Angelo watches her move from room to room. She drags the linen from the beds and piles it by the doors for the laundry service. Her hair is pulled back and he can see the fine lines of her face as she goes about her work. When she's finished she changes into bathers with shorts pulled over them and Angelo sees her walking towards the beach with a towel across her shoulder. Every day, she goes there. He sees her cross the highway and walk past the empty monument, down towards the shimmering water. When she returns in the early afternoon, there's already sales reps' cars waiting by reception and she walks past them with her hair shining wet and the towel wrapped about her waist. She waves her shorts at them and disappears inside.

Sometimes when the cars have gone, he'll see her knock at the door of number seventeen, of Victor's room, and hand him money or go inside with him and draw the blinds. He knows then that she may not come to him, or if she does she'll lie on the bed with her eyes glazed and unfocused, giggling at him, saying stupid things.

'You should talk to Victor, Angelo,' she'll say. 'He has some medication for you. Victor has all sorts of medication.' And she'll roll about on the bed, teasing him, rubbing her hands along her thighs. 'Give me an angel kiss, my Angelo. Come and show Lena how you love her.'

Angelo stays on the couch. He doesn't like her when she acts like this. He knows it's Victor who does this to her. He's seen him standing by his door with his shirt undone, showing the thin tattooed chain around his neck. He's seen the blue stars on the knuckles of his right hand. He's seen him blinking into the sun with the same dazed expression on his face that Lena has when she's been with him.

On those days, Angelo thinks of her as she appears to him each night, shining outside his window, filling his room with light. Sometimes she's no more than a dim glow in the distance. Other times he wakes to find her hovering above him, so bright he feels the room might suddenly erupt in flames. He lies there, letting the light wash over him, knowing he's safe with her.

One day she comes to him, late in the afternoon, from Victor's room. Her pupils are dilated and she stumbles in, rubbing herself against him, drawing him towards the bed.

'My baby,' she says. 'My angel baby. Come to Lena. Come and lay with Lena.' She brushes her lips against his ear and he can feel her warm body pressed against him. 'How old are you, Angelo? How old do you think you are?' And she laughs at him, pulling him towards the bed and falling onto it. 'Are you old enough, Angelo? How much has your daddy told?'

She opens her blouse and rubs her hands across herself, across the soft, brown skin which Angelo can't help but look at. He watches as she pushes herself towards him.

'Come, my baby. You're just a baby, aren't you? Come, my darling angel boy.' And she laughs again, pulling him onto the bed with her.

She pushes his lips to her nipple and Angelo does what he is told. He feels her fondling his groin, rubbing her hand along the inside of his leg.

'You're just like your daddy, Angelo,' she says. 'Just the same. Has he shown you one of these?' She pulls a plastic envelope from the pocket of her skirt. 'Has he shown you how to use it?'

Angelo watches her draw the rubber thing from it and feels himself being rolled onto his back. She sits astride him and fumbles with his zip.

'Lena can show you, angel. Lena can show you lots of things.' He feels the soft touch of her fingers as she slides the condom over him. 'Yes,' she says. 'You're just like your father. Just the same.' And she slips back off the bed, crying with laughter as she does her buttons up. 'Look at you,' she giggles. 'All dressed up. All dressed up and nowhere to go.'

She closes the door behind her and Angelo hears her laughing all the way back to reception. He lies on the bed with his trousers down, convinced that he's in love.

Each day, he watches her walk across the highway to the beach. He waits for her to return, wondering what she's doing there, imagining her brown limbs sliding through the water. He remembers her touch and thinks of following her down, past the monument, just to watch her swim. Through the winter months she wraps herself in heavy clothes and folds the towel across her arm. He can't see the shape of her body as she jogs across the carpark and he imagines her taking the clothes off, layer by layer on the cold beach.

When summer comes again, he's surprised to see how her shape has changed. Her stomach has swelled and the bathers stretch tight across it. She walks with her back bowed against a weight which wasn't part of her before. When she comes to his room to make the bed, he sees how awkwardly she smooths the sheets, leaning across to tuck the corners in. When she's finished she seems to glow. Her face is flushed as she sits on the couch to catch her breath.

'Do you like me, Angelo?' she says. 'Do you like the shape of me?' She stretches her dress across her swollen belly and splays her legs. 'Is it attractive to you, Angelo?'

Angelo doesn't answer. He walks away from her and turns the television on.

'No. Your father doesn't think so either. He doesn't want to know.' He pours her a glass of water from the fridge and hands it to her. 'You're good to me, Angelo. You're better than the others.'

He's noticed how his father's visits have become less frequent. Sometimes a whole month passes without the sound of his wheels on the carpark stones. And he's noticed how few cars pull up outside reception. Only Victor has a constant stream of visitors.

Lena continues to swim. 'It's good for the stomach muscles,' she tells him. 'I don't want flab.' He watches her struggle with the laundry then wrap her towel around her for the walk.

One day, he follows her down. He waits till she's out of sight then closes his door and walks into the heat. He can hear the television from Victor's room and hurries past his door. The monument towers above him as he crosses the highway and makes his slow way towards the shining water. Lena is almost at the bottom of the hill. He passes the old convent with its driveway over-run with weeds and hears the piercing whistle of cicadas in the trees. By the time he reaches the beach, Lena is already standing by the water.

All along the beach he can see the naked bodies of men and women lying in the sun or standing at the water's edge. Most of them are elderly. He sees them ease their withered bodies into the water, as though waiting for miracles to happen. Lena's bathers are draped across the towel behind her on the sand. He sees her swollen breasts and the brown skin of her stomach as she slowly immerses herself and swims away from shore. Fifty metres out she stops and rolls onto her back. Her distended abdomen rises from the water and he sees her floating, absolutely still in the warm water.

When she strokes back into shore, he turns and hurries up the hill again. Victor is standing by the door of seventeen, smoking.

'Been for a perv,' he says. 'Not much worth looking at down there.'

Angelo ignores him and closes the door of his own room, knowing that Lena will soon be back. When she comes to him it's late. He knows she's been with Victor and waits for the teasing to begin. She puts the tray on the television and lies across his bed. Her dress lifts and he can see the white triangle of her pants beneath it.

'Whose do you think it is?' she says. 'Whose baby do you think is in there?' She pulls the dress up to reveal her stomach and rubs her hands across it. 'Do you think it might be Victor's? Victor doesn't think so. Perhaps it's your father's, Angelo. Or yours.' She reaches out for his hand. 'Perhaps it's yours. The Immaculate Conception. My Angel Gabriel. Did you do this to me, my angel?'

She puts his hand against her belly and Angelo can feel something hard beneath the skin. 'Feel it. Feel your baby, Angelo.' He can feel the wriggling limbs inside her and the soft skin around her navel. 'Come and listen to its heart.' She pushes his head down against her and he can see the mound of pubic hair beneath her pants. 'Listen to it Angelo. It's alive. It's like a miracle.'

He pulls away from her and takes the tray from the top of the television. Next to the plate of food there are two white tablets and a glass of water.

'Don't forget your medication,' she says. 'Take it before you eat.' But the tablets are not like the Panadol she usually brings. 'You have to take your medication.' She gets up from the bed and takes the tablets in her hand. 'It will make you more relaxed.' She rubs her index finger around his lips and when they part, she pushes the tablets in. 'That's a good boy,' she says. 'Now eat your tea.'

That night, he wakes to the sweep of headlights across his room and the familiar thrum of his father's car. He hears a slamming door and the motor left idling in the driveway by reception. The digital clock tells him it's 10.15am. It could be any time at all. It's dark outside. He doesn't know how long he's slept. An hour? The best part of the night? It could be early morning with the sun about to rise, except that his father is here. He hears his voice over the thrumming of the car – urgent, angry – and drifts back into something close to sleep. When he wakes again to the bang of Victor's door, the car is still running and he hears Lena's voice arguing with his father, then Victor's footsteps hurrying across the stones. There is shouting; another slamming door. 10.35am. He feels he's slept for hours.

The muffled voices keep him half-awake – drifting – then his father is there, standing in his doorway, switching on the light.

'Angelo,' he says. 'Get up.'

There is no one else. His father takes Angelo's suitcase from the wardrobe and packs his belongings into it. He takes the shirts from their plastic hangers and folds them roughly into squares. He empties each of the drawers.

'Put these on,' he says. 'We're leaving.'

He tosses Angelo's trackpants to the end of the bed. A T-shirt, a pair of socks. Then he's in the bathroom, scooping his tablets and toothbrush into a plastic bag.

Angelo's head feels thick and heavy. His eyes won't adjust to the fluorescent light. He sits on the edge of the bed and pulls the trackpants over his pyjamas.

'What time is it?' he says. 'Where are we going?'

'Away.'

His father zips the suitcase and carries it to the car. The motor is still running; the headlights flare across the forecourt towards Lena's room. Angelo follows him out, carrying his shoes. The door of his own room is left ajar.

'Lena,' he says. 'What about Lena?

'Lena's finished,' his father says. He slides into the driver's seat and shuts the door. 'Get in.'

As he swings the car back out towards the highway, Angelo looks back to see Lena standing by reception. Her body is full and heavy, bathed in light from the open door.

'Don't look back,' his father says.

'Where are we going?'

'A new home, somewhere decent.'

Angelo lifts his hand to wave but Lena doesn't move.

'Don't look back. We're gone from here.'

Everything outside the car is dark except for Lena. She is ablaze with light, shining brighter and clearer than he's ever seen before, and as the car accelerates away she seems to float toward him, beckoning, holding out her arms. The headlights scan across the empty column.

Angelo knows that soon – tonight perhaps – the baby will be born. He knows it is his father's child. All of his memories start and end with her. Angelo knows he has been here before.

The Instigator

Sonya Hartnett

This is a true story. That's what makes it so awful. Not many people have their childhood end so cleanly, nor so dreadfully; not many can recall the experience like they'd remember a knife in the side. I don't speak about this often – I prefer never to speak of it at all. In my youth I crossed in an instant the muddy waters dividing an adult's sensibilities from a child's, sparing myself the untold dramas of making a slower voyage – but in my haste I disembarked upon a shore of shame.

The year was 1977: I remember the date with exactness because the summer of 1977 was when they released the remake of *King Kong* and there was a gigantic blow-up replica of Kong fastened by cables to the top of the skyscraper which reared behind our motel. This was one of the few skyscrapers sprouting in Surfer's Paradise at the time and it stood isolated by paddocks of weedy dry land, peering down on the smaller motels like some overgrown geek in a school yard. Wrenching against his chains, Kong gusted and heaved, hugging the tower like a parasite with great pillowing arms. The wind would press huge dents into him, flatten him and bulge him and snap him like a sail. Eternally grimacing, sandblasted by salty gales, the rampant ape held a frozen stare, not at the small planes that buzzed around his ears but over a shoulder, to the roof of our motel. I remember being told – perhaps by one of my uncles – that, despite appearances, King Kong wasn't a monster: Kong was a goodie, as innocent as a child. I was a child myself, then: in the summer of 1977 I was nine years old. My brother Jacky was seven, and although he plays a big part in this story, he is never crucial to it. I doubt he even remembers it. Certainly we've never discussed it.

In 1977, as I said, skyscrapers did not dominate the Surfer's Paradise skyline in the unpleasant way they do now. Rather, the most common kind of motel was something much closer to the ground, two or maybe three levels high, built along the lines of an angular horseshoe. The space created within the arms of the horseshoe was invariably occupied by the motel pool, which would be sunk into concrete and surrounded by slatted sun chairs. Concrete was a favoured building material for these motels and it was often elaborately stuccoed or baubled by pebbles or sprinkled with sparkles, which was the type I liked best; metal, too, featured prominently, bent into all sorts of shapes and designs so banisters sported waves and larkish loops and steel flamingos stood on spindly legs, flaking pinky paint. The motels themselves were white or salmon or baby-blue; plastic poolside furniture abounded, and although the expanses of concrete allowed for little vegetation there was always a parched frangipani or hibiscus leaf floating in the pool. The names of the motels were vaguely Spanish, as if conquistadors or maybe Mexicans had something to do with settling the tourist resort: El Dorado, Los Alamos, San Angelo, the Sierra and our motel, my favourite, the stuccoed, flamingoed, much-banistered blue Santa Fe.

My family – that is, Jacky, my mother and me, as well as my maternal grandparents, my aunt and her husband, and my two bachelor uncles – had spent every Christmas holiday at Santa Fe for as long as I could remember, and because we were such regular and reliable guests, and because my grandpa was a wealthy man who commanded a quivering respect, we were well known and much welcomed by the owners of the motel. They would put fresh fruit in our rooms before we arrived and tolerated the nosiness of Jacky and me; the pool-boy Lonny would pull the rings of our soft-drink cans and once gave me a puff of a cigarette. And my family were not just regular and reliable guests – we were also ever-increasing. A baby had been born in the twelve months since our last visit, a brother for Jacky and me. Eric had colic that summer, making him the vilest thing ever known. His ceaseless screaming drilled through walls and drove my grandfather, a curmudgeon in the room next door, furiously mad. His being mad made my mother mad, and Jacky and I spent hours hiding from the simmering rage, curled below the fire-escape stairs at the back of Santa Fe. There were silver skinks in the shade there, with lavishly discardable tails; from our cubby-hole we could also see Kong leering at us mightily, slapping with the wind. I remember how hot it was that summer, how the paddock separating Santa Fe from King Kong's skyscraper was brown as a dog and dry as its bone, how the stiff weeds snapped and the black flies swarmed. We ate icy-poles, which melted over our hands. Something bit Jacky and we watched, delighted, as his poisoned leg grew and grew. Mostly we were bored. Surfer's Paradise was full of activity and laughter and sunshine, convertibles, arcades and dreams, but we were just two children for whom adventure began and ended with a small space under some stairs.

We hungered, of course, to go to the beach, which was only a minute's walk away, but we were not allowed to go alone, and our mother could not leave Eric. Our aunt and her husband were newly married and there was nothing charming, to them, about the company of kids. Our grandpa scarcely left his room, and the heat swelled our grandma like a melon: why the pair of them routinely holidayed in sun-kissed Surfer's Paradise was a puzzle to everyone. For Jacky and me, our only hope, that summer, lay in the benevolence of our uncles.

Our uncles seemed quite old to me, but they must have been young, in their twenties – young men in their prime. Brothers, they were also best friends, separated in age by only a year or two. Jacky and I wildly adored them, and whenever

they could be persuaded to turn their thoughts from the passing parade of flesh and alcohol and the hangovers that
resulted from these, why, then Jacky and I simply revelled in
the warmth of their attention. When they were not otherwise
occupied, our uncles indulged us, taking us to the beach or
walking along the shopping strip. At bars they would buy us
strawberry fizz and in the ocean they gave us dolphin rides.
I liked it best when they hurled us from end to end of Santa
Fe's swimming pool – I still remember how it felt, flying
through the air skew-limbed. It was always with a heavy heart
that Jacky and I watched them climb from the pool each late
afternoon, sleek and brown as newborn sharks. The night
was calling them, and the fun for us was over. They would go
to their room on the upper floor of Santa Fe, there to get
showered and changed. Jacky and I would splash around by
ourselves for a while, but it wasn't the same. Our boredom
would move in like a cloud.

Things had been going on this way for a fortnight, maybe
more, when I had my idea. I was a shy and retiring child, but
also full of imagination. My idea was meant to surprise and
entertain, for I was a good child, wanting only to please: it was
only with the ghastly failure that I began to transform.

Jacky, as I say, was seven, as brainless as seven year olds are.
I told him it would be fun, that everyone would think it was
funny, and he believed me: I believed myself.

From poolside we watched our uncles amble down the
street, dressed to lady-kill. Maybe it was six in the evening. We
looked around the motel but only the pool-boy Lonny was
about, slouched in a puddle of shade, leaning against the
upper floor balcony and smoking a cigarette. When he'd
finished he ground a butt into a pot plant and, picking up his
bucket, strolled slowly away. Jacky and I watched him go, shiv-
ering in the shadow-struck pool. There was no one around,
now – not any of the motel's other guests, not our mother or
sunburned aunt. We could hear Eric bellowing; King Kong
glowered as he surged and writhed.

The three rooms occupied by my mother, grandparents and aunt sat side-by-side along one arm of the motel's horse-shoe shape, but our uncles' room was on the opposite side of the horseshoe, beyond the hibiscus and blue pool. Their room was not so classy as ours – they had neither lounge room nor rear balcony, and their kitchen was simply a corner filled with cupboards and a sink. Its two single, chenille-spread beds were kept apart by a small but muscular chest of drawers. In 1977 Surfer's Paradise was safe enough for people to leave their doors unlocked, and Jacky and I snuck easily into the room. We smelled a familiar aftershave and the stuffiness of male sleep. Quickly I pulled the blinds, not want-ing the surprise to be spoiled. I knew our uncles would be gone for hours and that when they returned they would be Worse for Wear, but our mother would call us in for dinner soon, and I urged Jacky to hurry.

My goodness, what a mess two children can make! We started off tentatively, hiding the ashtray under a pillow, tilting the pictures on the walls. Jacky upended a toiletry bag on the floor and his daring made us squeal; the ice broke with a crack. We plucked clothes from the cases and flung them around the room, catching them on the ceiling fan. We pulled out and gutted the dresser drawers, left them overlapping like bad teeth. We knotted the laces of the shoes and left them in amusing places, in the oven, on the toilet seat. We stripped one bed but left the other alone and I remember giggling, imagining the scene. How one weary uncle would grumble as he remade his bed, watching his luckier brother go straight to sleep!

Jacky and I were in the room for half an hour, I'd say – possibly less, surely no more. We chortled and guffawed while we made mayhem, and I would shush us silent. When we eventually slipped out the door, nothing in the room had been left untouched. The room looked as if it had been shaken, like a souvenir snow-dome; it looked like a hurricane had swept through it or some violent crazed animal had been let in the door. What we left behind was chaos splendid, and I was proud of what we'd done. I was certain that our uncles would recognise in the turmoil a work of endearing mischief, something not unrelated to art – I was so certain of this that it never *occurred* to me they might view it differently, let alone that they'd credit the work to anybody else. Jacky and I exchanged merry glances across the dinner table; by bed-time, what with intervening television and baths and baby tears, I'd almost forgotten what we'd done. I remembered quickly enough when I woke to the news that my uncles' room had been burgled and the police were on their way.

My blood, need I say, ran cold.

I was not a bold child, nor brave: easily cowed by anyone bigger than myself, I also hated and feared being in strife: the thought of my mother's disappointment was as dreadful to me as the thought of being carted off by the cops. Worse than this, however, was a sense of humiliation that welled up from my stomach and set fire to my ears. The thought of confess-ing to an act of such idiocy made me want to die.

Eric was screaming, stiff as a board, and while our mother was distracted I grabbed Jacky's hand and fled with him, through the burning morning and into the shade of the stairs. I was trembling, distraught; I was furious, too. How mean of my uncles, not to see the joke! Couldn't they see it was supposed to be funny? … And how stupid of me, how childish, to have believed the prank could unfold another way. In hindsight it was starkly obvious that an adult, opening a door to such disar-ray, would not think of bored children, but of criminal minds. That morning, hunkering below the stairs, I recognised the great gulf that divides a grown-up from a child, a grown-up's complex existence from a child's simple world, and I felt myself jerked clean of that innocence, knowing I would never dwell on those ignorant shores again. And I was glad to leave them, but I was still a child, surrounded by trouble like a sea.

Jacky was asking to see the policemen and I saw the mistake I'd made by including him in my scheme. He had a big mouth and was too little for lies; he'd throw me to the wolves in a wink if he thought that'd make my mother smile. I grabbed him by the elbows and shook him till his eyeballs rolled. Policemen are bad! I hissed, stones digging in my knees. Policemen will take Mummy away! If you tell anyone we messed up the room, Mummy and Granny won't love you anymore! He went white as a ghost beneath his sunburn, and I felt cruel but satisfied. If I'd been cleverer I might have left things, then, as they stood, and waited out the day, topping up Jacky's terror whenever it appeared to wane. But I was not clever – I was smarting with the very realisation that I was not clever – and the fearful threat of trouble washed over me. I told Jacky not to move and crawled out from under the stairs. The morning was dazzling bright and already hot; I could hear the passing traffic and the distant, restless waves.

My grandparents were in their air-conditioned suite, the pair of them sitting opposite one another at the newspaper-strewn table. I lurked around the room, gnawing on my nails. My grandma was bubbly with the news of the raid on the room; my grandfather even appeared to be listening. It could have happened at any time during the night, she was explaining gleefully. The boys didn't come home till morning.

Disgraceful, said my grandpa, and I didn't know which of her statements offended him more, or if it was just her way of saying them. I could hear Eric howling through the wallpaper. Can't your mother quieten that child?

Nothing's missing, said my grandma. Must have been disappointing, after turning the room upside-down. Have to try someone else's room now, and someone else's after that. I don't know how they'll catch him, unless they catch him in the act. I don't know – you trust a motel will be secure, and then you discover it's not. Spoils a holiday. She looked at me distantly, and something seemed to occur to her. Whoever did it must have known the boys were out for the night. I mean, who would risk sneaking into a room that might be occupied? Whoever did it must have known.

She frowned at me, and my blood ran colder still. Did you hear anyone yesterday, Poppy? Anyone hanging about?

Acting strange? Anyone near your uncles' room?

No! I yipped. I didn't see anyone. Only ...

Only? gasped my grandmother, widening her eyes.

Only Lonny, I whispered, with his bucket. I was telling the truth but my lip started wobbling, and I wanted to nip it off. He was on the balcony near my uncles' room, after they'd gone away.

Lonny! My grandma stared brightly at my grandfather, as if lights were going off in her head. Lonny tends the garden and the pool. The garden and the pool aren't on the second floor, are they? What was he doing up there?

Lonny's nice, I said, guilt engulfing me, making it hard to breathe. He plays ping-pong with us.

My grandmother tapped the newspaper. We should mention it to the police, Roy. We won't accuse him of anything, just say he was seen.

My grandfather grunted like he made no promises but I knew it would be done. I pinched the webbing of my fingers, I twisted a string of my hair. I needed, sickeningly, to pee. But I cannot deny I was pleased with myself, and felt as if I'd wriggled from the pitiless clutches of a fiend. My grandmother sat back in her chair, the air in its padding sighing through the vinyl. Lonny! she tisked. One expects better from an orphan.

I hurried away to Jacky then, and we huddled under the stairs. In the dry paddock the insects hummed and Kong's cables twanged, his skin crumpling like a parachute. The road in front of Santa Fe carried a zooming stream of traffic, happy tourists for whom this day had not dawned black and sour. One of those cars was a police car coming closer, closer. Jammed miserably into a corner, butterflies jangling in my gut, I was very nearly sick when I heard my mother call my name. I slunk out like a cowardly dog and stood miserably before her, the concrete searing my soles. I had met the bad child within myself, a discovery as surprising as finding my shadow asleep in my bed: this child unnerved me, but she seemed to be on my side. I wanted to know her better, to trust her, to let her keep me safe. I wanted her to lie for me when my mother asked about the burglary, I wanted her to be slippery as an eel. My mother brushed back my hair and looked me in the eye. Where's your brother, Poppy? she asked. Find him, then come and help me pack. We're going home. I can't stand another moment of your grandfather whingeing about the baby.

The clear sky grew impossibly clearer: sunlight caressed my heavy head and, all about me, angels began to sing. Any other summer I would have shrilly protested such a termination of our holiday – now I could not stuff my suitcase fast enough. Would it have made a difference if I'd known I would never see Santa Fe again – that my grandparents and the motel's owners would fall out over the honesty of the pool-boy and that our family would, in future, holiday at the El Dorado; that, when I was old enough to search out the motel, I found instead a forty-storey monolith clad in silver and gold? No, it wouldn't have made a difference. Such was my shame that morning, I could have burned Santa Fe to the ground. I quickly kissed my grandmother goodbye and climbed into the car, and before we turned onto the highway I looked out the rear window for a final glimpse of Kong.

Aquifer

Tim Winton

One evening not long ago I stirred from a television stupor at the sound of a familiar street name and saw a police forensic team in waders carry bones from the edge of a lake. Four femurs and a skull, to be precise. The view widened and I saw a shabby clique of melaleucas and knew exactly where it was that this macabre discovery had taken place. Through my open window I smelt dead lupin and for a long time forgot my age. Life moves on, people say, but I doubt it. Moves in, more like it.

Cast adrift again from middle age, I lay awake all night and travelled in loops and ellipses while an old song from school rang in my head.

> I love her far horizons,
> I love her jewelled sea,
> Her beauty and her terror,
> The wide brown land for me.

Before dawn and without explanation, I rose, made myself coffee and began the long drive back to where I come from.

The battlers' blocks, that's what they called the meagre grid of limestone streets of my childhood. Suburban lots scoured from bush land for an outpost of progress so that emigrants from Holland, England and the Balkan freckly types like us, barely a generation off the farm, participate in the Antipodean prize of home ownership. Our street wound down a long gully that gave on to a swamp. A few fences away the grey haze of banksia scrub and tuart trees resumed with its hiss of cicadas and crow song. Houses were of three basic designs and randomly jumbled along the way to lend an air of natural progression rather than reveal the entire suburb's origins in the smoky, fly-buzzing office of some bored government architect. But our houses were new; no one had ever lived in them before. They were as fresh as we imagined the country itself to be.

As they moved in, people planted buffalo grass and roses and put in rubber trees which brought havoc to the septics a decade later. From high on the ridge the city could be seen forming itself into a spearhead. It was coming our way and it travelled inexorably but honestly in straight lines. The bush rolled and twisted like an unmade bed. It was, in the beginning, only a fence away.

The men of our street went to work and left the driveways empty. They came home from the city tired, often silent. They scattered blood and bone on their garden beds and retired to their sheds. All day the women of the street cleaned and cooked and moved sprinklers around the garden to keep things alive. Late in the morning the baker arrived in his van, red-cheeked from civilisation, and after him the man with the veggie truck. At the sound of their bells kids spilled out into the dusty street and their mothers emerged in house-coats and pedal pushers with rollers in their hair. Everyone was working class, even the Aborigines around the corner whose name was Jones, though it seemed that these were Joneses who didn't need much keeping up with. We were new. It was all new.

At night when I was a baby my parents went walking to get me to sleep and while they were out they foraged for building materials in the streets beyond where raw sandy lots lay pegged out between brickies' sheds and piles of rough-sawn jarrah.

The old man built a retaining wall from bricks he loaded into the pram that first summer. A lot of sheds went up quickly in our street. All those jarrah planks, all that asbestos sheeting, those bags of Portland cement. It was all taxpayers' property anyway. Great evening strollers, the locals.

I grew up in a boxy double brick house with roses and a letter box, like anyone else. My parents were always struggling to get me inside something, into shirts and shoes, inside the fence, the neighbourhood, the house, out of the sun or the rain, out of the world itself it often seemed to me. I climbed the jacaranda and played with the kids across the street and came in ghosted with limestone dust. I sat on the fence and stared at the noisy blue bush and in time I was allowed to roam there.

When the road crew arrived and the lumpy limestone was tarred the street seemed subdued. The easterly wind was no longer chalky. In July and August when it finally rained the water ran down the hill towards the reedy recess of the swamp. Down the way a little from our place, outside the Dutchies' house with its window full of ornaments, a broad puddle formed and drew small children to its ochre sheen. The swamp was where we wanted to be, down there where the melaleucas seemed to stumble and the ducks skated, but our parents forbade it; they talked of quicksand and tiger snakes, wild roots and submerged logs and we made do with the winter puddle outside the van Gelders'. I remember my mother standing exasperated in the rain with the brolly over her head at dusk while I frog-kicked around in my speedos.

Eventually the road crew returned to put a drain in and my puddle became less impressive. Then a red telephone box appeared beside it. I suppose I was five or six when I learned to go in and stand on tiptoe to reach up and dial 1194 to hear a man with a BBC voice announce the exact time. I did that for years, alone and in company, listening to the authority in the man's voice. He sounded like he knew what he was on about, that at the stroke it would indeed be the time he said it was. It was a delicious thing to know, that at any time of the day, when adults weren't about, you could dial yourself something worth knowing, something irrefutable, and not need to pay.

When I was old enough I walked to school with the ragged column that worked its way up the hill for the mile or so it took. From high ground you could see the city and the real suburbs in the distance. You could even smell the sea. In the afternoons the blue bush plain was hazy with smoke and the dust churned up by bulldozers. On winter nights great bonfires of trees scraped into windrows flickered in the sky above the yard. Beyond the splintery fence cicadas and birds whirred. Now and then the hard laughter of ducks washed up the street; they sounded like mechanical clowns in a sideshow. When summer came and the windows lay open all night a noise of frogs and crickets and mosquitoes pressed in as though the swamp had swelled in the dark.

The smallest of us talked about the swamp. Down at the turnaround where the lupins took over, we climbed the peppermint to look out across that wild expanse, but for the longest time we didn't dare go further.

Bruno the Yugo went to the swamp. He had a flat head and he was twelve. He ranged down through the reeds until dark, even though his oldies flogged him for it. Across from Bruno lived the Mannerings. They were Poms with moany Midlands accents. I could never tell when they were happy. Their house smelt of fag smoke and kero and they didn't like open windows. George the father had very long feet. He wore socks and plastic sandals. His son Alan waited for me after school some days to walk behind me and nudge me wordlessly with a knuckle for the full mile. He was twelve and scared of Bruno the Yugo. I never knew why he picked me from all the kids in our street. He never said a thing, just poked and prodded and shoved until we came down the hill to within sight of our homes. He was tall and fair, Alan Mannering, and though I dreaded him I don't think I ever hated him. When he spoke to someone else beyond me his voice was soft and full of menace, his accent broadly local as my own. Some days he threw his schoolbag up on to the veranda of his place and headed on down to the swamp without even stopping in and I watched him go in relief and envy. Mostly I played with the Box kids across the road. There were seven or eight of them. They were Catholics and most of them wet the bed though it was hard to say which ones because they all had the same ammonia and milk smell. I liked them, though they fought and cried a lot. We slipped through the bush together where there were no straight lines. Beyond the fence there were snarls and matted tangles. We hid behind grass trees and twisted logs and gathered burrs in our shirts and seeds in our hair. Eventually the Boxes began to slip off to the swamp. I always pulled up short, though, and went back to dial 1194 for reassurance.

Another Pom moved in next door. I saw him digging and stood to watch, my shadow the only greeting. I watched him dig until only his balding head showed. He winked and pointed down until I shuffled over to the lip and saw the damp earth beneath my sandals.

'The water table,' he said in a chirpy accent, 'it's high here, see. Half these fence posts are in it, you know.'

The rank, dark stink of blood and bone rose up from his side of the fence. I climbed back over the fence doubtfully.

'Looks dry this country, it does, but underground there's water. Caves of it. Drilling, that's what this country needs.'

I went indoors.

Someone hung a snake from our jacaranda out front. It was a dugite, headless and oozing. My mother went spare.

Across the road one night, Mr Box left his kids asleep in the Holden and went indoors with his wife. It was for a moment's peace, my oldies said but a moment was all they had. The station wagon rolled across the road, bulldozed the letter box and mowed down our roses.

George Mannering with the long feet mowed his buffalo grass every week with a push mower. He liked grass; it was the one thing he'd not had in England though he reminded us that English grass was finer. My mother rolled her eyes. George Mannering bought a Victa power mower and I stood out front to watch his first cut. I was there when two-year-old Charlie lurched up between his father's legs and lost some toes in a bright pink blue. All the way back inside to my room I heard his voice above the whine of the two-stroke which sputtered alone out there until the ambulance came.

I forget how old I was when I gave in and went to the swamp. It felt bad to be cheating on my parents but the wild beyond the fences and the lawns and sprinklers was too much for me. By this time I was beginning to have second thoughts about the 1194 man. My parents bought a kitchen clock which seemed to cheat with time. A minute was longer some days than others. An hour beyond the fence travelled differently across our skin compared with an hour of television. I felt time turn off. Time wasn't straight and neither was the man with the BBC voice. I discovered that you could say anything you liked to him, shocking things you'd only say to prove a point, and the man never said a thing except declare the plodding time. I surrendered to the swamp without warning. Every wrinkle, every hollow in the landscape led to the hissing maze down there. It was December, I remember. I got off my bike and stepped down into dried lupin like a man striding through a crowd. Seed pods rattled behind me. A black swan rose from the water. I went on until the ground hardened with moisture and then went spongy with saturation. Scaly paperbacks keeled away in trains of black shadow. Reeds bristled like Venetian blinds in the breeze. Black water bled from the ground with a linoleum gleam.

From the water's edge you couldn't even see our street. The crowns of tuart trees were all I saw those early years before jacarandas, flame trees, and cape lilacs found their way to water and rose from yards like flags. I found eggs in the reeds, skinks in a fallen log, a bluetongue lizard jawing at me with its hard scales shining amidst the sighing wild oats. I sat in the hot shade of a melaleuca in a daze.

After that I went back alone or in the company of the Box kids or even Bruno. We dug hideouts and lit fires, came upon snakes real and imagined. I trekked to the swamp's farthest limits where the market gardens began. Italian men in ragged hats worked on sprinklers, lifted melons, turned the black earth. Water rose in rainbows across their land. I went home before dark amazed that my parents still believed me when I swore solemnly that I hadn't been down the swamp.

At school I learned about the wide brown land, the dry country. Summer after summer we recited the imperatives of water conservation. Sprinklers were banned in daylight hours and our parents watered glumly by hand.

One summer my mother announced that she'd come upon some Cape Coloureds at the nearest market garden. I thought she meant poultry of some kind. I met them on my own one day and was confused by their accents. We threw a ball for a while, two girls and me. Their skin had a mildness about it. They didn't seem as angry as the Joneses. The Joneses were dark and loud. Even their laughter seemed angry. I never had much to do with any of them. I rode past their house careful not to provoke them. They gave my little brother a hiding once. I never knew why. His nose swelled like a turnip and he nursed this grievance for the rest of his life. It made his mind up about them, he said. I kept clear. I already had Alan Mannering to worry about.

The Joneses never went near the swamp. I heard they were frightened of the dark. Their dad worked in a mine. Bruno said vile things to them and bolted into the swamp for sanctuary. It was his favourite game the year the Americans went to the moon.

One sunny winter day I sat in a hummock of soft weeds to stare at the tadpoles I had in my coffee jar. Billy Box said we all begin as tadpoles, that the Pope didn't want us to waste even one of them. I fell asleep pondering this queer assertion and when I woke Alan Mannering stood over me, his face without expression. I said nothing. He looked around for a moment before pulling his dick out of his shorts and pissing over me. He didn't wet me; he pissed around me in a huge circle. I saw sunlight in his pale stream and lay still lest I disturb his aim. When he was finished he reeled himself back into his shorts and walked off. I emptied my tadpoles back into the lake.

What did he want? What did he ever want from me?

I was ten when people started dumping cars down the swamp. Wrecks would just appear, driven in the back way from behind the market gardens, stripped or burned, left near the water on soft ground where the dirt tracks gave out.

Alan Mannering was the first to hack the roof off a car and use it upturned as a canoe. That's what kids said, though Bruno claimed it was his own idea.

I was with half a dozen Box kids when I saw Alan and Bruno out on the lake a hundred yards apart, sculling along with fence pickets. Those Box kids crowded against me, straining, big and small, to see. I can still remember the smell of them pressed in like that, their scent of warm milk and wet sheets. The two bigger boys drifted in silhouette out on the ruffled water. One of the Boxes went back for their old man's axe and we went to work on the scorched remains of an old F.J. Holden with nasty green upholstery. One of them came upon a used condom. The entire Box posse was horrified. I had no idea what it was and figured (correctly as it turned out) that you needed to be a Catholic to understand. Before dark we had our roof on the water. We kept close to shore and quickly discovered that two passengers was all it took. Some Boxes went home wet. I suppose nobody noticed.

Next day was Saturday. I got down to the swamp early in order to have the raft to myself for a while and had only pulled it from its nest of reeds when Alan Mannering appeared beside me. He never said a word. I actually cannot remember that boy ever uttering a word meant for me, but I don't trust myself on this. He lived over the road for ten years. He all but walked me home from school for five of those, poking me from behind, sometimes peppering my calves with gravel. I was in his house once, I remember the airless indoor smell. But he never spoke to me at any time.

Alan Mannering lifted the jarrah picket he'd ripped from someone's fence and pressed the point of it into my chest.

I tried to bat it away but he managed to twist it into my shirt and catch the flesh beneath so that I yielded a few steps. He stepped toward me casually, his downy legs graceful.

'You're shit,' I said, surprising myself.

Alan Mannering smiled. I saw cavities in his teeth and a hot rush of gratitude burned my cheeks, my fingertips. Somehow the glimpse of his teeth made it bearable to see him drag our F.J. Holden roof to the water and pole out into the shimmering distance without even a growl of triumph, let alone a word. I lifted my T-shirt to inspect the little graze on my chest and when I looked up again he was in trouble.

When he went down, sliding sideways like a banking air-craft out there in the ruffled shimmer of the swamp's eye, I really didn't think that my smug feeling, my satisfied pity about his English teeth had caused the capsize. He didn't come up. I never even hated him, though I'd never called anyone shit before or since. After the water settled and shook itself smooth again like hung washing, there wasn't a movement. No sign.

I went home and said nothing.

Police dragged the swamp, found the car roof but no body. Across the road the Mannerings' lawn grew long and cries louder than any mower drifted over day and night.

That Christmas we drove the Falcon across the Nullabor Plain to visit the Eastern States which is what we still call the remainder of Australia. The old man sealed the doors with masking tape and the four of us sat for days breathing white dust. The limestone road was marked only with blown tyres and blown roos. Near the border we stopped at the great blowhole that runs all the way to the distant sea. Its rising gorge made me queasy. I thought of things sucked in, of all that surging, sucking water beneath the crust of the wide brown land.

Back home, though they did not find his body, I knew that Alan Mannering was in the swamp. I thought of him silent, fair, awful, encased in the black cake mix of sediment down there.

The next year, come winter, the night air was musky with smoke and sparks hung in the sky like eyes. Bulldozers towing great chains and steel balls mowed down tuart trees and banksias.

I learned to spell aquifer.

Three doors up, Wally Burniston came home drunk night after night. His wife Beryl locked him out and if he couldn't smash his way in he lay bawling on the veranda until he passed out. Some school mornings I passed his place and saw him lying there beside the delivered milk, his greasy rocker's haircut awry, his mouth open, shoes gone.

New streets appeared even while the bush burned. I listened to the man from 1194 in the phone box that stank of cigarettes and knew that he was making the time up as he went along.

I saw the rainbow mist of the market-garden sprinklers and felt uneasy. I thought of Alan Mannering in that mist. He'd have been liquid long ago. I was eleven now, I knew this sort of thing.

As our neighbourhood became a suburb, and the bush was heaved back even further on itself, there was talk of using the swamp for landfill, making it a dump so that in time it could be reclaimed. But the market gardeners were furious. Their water came from the swamp, after all. Water was no longer cheap.

The van Gelders divorced. Wally Burniston was taken somewhere, I never found out where. One Sunday afternoon I found myself in the van Gelders' backyard scrounging for a companion when I came upon Mrs van Gelder on the back step. She had kohl around her eyes and a haircut that made her look like Cleopatra as played by Elizabeth Taylor and her short dress showed legs all the way up to her dark panties. She raised her chin at me, tapped ash from her cigarette, narrowed her eyes against the smoke that rose from her lips. I coasted near her on my bike preparing half-heartedly to ask where her son might be but she smiled and stopped me asking. From where I sat on my old chopper I saw the alarming shadow between her breasts and her smile broadened. Half her buttons were undone. She seemed sleepy. I stood against the pedals, preparing to take off, when she reached down and pulled out a breast. Its nipple was startling brown and it wore a green vein down its fuselage like a fuel line. I popped an involuntary wheelstand as I hurtled back out into the street. The slipstream of a car tugged at my shirt and tyres bawled on the fresh bitumen as someone braked and stalled. A woman began to cry. People came into the street. I swooped through them and coasted down our drive-way, trembling, and hid in the shed. Months later I woke from a dream in which Mrs van Gelder leaned before me so that her cleavage showed and I stared but did not touch as dark water slurped against the plump banks of her flesh. I sat up in bed wet as a Catholic.

From one summer to the next water restrictions grew more drastic and people in our neighbourhood began to sink bores to get free unlimited groundwater. The Englishman next door was the first and then everyone drilled and I thought of Alan Mannering raining silently down upon the lawns of our street, I thought of him in lettuce and tomatoes, on our roses. Like blood and bone. I considered him bearing mosquito larvae – even being in mosquito larvae. I thought of him in frogs' blood, and of tadpoles toiling through the muddy depths of Alan Mannering. On autumn evenings I sat outside for barbecues and felt the dew settle unsettlingly. At night I woke in a sweat and turned on the bedside light to examine the moisture on my palm where I wiped my brow. My neigh-bour had gotten into everything; he was artesian.

At the age of twelve I contemplated the others who might have drowned in our swamp. Explorers, maybe. Car thieves who drove too close to the edge. Even, startlingly, people like the Joneses before they became working class like us. The more I let myself think about it the less new everything seemed. The houses weren't old but the remnants of the bush, the swamp itself, that was another thing altogether. Sometimes the land beyond the straight lines seemed not merely shabby but grizzled. I imagined a hundred years, then a thousand and a million. I surveyed the zeroes of a million. Birds, fish, animals, plants were drowned in our swamp.

On every zero I drew a squiggly tadpole tail and shuddered. All those creatures living and dying, born to be reclaimed, all sinking back into the earth to rise again and again: evaporated, precipitated, percolated. Every time a mosquito bit I thought involuntarily of some queasy transaction with fair, silent, awful Alan Mannering. If I'm honest about it, I think I still do even now.

I knew even at ten that I hadn't willed him to die, good teeth or bad. I pulled down my T-shirt and saw him slip sideways and go without a sound, without a word. I faced the idea that he did it deliberately to spike me but he looked neither casual nor determined as he slipped into the dark. It was unexpected.

The brown land, I figured, wasn't just wide but deep too. All that dust on the surface, the powder of ash and bones, bark and skin. Out west here when the easterly blows the air sometimes turns pink with the flying dirt of the deserts, pink and corporeal. And beneath the crust, rising and falling with the tide, the soup, the juice of things filters down strong and pure and mobile as time itself finding its own level. I chewed on these things in classroom daydreams until the idea was no longer terrifying all of the time. In fact at moments it was strangely comforting. All the dead alive in the land, all the lost banking, mounting in layers of silt and humus, all the creatures and plants making thermoclines in water lit and unlit. I wasn't responsible for their coming and going either but I felt them in the water. I have, boy and man, felt the dead in my very water.

Not long after my thirteenth birthday we left the neighbourhood. We sold the house to a man who eventually married and then divorced Mrs van Gelder. News of the street trickled back to me over the years. I met people in malls, airports, waiting rooms. The man next door murdered his wife. Up the road, near the ridge, a man invented the orbital engine and the Americans tried to ruin him. Bruno went back to Serbia to burn Albanians out of their homes; someone saw him on television. One of the Box kids became a famous surgeon. Girls got pregnant. Families began to buy second cars and electrical appliances that stood like trophies on Formica shelves. The suburb straightened the bush out.

Years went by. So they say. For the past five the State has endured an historic drought. The metropolitan dams look like rock pools at ebb tide and it has long been forbidden to wash a car with a running hose. Unless they have sunk bores people's gardens have crisped and died. With all that pumping the water table has sunk and artesian water has begun to stink and leave gory stains on fences and walls. And our old swamp is all but dry. I saw it on the news because of the bones that have been revealed in the newly exposed mud. All around the swamp the ground is hardening in folds and wrinkles. The mud is veinous and cracks open to the sun.

From the moment I arrived in my air-conditioned Korean car I began to feel sheepish. Police were pulling down their tape barriers and a few news trucks wheeled away. The action was over. I sat behind the little steering wheel feeling the grit of fatigue in my eyes. What had I been expecting to see, more bones, *the* bones, perhaps, have them handed over for my close inspection? Would that suddenly make me sanguine about Alan Mannering?

The swamp has a cycleway around it now and even a bird hide. Around the perimeter, where the wild oats are slashed, signs bristle with civic exhortations. Behind the pine log barriers the straight lines give way to the scruffiness of natural Australia. The sun drove in through the windscreen and the dash began to cook and give off a chemical smell. Down at the swamp's receding edge the scrofulous melaleucas looked fat and solid as though they'd see off another five years of drought. I pulled away and drove up our old street running a few laps of the neighbourhood in low gear. I took in the gardens whose European ornamentals were blanching. Only a few people were about, women and children I didn't recognise. They stood before bloody mineral stains on parapet walls with a kind of stunned look that I wondered about. A man with rounded shoulders stood in front of my old house. The jacaranda was gone. Somebody had paved where it stood to make room for a hulking great fibreglass boat. No one looked my way more than a moment and part of me, some reptilian piece of me, was disappointed that no one looked up, saw right through the tinted glass and recognised me as the kid who was with Alan Mannering the day he drowned down there on the swamp. It's as though I craved discovery, even accusation. There he is! He was there! No one said it when it happened and nobody mentioned it since. People were always oddly incurious about him. He was gone, time, as they say, moves on. They all went on without him while he rose and fell, came and went regardless. And they had no idea.

It's kind of plush-looking, the old neighbourhood, despite the drought: houses remodelled, exotic trees grown against second-storey extensions. Middle class, I suppose, which is a shock until you remember that everyone's middle class in this country now. Except for the unemployed and the dead. The city has swept past our old outpost. The bush has peeled back like the sea before Moses. Progress has made straight the way until terracotta roofs shimmer as far as the eye can see.

As I left I noticed furniture on the sandy roadside verge around the corner. Some black kids hauled things across the yard in Woolworths bags under the frank and hostile gaze of neighbours either side. An Aboriginal woman raised her fist at a man with a mobile phone and a clipboard. I pulled over a moment, transfixed. Another man with a mobile phone and aviator glasses came over and asked me to move on. They were expecting a truck, he said; I complied obedient as ever, but as I gathered speed and found the freeway entry I thought of the Joneses being evicted like that. I was right to doubt the 1194 man on the telephone. Time doesn't click on and on at the stroke. It comes and goes in waves and folds like water; it flutters and sifts like dust, rises, billows, falls back on itself. When a wave breaks the water is not moving. The swell has travelled great distances but only the energy is moving, not the water. Perhaps time moves through us and not us through it. Seeing the Joneses out on the street, the only people I recognised from the old days, only confirmed what I've thought since Alan Mannering circled me as his own, pointed me out with his jagged paling and left, that the past is in us, and not behind us. Things are never over.

The Making of a Heart

Colin Oehring

Rain came, absolute and frightening. Cattle blundered about on the pavement of the square. Turf and vegetable carts made their way around little calves lowing on the flatness. Mist, white and cottony like a sheet hung out over them, over the buildings marking the square, over the formless hill shadows to the east. Kieran Kiberb ran the directest line homeward. The sparrows had other things to do: dropping from the trees to the pavement, pecking at the quarried water, looking for other fallen things.

Kieran was stopped by his new and now beaming neighbour Mr Culkin, who was framed like a portrait in his gate – an old sloping fellow who didn't seem to register Kieran's rush.

'Evening, boy. It's a wet one.'

'Yeah. Very wet.'

'Can't go anywhere in this rain.'

'No.'

'Spuds'll be washed out of the ground with this rain.'

Kieran nodded.

'My mother's waiting.'

He clenched his jaw until his temples ached; Mr Culkin persevered with the smile.

'Off you go then, boy. Say hello to your mother.'
'I will. She's waiting.'

She wasn't. His shout echoed down the hallway, ricocheting.
His school bag was in the hall by the hotpress which was piled
with clothes, mostly his own. The windows and curtains were
wide open and little pools of rainwater had stained the
windowsills. He battened down the hatches. The faucet kept
time with the downpour.

*

The grey road leading to the fort was not at all grey when
Kieran had walked it the day before. In spite of the stones, the
sea, the clouds, and the mist that blotted out the hills, July
had edged it with yellow ragweed and purple heather. Kieran
stepped back from the path and eased around to look at the
fort, his mind sped in rhyme: Up Down, valley vale glade glen
den fen hen shem sham at the hem; Up Down, glide fight
might meat mote; And Away, stay play –
    'Hey!'
    Kieran looked around, stunned. It was nothing. Nobody.
He shook the cry from his head.

The fort was a great stone ring with flights of worn-down
steps on the inside, each one leading closer to a parapet that
overlooked the coastal sands of the not-so-calm bay. There
were boats to be seen, sailing craft with small spare masts that
jolted on rough days like this; the wind-lashed deep.

Kieran, who liked the fort empty, was pleased that the unruly
boys he had watched chasing each other along the stone and
playing rugby on the ground beyond it, were gone today. All
he could hear were faint drizzles of water. At the base of one
inside wall he had discovered a secret passage, tight and black
at first (he had to crawl) before it opened up a little: there
was room to sit up, length enough to lie stretched. He lay

there, adjusting to the space. The vague round tightness of it melted into something that was just black. He touched the wrinkling moss of the walls; then, himself. It was like a cold front had descended on him; his balls were contracted, felt new, unexplored. The sound of water was louder here, almost a gush, and he was startled when he noticed someone creeping into the passage behind him. He called out. 'What the …?'

'Shut the fuck up,' came a voice, male and deep. 'Just shut the fuck up.'

Faithful chorus of the ocean.

There he was now, looking like a maimed thing, his words coming thick and slow.

'What do you want?'

'Like you don't know, you little shit.'

The older boy looked at Kieran, meditative and brutal.

'Do I have to spell it out?' he said.

*

Tank had broken him down, made him kneel, beg, scrape. Less jolt than collision. His pants were pulled down, his arse whitish-purple and bright as a flashbulb. He was washed in Tank's sweet breath. He fixed his eyes up high. Tank stretched out over him, backwards, reaching a sweet spot. Kieran's whole body tingled, felt the nascent strength in his own arms and back. Tank turned him over, exposed Kieran's hidden pink-white side, held his wrists of bone.

'No,' he said.

'It's easy,' Tank hissed back.

'I feel sick.'

He didn't actually, not much, just looked over his back at Tank's thing: *huge.*

'Keep going.'

Tank pulled at his hair, harder and harder, until Kieran yelped then yelled at him to Shut Up, curl up, shift here, there. Kieran's arm uncoiled beneath him and surgingly caught Tank clean on the mouth with the back of his hand.

'Fuck!'

Now that Kieran had started he wanted to keep on batter-ing him. But Tank forced his arm down and Kieran's centre of gravity slipped, moved hopelessly out of place. Then Tank's cock was pushing up through Kieran's slack fist. He sensed the implicit circuitry of this boy's body: two wires make a current, don't they? And something welled up in him like vapour, or sauce rising in a pan, on a stove ... And the smell. It was what he had quarried from all that tangle. The smell he'd never forget. Tank dragging hotly over him. Seed turned earth. And bleachy like chlorine. But the smell – it exhausted words, petitions. It would stay. It was over. They were sticky.

*

Kieran pitched his undies in the sink and ran hot water over them.

*

In a dream like this: the girl again, the girl on her horse. Wind in her hair, riding bareback, edging the cliff. He first dreamed those pictures two days after his fifteenth birthday, four days after moving South, eighteen days after being thrown out of the Fianna for shooting the wrong boy. Not a Protestant, not an informer – neither. A thickening in the air like dried skin, unlaundered laundry, musty hair, and that look of desperate enquiry in the boy's eye as he sprawled back jutting up the wall in his foul bed. He had shot the boy in the head with a .32 pistol picked up from a UDA arms dump. This kid: still dopey from sleep, his hair sticking up wildly, turning to run. Kieran had grabbed him, pushed him up against the wall. Tune in, level the gun. Boy collapse. *May what is false within you before your truth give way.* Gun recoil. Another shot and then out of there. That's what it should have been. But then that demented, distracted longing ... He lit a cigarette and smoked it with a flat kind of savour watching licks of smoke drift over the body. There was something by the bed.

What? Some kind of maritime toy, a wooden thing, blue and white.

> Removal to the Church of the Immaculate Concep-
> tion, Tullpoint, this (Tuesday) evening at 7 o'clock.
> Requiem mass tomorrow (Wednesday) at 12 noon.
> Funeral afterwards to Cross Cemetery. No flowers.
> House private.

Monday: three IRA youths were shot dead by the SAS from high ground as they crossed a field moving armaments. Kieran's friends, the three of them. Two brothers – twins – and a snooker champ, one year younger. The family had declined a military-style funeral opting for a modest service in the town church instead. Kieran stood outside, his mind wild with stray facts he could find no use for. Trivia about the dead boys. Favourite foods, peculiar habits. Parental visions. Kieran shook in his suit and tie, vibrating with the energy of fear and hunger. He offered up an abortive prayer when he saw the misery and grief in the mourners' eyes: their day-to-day avowals, perfectly good within their set application were of no use here; territorial imperatives became brittle and smug. But the SAS informant had been a boy from this town and Kieran had been given an address.

Before the service was over he snuck up the back way, along the river, to the pub. Most everyone over fourteen was let in on days like this; and Kieran, well, he got sinfully drunk. Most of the men drank standing up; Kieran's head lolled heavily, his legs kicked loose at his stool, at the counter. He ordered another drink and listened to the men, their talk about the wetness of the bog, machinery, football, the probability of the whole area being rezoned as EC Disadvantaged. Everything except what had happened to three boys in a field two days ago. Kieran began thinking as many blanks as he could. He drank more, entered a mostly snow-dark world inhabited only by a single silent servant holding calvary by a cross on a hill in the sweet light of failure, in the wind-still air, and he felt that the world held something for him, something beyond his circle of habit and he thought it might be the beauty of burnt wood. Whatever that meant. He giggled, fits of giggles until somebody thumped him on the back telling him to keep quiet now.

He'd taken a car that evening – from right in front of the pub. One of those A to B and back again cars. He pissed on the wheel, making it his, then worked the lock before jamming the nail-scissors from his pocket knife into the ignition. The engine took him as its own.

On the motorway it had started to rain. Driving was treacherous, visibility poor; and the rain ... A blankety wet stretching between Tullpoint and Leitrim right on over the west of the isle. Kieran's speed was down to fifty. On he went, through mountain roads with wide-spreading views, gorges and boulders. Green hedges, buds closed. Then high hills, blue-shadowed on olive ground; fields flagging young grass. Tender-leaved birches. Hazels and oaks. The road looked back at him in the rear-view mirror: first grey, then red, finally yellow.

*

Checkpoint: a dozen vehicles trailing along. A convoy of jeeps. Container trucks. A transit van with radio and signalling equipment. Scattered border security. Checkpoint? Meaning had trickled out of the question.

*

Kieran sprawled on his bed, half listening to the radio (*thunder only happens when it's raining, players only love you when they're playing*). He felt as if he were expiring by degrees, pinned down as if the stars outside were no longer glistening in high frozen concord, as if there were no dewy breeze below them, no muted television to his right flashing money indexes (decline of the pound, the dollar, the yen). He turned the stereo way up, the music cross-fading the world around him, racing through a track in his upper body. It left him feeling heavy and blank, as if he were waiting for an idea.

*

A group of boys – three of them – greeted him by the shed behind the fort on his third day in Brandontown with a ten spot of hash and a quart of whiskey. It was Tank and his friends. One – a Declan – leant back against the wood panelling, one leg up. He was shining in a cheap black T-shirt, his underarms were shadowed with sweat.

'Meet Kieran.' This was Tank.

Declan grinned. Kieran's voice thinned to a wisp, his soul softened to a bruise by the late afternoon. 'Hi.'

And Ash: he met this boy in the leather jacket, stockier than the others. Close-cropped blond hair and a broad, open face. The four of them pushed their way inside the shed. A dappled cool. Seatless chairs hung from the ceiling, swathes of calico lay on the floor under plastic bags of peat. There was a bench with tools, old tins, grease. And there was the threadless talk of the boys, the bragging loud and tough and wild. And that smell of childhood, dirty socks and shoes. Kieran's wariness deepened. He tried to relax, unclenching his fists and sat down, his back against some canister. Tank sat next to him and stuck out his sneakered feet. Kieran ached to hit him again, like in the Fort; but he liked him too as Tank smiled showing the jagged edges of his teeth. Ash turned to them, pointing gun-fingers at Tank.

'You sure messed up that goal last week,' he said. 'We could've won.'

Tank sprang up, made to punch him.

'Shut up, fuckface.'

Ash shrugged and made a disowning gesture – hands forward, palms up – before sitting down against an old sack, chewing his bottom lip, reading a grisly comic, looking up every now and then to see how the world was squaring up.

There was a knock at the door and a desperately thin, pale, stricken tree of a boy came in. He had sort of wrecked long black hair and a fag sticking out of his mouth.

'Hello, cunts,' he said.

'Hello, dick,' replied Tank.

'Right.'

The boy didn't seem to notice Kieran. He produced a cotton bag from under his sweater. 'Let's', he said slowly, 'get really really really stoned.'

*

Tank was smoking the joint now, a long one, sucking deep on it, eyes shut. Declan pulled it from his mouth and drew on it. Kieran vied for his turn, and, taking a moderate hit, was thrown by the smoky surge of calm. Pass to Ash.

'This is good stuff,' he moaned.

'You should come tomorrow. We hang out 'round the fort most days after school.'

'Or *during* school,' Declan added, gigglingly.

'Declan's a wanker,' Tank said. 'Eats ice-cream for breakfast. Shit like that.'

Kieran stretched out, looking up. The roof looked just about ready to fall in. He laughed.

'What's your opinion of Joy Division,' he asked nobody in particular. ''Cos I … I hate it that whatsit died.'

Silence.

'No, really,' he added. 'I mean, he couldn't help it right? Dying.'

He closed his eyes. One of the boys – he couldn't tell which, though he kind of thought it might have been Tank – told him that they – Ash, Declan and the new one – didn't like faggot music. Kieran opened his eyes.

'You like them?'

This was Declan. Kieran confirmed it in a quiet voice so that it didn't have to become an abiding abdication.

'It's shit music,' Ash said.

Declan turned on him, his voice harsh.

'Can you not be persecuting him, dickhead.'

'I just think it's shit music is all.'

Declan farted and reached for the bong. Laughter. The dope burned the cloud from his voice: 'Check this out.'

He blew three fat smoke rings.

'Don't waste that shit,' said Tank.

'Mine,' was all he said.

Kieran sat tall beside Tank and closed his eyes, unravelling.

*

The boys had gone, except for Tank who was studying him.

'Do you like your dad?' he asked.

'He's still up north.'

'But d'you *like* him?'

'I liked him. Taught me stuff.'

Oh yeah, like what Tank wants to know.

'Well, ah, I don't know really …'

Tank stood shakily.

'I should get back. Home.'

'Okay.'

He pulled Kieran to his feet and they staggered rigid-legged from the shed into the near-dark. The creek from the bay was noisy, disturbed and rising, and just starting to carry off an untethered black rowboat like a flag of anarchy.

'That's Sullivan's crap dinghy. He'll be …'

Tank trailed off and Kieran asked should they rescue it.

'Nah, fuck it.'

They walked to the 711 at the edge of town to buy corn chips, the lights from passing cars slashing across them. It was warm inside the store, much warmer than it had been on the street, and the oven where the bread was baked not just in the morning but right round the clock glowed as an alien might in a field on a cold night. There was a sweetness in being here with Tank, and something else, something like a lie: that they were friends, these two, that they had been for a long time. Kieran smiled cosily.

'You pay,' said Tank pulling out his (empty) pockets at the checkout.

'Unfair!' Kieran was loud-voiced in the quiet store: northern – that was what he sounded to himself. And, of course, there was no unsaying how or what he'd said.

When they had eaten the cheesy chips and the Mars bars, they balled and lobbed the empty bags and wrappers into the gutter and walked, following the road, back to Tank's place. Tank walked with a sulky slouch, the food weighing like ballast in his stomach. He kicked at the stones in his path until they faced gate nine.

'This is it,' he said.

Kieran nodded imperceptibly. The sun was almost gone but he could make out the farmyard: it was surrounded by a rectangle of outbuildings, most of their windows broken. Those of the house had been patched up with rain-warped plywood. There was rusted machinery and discarded sacks and the overturned hull of a car. They made their way to the house.

'It's a bit run-down.'

'Yeah.'

'Do you wanna stay a bit before you go.'

'Okay.'

So they sat down on the damp earth, the 6pm rain leaking into their jeans.

'Kieran Kiberb?'

'What?'

'Have you ever seen my knife?'

They were lying down now, under the night as it drifted across them. The moon, Kieran thought, looked wet.

'Your what?'

'My knife.'

'Don't think so.'

'Well, –'

Tank took Kieran's hand and he felt the blade, the cold cold steel. Tank had moved in on him, blocked out the weak rising moon. Kieran let his palm be guided up and down the cold steel. Tank stretched out his khakied leg and rubbed it up along Kieran's jeans. In the tangle, the blade-tip was, like, a part of Tank. Kieran pulled away. 'Don't cut me.'

Tank dealt out a cuff to the side of his head.

'Hey!'

'This', Tank said with emphasis, 'is a survivalist's knife. Special army issue to the SAS. And the Navy SEALS have them.'

Sure, it was a beautiful thing. Kieran examined the tungsten alloy laid over with Teflon and hafted by a brass tang to an ebony handle. His heart beat in a punishing Mayday rhythm; the knife – it had the dark polished sheen of obsidian. He held it gently.

Tank rose to his full height then stretched, straining up, head back almost touching his shirt which maybe was dirty, maybe just dusty, maybe both, and he let out a big strangled howl. Just for the sheer hell of it. Kieran sat back, impressed.

'Knife's great,' he said.

'Maybe,' said Tank.

'No, definitely.'

Tank bent over and put his fat lips to Kieran's, who imagined the kiss would be drier, who imagined adults or at least big boys had wetness under control. He tried to duck out from under him but Tank's body was huge and hot and unruly. He squirmed, then gave up: his shoulders stopped churning and he lay limp as Tank unzipped, wiggling his hardening cock. Kieran twisted out from under the body and ran, ran turning up his collar as he went.

'Hey!' Tank shouted, then coughed, deep and chesty. 'The knife!'

*

Kieran's mind wandered up the hill to Limerick: to Grandpa who'd had that raw reddish look in his eyes as if the road had run out on him – the web and tracery of blood vessels in his face. *Skinning. Hay on the floor.* Grandpa's gun-metal eyes moving onto Kieran who locked into the stare and stood stupid before him as he watched him lick blood from his hand. Licking it off good and proper. The body of the animal, that pared red thing, still steaming. Rag and bone. There was a pig-swell stench, sweet and hungry. Cold plants. Clouds.

*

Kieran was only half aware of the shadow figure approaching. It looked like a tree, a swaying trunk.

'You got the stuff.'

Tank nodded.

'Grand.'

'You?'

'I haven't forgotten,' he whispered, with feeling.

Tank blinked.

*

Tank and Kieran sprinted by the back of the house through the field and into the church ground. It was a sooty-dark night and they did their best, weaving through trees and head-stones until they reached the clearing beyond the graveyard.

'This is it, then,' Kieran said, swooping the torch in a low arc over the ingredients Tank had assembled, rather neatly, in two matching orange lunchboxes. Two long bolts, two nuts, copper piping (a foot long), a roll of insulating tape, a ball of twine and a small can of petrol to dip it in.

'You sure this is all we need?' Tank asked.

'Yep. I told you, I found it on the Net.'

'Cool.'

Tank shivered. Kieran stiffened.

'Fuck,' he said. 'The matches. Where the fuck are –'

'– I got 'em. Here.'

Tank reached into his back pocket and produced a box of matches.

'Hope there's enough.'

'This is the size you said to get.'

'Well, I meant bigger than that, but … OK.'

The boys sat down, divided the matches and started stripping the heads, Kieran with his pocket-knife, Tank with his special issue.

'Pisser of a job.'

'Shut up, Tank.' Kieran looked at him. 'It's gotta be done.'

After that they worked quietly, filling the tobacco tins with red grit.

*

When Kieran thought his note OK, he flicked his pen at the small bedside table where it joined a cassette of Joy Division, a paper bag with a little bomb in it and a freshly rolled, unlighted joint. 11.36pm. He drifted.

1.00am: his bones suffused with stiffness, his eyes still gluey with sleep. He raised his window creak by creak, his mind flaming with a double thought: wear dark clothes, keep to the shadows.

Rustle.

Kieran froze, urging time, Tank and everything to just hurry the fuck up. He snatched his Bic lighter and flicked on a flame, looking out: Trees streaking the ground – '*Tank*?'

No response. His heart beat like a dog's. He looked at his digital clock, touching it lightly. 1.34am. Then Tank's indecision – if that was what it had been – passed, and his hollow-bodied voice came: *Kieran?*

Tank was struggling against the tree now, boosting himself up, limb by limb. Then came a curse, a sigh and Tank, dropping straight down to the bottom of his room, sitting startled on his haunches, watched Kieran lean out, intention and impulse joining for a moment, to hug him. He held Tank's head, pulled it in close. A rush of breath. The boys frisked their pockets and made ready.

*

Fire lashed out. The full flame of it burning clear time's millioned accidents. A thunderous sound, like twenty drays let loose; the breath of the bang shuttling out at them. This one reflection of immensity stencilled itself into the earth, traced itself through the air. They hung around longer, really, than was safe, just listening for that new roaring silence that was about them. Then: a flint moment of clear thought and they ran –

– *we ran we ran man we ran.*

The two boys stood at the cliff, checking out the night-bay and parrying each others words, fogging the line between endurance and confrontation. Kieran began to explain why it had been *necessary*, to explain about, well, everything. But he let the sentence fizzle and Tank spat in the dirt. Kieran reached for his hand and held it a while, stiller than stone, before letting it fall.

A young girl riding bareback came at them, her horse treading the land, her hair loosed in the strong wind, falling soft and wild on the raincoat that was tight around her shoulders. She was eating from what looked like a bag of potato chips. Then the sirens started up and the two boys turned until the wind was at their backs, gusting them along towards the girl and her horse and the drop in the land where the sea, sudden and white, came up at them, massed like wild shifting stone. Tank had a thought and stopped where he was. Kieran, eyes fixed on the girl, walked on.

Road Kill

Anthony Lawrence

The roadside myrtles look startled, then spellbound in each sweep of the lights. Sleeves of torn lichen hang from the branches, though only one of the car's three passengers gives voice to their brief, lofty flaring. She is in the back seat, in the middle, leaning forward on the dark-haired shelves of her forearms. Her name is Alice. She is fourteen years old. Her father is driving. His grave expression seems more intense in the wash of green light from the dash. Alice studies the tide-line of his cropped black hair. Her hand moves towards his neck, then returns. Her mother is sleeping, her hair like a stalled, dark water spillage over the central armrest.

Look at the rotting material on that girl's dress, Alice says, pointing to a stand of lit myrtles.

Her father says something like What girl? or Lost world, then reaches up to angle the rear-view mirror to better see his daughter's face. A rectangle of dark glass contains her eyes, barely visible though wide and watchful.

Three people on a winding mountain road, late at night or early in the morning, entering a tight weave of rainforest, then the loose, vertical stitching of amber-barked stands of timber, now rainforest again, where bird's nest ferns fan and blow in the headlights.

The sound of a small animal being hit by speeding metal is a muted thing, as though someone near has palmed a watermelon, testing it for ripeness.

When the car stops, Alice is out the door and running. Her father reverses to where she's standing, then climbs out and goes to her. Her mother joins them, hurried from a fog of sleep. In the red glow of the tail-lights, they see a spotted quoll writhing in a roadside hollow, its body pasted with leaves and mud swirls, its back legs kicking into death. Blood drips from its open mouth, its claws rake the air. Then it dies. Alice kneels beside it. She strokes its head, traces the outline of its mouth. Then she places both hands on its back and strokes it. She can feel the ribs as the skin flows over them.

It's so warm, she says, before standing and turning away to inhale the heat on her hands.

Eight years on. A mountain road. Another state. Alice and her boyfriend Cleve were returning to Sydney after a weekend of caving and camping. Cleve was driving, too fast as usual, though this time the speed was palpable in another way. The unsealed road's corrugations and the rip of the tyres were intensified each time Cleve tensed his thighs or shifted position. With Alice's head in his lap, each tight corner made intense concentration essential. Alice liked fellating him while he drove, and she liked to take her time, teasing him into driving slowly, his head back, hands draped on the wheel, then using her tongue to urge him into sudden spurts of acceleration. But now she was uncomfortable. As she began using her hands, lips and tongue in the combination she knew would make him cum quickly, Cleve tensed, braked, and a loud hollow thump came through the floor as the car tipped, skidded and crunched to a stop.

In a cone of torchlight the wombat looked like a section of smooth dark stone that had fallen from a rock face. When they turned it over, one of its front legs almost came away. Cleve swore and lit a cigarette. Alice asked him to give her a hand.

No, not this time, Cleve said and stepped back onto the road.

Alice pleaded with him, reminding him of how much she'd been wanting to find a wombat. She said its family name: *Vombatidae*. She said Imagine how he'll look beside the paddymelon and the quoll.

Cleve flicked his cigarette away. It tumbled, throwing sparks. You're too obsessive, he said.

That's rich, coming from you, Alice said. Mr money market man. When you talk about the stock exchange your eyes glaze over. I always think you're about to start dribbling and rubbing your hands together.

Can we not do this? Look, let's just leave it here. Wombats are heavy. We won't be able to get it in the boot. There are a lots of other animals.

Alice trained the torch on Cleve's face. He shielded his eyes and said Fuck. Then she lowered the beam. Your zipper's undone, she said.

Cleve zipped himself up and said I really don't want this animal in the car. Are you coming?

No. I want you to help me. There's a groundsheet in the boot. I always make sure there's a sheet there, in case …

Cleve walked to the car and got in. Closed the door.

Alice moved the torch beam over the wombat's back and legs. There's not much blood, she called to the road. She put the torch down and rolled the wombat onto its back. It was heavier than she'd imagined. She tried rolling it up the slope, but its legs caught in the undergrowth and it fell back into place.

In the car she sat facing away from Cleve, looking out through a panel of speeding glass. Cleve had stopped talking. When she studied his reflection, she saw a man with no imagination, and it shocked her to realise she'd been with him for almost two years.

Alice lived in a two-bedroom caretaker's cottage in the south of Sydney on what was once a farm and series of orchards, before the land was divided and sold off as housing allotments. The road into the cottage was narrow, weed-lined and gutted. It divided two rambling sandstone horror shows with white concrete pillars and stone lions on the fencepost. The people who lived here thought Alice more than a curiosity. They avoided her. There was talk of her being on the run from something. This talk was not without some truth.

The cottage seemed to grow out of the end of a small paddock, where machinery parts gleamed, where a many-layered stack of tin sheet roofing remained as an apartment building for rats, mice, insects and the snakes that demand high payment. Out the back, the free-standing chimney stacks of a dead building; a large blue granite boulder like perma-nent, elevated shadow; mounds of bricks under the indigo bells of Patterson's Curse; the shell of a tractor; and three ironbark posts with no memory of the fence they once supported. From the outside, the cottage seemed conservative, deeply shaded by a sloping verandah. Two cane chairs on a concrete slab. A hammock strung between crepe myrtles. Inside, it was dark though comfortable: an open fireplace, paintings of birds and animals, a kitchen gleaming with hung pots and pans. Alice's bedroom was at the back of the house. Her bed was made by a woodworking friend – a queen-size, low-based bed made from rough-hewn redwood. The spare room contained the furred, feathered and scaled proof of her skill with what she called *the tangible afterlife*. The room was always closed, though its gamey smell was constant in every part of the cottage.

Alice did not encourage visitors. She'd been more or less a loner since childhood. Her small circle of friends knew better than to drop in unannounced. To socialise, she went to their houses. Cleve had given up on trying to change her. At first he'd called her eccentric, a word she despised. Then he called her crazy, his words carving a two-week silence into the air between them.

Alice had read extensively about taxidermy. Then she'd done a course, which ended when she felt she'd learned enough. She disliked conventional methods, feeling that not enough care was taken when attending to the animals. The furred shells of their bodies required tenderness and understanding, not just technical ability.

Her crows, wired into a stalled, gleaming flight under the ceiling, seemed to be fighting each other, or coming together in a mid-air coupling. A nankeen kestrel was dropping to a kill, the paired cages of its talons measuring the distance between the mouse and its death. Once, in candlelight, the kestrel had turned to look at her. She had asked What's the view like from up there? The kestrel had answered Excellent, and thanks for asking, then snapped its beak and looked down again. A flying fox moaned and wrapped itself into sleep.

Lying in bed, she would often hear the animals shifting in their skins. It was a comforting sound. She gave them names, voices. She positioned them in various locations, and on waking would see them again, their undersides lit with sunlight, their eyes hunting.

Despite her reservations about Cleve's ability to be spontaneous and wild, she liked the way he earthed her, when she needed grounding. He could be such a straight, boring man, and his temper had scared her on more than one occasion. But he loved her, he said so, he was generous with his time and money, and he gave her confidence, when she was *Out of her skin* – a term he once used when she was raving on, obsessively, about birds and animals. About the *afterlife* of birds and animals. Alice had come to see the term as a black compliment. She had written the words on a card and had pasted the card on the wall above her bed.

Being on the dole, Alice had no money for her taxidermy materials. Cleve provided these. At first he was more than happy to do so, but then, when he saw how much this activity meant to her, how deep she went into the craft, he became worried. His suggestion that she might be spending too much time with dead things was met with vehemence. She was happy while working, and he decided to let it ride, though it troubled him profoundly.

Road kills provided Alice with most of her birds and animals, but now that she no longer had a car, she relied on her outings with Cleve. These were too infrequent, and although he would sometimes bring her a possum or parrot, she needed more. She had asked farmers if they could let her know if any small animals had died, or been killed. There had been two phone calls. She now had a lamb and a kelpie pup.

Cleve suggested they go up the coast for a long weekend. A colleague from work had offered him the use of a shack on the beach, near Forster. He'd been talking about getting away for weeks, to do some fishing and walking. Alice responded enthusiastically. She'd not been well. A grey gauze of anxiety had been keeping her tethered, and she'd been inside too long, reading and sleeping, leaving the phone to ring out.

They left early, the car loaded with camping utensils, clothes and fishing gear. Driving out of Sydney, the Pacific Highway already thick with coast-bound traffic, Cleve talked seamlessly, brightly, about work, about how much he'd been missing Alice. She felt safe, warm, her fingers playing with the hair on the back of his neck.

At Forster, having unpacked the car and aired the shack, they went for a walk on the headland. Below, on a long stretch of beach, fishermen and children, dogs and gulls. Alice sat behind Cleve, her arms around his waist. Inhaling the scent of his shirt, she drifted off into a daydream layered with peace and quiet and long, slow sequences of lovemaking. Overhead, a pair of eastern rosellas clowned and leaned before they dropped and angled away, their heads like caps of flying blood.

They ate an early lunch in the shack's sunny front room. A bottle was opened. Then another. Pleasantly drunk, they made love on the floor, sliding on the lino in sweat and a wine spillage. Then they went to bed and slept, wrapped in each other's arms, waking and sleeping, listening to the surf and wind.

They woke late in the afternoon and drove down to a beach on the other side of the headland – a small, isolated cove bordered by dark basalt rocks and low scrub. The track to the beach was veined with deep ruts. It was overcast, the sky leaden with low cloud, a smell of rain on the make.

A lone fisherman wearing a yellow raincoat stood back from the waterline, his beach rod a tapering black line, threading the swell with gleaming monofilament. Back from the waterline, like a tapering, sea-polished length of tide-wood, was a huge mulloway, its silver scales glazed with sand and blood. Cleve had never seen such a large fish at close quarters before, and he asked the fisherman questions about bait, conditions, times and tides. The man answered him quietly, confidently. He was perhaps in his late seventies, his face lined deeply, with grey stubble on his jaw. As they spoke, Cleve kept looking at the mulloway as if its presence were casting the net of a spell. Alice left them and went to the water's edge, twisting until her feet were under the sand, going deeper with the flush and run of each receding wave.

Cleve returned to the shack to get his fishing gear. Alice watched the old man for a while, marvelling at the way he cast out and fed line to the sea, his graceful movements at odds with the bent back, the gnarled hands. Then she walked off down the beach, inspecting shells and driftwood. When she turned back, the fisherman was lying on the ground, his rod beside him on the sand. She ran to him and saw that he was pale and in trouble. He tried to say something, sweat beading his face. He grabbed at his raincoat and sucked in a loud lungful of air. Then he collapsed into himself. And did not breathe. Alice looked up. She shouted for help. There was no one on the beach. She did what she could with what she knew about the breath and the heart, when they faltered. She leaned into his chest, watching his face, amazed at the muted bone sounds that came from beneath her working hands, though it could have been the perished folds of his raincoat. She blew her breath into him. His mouth tasted of old bait and beer. She worked on him until she was sure he was dead, and then she fell away, exhausted. To look at him. To listen.

When Cleve drove onto the beach, he thought Alice and the old man were resting, talking quietly. She got to her feet as he approached. She told him. She seemed too calm. She walked away a few yards, and when she turned back Cleve was kneeling beside the dead man.

We should take him to the hospital, Cleve said. He was looking into the man's face. Isn't that what happens, when you find dead people?

I don't know, Cleve. This is a first for me. What about you?

Do you know where the hospital is? I think I saw a sign in town. It's a medical centre. Most likely someone there will know him anyway. It's like that in small towns.

Cleve got up and took a step back. Maybe we should just leave him here and go to the police.

Alice stiffened. No, let's take him with us. Come on, we'll put him in the back of the wagon.

I don't know. They say you shouldn't move a dead body. They'll need to check the scene.

Jesus Christ it's not a murder. The guy had a heart attack. I was here, remember.

Still, I think we should leave him. Cleve looked up at the sea. The tide's going out. He'll be high and dry for ages. It won't take the cops long to get back here and do their work. Look, even if we take him to the hospital, we can't just piss off. They'll call the cops. We'll be asked questions. Bloody hell, I mean, either way we could be up to our necks in questions and paperwork all fucking night.

Alice turned and looked at the dark place at the end of the beach where the track entered a dense screen of trees. We don't have to tell anyone, she said.

Cleve went to stand in front of her. He looked at her from under his eyebrows. No. Forget it. Whatever you're thinking just forget it. We're taking him to the cops. Come on. You get his legs. I'll take the arms.

Cleve gathered up the fisherman's rod and bait basket and put them into the back of the four-wheel drive. He put both hands deep into the cavity behind the mulloway's gill-rakers and hoisted the fish onto his shoulder. At least we've got dinner, he said, and lowered the fish into the wagon. Then he walked over and took the fisherman's hands. Come on, he said, grab the feet.

Alice hesitated.

You've got to help me. Take his feet.

When she didn't move, Cleve started dragging the fisherman towards the wagon. Fine, thanks very fucking much. Leave me to do the work. Why don't you build a fire and make a cup of tea, I mean we've got all night. The dead can wait, right? He struggled and cursed, staggered and then fell over.

Alice laughed. She tried to stop, but couldn't. She muzzled herself with both hands but the laughter came through, loud and cruel.

Cleve sat in the sand, a dead man's arm draped over his waist. He took a deep breath and held it. He took up a handful of sand and watched it pour from the end of a fisted cup. A black thought appeared and he welcomed it. The thought broke open inside his mouth like a seed under furious heat. You fucking bitch, he said. If I'd been the one to die out here, would you treat me this way? How long before you found me a warm place to lie down?

Alice did not answer.

Would you leave me here for the crabs and gulls? Cleve removed the fisherman's arm from his lap and got slowly to his feet. Come on, tell me. He took two steps and was standing close to Alice. How long? He tapped her hard on the shoulder. An hour? A night? He pushed her in the chest.

Don't do that, Cleve.

Don't do that, Cleve. Jesus, listen to yourself.

Cleve looked down at the fisherman. So, are you going to help me? Fuck it, Alice, if this was a kangaroo you'd be busting your guts to get it in the car.

Alice moved quickly. She slapped Cleve hard on the side of the face. Then she slapped him again. Cleve lashed out, punching her in the mouth. Alice screamed and fell over. When she looked up, Cleve could see that her lip was split and one of her front teeth was angled and loose. Blood was dripping from her chin.

Sorry, but you know … Cleve cut himself short and took the fisherman's arms, staggering under the weight in shifting sand. Fuck it, Alice, he said, pausing for breath. You deserved that.

Alice got into the four-wheel drive. Cleve dragged and cursed. As the fisherman's torso collapsed into the back, followed by his legs, Alice slipped over into the driver's seat, hammering the door locks down as she went. Then she started the engine and moved off. Cleve tried to stop her, clawing at the door, but the wheels found purchase in the tracks of other vehicles, and she was gone. Cleve shouted and kicked at the sand.

He watched her go. He watched until she'd turned onto the track and then he started walking, his head reeling between waves of fury and remorse.

It was dark. As he entered the track he could hear fruit bats coming over – the soft, blunt fannings of air, and the muted collisions of wings and bodies with leaves and sticks high in the canopy. He stopped to listen, to try and calm himself. His heart was racing. Ahead was a small, narrow wooden bridge over a creek. He thought he saw something move across it – a rat or bandicoot perhaps – and then, further on, a shape he could barely define, a shadow with no source of light in the middle of the track. As he stepped onto the bridge, a vehicle's spotlights blinded him. He covered his eyes and swore as the vehicle roared and came tearing down the track. He was hit at speed, his hip splintering as he was thrown into the railings, his head spearing into the main pylon at the beach end of the bridge.

His death did not come instantly. He lay breathing erratically, his ruptured organs shutting down like large sea anemone. Alice heard him die. She was crouching beside him. One long, uneven breath, then another, and then a loud, wet, lung-draining pulse of air.

The cottage chimney is smoking. It's winter. The grass and weeds around the yards have taken over. One light is burning.

One window the colour of amber. Alice is in a rocking chair in the kitchen, reading. The stove is ticking. Empty bottles line the floor. She turns a page and drinks deeply from her glass.

What's that? You're going to have to wait, she calls. I've nearly finished the novel.

She closes the book and looks over her shoulder. She goes to the stove, opens the door and checks the fire. She takes two small logs from the wood box and feeds the flames. Oh for fuck's sake, she says, can't you wait a minute? Oh alright then, I'm coming. She walks to the spare room and puts her ear to the door. She smiles. Opening the door, she stands outside and peers in. Walking back into the kitchen, she takes a flashlight from the shelf, clicks it on, and returns to the spare room. She trails the beam over birds, marsupials and dogs, fixed in various positions of stealth and repose. In the far corner, the beam finds a yellow raincoat, buttoned to the neck, then the face of an old man. His eyes are wide with amazement. He is leaning back, his body fixed to a darkwood post, his hands tense around the butt of a fishing rod. The rod is curving over, straining under weight. The line angles down to the floor. The monofilament gleams in the flashlight. At the line's end, a man's face with a large hook through his top lip, which has been pulled out dramatically. His eyes are closed. On his head, a blue woollen beanie. His head is all that remains of him. The skin of his neck merges seamlessly with the gill plates of a large fish, the scales on its long tapering body throwing muted sparks of silver. It's a wonder you can say anything at all, Alice says, the beam playing over the hooked and startled face. Who's out of whose skin? she asks, and kills the flashlight.

Kabul

David Brooks

*Why were they in Kabul? Chantal had no idea.
She wasn't sure if Charles knew either. They both
seemed to be spinning out of control. By now she
had abandoned herself to the challenge of surviving life with Charles. She had lost track of all
borders and distances ...*

The Life and Crimes of Charles Sobhraj,
Richard Neville and Julie Clarke

*There are things seen, witnessed, glimpsed in the
world beyond ourselves, that go immediately
inward, as if they were external projections of some
deep, internal dream – correspondences, that
should be asked not what they are, but from where,
what country within us they come, and why it is
that they should now, at last, appear.*

Correspondence, Alain Dufort

From one of the narrow side streets, an old woman
ambles into the parking lot, squats and defecates
between the cars. It is midday, Aix, the city of dogs.
We are only feet from the main thoroughfare, only
a block from the Hôtel Casino. No one else sees.

As she passes, her dress still caught up behind her, she glances at me as she might at a bird or parked car – or rather her eye falls upon me, without interest or defiance.

'Sophia,' the night porter says – I have not told him what I have seen, merely asked about the old woman in the square: 'That is Sophia,' as if she were well known in the town, as if he were pleased I had noticed her.

*

The nurses, if that is what they are: I cannot tell how many, or what is going on behind them, further into the shadow beyond the wide, open doorway of a barn or ancient stone warehouse – a *remise*. They are standing about a large bench that may be an operating-table, perhaps a mortuary slab. One holds up her gloved hands as if in defence or surrender, or simply to keep the blood from falling on the stone. Another's hands hang by her side. Between them, on the table, head falling back from it as if to look blindly toward me – as if he or she is too long, too tall for the space they're laid upon – is a man or a woman, I cannot tell which, only see, too far away to identify, a ghost-pale face, upside-down, and long black hair hanging limply from it, stark against the white of the sheet. Some of the nurses (*are* they nurses?) look up in my direction, as if sensing that somewhere out there in the desert heat – perhaps in the old bus that is slowly negotiating its way through the crowded square – someone is watching them. They are all wearing the same long gloves, bloodied almost to the elbow. Just as they slip from my view – just as the bus turns left at the corner of the square – one of them seems to reach deep into the body cavity. Correspondence. The beginning of a trail. A turn-off, between paragraphs, into the whiteness beyond.

I cannot tell why I think this is Kabul. The dust, perhaps, or light. When I think of Kabul there is not, at first, a great deal to remember. Some talk I once heard of a restaurant there, where travellers on the Asian Highway gathered; an image I once saw of a merchant standing on a cobbled street; stalls of carpets and brass-ware stretching out, behind him, toward the vanishing-point.

*

My friend tells me there is cannibalism in Kabul. The tense puzzles me. I would understand it better if he said *there had been*, as perhaps there was, in the time of the civil war, and the siege by the Russians, the Mujahadin. But *there is* is a different matter. So much so that I think he is saying something else, something quite other than that.

*

Dry. So dry. When a shell hits there is mainly dust, small puff-clouds seen through the binoculars. No particular target, unless rocks, hillside, something buried or dug in there, silence. And roads to the city, four of them, snaking out over the vast plain. Lorries, jeeps, trucks, sometimes carrying small platoons, sometimes farm produce, sometimes prisoners, often only the dust.

*

She told me that it was alright if I wanted to hurt her, but I didn't. There was blood everywhere — over the sheets, the pillows, my hand — but it wasn't that. She had to leave the next day, she said, and by noon she was gone. I wrote but there was no answer. The next time I was in the city I left a message, but she didn't return my call. When I found her apartment I thought I heard a sound inside, but when I knocked the door stayed closed. I was confused: if I had hurt her, would she have stayed?

*

At a dinner party I meet someone who has lived in Kabul. I ask him about the cannibalism but he is sceptical. He reminds me of the Zoroastrians, the Parsis, and the Temples of the Dead, the wooden platforms, exposure of bodies to the birds. Vultures eat the flesh of humans, he says, most certainly, but humans do not. An operation, on the other hand, or post mortem, these things were possible, given the exigencies of wartime. If, that is, it was not merely a dream; if I saw what I saw at all.

*

P. is a dark place, or was that winter, and cold, right through to the bones. An upper and a lower city, set on and around the hill. Arches, colonnades, places where people can meet in secret. A broad, cobbled avenue leading to the main piazza. Rude waiters, avaricious landlords. And at the end of a dark side-street the long staircase down to the Street of the Minotaur and its musty hotels, sad attic spaces, proprietors reluctant to show you their rooms because they know that you will not stay. A long, long staircase, almost a thousand steps.

*

*Ka*bul? Ka*bul*? I have heard it both ways, as if there were two places, split by the tongue. Is it necessary to know the actual city? Or would knowledge of the actual city mask the other, prevent us again from arriving? Entry from Pakistan or Iran is not easy. There are border-posts. And within the borders, the sieges, checkpoints, further borders. When the city is occupied by one force, it is the other force that prevents us. *If the city could be entered it would not be the city.* Hence the dependence on fragments, fortuitous glimpses: any other kind would undo itself. *Why would I go there*, my friend writes, *if I could imagine it?*

*

In Afghanistan they have been twenty years clearing the land mines. We see it repeatedly over the years, whenever something within us draws our attention there, as if it were a need, a part of us – images of people in makeshift hospital beds, their bloodied stumps balled in thick bandages, children growing up without hands, feet. There is violence even in the metaphor, if that's what this is, but perhaps that is the point; people straining out of the skins of themselves; in every construction, every artefact, these moments of rupture.

*

In a book about Charles Sobhraj, the gem-dealer–drug-runner who murdered so many on the Asian Highway, I read about him and Chantal, and how they were imprisoned in Kabul – how he escaped, in pyjamas, onto the Street of the Carpet-sellers, and went to Paris, leaving her in prison. How he drugged her mother at the Paris Hilton, to get his own daughter back, then was caught again and spent a year in a Greek prison before he made it back to Kabul, only to find Chantal gone.

*

A sparrow has flown in through one of the large, open windows and is hopping about between the restaurant tables under the feet of the waitresses. Out on the square a couple in their mid-thirties are arguing. They are trying to keep their voices down but their anger is evident. First one moves a pace or two away and the other follows, and then it is the other who moves away, as if the anger itself were a rope, only three or four yards long, tying them together, or this were a dance of prisoners.

*

Late at night, unable to sleep, I find myself thinking about Sophia: how, when I was leaving the city, I saw her sleeping, in her pile of rags, in the white marble entrance to the *Credit Agricole*. How I found her again, in a dream, on the long flight of stairs: the rushing, the pool of light, the people grouped about her body under the pile of rags. How the stairs continued downward, into a further dark that the dream did not let me bring anything back from. How I had realised, years later, that this dream may have meant that she was dying, that all along I might have known this without knowing. How there is no one, after all, no one to tell.

*

A television has been left on in an empty room. On the screen, several men are standing by a well in which they have just discovered the victims of a massacre. Some of the men have cloths over the mouths and noses, to shield them from the smell. I almost said 'over their faces', as if to shield them also from the sight, as if to shield them from knowing.

*

It is not always the body, not only. Kabul is within us, but is also a landscape of the days, a positive to their negative, a trace. Weeks marked by craters, explosions of shells. Months marked by lies and betrayal. A field-map of engagements, tracks leading inland. (There, on those ridges, a hideout. And if you could get to it, a view of the city. The minarets, the domes, convoys moving in or out. The land dry. The puffs of smoke where the shells hit. [Or in winter, when it is covered with snow ...])

*

On one side of the great plug of stone upon which P. sits – you could not call it a hill – is a rent or fissure like a crack in a curtain, though the men in the city have always had another name for it. Seen from the outside it is like the opening of a large cave, the entrance to an underworld, although in fact it is far taller than it is deep, and the people of P. several centuries ago tunnelled down from the main piazza to create a set of long staircases, hidden from their enemies, by which they could enter or leave the city. The modern city has widened the tunnel and replaced most of the stairs with escalators. You can see, each morning and evening, a long procession of people of all descriptions, standing almost stock-still as they are taken up or down into the darkness.

*

We exchange what we know: the long civil war, the damage, the land mines that turned the Dasht-i-Dargo into the Desert of Death. I talk about the Taliban and the restoration of the holy law, the executions, the severing of hands, the ineptitude of the peasant government. He tells me how the population undermines it – the small flashes of colour, the eyes – but is also grateful for the peace, a kind of hard certainty after the terror. Again Kabul is not the subject, or is, unexpectedly. One of us is weeping. *There is nothing to do but damage*, I tell him, but even as I say it I know it is the damage speaking.

*

We are in Kabul now, at the Intercontinental. The weather is hot and the air-conditioning is not working. The electricity goes off at night and for some stretches during the day. There is talk of rebels in the hills but the hippies seem to get through. You can buy lumps of hash in the markets for a song, good, rich stuff, and all sorts of drugs at the pharmacies. But the problem is getting it out, and there's a limit as to how much you can use while you're here. I prefer the icy vodka martinis, and the bar is a better way to meet people ...

*

Cannibalism, they say, is a site, a sign, a recurrence, whenever we fear the return of the repressed. Looking within, trying to seek out what is buried, is a kind of self-eating, or that other thing, an unleashing of something that might somehow devour us.

*

People on the long staircase at dusk, descending, widely spaced. A small group of students talking animatedly, a businessman, an elderly woman with a shopping basket – the couple from the square, part-way up the middle flight, the only people ascending, he a few yards ahead of her, studiously not turning, and she behind, climbing slowly, as if lost in thought, holding her scarf to her face against the cold wind.

*

No story is seamless. In every story there are unopened rooms, passageways, shafts leading to other stories, staircases, draughts arriving from dark, cavernous spaces that may be stories the mind is not ready for. Between one fact and another, one clause and the next. Even the long story of your life that you have been rehearsing over and over. You walk across a landing and a board breaks beneath you. You pause to let someone catch up and there is a door you had not seen before. You turn around, to tell them, and the person is gone.

He saw Chantal only once more, four years later in a house in London. He knocked on the door, she let him in, and they talked in the hallway at the foot of the stairs. He offered her money but she wouldn't take it. He seemed anxious to go, kept looking at his watch and back towards the door, as if there were a car waiting outside.

*

In the Hôtel Ana, a short street from the stairs, on the balcony of a room I had strayed into thinking it was my own, two doves were perched close together, so white, in the late light, with the dark cote behind them, they seemed to be haloed or to burn with a cool, invisible flame. I could not imagine creatures more perfect. Even now. It was as if I had discovered the city's secret, come upon it in a moment of great intimacy, nakedness. One expects fury, horror, the Minotaur, and instead this serenity, this pure, unsuspected light.

*

There are no endings, only sites, only moments of pause or clarity: landings, parapets, points where the stairs pass a window and you can look out briefly before descending – or climbing – into the story again. In one of his dreams he calls her at dusk after a day full of rain. She is driving through hills smoky with oleander. From the top of a rise she has just seen the sun setting, on the far ridges, into a nest of burning cloud, or the light from an ideal city they might soon be reaching.

In another dream he is in Kabul once more, searching for her desperately on the Street of the Carpetsellers, pushing through the crowd with an excited urgency, anticipation rather than fear, watching himself even as he does so with a strange, calm aloofness, as if from a balcony above the stalls. She is nowhere to be seen, he reflects from this vantage, watching himself flailing, nowhere, but an evanescence, a sense of her is everywhere.

The Resurrectionist

James Bradley

London, 1826

In their sacks they ride as in their mother's womb; knee to
chest, their head pressed down, as if to die is simply to return
to the flesh from which we were born, and this a second
conception. A rope behind the knees to hold them thus,
another to bind their arms in close and the mouth of the sack
closed about them and bound again, the whole presenting a
compact bundle and easily disguised, for to be seen abroad
with such a cargo is to tempt the mob.

A knife then, to cut the cords, and, one lifting, the other
pulling we deliver the sack of its contents, slipping them forth
onto the surface of the table, naked and cold, as a calf or a
child stillborn slides from its mother. The knife again, to cut
the cords which bind the body to itself, the cord and sack
retained, for we shall use them again, much later, to dispose
of the sacks and shreds.

Together then we take hold of them, forcing their bodies
straight once more. Although their limbs do not loll, nor are
they stiff, despite the chill that lingers in them, their rigor
already broken by the graveside as they were bent and bound
for sacking. Instead they shift beneath our grasp, moving with
the peculiar malleability of a corpse caught midway between

death and putrefaction. It is an ugly task, yet what ugliness it has lies not in the proximity of the dead but in the intimacy it demands of us, the closeness with the flesh and substance of their bodies.

When they are done, laid pale and naked on the table, we begin. First we turn them upon their faces, exposing the flesh of the back and buttocks, mottled purple and green with what might be bruises where the blood has pooled in the hours after death. If the flesh has begun to spoil there will be blisters forming soft, pale pouches of fluid which break when they are disturbed, but even if their flesh is still sweet the skin will be moist with the liquid that seeps from the skin and cavities like sweat. Sometimes the anus will have been plugged by those who dressed them for the grave, and if it has been, the obstruction must be removed and disposed of. Then, taking rags, and water, and vinegar, we begin the work of cleaning them, our hands moving carefully across their skin, the smell of the vinegar mingling with the darker scents of the dead, the movements of our hands economical yet not without tenderness as we wipe and wring.

Once the back and the legs are done we turn them over once more. We work from feet to groin, groin to chest, arms and hands, coming at last to the face. Here our work is most careful, our folded rags cleaning around the folds and bones, wiping the cheeks, the sunken pits of the eyes. Sometimes the lids will be open, caught in the stillness of death, and the eyes beneath them will be visible, their orbs cloudy and colourless as the eyes of the very old, as if pale with cataracts.

Once the washing is done we draw fresh water from the butt in the yard, fetch soap and razor. Cold water still, cold for the cold. Then, pulling the loose skin taut we begin to shave; first the scalp and face, the hair coming away in wet clumps to expose the knobbled dome of the skull; then the chest and armpits; then finally the cold instruments of their sex, the blade of the razor rasping across their skin. Sometimes we will nick them as we work, but no blood comes, the wound pale and empty.

How we know this is work to be done in silence I cannot say. Only that this is how it is, how it must always be. At other times we move amongst them as if they were not there, talking and laughing as we lug and cut and tidy the pieces, pushing them aside as casually as one might a book or a jacket which lies where one means to sit. But here we work quietly, speaking no more than we must. It is as if this is a ritual, this washing of the dead: as one washes a baby clean of its mother's flesh, so we wipe the grave from these stolen dead, bring them new into the world.

When our work is complete the sacks are tidied away, the buckets emptied, the rags rinsed and left to dry. There are books to be done: our master is most particular about the keeping of accounts, and so the payments we make to the men are carefully recorded. And so, while I mop the cellar floor Robert works quietly on the ledger, making notes of payments made, checking the balances against the contents of the cash-box, his face masked behind the look of quiet sadness he wears when he thinks he is unobserved. Tonight there were four, and by the time we are done, and we climb the stairs to the yard to wash our pails and hands at the pump, the sky has begun to lighten the high roofs which surround us. From far off there can be heard the ringing step of a horse upon the cobbles, but otherwise it is still, the air cold, the water from the pipe colder as we scrub our arms, over and over.

*

Mr Poll slips two fingers into the dead man's mouth, pulling the jaw open once more.

Death is a mirror, he says, in which life is reflected for our edification.

Beneath his fingers the dead man's tongue can be seen, purplish-grey like an oxen's on a butcher's slab, and beneath it the darker mass of the tumour, displacing it. As I watch he presses it down, tilting the head so the throat becomes visible. For several seconds he stands staring in, as if he has seen something that interests him then, his curiosity seemingly satisfied, he withdraws his fingers and pulls back the lips to expose the teeth, yellow and brown, higgledy-piggledy in the ulcerated flesh of the gums.

If death is a mirror, I find myself wondering, what lies behind it?

Finished with the mouth, Mr Poll turns to Robert.

We will begin with the chest. The state of the vital organs must be ascertained.

As he speaks a cough catches him midway. Turning away from us he withdraws a cloth from his sleeve and covers his mouth, stifling the sound. Robert and I watch him without a word. Once he is done he scrunches the cloth and secretes it back in his sleeve, the movement at once insouciant and furtive, as if its casualness were a show meant to disguise something he does not wish us to see.

A tremor runs through the body as the scalpel pierces the chest. Almost like a sigh, the gas that has swollen in the cavity is released, escaping in a soft breath. The smell is not quite foul, more the clinging scent of the butcher's yard, that peculiarly clammy scent of cut meat intermingling with the first sweetness of putrefaction. I no longer choke on the smell, indeed there is scarcely a smell a body can produce which still turns my stomach, but although I do not gag I am aware of it, even after all these months.

The skin divides in a wake behind Mr Poll's scalpel as he slices in one smooth motion from neck to groin. Carefully he makes more cuts at the top of the incision and at the bottom, then, with a practised motion he pushes his fingers into the incision and peels back the skin, revealing the bright red of the flesh beneath, the white ribs and bright yellow of the fat that nestles against it.

Releasing the flaps of skin so they drop down over the arms, he takes the bone saw Robert holds ready for him. Steadying himself with a hand upon the exposed flesh of the chest, he places the saw against the ribs and begins to cut. The teeth bite into the bone with a wet, splintering rasp, small flecks of meat and bone scattering before it, spattering the aprons we each of us wear. When he is done he lifts the sternum and ribs away, exposing the organs nestled in their broken cage of bone; grey, blue, black. Extending a hand he touches the heart, his thin fingers lingering upon the bluish muscle.

It does not beat, he says. I do not answer, for the statement seems incontrovertible. But after a moment Mr Poll looks up, his watery blue eyes fixing me with their cold stare.

Why not?

Still I do not answer.

Do you think it a foolish question, Mr Swift?

I shake my head. No, sir, I say.

Perhaps you think its author a fool instead?

No, I say again. I can see Robert watching me beside Mr Poll. His eyes are steady.

Then why does it not beat?

Because he is dead, I say, but even as I speak I know I sound half-witted. Mr Poll regards me disappointedly, then returns his attention to the corpse.

And I suppose when once it beat, it beat because he lived, he says.

He does not look at me as he speaks.

*

When our work with them is done, we sack the remains, pile them in the cellar. It is ugly work, for even in November the scraps turn rotten and begin to stink, and the limbs and torsos grow swollen and foul. Robert tells me that this is nothing; in the summer the sacks are almost liquid sometimes. A man comes before dawn each Thursday, and Robert and I load the sacks into the cart in the half-light. The houses opposite stand silent, still sleeping. Mr Poll's neighbours know our business, yet it is wise not to remind them of the facts more than we must.

The man who comes for the sacks is a former soldier called Miller. He does not meet our eye as he takes the sacks, just grunts and thrusts out a hand for his fee. Robert has told me that once, two years ago, it was Mr Poll's wish that he travel with Miller to see that the remains were disposed of discreetly and completely. The day chosen was in late spring, a fine, summery day. Robert rode beside Miller, his companion never speaking, so they travelled in silence, the cart jolting beneath them. All through the long morning and into the afternoon they travelled east along the river, until they came to a low field, surrounded on one side by trees, and bordered on the other by the river flats. The place was silent, no birds singing, save for a flock of geese, who rose as one, honking and shrieking as the cart approached. In the centre of the field the grass was burnt away, the ground scorched and filthy. Robert helped Miller unload the sacks. When they were done, Miller took the wood he had piled upon the sacks to disguise them for their passage through the streets and built a pyre. Then, one by one, he shook the sacks out, spreading their contents thinly across the pyre. Finally Miller set it burning, stoking and tending it as the flames consumed the rotting remains. The fire spat and crackled where it took the fat, the flesh bubbling and blackening where it lay. Robert said hell might look like this, legs and arms and heads, jumbled and broken and burning. The smoke that rose from the pyre was oily black, and evil, and Robert said it clung to his clothes like a stain. It was dusk before the fire was done, the embers glowing in the fading light. And in the gathering darkness Miller took up a post from the cart, and, stepping out across the remnants of the pyre, brought it down again and again upon anything that remained; bone, skull, jaw, sparks rising in clouds around him, like fireflies or shooting stars against the great space of the night.

II

But what of the soul? demands Marshall, his voice breaking across Mr Poll's.

Mr Poll pauses, regarding Marshall coolly.

My apologies, he says, although all know he has heard Marshall well enough. You have a question?

I asked, what of the soul?

Mr Poll stares at him for long enough for all present to comprehend the foolishness of Marshall's tone.

And where might this soul have its seat? he inquires at last. Raising his eyebrow he taps the bisected heart with one finger. Here perhaps?

When Marshall does not answer Mr Poll scoops up the brain from the dish in which it lies.

Or maybe it is here?

Looking down at the brain he weighs the ghastly thing in his hand, as if considering it. Then with a smile he looks back at Marshall.

No doubt there is a gland somewhere, some fattened lymph or somesuch which you have in mind. After all, were not toads said to have jewels within their skulls?

Marshall licks his lips, his face reddening. He is an oafish, bullying sort, and like many of his kind is skilled only in the infliction of ridicule, not its receipt.

Please, Mr Marshall, if you know where this gland might lie I am sure we would all care to be informed.

Nervous now, Marshall looks about himself, no doubt hoping to spy support in the faces of his fellow, but they avoid his silent appeal. Perhaps like me they have been on the receiving end of his jests. The brain still in his raised hand, Mr Poll stands, waiting. From behind Marshall comes a snigger – it is Hibbert, a nervous lad, but handy with a knife – and for the first time a flicker of amusement appears on Mr Poll's face.

I cannot say, Marshall says all at once, his manner bold, as if he still thinks he can bluster his way out of this.

No, says Mr Poll, his voice heavy with sarcasm, I daresay you cannot.

A ripple of chuckles moves through the assembled students. Mr Poll does not acknowledge them, but he lets them take their course. It is a peculiar vanity of his, this grim theatre of the dissecting room, in which he plays his part with relish. Not just the ritual of the cutting itself, although there is theatre enough in the precision of his cuts as he opens the belly or unpacks the innards, as there is in the deadpan humour with which he works, but in his role as the great man, impatient with the foolishness of the world about him.

Like a true showman he does not let the moment outplay itself. Before the chuckles have died away he silences the audience with a raised hand. The room falls expectantly silent, watching Mr Poll as he wipes his hands upon a cloth, then, reaching into a pocket beneath his apron, he produces a small vial. Reaching across to me he takes a piece of paper and places it on the table and shakes the contents of the vial onto it.

Iron filings, he says, his eyes watching his audience carefully. They assume no shape, respond only to the forces that act upon them: gravity, movement in the air. They are inert.

No one speaks. Watching his audience, playing them, Mr Poll produces a small rod of metal from his pocket.

Yet if a magnet is introduced, we see something quite different. As he speaks he places the magnet upon the paper, and the filings begin to quiver and move, marking out the lines of force that surround the magnet against the paper's pale background. In the hush of the room the sound of their motion upon the paper is audible, a soft rustling.

No agency is visible, no collision of atoms, yet the filings move. How?

Magnetism? interjects one of the students.

Mr Poll regards him chillily. An astute observation, Dawson. I only hope for your patients' sake it is not typical of your powers of diagnosis.

Several of the others laugh, but Mr Poll stills the levity with a glance. Indicating the subject who lies before him, his brainpan open and brain disgorged into a bowl, Mr Poll continues.

Consider, gentlemen, the man that lies before you. Once …

He looks down at the figure before him. In the light from the window the skin has begun to mottle, as if fading bruises swim beneath the skin.

... perhaps not quite as recently as we might prefer, he lived. His heart beat, blood coursed in his veins, his form was wracked with all the appetites, suffused by all the joys of life. Yet today he is cold, the movement of his heart and blood stilled, the life that inhabited him, as meaning inhabits a word, fled. Already this shell he inhabited begins to decay, in a week it shall be rotten, in a month worm's meat, in a year little shall remain. Yet what has changed? What force that once held his tissues back from this inevitable decline has failed? What is it that has fled?

His soul, quips one of the lads, Hibbert, I think, and a smile flickers across Mr Poll's face.

It is an idea you are reluctant to let go of, this soul of yours. But we are scientists, gentlemen; we seek to cut through the veil of superstition, to pierce the very fabric of existence. Would we not turn away with pity from a savage who invoked witchcraft to explain the movement of the filings upon the paper? Then how can we let ourselves accept such poor answers to our own questions? It is our purpose, our duty to strive to elucidate the nature of the force which gives breath to our clay.

He pauses, watching his audience. When he continues his voice is softer.

Our answers lie here, in this cold flesh. For in these tissues we shall divine life's shadow, the ghost of the force which once gave his body its vitality, which drove his heart so it flickered and beat. Just as these base filings find order in the magnet's field; just as electricity will make a newt's leg twitch, so too there flows a force within our selves, a force which drives the fuse within these shells we call our bodies, no more and no less mysterious than the invisible lines of force which move these filings. This gentlemen, is what we seek, the nature of this force. The secret, in short, of life itself. Perhaps like Marshall you might think soul to be an appropriate name, but if it is, then it is a soul we shall soon be able to measure with the instruments of science.

*

When the lecture is done I stand in the library window and watch the students file from the house into the street below. A blustery wind is worrying itself about the street, whipping leaves and grit between the narrow buildings, and as they mill about, talking and laughing amongst themselves they seem to lean into it, their arms folded against its chill. No doubt it is their intention to repair to some tavern or other, but for now at least they seem in no hurry. Marshall does not linger, nor, as he strikes off into Soho with Dawson, do I think he will be back: at two guineas a session it is an expensive way to be made a fool.

The others will return though. Even at such a price these lectures of Mr Poll's are sought after. Not all who seek admission may have it, for unlike van Hooch and Carpue and the others who offer private instruction in the science of anatomy, Mr Poll is a man of considerable means, and need not tolerate a dissecting room crowded with the sons of shop-keepers and clerks at a sovereign a time.

His achievements are many – surgeon, anatomist, scientist – since Hunter no man has done so much to advance the cause of each. As a surgeon he has few peers, his services commanding a fee second only to that of Sir Astley of Guy's, and although to be thus exceeded rankles with him, there are many who declare him the greater of the two, and point to his less eager courting of the blandishments of celebrity.

But for all his proficiency in the craft of surgery, Mr Poll's true achievements are greater, and deeper. Although the great work that shall form the cornerstone of his enduring fame remains unfinished, he has spent a lifetime dedicated to the task of deciphering the book of Nature. From morning until night he works, his restless energy filling the house, his curiosity sometimes seeming more like an appetite, a monstrous hunger which burns within him. Through our doors pass many in whose cases Mr Poll has taken an interest, sometimes living, sometimes dead; from each he gleans something more to assist him in the task he has taken upon himself, that of understanding not just the structures of the body but the very essence of life itself.

In his quest for understanding he has dissected all manner of creatures – dogs and horses, rats and apes, insects, snakes, even once, so Robert tells me, a rhinoceros, late of a menagerie in Chelsea – seeking in each to divine the structures common to all. And I have seen him perform experiments that seem to insult the will of the Creator – a human tooth, pulled still living from the mouth of a baker and sewn into the comb of a rooster which took root and grew, the corpse of a newt given brief and slippery life by the application of electricity, a false womb made from the bladder of a horse, in which a blood-slathered lamb foetus grew still and cold. So too does he seek out the monstrous and misshapen, those freaks in whom the script of Nature does not read true, for in their imperfection we might, he thinks, find the image of perfection.

Nor is just the dead who must bend to our will. I have seen Mr Tyne catch cats in a wicker trap of his own making, and more than once bring men here, bought for a florin in the ginshops of St Giles so they might sample some medicine or other and their reactions be measured and recorded. And a week after I came here I lured a dog to the house with a piece of meat in order that Mr Poll and Charles might open its chest, feel its living heart jump like a fish against our inquiring hands.

*

In time the last of them move away along the streets, no doubt to some tavern, in which they will drink and laugh and take their ease. I return to the table. It is a messy thing, to open the dead, and it is my duty to ensure no trace is left. Beside the basin that contains the heart, bisected to reveal its fat-clogged interior, the piece of paper Mr Poll used in his demonstration still sits where it was left. For all its theatricality his demonstration has nonetheless unsettled me: it is a fearsome thing this atheism of his; to put aside all belief which cannot be measured, to leave behind the strictures of what the world calls morality. Taking up the magnet I weigh it in my hand. On the paper the filings mark out the ghost of its presence. For a time I stand looking down at the pattern, then I take my hand and brush it through, the filings rustling as my hand sweeps them before it with a sound like dead leaves. The passage of my hand lies across the paper, a long mark erasing the elegant whorls; without the magnet's presence they do not return to their former patterns, instead they lie inert, unresponsive. Such thin things, these lives of ours; cheap got, cheap lost, mere flickers against the ever dark, brief shadows upon a wall. This life no more substantial than breath, a light that fills the chambers of our body, and is gone.

Jack the Dancer Dies

Wayne Macauley

They are digging a hole for me somewhere, out where the horse paddocks start. What I have visited upon all their loved ones they will soon visit upon me. They will all be there: mothers, fathers, sisters, brothers, aunts, uncles, cousins, friends. There will be beer and sausages, party hats and fairy bread. They will all take turns to spit in the hole, unseat their pants and with their legs astride it do what I dare not mention in such polite company as this. But I will go peacefully, I will not fight. I do not have the spleen. They will bury me standing up, no doubt, the easier to jump on my head.

My name is Jack the Dancer; it is not a name I chose myself but I have lived its meaning out. When they trip lightly into my arms and dance with me in the dark they feel better for having given the nameless a name, and a good laconicism at that. They might have called me other names – recently they have – but this one had me written all over it. I know all the steps, can sweep even the tangle-toed off their feet. And they come willingly to me, that is what those ignorant killers with their picks and shovels will never understand. Did I ever dance with anyone who did not want to dance with me? Have I ever taken anyone who did not want to be taken? To each their time comes, and for each the dance that is theirs alone.

It all began a long time ago, I do not recall it exactly. Come on down, Jack and dance for us, they'd say, come and show us those steps again! Oh yes I am a dancer all right, a real Fred Astaire: I was ballroom champion in my day. Around the bar I would dance, to the music and the clapping, until someone was thrust with drunken hands into my open arms. This night it was Jenny, Sam the publican's wife, and to the laughter and the whooping I took her thin body close to mine and danced her out into the car park and the dead urban boondocks beyond. She was found come morning with not a mark on her and my reputation was made. *If you've had enough go and dance with Jack, he'll take you out of here.*

After three days' grieving, Sam the publican barred me and bade me never return. You are an evil man, he said, and your reckoning time will come. (I am not evil, I am not good, I am a necessity, that's all.) For years I wandered, cast out like Cain, through suburbs, towns and cities. I slept below bridges, in back lanes and bus shelters but I could always find someone ready to dance and I danced my fair share away. Man, woman, adult, child, I did not discriminate, I took them all. Sometimes I took groups, like a kind of barn dance or eisteddfod, off we all went to The Great Beyond, in a conga-line, bumping our hips. Everywhere my reputation preceded me, everywhere my customers pursued me, but everywhere, too, the selfish bereaved tracked me down, beat me with sticks and drove me away.

I settled down in a suburb on the edge of the city and made there a quiet home for myself behind the changing sheds at the local football ground. It was a house open to the weather on three of its four sides. By day I hid in the storm-water drain; at night I sat drinking on the orange plastic chair beneath the flickering fluorescent light. It did not take long for the soul-sick to find me. The grapevine is long, its tendrils innumerable; they slither through half-open windows and touch you gently on the cheek. Once called you rise willingly, find your keys, go to the fridge, make up a plate. You kiss your partner, put out the cat, check the children, tuck them down.

The air outside is still and quiet and the stars above pulse and shiver. You are going to see Jack the Dancer – from far off I hear a car door slam. I comb my hair, trim my cuffs. I still get nerves even now. I go through a few quick steps with the broom and sweep away the broken glass. I set up the old Sanyo on the orange plastic chair. Come, come, I say, don't be afraid, give me the tape and let's hear. They choose the music, and therefore the dance; some say goodbye to this idiot's tale with an overture from Mozart, some with their favourite pop. We eat a little of the food they've brought and drink the wine, spirits or beer. I did not then and have not since asked for any more payment than this. Come, come, I say, don't be afraid, step over here out of the light.

Young Sandra McLain, that's where I went wrong, I should have sent her back straight away. She came to me pregnant with a pain in her gut. It kicks all day long, said Sandra McLain, and talks to me in the night. It doesn't want to be born, but I am almost full-term – what am I going to do? I sat her on the chair and put my ear to the hump. The best thing for man, said the little voice inside, would be to die quickly – better than that, never to have been born. Are you quoting? I asked. Yes, said the voice. I relayed all this to the mother. It's like this every night, she said, I can't stand it any more. But I cannot take the child without taking you, I said, this is really outside my brief. But Sandra McLain did not want to be taken. I put my ear to the hump again. You in there, listen, what you're asking is impossible, I do not do unborn deaths. What are you, said the little tyke, have I brought my poor mother here for nothing? I want to go back where I came from. Is your name Jack the Dancer or not?

Yes, my name is Jack the Dancer; I am a real gangly-dangly vaudevillian Fred Astaire, and that night I danced the most peculiar dance with steps I never thought I had in me. Part jitterbug, part tango, part waltz, part jazz ballet, and yet none of these; singular, unique; with moves so original I surprised even myself. One moment the child was my partner, then

Sandra McLain, then both; one moment I saw the door open and the light far off, far away, the next the door closed and we were spinning in a vortex, my feet going nineteen to the dozen. This went on all night and well into the following morning; I could hear the trucks out on the highway but I could not stop the dance. Sandra McLain was gone now, had gone with the first light of dawn, all that was left was her shell and the hump and the belligerent child inside. Do you want to go or not? I asked. Of course I do, it muttered: for those who have already lived, it said, a short dance is enough, but this is life and death for me, I want to enjoy it while it lasts. My God! Is there no end to our selfishness, when even a child in the womb can demand a birthday party that goes on all day!

By lunchtime I was exhausted. I am an old man and not as fit as I was. By the time the child let go and swam dog-paddle through the air down the corridor towards the light, I could hear the distant clatter of football stops in the changing rooms and a siren blast in the afternoon air. I retreated to the storm-water drain, like an injured dog licking its wounds. I had taken them both, mother and child, and with it brought down years of unleashed vengeance upon me. Sandra McLain's de facto hired a plane and had the skywriter write high up in the blue ether: Jack the Dancer Must Die. They hunted for me by torch-light and paid children for news of my foxholes. Medicos stroked their beards and said they knew about me all along. By night I moved from one hideout to the next, a fugitive damned for doing only what he had been asked to do. In a wrecking yard I hid in the boot of a Volvo sedan and listened like a frightened mouse to the crying and caterwauling outside. So they will kill me, I thought, but then who will kill them? Who will take them down to the river and bathe them in blood? I am not evil, I am not good, I am a necessity, that's all. Without me they will live forever – let's see their faces then!

A child punched a hole with a hammer and nail and put his eye hard up against it. I watched the pupil widen. You have just looked Death in the eye, I said, now go back and tell them you've found me.

Out on the horse paddocks the preparations are almost complete. The hole has been dug, the trestle tables laid, the fence festooned with streamers. Some mother has baked a cake, the children all wear fairy wings. They will be given little plastic toy trumpets to blow, just like Gabriel did. Through the nail-hole I see violet, giving way to a dirty pink. Night is falling, they will soon be here. I hope the killing is quick.

From the Fake to the Real

Ellen Rodger

'So I said to him, when are you going to get those black stumps fixed? What girl is going to go out with you with a mouth full of black stumps like that? This is how he laughs. He's trained his laugh so that his top lip covers his black stumps. And this is how he walks. He hitches his jeans up like this. His jeans are so tight it's like he puts them on, separating his balls first, one on each side of the seam. And his hair's like this. Like steel wool.'

Jasmina's elbows are bent, hands up around her ears. Fine strands of elastic have snapped in the straps of her bra and poke through the fabric. Her back, grey looking from hundreds of moles, appears to be full of wriggling, tightly wound nerves.

I turn away from the mirror and run a finger down the sharp bone of Jasmina's nose. Up close her face is fraught with vicious thoughts. And yet Jasmina calms me. She can take my hand, unfold the fingers, look into my palm, and show me particular points that when stroked, alter your body's entire chemistry. Jasmina can put me to sleep.

'George is waiting,' I say.

'Talk him into having a double. I want to see what you're like in the room.'

Jasmina and I have never done a double. I'm not sure that I'd want to.

I walk down the hall to Room Five, the height of my sandals making my knees crunch and torturing my calves into tautness. I think of my calves as the muscles that hold my ego up. In the corner of the room is a new addition, a white metal structure shaped like a body for clothes to hang on. No one has hung his or her clothes on it yet. The shape is right, but its hollowness makes it eerie.

George looks up from drying his toes.

'George? Do you want to see Jasmina as well?'

George says no. George wants just me. George has a thing for me, and I would be disappointed if he'd said yes.

In the girls' room I squeeze lube onto my finger and reach up under my dress.

'George doesn't want a double.'

'Paul's coming in later. Maybe he'll want one.'

Paul won't want a double. Paul is in love with Jasmina, and thinks she loves him too.

'You prepare our snack,' I tell Jasmina, 'and when I'm finished we'll sit together and eat.'

George's clothes are not sitting on the cane chair or hanging from the hollow white structure, but are folded up on the floor, tucked away in the corner like the belongings of a very neat serial killer. A packet of Panadol sits upright in one shoe. In his long, flabby earlobe is what looks like a tiny diamond stud. Up close I see it's a droplet of water.

George! Watch!

I roll my dress down my body, step out of it, and for a moment stand in my underwear, then I stroll around the room in just my sandals. Unsettled if my dress isn't folded properly, I fold it up and place it on the white shelves.

No need for preliminaries with George. I climb straight onto the table and let him feel me. Just in time I see a small grey velvet bud I have almost squashed, picked from the backyard by Jasmina and placed as a memento on the towel at the bottom of the table. I see it just in time and take it between my fingers. Shaped like a toe, it feels warm and plush and alive. Little stabbing pricks from the pimples on my knees, caused by kneeling on oil-sodden towels, remind me to tell Julie that cold water will never remove the oil.

'I saw you the other day,' George says, trying to locate my g-spot, looking over at the white hollow body as if an obscure source of eroticism lay there. 'You walked right past my shop. You looked so ordinary, compared to now.'

I saw George too, on my way to the supermarket, and got such a fright I went home without doing my shopping. I've seen clients in all the shopping centres in my area now.

Desensitised by compulsive visits, and only half-hard, George decides that today he'll pay extra and have sex. He gives me the money, at pains to remind me that he doesn't normally do this, and it's true, at least with me, that usually it's just hand relief.

I do my best with his cock, folding it up inside me, and chant a seamless story about Jasmina and me, and though George says he knows it isn't true, that Jasmina and I have never been together, his cock doesn't know and quickly straightens out.

And while I tend to George my mind is on another story, an unfinished one that wouldn't interest him, which begins with the thread of an unraveling sleeve, and a tiny ball of spit that landed on my shirt, and a coat taken off and put back on and taken off again. And thinking of it moves me so quickly from the fake to the real I lose track of George, only to find him in the middle of a conversation I've been absent from.

'The truth is, I was going to kill myself. I was going to end it all. You wouldn't think I'd think like that, would you? Looking at me now, and knowing what you know.'

'No,' I say, but I could.

And then it's over for George. Strangely, I'm never in a hurry to get dressed. George chats about the time he was a Scientologist, and I lay out fresh towels while he has the first shower, and then I have a shower and put my clothes back on with some regret.

'You know what that bastard did? That bastard just made me come.'

Dolly's antique stilettos, attached to her feet by two very thin gold straps and laces that tie in bows around her ankles, cause her to wobble and stand on her tiptoes, never applying her whole weight, fearful that the delicate heel will snap. The burns on her face, hair remover left on too long, have settled into three finger-length streaks. Around her shoulders is a towel distractingly discoloured with spilt bleach; she is cutting her hair and stuffing bits of it down the hole in the floor through which a beautiful blue light glows, a reflection from the plastic tarpaulin that protects the renovations downstairs.

Describing the bastard only as 'Ugly! A real ugly bastard,' I am unable to identify him from the others, but Jasmina knows who Dolly means and draws a sketch depicting his posture on the table – body curled up, shaped like a prawn – and suddenly it's clear.

I hand the toe-shaped bud to Jasmina, difficult to relinquish once it's been in your fingers, and then she stands behind me with the toy cock positioned against my body, teaching Dolly and me how to do trick sex. The tiny black heart at the top of her thigh seems to have retained the heat of the instrument that applied it, which passes through to me. Wetness beneath my toes – Dolly's spilt foundation – ends up trodden all over the floor in little pink dabs.

Lesson over, we throw the cock at the wall, its jelly consistency gluing it momentarily and leaving damp marks when it releases, the carpet's blue fibres adhering and turning its pink surface muddy grey. New, it smelled like a miniature pink umbrella I was given as child, so feminine it was almost sexual, with cartoon girls holding parasols in each flared segment. Now it smells of nothing.

Out in the backyard, banked pink and yellow clouds have turned the pale grey concrete steps very white, as if lit. We eat our snack, toast left to cool topped with ice-cold shavings of butter, and through the slats in the fence watch a small girl with conical limbs grab a ball from a boys' game in the backyard next door, holding on to it with a nuisance's tenacity, screaming and handing it back only when one of the boys approaches her case of Barbies.

Jasmina loops her legs across mine.

'I used to sit like this with my father when I was a little girl. I used to say to my mum, eat your heart out, Mum, eat your heart out.'

She says eat your heart out slowly, long spaces between each word.

'Imagine saying that. Imagine saying eat your heart out to your mother.'

She looks childishly triumphant for a moment, then turns despondent.

'I just wish my mum could have been happy for me, that's all.'

Jasmina touches my hand and I have a small sleep, and when I wake up Victoria is there, wearing a short dark-blue skirt with a patch pocket at the front and a sleeveless black top which flattens her breasts. There's something dignified about the way Victoria flattens her breasts for work. She pats metal-coloured lip-gloss onto her lips with a small foam wand.

'Has Shane been in?'

Victoria and I share Shane, but really he belongs to her. Shane hasn't been in.

'He phoned me this morning and asked when you were working next. He said he'll be coming soon.'

Tiny beads of water cling to the hairs inside Victoria's nose. Her black tights, so dense there's nothing to see through them, are flecked with papery petals of disintegrated lavender flowers. At first I thought the small grey balls that fell from her washing were rolled-up spiders and jumped back, but they're lavender heads that she picks from the backyard and puts in the dryer with her clothes. I have put my nose to her clothes but I can't smell the lavender.

Sharing Shane causes me to be shy with Victoria; we sit together mostly in silence. Sometimes she'll tell me which girls are offering particular services and how much they charge, which she discovers by listening at closed doors. I wonder if she listens at mine.

Victoria needs the spa in Room Five so I use Room Two. Room Two's mirrors, on opposing walls, offer up a sickening infinity of reflections. Water from Room Three, Jasmina's room, gurgles along the pipes beneath the floor. I'm hugged, and given a series of dry kisses on my shoulder.

'Are you going to be, like, passionate? 'Cause that's what I'm missing. That's what I'm not getting at home.'

Purple holes in his back where pimples used to be disappear as his skin turns the colour of tomatoes. His boots, limp on their sides near the chair, are so old and broken down I'm drawn towards sympathy. Lodged in a corner of the ceiling in Room Two is a grasshopper which Victoria refuses to remove. Over and over the grasshopper hooks a feeler with one foot and folds it down to its mouth.

'How much time is left? I wish it didn't ever have to end.'

I straighten out his fingers, which curl up as if the skin is drawn too tight.

'Like this?' he says, trying to grasp the subtleties.

'How'm I going?' he asks, plodding on.

I lay him down and have to ease his arms apart, placing them alongside his body. His eyes are closed tight, and what at first I thought were crooked teeth are actually two sets of front teeth, one behind the other. When he rises up to kiss my neck I gently push him back down.

Dark leaves brush the sliding-glass doors which are covered by cream vertical blinds that never sit neatly together. Renovations downstairs proceed deep into the night, and he keeps opening his eyes, thinking someone is banging at the door.

Afterwards he looks as though he's woken unhappily from a dream. I pull him up by the hands and turn the shower on, and he stumbles around, asking my name, then drags his sad boots on, not looking up at me again.

'One of your admirers was just on the phone.'
I want it to be Shane.
'Who?'
'Shane.'
He comes in, eyes hooded from smoking too much pot, face heavy and swollen with the held-back appearance of someone on the verge of tears. When I try to find out about him he doesn't know what to say, and blushes, embarrassed that I'm interested. He says he hasn't cried in years. But life is bleak, he says, sprinkling Dettol on the shower floor, because the apartment he lives in, a drug dealer's apartment, is so large and high up and has so much glass, it's impossible to keep warm. There isn't any furniture except beds.

Sounds from the girls' room are like clouds at the window of a room in which you've been lying for days, alone and sick: a reminder that a room is not the world. It's disappointing sometimes, to realise it's only a room. Steam from the shower reveals circular patterns of mould on the ceiling, and the sweep of a mop that tried to remove it. It's almost dark. My heartbeat resolves to intermittent beats, and at the backs of my knees and in the arches of my feet is the suggestion of a collapse. I want to lie down, huddle, turn to one side, hold soft clothes. I want to fall asleep.

Shane's tongue, the palms of our hands, my fingers, all touch very lightly. Everything touches lightly, except when I'm holding his cock. I'm above him, and one of his hands is on my back, encouraging me down. He calls me girl, and we kiss, and my mouth seems to fill with water.

I don't want Victoria to know this. I don't want her to know I kiss.

My room feels very empty when Shane leaves.

Overwashed, my hands carry the residue sting of antiseptic soap around the nails. The faintest red map – an irritation, an ambivalence, a kind of rebellion – appears beneath my fringe. I lift my hair and apply the tar-based cream we use for skin complaints, which smells vaguely of roadworks.

In the fierce laundry light Jasmina's lashes shadow and lengthen on her cheeks. A trail of ants pause along their path from the window to the sink, a crowd of dead ones decorating a small gold pool of poison, mouths pointing at the liquid, bodies facing away. Jasmina wipes her face with a handful of toilet paper, roughly pulling the skin.

'Be careful,' I tell her, 'treat yourself more gently,' but already she is walking away from me to stand at the door and receive cool air from the backyard. I reach around; her nipples coldly brush the undersides of my arms. An earring lands soundlessly on the floor. I pick it up and see webs of hair, glossed over by the vacuum cleaner.

Footsteps echo on the terracotta tiles in the hallway; in the glass brick wall the colours of business shirts pool, elongate and disappear. And we wait, eroticism and the dollar pulling us towards the ring of the doorbell, revulsion and the company of each other pulling us the other way.

'An engagement!'

Dolly's cut hair lies in damaged piles at Paul's feet. Jasmina holds out her hand, meagre blue jewels hardly glittering, tears in her eyes for all the wrong reasons. Freckles I'd never noticed before stand up on her face like an illness. Paul moves towards me, then recedes when he realises I'm not going to be kissed, then I go towards him out of embarrassment, but he's already moved back. Finally I connect with his cheek, the skin transparent with happiness and smelling of Jasmina's transferred perfume. As my eyes sweep past the kitchen I see that it's been rearranged: old scraps of lino pulled up, the table moved. Dolly is scrubbing down walls. The burns on her face have fried and formed blisters beneath a coating of moisturiser.

Julie looks in the fridge for something to toast with, but there's only orange cordial. Paul says he'll go to the bottle shop, and as I let him out a young man in an oversized turquoise suit, dark curly hair blonded at the front in orange wings, approaches the door, trying to sell mobile phone plans. I dismiss him brusquely and as he walks away, body miniscule in the baggy suit, I imagine him in a greater, sadder context: financially competitive amongst friends, full of thwarted ambition, held just afloat by hope.

I don't want to go back into the girls' room yet, don't want to see Jasmina's forlornness at the months of futile effort she's put into Paul. I want Paul to hurry back and bring with him my cold shield of contempt.

'To my Miss Australia.'
  'Miss Nude Australia.'
  'Don't say that.'
  'That's what I was. I wasn't a Miss Australia.'
  'You're my Miss Australia.'
Twice as old as Jasmina, Paul rarely sees her outside the parlour. That he doesn't complain makes him seem complicit in Jasmina's deceit. Once I saw him in a mall in Chinatown, sitting at a table, head low, eyes scanning his surroundings. 'Looking for young Asian girls,' Julie said.

After he leaves Jasmina changes out of her work clothes, nipples soft and withdrawn through her singlet, then phones her boyfriend to tell him the bad news about the worthlessness of the ring. She slips the toe back and forth through the band as she speaks, crying softly. Dolly, unable to process another's unhappiness, continues scrubbing the wall with a scourer whose leaking green dye discolours the paint.

My client, all lugubrious eyes and pretzel-shaped cheekbones, seems unaware that we went to high school together. In his agitated state he is hardly looking at my face. He sits in the waiting room, eyes mostly downcast, opening his briefcase to show me that he has brought his own scissors, a small pair that he has just now purchased from the supermarket in the mall. The price tag is still on them.

A pitiful gratitude hovers in his voice. Grounded only by the briefcase on his lap, he looks hopeless and stupid and seems to be asking, Am I? I take his hand and lead him to my room as if answering, No.

In the tenderness I feel towards him, partly because I recognise him from school and he doesn't appear to recognise me, and partly because of this dear little act of buying scissors, I give him a very good price for his request. And though I don't like the way that lying down causes my hair to fall away from my face, I lie patiently as he trims my pubic hair.

My schoolmate is in a hurry. There is a sense of compulsion about his visit, which increases the tenderness I feel towards him. He would have rushed from work to get here, stopping at the mall on the way, and he'll be on the train soon, and only a little late home. I imagine he has a wife and that he doesn't trim her pubic hair.

And suddenly I recall sitting next to him at a party when I was twelve, and my best friend's devastatingly handsome older brother observing me from across the room with cold, erotic condescension as I ate a slice of bomb alaska. That night, lips pressed to the flyscreen grid at my bedroom window, I smoked and tried not to think of my own brother's bedroom which now seemed much too close.

Trimming over, my schoolmate pours oil on me then climbs up onto the table and rubs his bare pubic bone against mine. Finished, his eyebrows shadow at thoughts of later trouble; he has stomped lasciviously through the puddled streets of childhood and now must arrive home with wet ankles.

Beneath bright candelabra lights I gather up trimmed pubic hairs, then turn the lights down low and close the door gently on eroticism's indefatigable attempts to make an absence of everything else, and the inevitable jar of absence's tissue breaking down.

I get rid of the boy who does his usual weekly trick of slobbering all over me then not staying, after all that. But afterwards I worry. I have a suspicion that the boy is retarded, and that his weekly visits here, which never progress to an outlay of cash, are perhaps the closest thing he gets to sexual intimacy.

And I think of my own concessions to the real thing – the thread of an unravelling sleeve, a tiny ball of spit that landed on my shirt, a coat taken off and put back on and taken off again – and I run back to the door, intending to tell the boy that I don't mind that he never stays, but of course he's already gone.

A sediment of skin and dirt lies in miniature sandbanks along the turquoise step of the draining spa. Slowly, unmethodically, we clean our rooms, unwrapping Minties from the bowl at reception, disturbing tiny puddles in the indentations of the terracotta tiles in the hallway, reaching out to brush another's hair, lift a fallen strap, just to touch. A mild tug that we're hardly aware of delays our leaving. Conversation dribbles out, sentences don't quite match up; we're dumb with the comfort of money.

Unable to get a taxi, Jasmina and I walk to the train station, money stuffed inside our shoes. We hardly speak. We sit on the platform and watch mice dart from one shadow to another. Jasmina takes the ring from her purse and savagely scratches the finger it's meant to be on. Eyelids pinkly translucent from crying, she looks beautifully made up but in a slightly different way.

Glum-eyed station staff lean tiredly against mustard-coloured tiles that line the tunnel wall. A noisy drunk man approaches a woman holding a baby, and fondles the baby's fingers. Expecting the mother to recoil, I'm surprised when she smiles and seems comfortable with the drunk, as though the baby's presence neutralises any possibility of aggression. The woman's husband looks momentarily alarmed, but is eventually charmed by this brutish man whose body has softened. All around, people smile at the redemptive power of a baby.

And then the train pulls in, and the drunk man wanders off down the platform, pausing behind a young teenage girl. As they wait for the carriage doors to open, the man grabs her bum, digging hard between her legs. The girl looks around in shock, then half-smiles in shame. The man has disappeared. The audience has turned the other way.

The three lights on my answering machine look absurdly distant from my bed, as though I'm on a hill looking down at a sparsely inhabited town, reminding me of a morning long ago, on holidays overseas, when I was running away from a madman who'd employed me to clean up his hotel. As I ran, the backpack on my back caused the top of my body to over-step my feet so that I kept almost toppling over. 'Don't look back,' I thought, 'don't look back,' and when I got to the top of the hill I looked down to the other side and saw a small town, mildly lit, on the cusp of waking up.

The Cellist

Luke Davies

The world is so big, and we are all so concerned with our own affairs, that it is often a jolt to consider all those separate lives, all those billions of events, going on at any given time. Trillions, if you include occurrences at the subatomic level. Four years ago, on 22 October, I split up with my wife – at least, that was the formal date. Four days ago I met Stacey, whose entire stay here is to be five days, which is to say she leaves tomorrow. Today, surprisingly, we were making love. Or fairly surprisingly to me. Four days ago I wouldn't have predicted it. I hadn't noticed her much one way or the other, no more than I'd noticed anyone else here. It was something of a crash course in each other's lives, the aftertalk in bed, and possibly utterly pointless as we will most likely never see each other again, she being an American living in Italy and me having not much to do with either country. Stacey told me that while jogging at six o'clock one morning four years ago on the sprawling campus of the University of Iowa she was dragged into some shrubs by two men and raped. I was not specifically interested in dates but the story had horrified me, the suddenness of the awful events she described, and, to be honest, I had wanted to get a clearer mental image of the morning – was there frost on the path? was it light or dark at 6am? But I had simply asked, 'What time of the year was this?'

'October,' she said. 'October twenty-second, to be precise.'

I could no more tell you the date of our wedding than I could build a submarine by hand. But for some reason this date – October twenty-second – flashed in my mind, the instant Stacey said it, as being the date I'd moved out of our home those four years earlier. It is all so puzzling – all the trillions.

Stacey is one of the world's best cellists; according to the others staying here, maybe one of the best two or three, and apparently quite well known, as classical musicians go. Me, I tend to buy CDs according to composer, when it's not just a specials bin thing. I'm not one for reading the covers in detail, nor for remembering names. Faces, yes. And: Stacey's pungent musk, already (I imagine) lodging itself deep inside my memory banks as I was peeling off her underpants and burying my face in that part of her which had so little to do with her abilities as a cellist and which, it rapidly transpired, loved to bump and grind so. She had been invited to Iowa for the Pablo Casals Festival, which was being held in honour of the twenty-fifth anniversary of the great man's death. The fact of the festival's existence in Iowa is a disturbing piece of trivia which even now is nagging me, at least eight hours after we made love, in the form of a question: what's the connection between the Iowans and the Spanish cellist? The fact that any number of events could be occurring at precisely the same time your marriage formally ends, despite the logical certainty of it, is, as I said, something of a jolt. 'It was a turning point in my life,' Stacey said, 'because it was a near-death experience. Before this, I kind of had an eating disorder. I was, like, totally bulimic. I know it's weird to suggest that a rape could have a positive result, but I haven't been badly bulimic since. Plus I went off my Prozac three days later. This was all a very weird time for me. Those two guys were criminals, evil. But it's like I was lost, and self-destructive, and the rape snapped me out of a dream.'

Stacey is quite striking even though her teeth are a little grey, something that happens, I'm told, when stomach acids and tooth enamel cross paths on a more or less regular basis.

My own guess is that being raped is powerfully dreadful, possibly worse than being murdered since after you are dead you don't have to deal with the continuing consciousness of the horror of the event. It does not seem too much to imagine a world in which the giving or withholding of *permission* is respected as sacred and inalienable but this is certainly not that world.

In any case, one assumes that we move on, at times, from calamity and trauma, and now and then might find ourselves able to relax in the middle of mutually consensual sex. And yet now, eight-and-a-half hours or so after the event, I feel paralysed by a deep concern that Stacey will never be free of the rape, that even when she kisses someone (me, for example) those twenty rough fingers and thumbs will dig into her skinny wrists and shoulders and tear away her track-pants. Concern number two is that she seduces men she will never see again in order to engage in fleeting moments of near-anonymous sex, and that therefore I was not, in fact, just a guy she found so irresistible she had to jump him. Concern number two (a), just to bring things back into the present here, is that concern number two seems to deal exclusively with my ego and the question of 'How did sex come about?' rather than, 'Should I have had sex?' Concern number three is the logical extension of two but seems worse: what if Stacey's desire for sex had nothing to do with the desire for sex – say, for example, it was a compulsive need for approval – and she merely had this finely-tuned radar which was very adept at picking up that telltale sonar ping that showed another sick person in the vicinity? A person with, how shall I put this delicately without offending myself, less than the full six cylinders firing? Or eight, as the case may be.

What no doubt adds to my sense of unease is the fact that Stacey was married sixteen days ago. Her husband, a Russian, is one of the best violinists in the world. Perhaps some background is necessary. I have to admit the bare facts seem odd. We're in the north of Scotland, Cramb Castle, an artists' centre run by an eccentric millionaire, for which bursaries are sometimes available. I'm here for three weeks as part of a European Economic Community program for translators – I translate children's books from French into English, English to French; I'm completely bilingual, can go in either direction. Stacey's preparing her program for the upcoming year. Bach, Elgar, Schumann, don't ask me who, drift to us faintly most days from the music room. (Except a big chunk of today, I guess.) Stacey and the Russian spent their ten-day honeymoon on the Greek island of Samos, after which she had to give a series of concerts in Stockholm and Copenhagen before coming to Cramb Castle. The Russian husband had a prior guest engagement with the Chicago Philharmonic. Stacey had been offered the Cramb residency a year earlier, before the wedding had even been planned; the couple decided to go ahead with their original itineraries. (Career advancement, she told me, the who-did-what, the when-and-where, was more ruthless at the high end of classical performance than in the world of Formula One racing, though how she could verify this is beyond me.) The rest of us, myself and the other artists here, treated her with that cooing warmth the world reserves for new brides. At dinner last night Martin, the sculptor, commented that it must be tough to interrupt the marriage so early.

'We've lived together three years already,' Stacey said. 'We're used to different schedules.'

Still, I was more than a little taken aback when late this morning as a group of us (Stacey included) sat at the kitchen table avoiding our work and the conversation fluttered rowdily and without seeming pattern backwards and forwards, Stacey caught my attention for a moment and said, almost covertly, 'James. Can I talk to you? Up in the music room?'

And yet it wasn't covert. She had to speak loudly enough to be heard over the others. People talked here all the time. They didn't pre-arrange trysts to do it. And almost immediately I knew something was up. And I knew I had to act as if *nothing at all was strange about her request.*

I didn't ask the obvious, the reasonable question, 'Why? What about?' I said, 'Sure. When?' She shrugged and said, 'Half an hour?' I knew right then we were going to fuck. I wasn't even certain I wanted to. I felt the inevitability of compulsion. This thing had a tick to it, a loud internal clock.

I *felt* … a dryness in my throat, as if I'd been called to the headmaster's office.

'Can I talk to you? Up in the music room?' It was as simple as that. And one or two of the others, the women in fact, heard it, noted it, registered it. Lodged it away. That little gathering around the kitchen table was fairly bursting to pry.

And I looked at my watch. 'Half an hour …' I said. 'Umm, sure. I have to go back to my room and do a few things, so, er … half an hour is good.' As if we did it all the time, arranged meetings like that!

But at exactly this instant, the instant I was absolutely certain we were going to fuck, I thought of the Russian husband and, assuring myself I was in fact wrong, tried to find other explanations. I thought, absurdly, that maybe Stacey had a bright idea, perhaps something involving a collaborative project. Cramb Castle was an artists' colony, after all. The brochure even talked about 'the cross-pollenisation of ideas through and across the various disciplines'. I thought, absurdly, that she would suggest we turn some obscure children's story into a cello concerto, libretto James Middleton, score Stacey Stoyanovich. Yes, she had the Russian name even before the husband came along.

Yet what did I do in my room for that half-hour? *I took a shower. I left my head dry so it didn't look like I'd taken a shower. I paid special attention to the soaping of my balls and penis and hairy bum.*

I might as well have been sleepwalking.

Applicants to Cramb Castle must submit examples of their work, which go into the library for the benefit of all. When I walked into the music room Stacey was seated in an armchair in the window alcove overlooking the herb garden, facing away from me. The cello leaned against a wall. Stacey stood and walked towards me. She held up a copy of my ground-breaking *Chat/Chapeau,* a radical re-translation and reissue of Dr Seuss's classic *The Cat in the Hat,* for which I had won the Enfant Terrible d'Or the previous year.

'I love this! I absolutely love this!' she exclaimed.

'You read French?' I asked hopefully.

'Oh no – I just think it's so cute and all. These are really strong images from my childhood, and to see them with the French words – I love it!'

Well, I was pleased enough. It wasn't really any kind of response to my work; but after all, as I've said, I was a trans-lator of children's books. It was nothing new to me.

Nine hours after the event I find myself asking the ques-tion, What would I have done if she'd brought up the rape *before* we made love? It was strange enough coming after-wards. I might have heard alarm bells had it come earlier – something a little stronger than the ticking of the clock.

As it was, she put down the book and said, 'So ...'

'So.' I shrugged my shoulders. Oh, most delicious of antic-ipations and awkwardnesses.

'It's been nice getting to know you.'

'And you likewise,' I lied. Not that it hadn't been nice. Just that we hadn't, by any reasonable definition of the term, been getting to know each other. The place was huge; people worked; Stacey rehearsed; I translated (right now, Russell Hoban's *The Mouse and His Child*); random clusters would form in the kitchen as people took breaks; at night everyone came together for dinner at the Big Table. Three nights ago a group of us went for a walk to the local pub, forty minutes away. We drank and played pool. It was good to relax; one could go a little stir-crazy in the Castle. Stacey was among that group. We chatted a little. She said the crows reminded her of the crows in Wyoming. I can't remember much else that passed between us. An entirely affable American.

But afterwards, in the aftermath and the aftertalk … no, that is not correct. It was *during*, it was in the breathlessness, it was as our clothes were coming off, I said to her, 'I totally don't get this. You just got married.' She said, 'My husband and I, we have a strange relationship.'

I said, 'No doubt, no doubt.'

Afterwards, in the aftertalk, we hadn't said a lot, or not at first. Then suddenly, the story of the rape. And right away I began to feel a fuzziness, a tiny knot in the stomach, which began to grow and even now, nine-and-a-half, ten hours after the event, is tightening and contracting inside me. Because *there is nothing I can do to help her*. Was nothing then, and never would be. There was a time she experienced terror, worse than anything I'd ever know. I was bewildered, lost, walking away from the ruin of my old life and experiencing cripplingly high anxiety levels about the unknown expanse of the new one. I thought you could get liver cancer from fear so big. And these two things, these events, were happening at the same time. *What can you make of that?*

How on earth can we be expected to cling to a sense of continuity in the face of the violence of parallel existences, multiple universes?

I had stroked her face. 'Your husband, does he do this too?'

'My husband is a good man. You know what a power marriage is?'

'I guess I can work it out,' I said.

A while later I asked: 'Are you happy?'

She thought for a moment. 'I like my life,' she said. It was as good an answer as any.

Stacey spooked me a little. I fell into there so fast, that old clock ticking, and came face to face with her own lockdown. You know what else about bulimics? Her skin was slack, and papery, like folds of silk. She was only twenty-nine. She shouldn't have looked like that.

Arrayed in All Her Glory

Gerard Windsor

I

It was the Princess de Broglie's satin that landed me. In spite of my having always been quite indifferent to fabrics. Her blue satin is perfect in its arrest. Even in its glory it's being played upon by the great forces of change – the light and the shadow have fallen into place, the folds and the creases are established. This material should now start to fade, to fray and to wither. But for this moment, and forever, it's supple and incandescent. The planes and undulations of the blue sheen go on eternally. Here is the waterfall of the Romantics. The pool of the skirt widens from the waist, and cascades in an unbroken circle. As light skims the barely depressed hollows of the satin, white funnels unevenly down through the blue, and plunges through its own motionless spume. The satin re-establishes its tension, and the gleam disappears, catching just briefly, here and there, in the crinkled interstices of the grand descent. When I look at Madame La Princesse de Broglie, it's with the billow of this skirt that I start. And even after I have pulled myself away I keep returning to it. Yet it's the woman herself that enthralls me, not some mannequinned textile.

I fell for Madame la Princesse, not merely for Ingres' astonishing portrait. Why shouldn't I? If I can cry for little Nell and rage against Iago, why shouldn't I fall in love with the one-time Joséphine-Eléonore-Marie-Pauline de Galard de Brassac de Béarn, now and forever the Princess de Broglie? How could I not make a litany of her like that? The names and the titles have a part in it, I know. One of my mother's party tricks has always been to reel out 'Edward Albert Christian George Andrew Patrick David', the given names of King Edward VIII, an apparently dull man but one allowed a certain charming memorability by this string of names. But such a torrent of plosives is gross and graceless set beside the echoing vowels and the truly aristocratic lineage and even the linking hyphens of the Princess de Broglie. I remember that once, in the town of Riberac in the Dordogne, a young Frenchman confided to me that the Germans were essentially *unspirituels*. I understand. The motion and the sound of the names proclaim it.

Jean-Auguste-Dominique Ingres painted many grand names. Madame Paul-Sigisbert Moitessier, née Marie-Clotilde-Inès de Foucauld; Baronne James de Rothschild, née Betty von Rothschild; Vicomtesse Othenin d'Haussonville, née Louise-Albertine de Broglie; Mademoiselle Jeanne-Suzanne-Catherine Gonin; Queen Caroline Murat; Madame Philibert Rivière, née Marie-Francoise-Jacquette-Bibiane Blot de Beauregard. None of them however has the soft, lingering liquidity of the Princess de Broglie. The quality appeals to me, I admit it. Although it's only words I'm talking about. Her name. And her dress. The hooks of an infatuation.

Why should she transport me so suddenly? Ingres' figures have hung in my memory palace nearly all my life, unsigned and unacknowledged. *Jupiter and Thetis*, the young hippy god indifferent to the naked nymph leaning across his thigh; *Oedipus and the Sphinx*, the riddlemaster still on the front foot; *Napoleon I on his Imperial Throne; Joan of Arc at the Coronation of Charles VII in the Cathedral of Rheims*. Picture book desiderata all these, mythology and history rendered heroically and with the most detailed realism. Ingres one contributor among many. His master, David, and the launchers of Scots Greys charging and thin red lines holding, and pre-Raphaelite enchantments, and even Holman Hunt offering the *Light of the World*, a Christ immediate to me as no Old Master Saviour had ever been ... I felt that I had been there, that the viewing platform was perfect. The past done more sparsely than this, more impressionistically, seemed inauthentic.

These were all triumphal moments. No fury and mire in any of these veins. The only emotion was solitary exaltation, cold and implacable in the case of Jupiter and Oedipus and Napoleon, more warmed-up and lofty with Joan of Arc.

It was the narrative drive and the exactitude of human impedimenta – armour, weaponry, clothing, hairstyle, decoration – that gave me what I wanted. I had no interest in expression or subtlety of emotion or even the symmetries of tableau. Now that very passionlessness has me pacing through the galleries or turning the pages without pause. All these props of history were shifted into my imagination long ago, and now I'm wanting the sound and the fury and the lasting significance.

If I get rid of the trappings, or most of them, I get Ingres' best-known image. The *Grande Odalisque* is nameless. Nude, chief prize in the seraglio, yet something of a sovereign within that cage, she has so many of the assets of allure. The long curving half moon of a back; pride in her nakedness that is then set off by the trappings of opulence – the pearl-encrusted ruby on her hair-band, the gilt-heightened, peacock-feathered fan, the thick tassels of the headscarf on her neck, the sweep of its silken tail down her arm; the commodious divan, the hookah and its boiling water within easy reach; the damask curtain, of Tyrrhenian blue, being drawn aside and the dark mysterious triangle opening up. Above all, her turned head, and her eyes directly on the viewer. Yet, for all this, I don't know that even in my most febrile days my blood stirred very much at the *Grande Odalisque*.

She isn't sexy, the painting is not erotic. No wonder W.S. Gilbert could include her in a patter song; 'the grace of an odalisque on a divan' is an ingredient in the recipe for, of all things, a Heavy Dragoon. Her face is blank; there's neither invitation nor modesty to it. Above all Ingres' sole concern has been with composition. The haunch of her further leg is invisible but impossibly long; her right breast is a circular growth sloping upwards from just beneath her armpit and hiding its nipple behind her arm. In fact she is all monochrome skin – no nipples, no nails, no hair below her high forehead and her ear, no cleft between her buttocks. You could say there is no opening, no handle for desire. This is a young, handsome woman naked, and her name, her title, defines her by her sexual role, but in fact she is a latitudinal expanse of creamy white set off by – or maybe itself setting off – rich polychrome fabric. I gave no more of a second glance to the Grande Odalisque than she gave to me, or to anyone.

So I swept on, into Ingres' portrait galleries, and suddenly I am shaking my head and trembling – there are all these wonderful women. Yet now, barely four months after encountering this riot, I am settled with the Princess de Broglie. And nor has it been a matter of weighing up and choosing among all those riches. Initially yes, I was the child shown into the lolly shop. Everywhere beauty, elegance, poise, but also naturalness and accessibility to me. These were neither the heroines of history and mythology, nor the wigged and cloud-topped *grandes dames* of eighteenth-century portraiture.

This is all infantile? Why so? What other effect can be expected from the application of such exquisite painterly technique to the portrayal of young women? These were women such as I knew, or could know. When one of them looked out at me, I shivered under the gaze. This was no low-key, picking-up-the-children, trawling-the-supermarket-shelves kind of meeting. These women were, and still are, out to impress, to charm, and I am susceptible.

The first I saw was Louise-Albertine, the Vicomtesse d'Haussonville. The informality of her in her battleship grey silk taffeta, leaning back, her buttocks taking the pressure against the console table, her right arm draped across her forward-thrust belly. That downward gaze of the tilted head, the chin resting on the left hand and the index finger moving away, propping by itself up into the neck – there is just a shade of the coquette here. But the intimation is just as strong of a thoughtful woman, a challenging woman – or at least of the aspired-to desirability of those qualities. I can fall for Louise-Albertine with a clear conscience. She is much younger than I, nearly thirty years, but that age difference is somehow evened out by her being, I calculate, of my great-great-great-grandmother's generation. There is an equilibrium in our relationship.

Yet I suppose it is a matter of days that I remained fixed on Louise-Albertine. Even in that time I never thought of her as the Viscountess – her youth, the pose that I couldn't take quite seriously, and yes, her face. It's pretty enough, but it's not distinguished. It doesn't go so far as being common (a slur word, I know, but one I find I still have some use for). It's sweet, but the nose has no lines to it, and the wings of the nostrils are set back too hard against the cheekbones, and the complete lack of angularity presages a future falling into flesh. I don't remark these things when I first meet her. I'm entranced by the gaze and the frank pregnancy of her and the shimmer of that taffeta. Then I spend some time with her, and I think I have seen all there is to see, and my interest thins.

Any feeling I have for her is blown away when I meet the Princess. I should be precise about the chronology. The misgivings I have about Louise-Albertine aren't even emerging when I meet the Princess. Then I lose interest quite suddenly, I go cold on her. I look at Louise-Albertine and I'm puzzled by myself. Was I really swept away by her? But where is the enchantment? I look around uneasily. How foolish am I? It's then, with clarity, that I tick off the commonness and the play-acting and the rest of the flaws that I'm now embarrassed about, not so much for Louise-Albertine's sake, but for my own because I didn't immediately see them myself. But all this is after Joséphine-Eléonore-Marie-Pauline. The moment before I'm introduced to her, I think I'm still bedazzled by Louise-Albertine. The Princess, melancholy if anything, looks out at me, and one whole emotional seizure is trashed and I start again. Some time later Louise-Albertine stands in front of me again, and yes, I'm even-handed enough, but that says it all. I'm coolly bewildered by my past, even a little ashamed.

I'm entranced by the Princess de Broglie. I'm detached enough to acknowledge that she has a particular appeal for the late-middle-aged man. Not that she's that age herself. At the most she's twenty-eight, as she was when Ingres finished her portrait. But oh, she has all the bloom, the flawlessness of youth, but so too all the settled, sombre, wise compassion of maturity. Her grooming is meticulous, not a filament of hair loose, but the pearl-pale shoulders rise out of the diaphanous lace trim, and for once among all these plump-planed women, there is the delicate jut of bone, taut line of muscle, dimple at the throat. The seat of her gown, all we have of her form in that area, rears high and attention-demanding, but her eyes are heavy-lidded and sad, and the lashes hang as shade against the brightness. One hand hides itself away, awkwardly even, but the left hand dangles, almost in the centre of the picture, the fingers apart and idle and ready for use. My eye catches on these fingers; they are exciting, long and exquisitely tapered. The wide-band ring doesn't interfere with their efficiency; these are active hands, not mere carriers for ornamentation. Yet I look more closely at them and I realise they're as sexy as they are because the fingers are broken-jointed. Ingres has snapped her bones. He has treated her as one might a dead woman. The clinician reads his subject with accelerated forsight.

The young Princess has only seven years to live.

These are trophy women, I know, Louise-Albertine and Pauline. They are to hang on the walls of their husbands' homes. The husbands themselves are not painted. 'Have your jewel case with you,' said Ingres. For the Princess he chose her seed-pearl earrings, her ruby and diamond bracelet, her pearl necklace to be worn entwined as a cuff, her gold Byzantine-style pendant whose central ornamentation is a cross. To the flawlessly divided gatherings of her hair he attached satin rosettes and from them he hung marabou feathers sprinkled with gelatin sequins. Too much, too much, vulgar and ostentatious, hasn't the man better things to do with his art! But in this case it's not too much, and he's done wonders with his art.

The Princess has come into the room, and there are people already there, seated. She joins them, but with the utmost natural casualness, leaning forward against the back of an unoccupied chair in their circle. She leans on her right-angled arms, one hand tucked into her oxter, the other hanging quite idly. Oh yes, she is sumptuously dressed, she has just come in from the opera and has dropped her shawl and her gloves and her fan on the chair. But she is joining in now. She's not standing on dignity nor striking a pose. She wants to know what's going on. She's not staying, she hasn't collapsed into a chair, content to be carried along by whatever's already happening in the room. She's both too independent and too shy for that, but she's open and curious enough to stop and see what's in the air.

Ingres hasn't found a pose for her. He has cut the lowest of low-key actions out of nature. This woman is moving, this is a life drawing, this is what she does when the artist is nowhere around. Striking an attitude and holding it is not how he sees her, not how anyone sees her now. I think she is perfect.

A few rooms from where the Princess now hovers in the Metropolitan Museum in New York, Galatea feels the blood coursing from her unlocked heart. Pygmalion has chipped out the woman of his dreams and his own warmth and excitement has penetrated the pedestalled marble. He stands not on the floor but on the lowest box; he has been working on the small of her back, chipping in the delicate concavity that spills out onto the high slope of her buttocks. She has felt the heat moving forward through her belly and she arches her back and swings her torso towards him. He's taken by surprise, but already his fever for her is intense, and he drops his mallet and flings his muscular arm, clawing, around her waist, and stretches on tiptoe to reach his lips to hers. She slides her arm around his neck and leans, with ideal suppleness, sideways from the waist to meet him. For a few hours more he will forget to ask whether she is the best he could have done, whether one more attempt mightn't yield him a beauty and a satisfaction he couldn't previously have imagined.

II

The portrait by Ingres that commonly has applied to it such epithets as seductive, voluptuous, enigmatic, is that of Madame Duvaucey. She was painted in 1807 when the artist was twenty-seven. I see what the commentators mean. It's all in the face. Madame Duvaucey cannot be more than twenty, and her direct gaze has an imperial confidence. Her features are wholly symmetrical, varied only by the room's shadow on one side and the most delicate of beauty spots on her chin. In the almonds of her eyes the pupils hang dead centre and their lustrous, unblinking dark is some shade halfway between the deep brown of her hair and the black of her dress. Oh yes, she's a contained beauty, just the first shadow of a cleavage below the unflashy amber and gold necklace, her right hand in the act of unclenching, the cape barely clinging to that right shoulder. No doubt some minute frisson shakes me when I learn that Madame Duvaucey is not really one of Ingres' grand matrons, that Monsieur Duvaucey is irrelevant and not on the scene at all, that Madame Duvaucey is here, bewitchingly, in the twenty-first century, because she is the mistress of Monsieur Alquier, the French ambassador to the Holy See no less. Yes, Madame Duvaucey need do very little to be presentable at a papal audience.

Yet she looks so young. I'd have qualms about falling for her. The barriers between us seem rock-solid – such a disparity in age, and then her status as a popular object of desire. A sense of responsibility, and a vanity set firmly against being obvious or gadarene, are my protectors. I'm not doing violence to spontaneous inclinations. I'm not already nursing a secret yearning. Yet I know her severity appeals to me. Whereas there is nothing severe at all about the Princess de Broglie.

III

Ingres did a nude study for his Princess de Broglie. The woman has the shape of a centaur – but uniquely a female centaur of course. The artist has leant her forward, half side on, and the dark recess of her navel marks the geometrical centre of the page. The heavily blacked patch is an omphalos all right. For the hub of this drawing is the precise point where the human figure merges with the animal. The small of the back is a right angle. What we see, I suppose, is an elongated haunch, and behind the haunch the buttocks jut towards the side of the frame. They are reared. The artist's framing line first bisects the woman's back just as it starts its slope away to the horizontal, and then the line progresses in its strong rectilinearity down through the pubic area. The artist has rubbed the graphite hard to leave a dark stubble of pubic hair, and a strong linear fuzz links groin and navel. This marking of pubic hair is not found elsewhere in Ingres' work, except in a sketch of his own wife, Madeleine, surviving only on a daguerrotype. Otherwise the odalisques, or Thetis, or Angelica being freed by Roger have their pubic area curtained or it's hairless and undifferentiated from the unbroken snow of the belly. Nobody says that the Princess posed for this drawing. Ingres took his lead from his master, David. He wished to see how the body, leaning this way, thrust that way, might relate to the costume it was given. In David's day, in Ingres' early professional years, this made obvious sense; the light, high-waisted shifts of the first Empire, the men's trousered tights, followed the outline of the breasts or of the thighs, and followed the contours of the body when it arched or when the legs moved out of alignment. The material hugged and revealed the flesh.

By 1850 when Ingres began on the Princess de Broglie, fashion had smashed through the classical lines. The look was, well, swollen. Costume and adornment opened up; it was the circular motion of the bud towards full blossom. Hoops and bustles displaced the human form as the frame for clothing. Yet Ingres did a nude study for the Princess. I imagine he kept it beside him as he worked on the portrait, that he took it with him when he went to the de Broglie residence in the *rue de l'Université*.

He was over seventy by this time. He had been widowed in July 1849. By September he could no longer bear to stay in the apartment he and his wife had shared. In January he was invited to dine with the de Broglie family, specifically to meet and view Joséphine-Eléonore-Marie-Pauline. It was observed that he seemed to be very happy with his model. By March, as winter turned into spring, and the lengthening days allowed him more light, he was starting to work. In June 1853 he considered the painting was finished. 'To the applause of everyone,' he said, and added, 'it is, to tell the truth, really beautiful.' A year before this, two-thirds of the way through the commission, he remarried. He was seventy-one, and his new wife, Delphine, was forty-three. Studying a young woman month after month, referring to his sketches or imagining the lines her body followed under the grand drapery, what effect might this have had on his bereft and lonely spirit? Another woman, a younger woman, could take the place of Madeleine, his first wife. After all, he had proposed to Madeleine herself six months after calling off an earlier engagement. Throughout these years the Princess de Broglie had kept her shy sombre eyes on him. Wouldn't it make sense that he would need to displace the enchantment she must have had for him. Perhaps he didn't throw it off completely; shortly after his marriage he was planning to move into a house in the *rue de l'Université*.

What doesn't make sense however is that Ingres' infatuation was actually elsewhere. He painted Madame Moitessier twice, beginning his second portrait in 1848 but not finishing it till 1856. Eight years he worked on this woman. His letters to her are as much playful as professional. Constantly he referred to her as 'my beautiful and good one'. Madame

Moitessier is a dumpling of a woman, her puny features receding visibly over the years into her expandingly pudgy face. Her younger self is perhaps ill at ease, her older self merely nondescript. Her fame rests on two features; Ingres has her right hand in a starfish splay against her head; it is an Olympian gesture. But Madame Moitessier is no Juno. Secondly, he chose to dress her in a spectacular brocade. Posied flowers riot across the silk. This is a tour de force of the painter's minute reproductive skills. But the vivacity of the pattern, spread-eagled across the entire breadth of the canvas, is too overwhelming for the plain woman emerging from its summit. The Olympian hand is nullified; the arms held high can't stop her from drowning. They're too plump – even after mutual friends have had a quiet word (Madame Moitessier herself would be mortified to know of the intervention) and Ingres has pared them. Yet before he has met Delphine or the Princess de Broglie, and then long after he has finished with the de Broglies and married Delphine, Madame Moitessier is always his 'beautiful and good one'.

When he married Delphine, Ingres destroyed the nude sketch he had done of his first wife, Madeleine. Upon his own death, his effects included his nude studies for Madame Moitessier and the Princess de Broglie. In 1876 his widow, Delphine, consigned them to auction. Monsieur Moitessier took legal action about the nude sketch for his wife. He demanded that it be handed over to him or else burnt in his presence. The Civil Tribunal ruled that such sketches were the artist's property, but 'could not, without violating the sanctity of domestic privacy', be exhibited or offered for public sale. 'Study for Madame Moitessier (Nude)' remains in private hands. 'Study for Princess de Broglie (Nude)' is on public display in Bayonne.

IV

When the Princess moved into her thirties she began work on her *Christian Virtues Explained by Examples Drawn from the Lives of the Saints*. It was, as it were, her sixth child. As her lungs were gradually shredded and the blood retreated from beneath her skin and was coughed up in tissued gouts, it was the book that consumed her. At first seated by the fire, and then propped on her bed she meditated how the designated just men and women coped with the splendour and brutality of the world.

The Prince installed a curtain to cover the portrait.

'Don't draw it. Not yet,' she asked him.

Looking up at it she saw the shimmer and cadence of her enclosure, and instinctively, there in the bed, she put her hand to her neck and drew it down across the greying pallor of her chest. The fingers lodged against her nipple, and she was jolted by the texture, rubbery and manipulable, not fine and delicate in any way, but of immense comfort and unspectacular durability. The satin in the portrait trembled, and she retrieved her pen and began to scratch away at a classic tale of the body and its raiment.

When she died the Prince drew the curtain across the portrait and prepared her work for the press. It was published in Paris in 1862 and contained her meditation on the defining French story of Martin of Tours.

One feature of the best-known incident in the life of Saint Martin of Tours strikes me as odd. One night, in the depths of winter, he was confronted by a beggar woman. Threadbare rags were barely more than patches on her exposed body. Martin, on his way to or from his barracks, was in uniform. He was wearing armour and over it his large military cloak. Importuned by the woman, he released one shoulder clasp and swung the heavy material into the crook of his left arm, and using that arm as a hanger he jiggled the cloak until he had two equal lengths hanging parallel. His arm swivelled against his chest. He drew his sword with his right hand, slid the blade in between left arm and cloth and yanked the razor edge up and along the clamped material. To the beggar he gave the lower half, unencumbered by any cold heavy clasps.

He did nothing of the kind. He had no thought for himself. Why would a saint be so calculating and reserved in his generosity? The niggardly idea of halving his cloak would never have occurred to him. Does not the gospel itself say that if a man tries to take your cloak from you, you must hand over to him your shoes and your purse as well? The careful Christian will never find a place among the saints. Martin was accosted, and without pause he gave to the woman all he had, all that could be of any use to her.

That's not what the stories say. Not one of them. He halved his cloak. There is truth in the unlikely, reiterated story. Let us imagine how the saint's mind must have opened out. For this was a moment of revelation and progress for him as much as it might be for us. The woman might as well be naked. There, at the gate of the city, a convergence of streets and alleyways drawing the winter gales bouncing and whipping along the passages, the few rags she is wearing ridicule any attempt at modesty. They lift and flap and flail against her, and pour scorn on the very role they've been assigned. It's the devil's own mockery the way those intimate surfaces of her body are whipped into view and almost teasingly covered again, for an instant, or for a long sighing drop in the wind, before perhaps another sustained frenzy of blinking, beaten exposure.

The saint does not see whether it is a worn body, or a young one. It's a matter of indifference to him. Any body, scourged like this, shrieks to him. His own shoulders are warm under the heavy wool, and to the woman he is no more than eyes and a mouth, an intelligence peering at her, making something of her. He feels a fool, a parody of a god who has not become incarnate. The woman is a creature in the world of flesh, he an unmoved mind surveying from his eminence. He reaches out his arm, then withdraws it with a jerk. The wretched animal doesn't want the sham deity. So he takes a pace back, no longer threatens, unsheathes his sword, and shears the cloak in two. He hands the lower half to the woman, he doesn't drape her himself. Diminutive and huddled she heaves it around her shoulders and her arms lock in the front and she shudders in a rush of pleasure. The roughly serrated wool hangs to the back of her knees, and her newly enlivened legs stamp, almost dance, in the mud.

GERARD WINDSOR

*The saint feels the icy bite around his thighs, his calves. Foreshort-
ened like this he feels for a moment absurd, he knows that others
will see him so for longer than a moment. But he is watching
the woman. What is it he's done? Or maybe just what is it that's
happened? She has lifted her head up, the dark pools of her eyes
have gleaming surfaces and he reads wonder and gratitude and
wariness and even amusement there. He notices her bare legs bend-
ing and straightening together, hugging one another, more in delight
now than in desperate misery. I could hold this woman, he thinks
to himself. Perhaps too she could hold me. Both of us are stripped,
and dressed, the perfect equilibrium for the divine animal, bare skin
and flesh crying out its pathetic contemptibility, and in the same
voice singing its own gorgeousness. I have heard both together. The
body in ruins, the body enhanced, simultaneously. The naked body
in its prime, or Solomon arrayed in all his glory – both are vitiated,
both imperfect.*

The Place of the Paintings

Graham Henderson

Unlike the others he had never been afraid of the place of the paintings. Yet this day was different. His body shivered even in the sun and gave off a smell that did not belong to him. For the first time he felt something like disquiet as he approached the place of rocks where he would paint the men who had died.

It was a feeling he had carried since morning. The sun was already hot by the time he woke. He lay on his back and listened to the muted sounds of the day. There had been a dream, but all he recalled of it was an oppressive darkness and a sudden overwhelming urge to wake himself. Somehow he'd forced open his eyes and was startled by the brightness. He closed his eyes again. There was something he'd forgotten. Something had happened when he was asleep, but many hours ago, when he was asleep and it was still dark.

He slowly became conscious of the pain in his side, the strange smell which covered him. And the feeling began to grow despite himself, the inexplicable feeling that his body was not really his own anymore, that somehow his own body no longer entirely belonged to him; that some part of him had been taken away in his sleep, taken far away and left in the open to be devoured by sun or animal. He sat up and scoured his torso for a tiny smearing of ash or semen, a sign that he had been visited in the night by an enemy or by the dog-faced spirits beyond the river. He stared at his palms, then ran his fingertips carefully over the soles of his feet. He rocked himself on his haunches, gently backwards and forwards, and the pain seemed to die down a little.

They all watched as he dragged himself down to the mudflats. He lay in the faintly warm mud and looked up at the cloudless sky. He caught himself waiting for a flight of birds to cross his vision. Long ago he had taught himself to fix their passage in his eyes, to see the vanished sweeps and arcs of many birds in the sky as if they were being traced out by his own hands across a smooth rockface. But nothing disturbed the deep blue stillness. When it was empty like that, with not a cloud or bird anywhere, the sky was almost like a blindness. That blue, there was no name for it, no colour on his earth to mirror it; it was almost like a huge breach in the constant world of the visible.

Once, when he was a boy, they'd stood on a rocky outcrop which had towered high above the surrounding land. They'd arrived there after many days of hard walking. Perhaps they were fleeing, he no longer remembered. But for a short time they had all gazed across from the heights at a vast blue stretch of plain on the horizon. He had cried out in something like fright to see this blue that wasn't sky. He was exhausted and had hardly trusted his eyes, hardly recognised the joy that escaped in his cry, a searing joy even stronger than his small boy's fright of the unseen. But they had not gone towards it. They went back across the sparse grey plains towards the sunrise. No longer a boy, he'd tried to ask one of the old men what they had seen that day but he could not find the words.

No one came to him as he lay there in the muddy warmth and after a time he felt some of his strength returning. Yet still the unfamiliar smell was with him. Even the sharp smells of mud and weed and wallowing animal could not disguise it.

But now, many hours later, the worst of the journey was behind him. It had taken much longer than usual to follow the steep rock ledge. He was often forced to stop and catch his breath, and yet the deep gasps of air gave him no relief.

It was as if something far off, some furtive and implacable will, was working against his progress. He edged his way along and tried to cast his mind back to the night. For a moment he thought he remembered: strong fingers pressing down on his eyelids, keeping him there in darkness. But there was nothing before or after.

He crawled through the narrow cleft of rocks that led to the place of the paintings. Then he stopped and listened for the voice, the voice that told him again the reason of his journey. He listened for it above the pounding of his heart and the quick rasping swallows of breath. Since he'd set out the voice was with him, telling him the ordination of the three figures. He heard it as he heard the sound of his own footsteps, constant and reassuring, at the threshold of thought. But whenever he stopped to catch his breath the smell of his own body was suddenly very strong again, and he realised that the voice was almost lost to him. It was only the faintest murmur.

He rested his back against the cool rock and wiped the sweat from his face. He closed his eyes and felt himself falling into the sudden quiet. A sour taste, like mud, rose up into his mouth. He spat it out. In his mind he saw the old woman carrying the girl's severed finger, wrapped in dry grass, towards him. He saw the girl being led down to the river, whimpering and faint. She held her mutilated hand out in front of her. It was bloodreddened and trembling. The women comforted her and made a poultice of mud and leaves. The old woman stopped in front of him. She knelt and laid the small ball of bloodied grass on the earth. She looked up at him with her white, clouded eyes. Grown slowly sightless, she had somehow taught her hands to see beyond the reaches of gazing. Somehow the shape or weight of a stone in her hand could reveal the coming of a storm or a snake's hidden closeness.

Then suddenly he was no longer seeing her in his mind. It was the three figures. They had all seen them, at dusk the day before, the bodies of the three men floating down the river. The strangeness of it had defeated recollection, defeated the wordless voice that carried the seeds of their depiction. And yet they'd all recognised them soon enough. The three were borne along on a log. They seemed bound to it in some way, and their limbs had coiled together. The log sometimes dipped over in the calm current, submerging them. But always they returned to the surface, still held fast to one another in their placid lolling embrace. It was a long time passing out of sight. They had all gathered on the bank, their sorrow briefly stilled by confusion or foreboding at the inexplicable bonding of the three men and the great ravages to their bodies. The three had only set out that morning and yet their flesh was greatly broken, as if they had drifted the sleepy waters for day upon day. They grieved into the night that the bodies of the three men would not pass through the fire. Instead they would journey on and on down the river, unresting beneath the sun and stars, on and on to the edge of the world.

His progress had been so slow he had missed the light. On other days the sun slanted down through an opening in the rocks high above. The light fell directly across the rockface. But today the sun had already passed the zenith and the paintings were shaded and strangely sombre. He had never seen them like that before. It was cool here in this outer rock chamber, and the quiet was not within him anymore but in the air, in the dimness. He felt his breath come more easily. Many times he'd searched among the rocks for such a wall, for a surface as smooth and sheltered as this, but he had never found one. Many had been here before him and their faded paintings were still visible beneath his own. The ones who had made them were long gone from the river. He ran his fingers over the dull ochre lines which those vanished hands had once traced. Always he felt a strength come to him when he touched the lines; felt some sleeping part of himself stir and come to life like a sudden hunger. Yet this time there was only a solitude and a deep weariness. The alien smell of his body crept back. He began to shiver.

Above him, well out of his reach, were the striped gazelles, creatures made solely of lines winding across the contours of their bodies. From the beginning they had fascinated him. Their markings were a great mystery. He wondered at the men who could have painted them there, so high on the rockface. But perhaps they weren't men at all. Perhaps they were only the shadows of men – the sleepless ones from far away – who had made those paintings so unlike all the others on the wall.

Once, after a day of heavy rain, he had sat in the mud with a twig and tried to trace the lines of the striped gazelles, just as he had seen them on the rockface. He'd closed his eyes. In his mind he saw the simple, faded lines come to life. The contours of the gazelles coursed swiftly in the darkness, and their lines hummed and sang. He opened his eyes and tried to trace them in the cold mud but the lines would not be drawn. He sat there until the rain returned to wash out his lifeless marks.

And once, when the sun was setting in a red sky, he'd lain stretched out in the long grass and watched the gazelles drinking at a waterhole. The light was thick and yellow, and the water darkest green, trailing silver at their hocks. He remembered how still they were, silhouetted against the dark water, each a single line of sinew and bone, a bright line full of darkness. Today, because the light had passed, he could barely make out the lines of the gazelles on the rock, only the deep red outline that contained the swift darkness of their flesh. Yet still it was not as he had seen them in the dusk. He remembered the taut arch of the gazelles' necks as they dipped to drink, the invisible power that surged within them like the hum of the wind through the rocks.

He opened the skin bag and dug his fingers into the fat, slowly kneading in the reddish ochre. The familiar smells soothed him. He listened for distant sounds. It was very quiet, the face of the land hardly moving in the afternoon heat. For a moment he wished he'd brought the boy with him, just to be watched by curious eyes as he made the preparations. He sensed the boy was somehow like him; recalled how he some-times looked at things, held them in his small hands, staring with a dark curiosity, almost as if he were on the verge of anger.

With a shudder he thought again of the three men and their deaths that still had not ended. He thought of the river. The river that was lines. The river that drew all creatures to its banks in the fading light. He wiped his hands and ran his fingers over the lines of the river he had once painted, and over the figures of the bathers, the women and children running from the water. As he touched the dry ochre lines their laughter came back to him, the glistening wet brightness of their limbs. His own figure was there, a tiny dot a yellow clay beneath the feet. It seemed to him strangely still among the careening women; stiff and weighted down by some invisible burden. He began to paint a body beside it, a small body, walking as if hand in hand. He gave it the head of a dog. The sour taste came into his mouth again. He felt dizzy and his legs had begun to ache. He let himself sink down onto his haunches. The rushing figures blurred above him and he wiped the stinging sweat from his eyes. He could feel himself falling asleep, giving in to the heaviness of his body. He was at the river again. The splashing arms and swaying torsos of the bathers filled his vision. They stood against the sun. It broke through their bodies in blinding flashes. For an instant he would recognise one of them but then the face was swallowed up in the swishing water or lost against the sun. The figures seemed to be swirling around him in the water. Then, as if she had called out to him, he turned his vision to the water's edge. She was standing quite still, her feet sunk into the wet mud. She seemed rooted in the earth. She held a small child in her arms and stared out at him. Her thighs were splashed with mud, moist and glowing. The familiarity of her body made him feel inexplicably helpless. She was always at the threshold of his thoughts. Sometimes the others seemed hardly living at all, just mute unseeing presences, but she was never like that. She was always agonisingly, tremulously alive. Suddenly her face was very close and she looked at him as if from another world, a hidden and forbidden place that would never reveal itself in red ochre lines, never submit to the will of seeing.

He shook himself awake and struggled to his feet. The light had grown much weaker. He peered up at the wall but the striped gazelles had vanished from sight. The voice was louder, recalling him to the three lost men journeying still. He began to paint the figures of the three men low down on the wall. He painted them standing side by side. The one with the twisted leg, the weakest, he placed in the centre. He drew beside them the lines of the fire. When he'd finished he stared at the ochre figures and tried to summon up their faces as he had known them in life. The three men were so familiar to him and yet now he saw in his mind only their dimness and their agony, their eyes breaking in death. He shuddered, sensing somehow their panic and the last helpless threshings of their bodies, the savage futile strength that must have entered them. For a moment it was like a roaring scream in his ears, a scream that seemed to swallow him up, like night swallowing up the land. But now the three dead men stood in the warm shadow of the red ochre fire. Their bodies were no longer ravaged by the river's endlessness. Their journey was almost over.

He began to make his way towards the inner rock chamber where he would paint them again. A narrow sloping shaft led down to this inner chamber. He tried to move quickly, groping for handholds on the rock to pull himself along. He knew the chamber would soon be in darkness. Sometimes his shoulders swayed heavily against the narrow walls, grazing his skin. His body felt huge and trembling. Several times he stumbled over rock shards, blindly pushed out his arms to break the fall. He felt the sweat coating his whole body in a sickly smothering warmth. He felt himself rushing blindly through the eye of a dream. The walls seemed to be moving, crushing in on him. He was conscious of the tearing pain in his side. Perhaps it was there they had wounded him. He pressed his fingers against the spot and the pain leapt through his body. The dog-faced spirits must have wounded him there in the night and the dark had swallowed up all trace. And then they had confused his dreams so that he would not remember their coming.

He felt his legs give way under him and let himself sink down onto his knees. The sour muddy taste came into his mouth again. He tried to spit it out, heaving for breath. He closed his eyes. A voice echoed around him, strangely loud. He was calling her, making the sounds only she would recognise. He saw her again, standing by the water's edge. But this time there were no others. It was like early morning. He saw her only distantly, through the river haze of early morning, as if he were standing on the other side. She was carrying the child inside her, and the women had covered her body with red ochre and kept her apart. He remembered that time, those nights when she was not near him, when he'd called to her silently through the night and she had not come.

He forced open his eyes and walked on. The passage widened out and the stones grew smoother under his feet. He entered the inner chamber. There was still enough light. He knew the place on the rockface where he would paint the three men. He laid down the small ball of blood-matted grass and picked out the girl's severed finger.

For the first time he wondered how he would find his way back when he had finished. He wondered what would happen to him if he fell asleep in that half-light, there, among the secret images of the dead. He daubed the severed finger with ochre and began to draw with it the three figures lain side by side on the earth. As he painted the figure with the twisted leg he felt a sudden pity for this man who had often been in pain and did not laugh like the others. He drew a line across the three men. They would remain together even in death, bound by the line as their bodies had been bound by log and river, and by the strangeness of their recollection.

He decided to rest briefly before making his way back. The pain had subsided a little and he felt calmer. He listened for the distant sounds of duskfall, and pictured to himself the weary herds drifting towards the river in the last tepid light. Even the smell of his body seemed less familiar now. The sweat had begun to dry on his skin, almost cold in the faint hum of breeze. The unaccountable urgency he had carried with him since morning had gone.

He squatted down close to the wall, peering hard at all the figures, the many dead, watching them vanish in the last glow. The slender ochre figures seemed to shimmer against the dark rock, hovering at the tremulous edge of stillness, as if they somehow struggled against their vanishing. Only the tall profiled figure of the reed player seemed at rest, stilled against the darkness of the rock. Dots of yellow clay danced around the tip of the reed in a mute semblance of its sounds. He'd only ever heard those sounds once and had never forgotten the mystery of it.

There had been no rain for months and fires had blackened much of the land. That day they'd watched a fire roar through the grass on the other side of the river. They'd seen many fleeing animals and the smell of scorched carcasses filled the air. Then they heard the sounds. Two figures wandered through the coils of smoke and smouldering stubble. The two stood in the far shallows and gazed at them with hollow eyes while the sound of the reed floated across the water. The two men had huge heads and the expressions of their grief did not change. They walked away through the smoke, soon invisible. Slowly the sounds were swallowed up in the silence.

When he woke again it was dark in the chamber. He had dreamt of snakes. He was beside the river, walking upstream. He carried a heavy stick. The snakes were coiled together in the mud, a thick writhing mass. He watched them in terror and fascination. He beat out with the stick, thrashed out at the swarming mass. A dark sinuous shape flashed at him, and another, but he no longer felt any fear. He let the stick fall from his hands and stepped into the water.

Only when he stretched out his arm in the darkness and touched the rockface and the small mound of ochred fat did he recall where he was. His body shivered with cold and the pain in his side made him cry out. His mouth was filled with the choking sourness and his whole body heaved to be rid of it. He stared with wide-open eyes into the huge smothering darkness. He felt as if he were lying on his back in the mud, sinking slowly through a muddy gaping darkness that would never end.

He dug his hand into the fat, kneading it into a lukewarm paste. Without memory or hope of seeing, he rubbed the red paste over his side and chest, rubbed it across the risings of his face and the lengths of his arms. Then he lay still. He let himself sink painlessly through the warm, blindly churning mud, deeper and gently deeper.

At the end of the falling he found himself on the earth again, in the body of a boy, standing in the dizzying brightness of the plain where he had once seen a white leopard stalking through the watery waves of heat, shimmering at the will-less edge of seeing.

The Shark

Kim Mahood

A fishing trawler had gone down somewhere off Cape York with a crew of three, two men and a woman. They had life jackets and a raft. The weather was calm. They got an SOS signal off before the boat went down. When the search plane spotted the life raft three days later there was only one man aboard, the owner of the trawler. He told his rescuers that a shark had taken the other two, separately, hours, maybe days apart. He was big and young and exhausted, lacerated by days of salt and sun. The tears ran down his blistered face before the relentless cameras. He turned his head away, as if ashamed. 'It got both of them,' he said, over and over. 'It got both of them.'

Janis was distracted from the small, energetic bodies of her children, freshly bathed, so vulnerable and alive and *hers* to protect from sharks and other predators. There was a tone in the news reporter's voice that suggested something unfinished, unanswered. *You were the one in charge*, it hinted to the big weeping man as the stretcher carried him away, *why did you survive?*

Why did you survive?

She went back to her children, read them a bed-time story with the smallest on her lap and the other two leaning into her, enthralled at the tale of children who had marvellous adventures, flying away at night with a magical boy while their parents dined out and the dog who might have stopped it all was chained in the yard. She answered questions, tucked them in, kissed them, discovering them anew as she always did.

There was a time, before Larry and the children and the suburban security of her present life, when she had known that violent indolent coast, known men like the fisherman with his leaky trawler. She felt the memory of it in her gut with a kind of terror, later in the evening when Larry was home and they watched the late news together. There was a fuller account of the story, the fisherman in a hospital bed now more composed, though he broke down at the re-telling of the story.

The trawler had begun to take water in the morning, and by midday they knew it was sinking. He'd sent out the SOS and given their position before they bailed out and watched it go down. The life raft was too small for three, and they'd hung on the sides of it in their life jackets. The shark came onto them fast, as if it had been following the boat, and bit off his mate's leg. Saw it trailing in the water and bit it off. It could have been any one of them. It swam off then, circled them at a distance. The man whose leg was gone said to his companions, 'The cunt's got my leg off. He'll come back.' He said, 'Jesus fucking Christ,' and swam back to meet the shark. They saw him come up to the place where the fin cut the water, and for what seemed a long time nothing happened. And then there was a flurry of water and blood and he began to swear and scream, and he was gone.

At this point the fisherman began to weep again. Janis could see the transparent blood-streaked water and the maimed man swimming across the empty stretch of sea towards his fate, an act of courage so outrageous she gagged on it. It was the fact of his swearing at the shark she found unbearable, that heroic moment of profanity and terror.

'Jesus,' Larry muttered beside her.

The two survivors, the girl and the man, had dragged themselves as best they could onto the dinghy and drifted through the rest of the day and the night. Sometime the next day the shark came again and took the girl. She was half off the raft, and she went without a sound. The shark stayed with the fisherman after that, through the night and into the next day. It was a full moon, and he could see the fin at the edge of his vision. By this time he was beginning to hallucinate and lose consciousness, but he knew the shark was real, stalking him across the moonlit sea. The rescue plane confirmed that when they located the dinghy and its occupant they had sighted a large shark a few hundred metres away. The water is very clear up there, and from the air the submerged reefs look like pale green islands.

That night Janis slept hardly at all, and when Larry touched her reassuringly she squirmed away from him. She dreamed of the fisherman, curled like a foetus in his flimsy craft. The shark swam nearby. She swam beside it, and when she turned to look it was not a shark but a man, long and pale, with his leg missing and a thin stream of blood coming from his smiling mouth. She knew her children were in the dinghy with the fisherman, and if she didn't get to them he would push them off into the water, because there wasn't enough room. But the water was warm and thick and she could barely move her limbs to keep afloat. The shark man swam ahead and the dinghy drifted away from her, faster and faster. Her body ached with the effort of movement, a kind of menstrual ache, sluggish and heavy. The physical sensation woke her, and did not recede immediately on waking. She dragged herself from the bed to the children's room, where she stood in the doorway with her heart pounding.

*

Back then, she'd had the beach to herself most mornings, for she had become an early riser. The salty, ozone-crisp air held, even this early, the promise of the afternoon's thunderous downpour. She would walk, watching for stingrays, among the granite boulders that extended for some distance into the sea.

The place was beautiful, but it was not its beauty which set it apart. There was a smell, an aura that belonged to places which have never been subjected to more than marginal European habitation. The rainforest came to the edge of the sand, without the tangle of undergrowth that choked the forests further south. Bush turkeys pottered in the leaf mulch which insulated the forest floor, and the great Palm cockatoos screeched in the canopy. Among the few visitors who found their way to the beach were birdwatchers, in search of exotics like the Trumpet Manucode, the Magnificent Rifle Bird, the Red-footed Booby.

There were as many rare and endangered species of humans secreted in the forest. Janis made up bird names for them. The red-necked kneejerker, the lesser-crested work-dodger, the floppy-breasted cocksucker. She didn't acknowledge how isolated and lonely she was. The man for whom she'd come to this place kept her emotions so skewed she couldn't make the judgements which came naturally to her. It was only by retreating into private family games that she could touch something in herself she recognised. Yet if she exposed this to him, she knew that he would make her ashamed of it.

The life she shared with him had nothing to do with her past, her family. She didn't examine the need she felt to protect both from him. The seed of scepticism invented bird names, but she did not challenge him. When she smoked herself into euphoria she could believe his diatribes against the comfortable society which had produced her. She believed it was good to be challenged, to be forced to examine one's beliefs and prejudices. She did not understand she was being challenged by a more primitive and simplistic set of prejudices. An intellectual and restrained girl, she was easily overcome by the impetus of his resentful, manic, charismatic personality.

It was obligatory to reject the affluent middle-class world, especially if you'd grown up with all its advantages. That's when she changed the spelling of her name, after Janis Joplin. She was in fact appalled by the singer's self-destructive career, and couldn't accept the romanticised view of the tragic heroine. But it suited her to discard the suburban Janice for the husky, dangerous Janis. It really did make a difference, for it allowed her to identify with what was less conventional in her nature.

She met Rudi at a student protest. He was passing through on his way back to the Cape after three months spent in prison on a marijuana charge, and was drawn to the agitated ineffectual energy of the protest. Things tended to run out of steam in the tropics. It was difficult in the splendid enervating sunlight to take anything too seriously.

He was a good deal older than she and her student friends, and his thin, handsome face already showed the marks of a past of some kind. His accent suggested something Middle-European, overlaid with broad North Queensland vowels which sat oddly with a staccato delivery. Janis was impressed with his passion and vigour, which showed up the limpness and lack of conviction of her friends. He impressed all of them. Among all that lacklustre cheesecloth and wispy facial hair he was like a cheerful brigand.

After the protest they went to the Strand and smoked dope and drank tequila. He told stories of his adventures and invited them to visit him on the Cape York coast, in paradise. They said 'Yeah man, sounds great,' but she knew none of them meant it. They didn't believe you could change your life or live outside society, in spite of what they said. So in the end she was the only one who went.

She'd have gone to bed with him on that first occasion, if he'd shown any interest, which he didn't. In fact it was a year later that she went north, not really expecting him to be where he said he'd be. By this time she'd dropped out of university and was burning bridges. Janis understood something fundamental about herself, which was that she was a timid person, and that if she allowed herself any escape routes she would use them. At twenty-two she took herself and her life seriously. Her intellectual bravado concealed a fragility even her parents did not guess. She knew she was rather ordinary, and wanted to be extraordinary.

*

'Bad night, sweetheart?' Larry said to her next morning, and it was obvious enough from the rings under her eyes.

'I had bad dreams,' she told him. 'Couldn't get that shark story out of my mind.'

He agreed it was a bad business. 'I can see the shark taking the first bloke like that. But not the girl. What kind of bloke would leave a girl trailing in the water when there's sharks about?'

This possibility was so far beyond Larry's comprehension that it disturbed him far more than the man swimming back to the shark. That made sense. It was the kind of thing Larry himself would have done.

He patted her, and patted and cuddled the children, who took for granted that large gentle men were synonymous with fathers.

She delivered them to school and kindergarten, a youngish mother among young mothers, who talked at the school gate or waved from cars. Her own children went confidently, trusting her to extend her protection over them from afar. Last night during the story, Ben had been distressed by the Lost Boys. 'But what about their mothers?' he wanted to know.

'The Lost Boys haven't got any mothers,' she told him. 'Sometimes that happens.'

He pondered this, unable to imagine a place without mothers, until Eddie pointed out that Wendy would be their mother whenever she came to Neverland, and that satisfied him.

Well, Janis had flown off to Neverland and found Peter Pan and the Lost Boys, and the Lost Girls too. But she didn't have Wendy's moral fibre, and anyway it wasn't mothers that particular band of Lost Boys were looking for.

*

Rudi was delighted to see her, though she doubted he actually remembered her. They went to bed almost immediately, since that was clearly part of the purpose of her visit. When he leaned above her, his dark head framed by palm fronds and moonlight, whispering absurdly passionate endearments, she knew she'd begun to change her life irrevocably. Something surged in the back of her mind, part irony and part dread, which she quenched instantly, and did not remember until much later.

In the following months she learned to fish and sail, collect seaweed to fertilise the garden he'd established, and coconuts which provided a staple of pawpaws and fish. Rudi was almost self-sufficient, with a small marijuana plantation hidden in the forest and the only vegetable garden on the beach. He traded vegetables, and sold dope to the locals in the settlement across the bay.

In the beginning Janis was fascinated by the other inhabitants of the forest's edge. Like the bird life which flourishes where habitats meet, the zone between beach and rainforest was home to a handful of survivors, one-offs who could exist nowhere else. Jack Beanstalk was one of these, a refugee from the police raid on Cedar Bay which had shattered the hippy community and driven the remnants deeper into the wilderness or back to the fringes of the society they'd rejected. Beanstalk had been a bank clerk in a past life, which began in Switzerland and led by some weird logic to a beach on the rim of a reef-strung southern ocean. Janis was unable to establish whether he was mad or merely stoned all the time. Thin to the point of emaciation, with rat-tails of hair which reached past his buttocks and claw-like fingernails, he wandered about naked or wrapped in a ragged sarong. His home, a canvas and corrugated iron structure open on all sides, was on a promontory which jutted into the sea and sloped back to the forest. Most of his time was spent constructing mobiles from the flotsam which arrived on the beach near his cliff. The first time she came on his part of the forest she thought she'd stumbled into the den of a lunatic macrame artist. Rubber thongs were the central motif, suspended eerily like so many footprints in the spaces between tree trunks, the strings which held them threaded with shells and fragments of driftwood and bone.

You didn't have conversations with Beanstalk, but simply fielded the statements he flung about and translated them to suit yourself. And yet Janis didn't believe he was as childlike or as harmless as he seemed. There were times she caught a hard glitter in his eyes before he turned away and threw out one of his gnomic remarks. He and Rudi sat for hours, smoking and discussing esoteric philosophies until Janis was driven to escape to the beach, to walk and dream and pick up fragments of beach wrack.

She preferred Rachel and Morry, when Rachel was sober, which was a good deal of the time, since alcohol was fairly hard to come by on the beach. Rachel was in her late forties, a big red-haired woman who had been a flamboyant beauty. A self-confessed slut and drunk, she had been married and had two daughters who lived with their father and came to visit in the school holidays. Morry was an amiable young Maori half her age, good-natured until he joined her binges, when he became morose and furious. At these times he stalked along the beach muttering to himself, his eyes slitted to nacreous chips, his usually fine-featured face congested with undirected rage. Rachel was dry, a hard case. She parodied herself, though the parody by now was closer to the truth. She adored Morry, who had drifted in from one of the fishing boats and would sooner or later drift away again. 'Like the bloody garbage that floats up onto the beach, and washes out again on the tide,' she said, inviting him to contradict her, which he did not.

Janis had the fair, glossy Australian looks that had more to do with health and youth and optimism than with intrinsic beauty. With her long tanned legs under the flimsy sarong, her hair bleached into a tangle of wild curls, she was beautiful. She knew it was her body that held Rudi enthralled, and she enjoyed the experience of sexual power. Physically she had never been so much in her element. The sun and salt and sea kept her in a constant state of semi-arousal, and she was a willing recipient of Rudi's obsessive attention. She couldn't say whether she loved him or not, but she loved the adventure of being with him.

Once she asked him if he would continue to live this way.

'Why not?' he answered. 'You know anywhere better than this?'

The circumstances of his arrival in Australia were never clear to her. He refused to tell her where he came from. 'Doesn't matter,' he said. 'Doesn't exist any more. Now I come from Australia. I am a new Australian. Brand new, from nowhere.' He bared his teeth in his white grin.

Wherever it was he'd come from, he brought with him a hatred of authority which did not discriminate between the oppressive regime he had left and the mild political climate of his adopted country. When she protested at one of his wilder accusations against middle-class urban Australia, and by implication against her, she saw a flash of something in his face which frightened her. But she suppressed it, as she had suppressed the earlier surge of dread.

The scattered community consisted of two settlements, the beach and the slightly more respectable bay, where the lighthouse-keeper and his family lived, and where the barge called in once a month to deliver supplies. Janis knew all the locals by this time, knew their stories, in fact was profoundly bored by most of them. Although still too sexually infatuated to admit that Rudi belonged in the same category, she discovered that eccentrics with a grievance are too self-absorbed to be interesting.

They were thrown together only by a shared inability to tolerate the boundaries of ordinary society. From time to time, driven by an impulse to behave like a proper community, a celebration was declared on some pretext or other. Janis had been on the beach for several months when she went to her first fancy-dress party, in celebration of Labour Day. It was an irony appreciated by everyone, since no one in the community worked in the conventional sense.

Beanstalk came as a mobile, shells and coloured rope threaded into his hair and about his naked torso, his genitals partly concealed by a thong. Rachel wore a tight green satin ball dress, stained with mildew and sweat, and looked opulent, raddled and magnificent. She'd found a frayed evening jacket for Morry, which he wore over a skirt of palm fronds. Joseph the drug dealer was a pirate, which hardly required the red bandanna tied over his oily hair, so in-character was the role. Most people had settled for a re-arrangement of the colourful rags and sarongs they usually wore, with flowers and shells as decoration. Janis toyed with the idea of being Wendy, but no one would have picked up the references, so she was a mermaid, with a string of shells wound about her hair and a bikini top. Rudi, wrapped in a cast net and carrying his garden fork, was Neptune.

Among the visitors from the bay were a couple of new faces, from the barge which had called in on its monthly supply run. The bargeman's offsider was a young Dutchman with bright curious eyes and clipped English. He took in everything with delighted amusement, a fresh-faced observer of the natives at play in their skewed Eden. When he spoke to Janis later in the night, he took for granted that, like him, she was simply passing through.

'I live here,' she told him. 'With him,' pointing out Rudi.

'But you do not belong here,' he said. 'This is not the real world. You are just playing.'

'For some people this *is* the real world.' She was sharp, resentful of being patronised.

'No.' He shook his head with slow emphasis. She realised he was rather drunk. 'This is a fantasy. Look at the faces of the people. Everybody here is running away from something. They are all lost souls.' He made his pronouncement from the height of his youthful sophistication. Janis knew he was right, but he reduced to cliché something more profound than he could understand. She thought with some irony that more than half the people here were from his hemisphere. Apart from Rudi and Beanstalk there was Paul, the French artist who read trashy novels all his waking hours, whose rationalisations for his inability to paint were an art form in themselves. Ugly, intelligent Lena, a Czech, with her Australian boyfriend who was beautiful and almost half-witted. Old Judith the Polish Jew, a concentration camp survivor who'd come to Australia and married a lighthouse-keeper, staying on after his death, her corrugated iron shack as dim and memory-laden as any European interior. Gross, malevolent Joseph, the American Vietnam vet, probably a deserter, who trafficked in drugs and was the one real villain among them. Joseph came and went, accompanied from time to time by a retinue of desperadoes. He had a big marijuana plantation somewhere in the forest, but his real business was smuggling hard drugs. For Joseph, at least, this was the real world.

'So what about you?' said the Dutchman, watching her with his clever eyes. 'What are you running away from?'

He had begun to irritate her. In the firelight Morry stripped off his dress jacket and began to sway slowly, raising his arms. The others fell silent, giving him room.

Morry's performances of the haka were legendary and rare. As he began the angular pounding rhythms his bland face seemed to dissolve and re-assemble. Rachel's good-natured toy boy might never have existed. In his place some ancient presence manifested itself, a warrior on an alien shore, hurling his ritual fury across the sea. Janis felt the hairs on her arms prickle. The watchers began to chant and howl. Beanstalk became hysterical, spinning and shrieking like a demented toy. Joseph leapt up and beat his chest, his hairy belly bouncing. Half out of the light, Rachel lay stranded in her green satin, too drunk to move.

The following day everyone was morose and hung-over. Morry disappeared, which he did whenever he danced a haka. Rachel continued to drink until she had exhausted her own supply, then staggered down to Rudi and Janis and fell asleep on their bed, the green satin dress torn and stained with urine. Up and down the beach the casualties of the previous night slept it off in the mottled shade of the forest edge, crawling into the sea from time to time to lie in the shallows.

The Dutch boy's assumption that she was merely a visitor had unsettled Janis. She was in the habit of taking each day as it came, adjusting her own protean nature around Rudi's volatility. The suggestion that she was running away from something continued to irritate her. 'Arrogant prick,' she thought. But she was depressed, and suddenly couldn't bear Rudi's pacing and needling. His brooding Middle-European intensity, which had once seemed so dangerous and attractive, now merely oppressed her.

'You liked that Dutch fellow? He was like your friends from the university.'

'No. I didn't like him.'

'You talked to him a long time.'

'Everyone else was drunk.'

'But not you, of course. You don't get drunk and dance. You are too refined for us peasants.'

This shocked her, for there was an element of truth in it.

'Oh yes.' He was grinning at her balefully. 'You sit there with your princess look while the rest of us become fools. Well, you are the fool, with your cosy little arrangement you make with life. You will go back to your nice life and tell your friends about the time you spent with the mad people on the beach. But you don't know how to live. You keep it all tied up inside in neat little parcels, and all you can do is unwrap them one at a time.'

Janis began to cry, having no idea what else to do. He was contrite then, though obscurely pleased, and made love to her with gentle passion.

'I am afraid to lose you,' he told her. 'I love you.'

A shark was caught by a sports fisherman off Cooktown, and a human forearm was found in its stomach. The incident subdued the beach dwellers. The arm wore a distinctive tattoo, which resembled the tattoo on the arm of Joseph's unsavoury sidekick. The sidekick, whose name was Spook, hadn't been seen for some time. Black humour competed with bizarre rumour. Rachel remarked that she always thought Spook was 'armless. The park ranger visited the beach with two police-men, and questions were asked. No one revealed what they told the police, but it was clear enough that fear of Joseph had far more authority than the conventional forces of law. Janis noticed how unreliable everyone looked in the presence of the police uniforms and the ranger's pressed khakis.

Her supply of contraceptives ran out, and shortly after this she suspected she was pregnant. She went to the clinic at the Aboriginal Mission to have it confirmed, and didn't tell Rudi immediately. The sister at the clinic treated her with exasper-ation. To her, Janis was just another irresponsible promiscuous hippie girl with more hormones than sense. For the first time, Janis saw herself through the eyes of the world she had so casually wandered away from, and was shocked. She was a romantic, not a rebel, and had no armour of convictions.

Rudi, when she told him, was ecstatic. She was vaguely aware by this time that she didn't really exist for him except as a mirror to reflect him, as a receptacle for his fantasies, and now for his child. Janis, who had always depended on the approval and expectations of the people she loved and admired, felt herself disappearing into the voluptuous prom-ise of her body. Rudi's appropriation of it, at once sentimental and predatory, left her chilled and isolated, and she respond-ed to him frantically because there was no one else. She knew she should leave but she could not.

Rachel seemed to understand something of this and offered to help Janis if she wanted to go home. But her passivity, made more acute by the oppression of the tropical summer, and Rachel's own ironic haplessness, made the offer impossible to act on. Janis borrowed books from French Paul and old Judith. She understood Paul now, who used reading like a drug, for she was the same. Between books she suffered withdrawal symptoms, read sometimes through the night, using up the battery reserve from Rudi's solar panel, resort-ing to candles when it ran out. When she couldn't read she walked, picking up shells and bits of driftwood, most of which she gave to Beanstalk. Rudi treated her with indulgent uxoriousness. She no longer listened to his rantings, though sometimes she was shaken by glimpses of the fantasy he was building around her and the child. She didn't want to understand what drove him.

One day he took her out in the boat, to visit an estuary some miles to the north. She didn't much want to go. The weather felt unsettled, but he coerced her into it. In the afternoon, squalls began to blow over, and then the sky dropped on them suddenly, violent purple clouds full of lightning and wind. The boat was small and none too seaworthy, and she was afraid, as much of Rudi as of the sea. The storm seemed to unleash in him a parallel violence with which he fought both vessel and sea. When finally he brought the boat into the estuary it seemed to Janis that he had conquered it through nothing but defiance. They spent the night bailing out the deluge which threatened to swamp them, and by morning she was exhausted and very ill. On the way home through wallowing seas she began to miscarry, and by the time they reached the Mission clinic some hours later she had lost the baby.

It was routine in serious cases to fly patients to Cairns Base Hospital, and Janis was too numb with exhaustion and loss of blood to pay much heed to Rudi, a forlorn and peripheral presence, as she was loaded onto the plane. Some days later, when she was recovered enough to take stock of her circumstances, she had a curious sense of having escaped. The baby had never been real to her; she had felt marooned in her pregnancy, and while she mourned its loss, she felt the possibility of pulling free of the passivity which had gripped her in these past months.

*

There was to be some sort of enquiry into the sinking of the trawler and the subsequent shark attack. Newspapers kept the incident alive, and Janis came across a story in one of the tabloids which hinted at sexual jealousy and revenge at sea.

It was full of conjecture: a shark would not kill again so soon after it had already eaten, if there were a shark at all; there had been a ménage à trois, the girl had been the cause of friction and jealousy between the men; drugs were somehow involved. It was all possible, Janis thought. But she believed in the man swimming back to the shark. It wasn't the kind of thing anyone would make up.

She'd never told Larry of her time on the beach. In her late thirties the gloss of that younger self was gone, her body thickened from her children's births. Her hair was still her best feature, though now she coloured it to disguise the fact that it was fading. After her escape from the beach she had gone south and lost herself in the city. She thought about going back to university but couldn't muster the incentive. It seemed that the torpor of the tropics had seeped into her bloodstream, like one of the internal parasites which thrived in the swamps and forests she had left. She went from job to job, living in communal households and squats. She joined the Rajneeshi and got a curious pleasure from dyeing all her clothes, watching the red stain overtake the fabric until everything was uniform, anonymous. But the self-absorption of it was too much for her. She wanted only to disappear, and found herself continually in the self-reflective embrace of some cult or group or household.

For a long time Janis didn't take seriously Larry's interest in her. He was overseeing the construction of a block of flats on a site next door to the house where she rented a room, and had taken to chatting over the fence when she sat outside in the late mornings over her breakfast. She worked nights in a bar and went intermittently to meditation evenings at a local ashram. Once he knew where she worked he came sometimes and ordered a beer, and if she was on an early shift drove her home. She began to take for granted his slow, undemanding presence. He made no sexual advances towards her. There had been affairs since Rudi, brief liaisons that convinced Janis she lacked the capacity to meet emotional demands. With Larry there was simply a reassuring masculine presence, punctuated with small courtesies which constantly surprised her.

It didn't occur to her that he might be in love with her, though sometimes she found herself fantasising about marriage and children, the accoutrements of a normal life. But she felt herself so contaminated by her time on the beach that she thought it was impossible to achieve ordinary happiness. When Larry said matter-of-factly that he loved her but guessed something bad must have happened, and he was happy to wait around for a while yet, her first instinct was to run. But she had seen him clearly for a moment, his humorous, monkey-like face, his physical grace masked by the slowness of his movements, and saw in him an equal grace of character.

He took her to meet his family, and her intuition was confirmed. She felt herself in the presence of a gentler species than she was used to. Still, she might have run away if she'd been able to rediscover the girl who'd thrown off caution years ago and gone north. But she couldn't shake the passivity which had overtaken her, and the tribe of good-natured giants which was Larry's family (even the children seemed larger than normal) simply appropriated her. Her own sharp, clever family, who came to the wedding, seemed spindly and shrill. They were clearly relieved that she was settling down but couldn't hide their bemusement. She continued to go to the ashram to meditate, but abandoned it in the late stages of her first pregnancy. There was a point during the pregnancy when she became terrified she would lose the baby, and told Larry of her miscarriage, though not the circumstances. But she gave birth without mishap, and the strong little animal she miraculously brought out of her body seemed to offer proof of her own vitality.

If her life sometimes seemed provisional on her luck holding, she did not waste time in questioning it. This at least she had learned from Larry.

But now the shark incident had penetrated her life at an imaginative level, swimming under the layers of consciousness.

She felt it surge at unexpected moments, when she emptied tea leaves in the back garden, or looked through frosted glass doors at frozen supermarket food. She remembered something she had read about sharks, that they had no buoyancy, and must keep swimming or die.

*

It hadn't occurred to her that Rudi would come for her, but he did. After the loss of the baby she felt that her connection with Rudi and the beach was severed, as if she had expelled from her body with that bloody scrap the part of herself that was joined to him, rejecting convulsively his power over her. His presence at the side of the hospital bed filled her with a dull fear, but she was too tired to resist him. He had borrowed a car, and when the hospital released her she went with him into the hot town, which was full of tourists and noise, and nauseated her. They spent the night in a cheap hotel room, a humid cave with orange furnishings and a stained carpet. When she shrank away from his caresses he raped her, forcing her down into the nylon counterpane, and wept when it was over. Spread-eagled and unmoving beneath him, she felt herself crawl away into some secret part of herself which he could not reach, which had nothing to do with the body he had just violated.

The return journey to the beach was a nightmare. The wet season was threatening and storms had already made the road precarious. Rudi drove as if he could push the vehicle through the muddy tracks by sheer force of will. Janis was reminded of the night in the boat. She saw with detachment that he didn't use the evidence of previous experience to modify his driving methods. Again and again he attacked the muddy stretches at speed, again and again the vehicle slewed and spun and bogged. It took them ten days to negotiate the several hundred kilometres to the beach. By the time they arrived she could no longer imagine any reality beyond the nightmare of dripping forest and oppressive heat, biting insects, heavy bruised skies. And Rudi. She realised that in the beginning he had made an enormous effort to inhabit the best part of himself for her sake.

Now he had stopped trying, and she saw a querulous man driven by a niggling anger, a man with few resources beyond the unusual physical energy which drove him. Oddly, now that she saw the real man she felt a kind of bleak compassion for him, which disturbed her more than her physical fear at his violence. Always after the violence he would weep and insist that he loved her, and she knew that in a curious way it was true.

Her return to the beach was greeted by the others with an enthusiasm which surprised her. They hadn't expected her to come back. Rachel offered a caricature of motherliness which was almost comforting. Rachel had a long acquaintance with violent, unhappy men. She understood Rudi as Janis could not, for they had both gone beyond the pale and set up camp there. Although the woman in Rachel sympathised with Janis, her real empathy, beyond morality, was with Rudi.

As for Beanstalk, Janis saw in his reaction to her return a satisfaction that she had been brought to heel.

She didn't remember much of the time which followed. The wet season ran its course, the damp and mildew and mosquitoes gave way to clear days, the beach recovered its primordial beauty. Always prone to insomnia, Janis took to wandering the beach, dozing at intervals throughout the day. She felt bound to Rudi, and thought dully she would eventually die of it. She smoked marijuana continually, which made his use of her body more tolerable. His behaviour towards her became subdued, almost ingratiating, punctuated by bursts of rage. He began to tell her about himself, the cold mountainous country of his homeland, his mad parents, the narrow streets and the ancient, rich, oppressive culture which had shaped him. He described the invasion by the Russians, the crushing of what had seemed like the beginnings of something clean and open, and his own flight, which became confused in her mind with novels she had read.

The details of his story she barely took in, but absorbed only a general sense of darkness and weight and unpredictable danger, and a monotonous anguish seeping through it all. It made her think of *Gormenghast* and Kafka and that mad strange novel by Alfred Kubin, *The Other Side*. The stories revealed a world both primitive and over-civilised; it was inscrutable to her but it haunted her just the same. The beach somehow became a part of it, as if on the other side of the forest a dark and crumbling world existed, from which they had escaped and now lived in exile.

On the day they sailed to the reef Janis had a premonition that she would die. It was a place Rudi insisted she must see. He had discovered it accidentally, and had clearly felt some sort of epiphany there, as though the place had been created for him alone. The tenor of his stories had changed recently. He no longer talked about his homeland but of his early days in Australia. They were stories of confrontation, and of bitter grievance that in this new place which offered such promise still he had not been acceptable. He seemed to hold Janis responsible, as if she was the vehicle for the conventions and values which had shunned him. She could see the justice in this, because according to those values, the same values which had shaped her, he was quite unacceptable. He was excessive, emotionally dramatic and transparently manipulative. He was a Middle-European stereotype, transfixed by the drama of his own existence. She imagined him through the eyes of her family and the friends she'd once had, their cool patience. There were moments when she loathed him with a loathing which was rooted in class, and understood the perfect justice of his hatred for what she represented.

Odd, it should come to this. She didn't resent him for his abuse of her, in which she had in some sense been complicit, but the way he ate made her ill. A series of small prejudices accumulated into a revulsion that carried in it the stuff of real prejudice, an annihilation, of shared humanity. She understood how it was possible to feel about other people, even a whole race of people, that they were not quite human, and why that person or race of people must resist the negation of their humanity by whatever means they had at their disposal.

Janis didn't want to feel this way towards Rudi. His excessiveness offended her to the roots of her being. It shocked her to discover how relentlessly her upbringing had tracked and caught up with her. She had thought herself free of prejudices she had merely been too timid to assert.

Her distaste gave her new energy, though not enough to leave him. It became a contest between them for her to indicate through nuances of body language and the withholding of comment how his behaviour fell short of a standard only she could apprehend. It touched a nerve in him. In a curious way he was cowed by it, though at other times it provoked tirades which exhausted them both, and made Janis want to kill him just to stop the noise.

She felt, too, a peculiar pleasure in the thought that if he killed her in one of his rages he wouldn't recover from it. Now that the sexual infatuation was gone, she had finally come into existence for him. He wanted her approval, and she would not give it.

On this perfect morning, the two of them sailing away from land and towards the ocean swell which rippled the horizon, Janis could see the moment's symbolism. In his desire to show her the sliver of sandy atoll miles from land, where he had felt himself touched by some kind of magic, he was attempting to show her his soul, which she did not want to see.

It seemed impossible that they would find the reef in all that open water, but it was there, a perfect crescent of sand surrounded by sea. They snorkelled about the coral cliffs, visitors in an inhuman wonderland. A hammerhead shark cruised, watching them from a lateral eye. It was small and timid, and entirely without menace. Later, on the atoll, they shared the picnic of fruit and fish Rudi had prepared, and a bottle of white wine saved from Rachel's depredations. Between them there was something like companionship, which Rudi destroyed by attempting to make love to her.

Janis fought him off, feeling his rage leap up and something intractable in her rise to meet it. 'Now,' she thought. 'Now he'll kill me.'

But he didn't kill her. He fell back and began to weep, and she left him and swam out to the boat. When she started the outboard he ran to the edge of the atoll, but didn't pursue her. She pulled away and he made a sound, not her name, a wordless howl which followed her across the water.

Janis had only a general sense of where the coast lay. In any case it wasn't the coast she was seeking, but simply to be free of Rudi. When darkness fell she cut the motor. She made a nest in the hollow between the seats and half-slept in intervals, waking in leaping jolts of expectation that Rudi's head would appear at the boat's rim. The first sunrise stayed with her, the light breaking over the sea, followed by the gold ball of the sun, like the face of God. After that she didn't know how many sunrises came and went before the boat grounded in shallow water, and the startled black faces of fishermen loomed above her. They didn't touch her, thinking she was dead, but brought the policeman from the Mission. Her tongue was too swollen for her to speak, and in any case she couldn't remember who or where she was. All she could say, when she regained some semblance of memory and health, was, 'He's gone,' and cry. It was surmised that Rudi had gone overboard and drowned, or been taken by a shark.

Janis's family was traced, and her parents came in flustered disbelief to collect her. She stayed with them long enough to know, and for her parents to know too, that they had lost each other.

*

Janis never knew if Rudi survived. She believed he was capable of swimming the distance to the coast. His body would follow the dictates of the will which drove it. And if the will was not there, it was not her doing. It wasn't the possibility of Rudi's death which had come back to haunt her, but the person he had revealed her to be. She lay awake and felt the presence of her children through the walls, and in the cells of her body. She knew what was good in her came from Larry, that without him she would not know how to recognise it.

In the darkness, the body beside her might have been Rudi's. She inhaled the pure stuff of his anguish. He had offered her the best he knew of himself, and she had risked the sea to escape it.

She'd lost a part of herself to the shark, back then. But she hadn't swum back to let it finish the job. She'd bled and flailed and clung on, endangering everyone. And now her memory was being breached by the part of itself it had left behind. The shark was swimming in the reaches of her mind, with the smell of her blood to guide it.

Notes on Contributors

Murray Bail's books include *Eucalyptus, Holden's Performance* and *The Drover's Wife*.

James Bradley is the author of *Wrack* and *The Deep Field*. His third novel, *The Resurrectionist*, will be published in 2002.

David Brooks's work includes *The Book of Sei* and *Sheep and the Diva*.

Patricia Cornelius's first novel, *My Sister Jill*, published by Random House, will be released in 2002.

Luke Davies is the author of four volumes of poetry including *Running with Light*, and two novels, *Candy* and *Isabelle the Navigator*.

Robyn Davidson's books include *Tracks* and *Desert Places*.

Liam Davison's novels include *Soundings, The White Woman* and *The Betrayal*. His *Collected Stories* was published early this year.

Kate Grenville's books include *Lilian's Story* and *The Idea of Perfection*.

Sonya Hartnett is the author of *Sleeping Dogs, Wilful Blue* and *Stripes of the Sidestep*, among other books.

Susan Hancock's first book, *Sailing through the Amber*, was short-listed for the Steele Rudd Award in 1996.

Graham Henderson is author of *The Mountain*.

Thomas Keneally's books include *The Chant of Jimmie Blacksmith*, *Bettany's Book* and *The Great Shame*.

Anthony Lawrence has published six books of poems. His novel, *In the Half Light*, was published by Picador.

Wayne Macauley's short fiction has been published in *Meanjin*, *Overland* and *Westerly*.

Kim Mahood's work includes *Craft for a Dry Lake*.

Gillian Mears' collection of short stories, *A Map of the Gardens*, is being published by Pan Macmillan in 2002.

Gerald Murnane's fiction includes *The Plains*, republished by Text this year.

Colin Oehring is currently writing his first novel.

Hannie Rayson's plays include *Hotel Sorrento*, adapted as a feature film, *Falling from Grace* and *Life after George*.

Ellen Rodger's short stories have been published in *Hecate*, *Ulitarra*, and *Going Down Swinging*.

Nadia Wheatley's most recent publication, *The Life and Myth of Charmian Clift* was the *Age* Book of the Year for Non-fiction 2001.

Gerard Windsor's most recent book is *The Mansions of Bedlam, Stories and Essays*.

Tim Winton's most recent book is *Dirt Music.*.

Amy Witting, writer and poet, died in September 2001. Her last book is *After Cynthia*.

Publication Details

Stories and extracts by **Anthony Lawrence, Ellen Rodger, Sonya Hartnett, Patricia Cornelius, Susan Hancock, Colin Oehring, Graham Henderson, Nadia Wheatley, Luke Davies** and **Kim Mahood** appear for the first time in this anthology.

Murray Bail's *Camouflage* was published by Text in 2001.

Wayne Macauley's 'Jack the Dancer Dies' appeared in *Meanjin*, 2000.

Hannie Rayson's 'Inheritance' is an extract from her play commissioned by the Melbourne Theatre Company.

Tim Winton's 'Aquifer' appeared in *Granta* 70, 2000.

James Bradley's 'The Resurrectionist' is an extract from his forthcoming novel, to be published by Sceptre Australia in 2002.

Amy Witting's 'Isobel, Anna and Stan' is the first part of a novel left unfinished at the time of her death.

Gerald Murnane's 'Last Letter to a Niece' is to be published in the next issue of *Verse*. 'As It Were a Letter' appeared in *Southerly*, 2001.

Kate Grenville's 'Bushfire' appeared in *The Bulletin*, December 2000. 'Mate' was published in *Granta* 70, 2000.

Thomas Keneally's 'One Sunday in February, 1942' is part of a forthcoming novel, to be published by Random House.

David Brooks's 'Kabul' is to appear in an Australian edition of *The Literary Review* (USA).

Robyn Davidson's 'The First Sense' is to be published in the next edition of *Granta*.

Gerard Windsor's 'Arrayed in All Her Glory' was published in *The Mansions of Bedlam, Stories and Essays*, University of Queensland Press, 2001.

Gillian Mears' 'La Moustiquaire' was published in *Southerly* 61, 2001.

Liam Davison's 'Motel Morning-Star' first appeared in his *Collected Stories*, University of Queensland Press, 2001.